Fourth World

By Chee C. Chow

This novel is dedicated to

Joan, Kimberly and Christopher,

with gratitude for their unfailing patience,

understanding and love.

Table of Contents

Prologue

Face it, Benn, whispers a small, arch voice: you're dreaming again. It's very close to the same dream, but this time he feels... maybe ruffled? The voice taunts him: that's all you've got- *ruffled*? So many options to consider: Is he triumphant? Exalted- or, rather, up in arms? Buoyant, yet exasperated at the way things always turn out? Isn't this what they called, let's see, "a royal pain on the ass" back in the twentieth century, when royalty still existed, and language was so much meatier? One thing for sure: it's Q, to hurl himself into this dream sequence again. Q! That howling quantum leap they all rave about, those who've melted their mental boundaries by over-indulging in psychopeptides.

It is Q, and yet he can't quite place it: there's a clear impression that he's acting a role, passively following a script in some holoplay. In that context, the director, after yelling "Emote, Benn, emote!" has suddenly disappeared on his lunch break, leaving Benn completely unprepared. You should have studied, Benn, the small voice scolds. Should have been paying closer attention, it piles on needlessly. He stands shivering at the center of his hypothetical, amazingly realistic stage set- a snow-packed Alpine mountain- gazing out at an invisible but highly critical audience. Who are these people? Sure, as an actor, he needs to channel the emotions of his character for the audience. But his efforts are undermined by a lack of clarity: for example, is that character thrilled, or otherwise jammed, to be in the dream play? Is he humiliated in his role? Or does he simply feel *ruffled*?

Glittering snowflakes have attached onto the drab green shoulders and sleeves of Benn's ecosuit. Why, they look just like little sequins, he notes warily, as a familiar snare drum begins to roll in a dark corner of his mind: an agitated, rebellious realm lying somewhere beneath his conscious thoughts which Benn has, without a trace of irony, labeled his Under Mind. Even though deep in sleep, Under Mind makes a fast pitch (drumroll crescendo): Couldn't you call these snowflakes... your *dream sequins*? Hi-hat and cymbals crash, holostage left, Ba-da-BASH! Benn dearly wishes Under Mind wouldn't cackle like that. Oh, Dream Sequins, I get it- ha-HAH, that's terrible! But it's also terribly insightful, isn't it: editing his dream sequence *while in progress.* No less remarkable than operating on his own appendix.

Right at eye level, thousands of silvery, crystalline seeds stretch out of black nothingness. They extend tiny, beautifully symmetrical branches and then flutter across the frigid orange-gray landscape, stirred aimlessly by a mild breeze. A deceptively benign breeze, which Benn knows will soon gather its full, terrifying force. For now, suspended against the dense sweep of stars in the Martian sky, his sparkling Dream Sequins dance in the serene glow of two moons, Deimos and Phobos: Panic and Fear, constant companions of the ancient god of war.

Benn's Under Mind, fussy as usual, whines: Deimos and Phobos? You can never see the moons of Mars from either pole. They orbit over the equator- as any young schoolchild knows. Also, there are no mountains like this at the North Pole. Listen, Benn, your holoplay is flawed and needs editing; this whole scene is clearly impossible!

And yet, in the next breath, the voice pokes at him, pointing out the shiny red Ares racing skis beneath his feet. Very well, Benn, Deimos and Phobos can stay- your fantasy, after all. But then why don't you make the most of it- *go on*, the voice whispers hoarsely. Dreamt of skiing in the Alps? So do it- *now!*

Really, Under Mind can sometimes be a bit much to take.

As Benn finally pushes off- all right, that was a little tentative, he admits- the gusting wind whips at his weathered faceplate. How strange: now he seems to be watching events from the audience's point of view- at a safe distance (although Benn would never put it that way)- while, *at the same time,* struggling to prevent his skis from heading off in different directions. Anything's possible in a dream, and he has to concede that it *would* be prudent to keep one foot in the audience, where he could retreat if things were to get too rough. From this removed angle, he looks like a boulder slowly rolling downhill, about to trigger an avalanche. The run is steep and bumpy, at least a triple-black-diamond. So come *on*, urges the voice- *attack* the hill this time! Tensely, he watches

2

himself crunch a meandering path through the hard crust of dry surface ice.

And it is, literally, dry ice. What you call "snow" is actually frozen carbon dioxide- a far cry from Alpine water, the little voice points out. Not even water at all. And consider the ambient temperature: hardly spring skiing, is it, at minus 120 degrees Celsius? The annoying voice confuses the issue every time with these mundane facts, which Benn impatiently sweeps aside. He wishes Under Mind would make a firm decision: attack the slope, it says, but then this isn't real snow. Do it *now*, it insists, although the scene is clearly impossible.

After a brief pause for careful consideration, Benn decides to ignore Under Mind's contradictions and to take action (that is, to edit his holoplay). It's bold enough, but also easy: in the blink of an eye, he transforms into a supreme, god-like skier- Mercury on winged blades- soaring effortlessly across the mountain's placid face, a slick serpentine path in his wake. Turn, traverse, turn- a brilliant display, especially considering that Benn has never in his life come anywhere near snow! His slalom technique becomes ever more impressive with practice- but he wonders, can you perfect any skill in a recurrent dream?

Down in the broad valley, Benn makes out the lights of a village, glimmering through the gray haze. He speeds downhill, accelerated by a powerful sense of... yes, homecoming. The conquering hero returns home, brimming with victory, a glorious song in his heart! But Under Mind objects again: Home, Benn? As you well know, all five colonies lie near the equator- there's nothing but wasteland this far north. Benn, Benn, Benn. Gravity, Benn. You're accelerated downhill by a powerful sense of *gravity*- nothing more.

All valid points, nonetheless irritating. First the two moons, and now this....

But there's no time for further editing: here comes that sharp curve, and the terrifying drop that lies just beyond. Benn truly dreads this portion of the run, and has begged himself many times- begged in vain, he's proud to report- to please, *please* choose a less hazardous route. Flinging himself blindly around a towering black boulder, he falls through its dense shadow, knees buckling as he slaps onto a sheer cliff-face littered with jagged rock shards and blocks of purple ice. Q! Benn lurches forward, now barely upright, his skis bouncing off deep ruts and moguls. Stop! Before you kill us both! the little voice hisses. Observing from high above, Benn replies with a calm shrug, Too late. No way to break the free-fall on this (impressive!) vertical sheet of ice.

Despite having flashed through this scene- what, two dozen times?- before, it still catches Benn- the Benn sitting in the audience *and* the one hurtling downhill- by surprise: suddenly comes a rude THUMP. He teeters. His left leg darts sideways, the ski flapping back and forth in the wind- as though taunting him, waving him a fond farewell! Amazed by this treachery, Benn watches himself, one-legged, pivot in slow motion for agonizing seconds on the opposite ski. His motion slows even further. He is leaning much too far to his right: mouth dumbly agape, olive-green sleeves raised in abject surrender, ski poles flailing behind. As annotated in the holoscript, his ludicrous slapstick pose seems frozen in time (and it is certainly cold enough, Under Mind chimes in with a half-hearted drumroll). Then, just as Benn recalls the next turn of events- a low groan oozing like bilious syrup from the back of his throat- a second skier suddenly intrudes upon his private holostage.

Plummets onto it, more precisely. Launched off a low rise over Benn's right shoulder, a shadowy figure sails like an errant missile, its flight path predictably intercepting Benn, who is already in mid-collapse. This is no longer funny, he tells himself. Their skis clatter like duelling sabers; their bodies tumble downhill in a rapid blur (bending in places and angles, Benn notes with increasing alarm, *strictly forbidden* by human skeletal anatomy) and finally snap apart in an angry shower of red sparks. For just an instant, Benn glimpses a young woman's face, her pale blue eyes flaring at him in accusation and shock. Excuse me, I don't see how it's my fault at all. He averts his gaze as she spins off to the left.

The collision, although way off the Richter scale, fails to rattle Benn from his deep sleep. Oh, but wait for it, here they come, he moans: the ensuing tsunami, a hundred-foot wave of muddy sensations sucked up from the bottom of the ocean, knocks down his protective levee and floods the dream with a polluted, jangling mix of emotions. He has long since classified these feelings as negative. Definitely negative, for example, agitated. To be expected, of course, following such a violent collision. Might he be

4

resentful as well? After all, she's the reckless one, but appears to blame him for the crash! So, then: definitely agitated, and very likely resentful as well, Benn somersaults for some distance before rolling to an undignified stop.

Dangerous moron! Reckless, irresponsible...

Breathing hard, Benn struggles to his feet, which by some miracle are still fastened to their boards. Bloody idiot! Quite literally, bloody idiot. The woman skier, lying ominously still in a shapeless heap fifty meters uphill, deflates like a leaking balloon. A leaking, reckless, irresponsible, bloody idiot balloon. Benn cups his hands and yells: "ALL RIGHT?" Her clothing flaps in a steady wind. Face hot and flushed, he begins to side-step up the slope, but finds himself gasping after only a few steps. It's the attitude- I mean altitude, Ba-da-Bing! Thin mountain air. One hundredth. Normal pressure. Not to mention the. Carbon dioxide atmosphere.

A second try: five grunting lunges up the hill, sliding down backwards like Sisyphus on skis, sweating in a febrile heat while trying to keep his mind coolly focused on her blue eyes, at once intriguing and infuriating. Again Benn stops to catch his breath. No good- get help from that village below. Look, he reasons, even if he did manage to climb up this steep wall of ice, how on Mars would he bring her in? Really there's no choice- better leave her behind (although there is a huge storm coming, so be sure to get back here soon). Anyone can plainly see that Benn is reluctant to abandon her, as he finally points his skis downhill and pushes off.

The dream always ends with his long descent through a deep canyon of light and shadow, alternating in a strobe-like, hypnotic rhythm. Remnants of moon-glow fade before the gathering storm, and just behind him, gusting streaks of snow have completely veiled the mountain. The village ahead beckons with the warm glow of lamps in every window, and as he approaches, he hears the rich tones of a grand piano, played rather well! Instantly he recognizes the piano as a Hamburg Steinway, and the challenging piano piece as the Schumann Fantasie in C Major.

But looking down on the scene, Benn can hardly recognize himself: an anonymous blur, wending his way through a maze of narrow alleyways. He finds the town square deserted- no doubt due to the storm, now thundering directly overhead. The piano falls silent as he glides to a stop. What was it he needed to do? Leaning

5

heavily on his poles, he struggles to recall: something back on the mountain. Benn slowly turns to survey the holostage, looking for any clue. Dark, shuttered buildings tilt inward to seal off the square; masses of Dream Sequins are piled high within recessed doorways; his own faint tracks have long since been whited out by the blizzard. Then suddenly he remembers, and searches upward- but the moons of Mars have fallen from the night sky.

Chapter One

"You've got Vi-i-i-sion, Orbitvi-i-i-sion." Benn had personalized the quaint old musical announcement for his inbox, sung by a jaunty female voice emanating from under the bed. The choice of this outdated greeting ("retro-reject," one schoolmate- no longer invited over- had cracked) was his homage to the corporate giant. Like all children in Tharsis Colony, Benn had grown up regaled with the pioneering exploits of Orbitvision, the largest Earth mega-corporation commercially active on Mars. Orbitvision, builder of extensive orbiting satellite systems which surveyed the planet's surface with pinpoint resolution and provided communication links between the Mars colonies, Earth and Luna Station. Orbitvi-i-i-sion… the little ditty may be retro-reject, but he preferred it to those stiff colonial holo-butlers currently in fashion. Pompous, nasal voices and pretentious accents. Servants of nineteenth-century expatriot British aristocrats, or so Benn imagined: Jeeves at your service, what? He could perhaps understand the rationale: residing in a distant, God-forsaken colony, one might as well choose the part of Viceroy. Talk about retro-reject! Good old Orbitvi-i-i-sion. *Plus*… eyeballs were also called orbits, weren't they: therefore, technically, *all* vision was Orbitvision, Ba-da-Boom! He found the double-meaning irresistible.

"Tell only," said Benn, emitting a leonine yawn as he shuffled across the cold tile floor toward the bath area. He wasn't dressed for a visual- and after last night's heart-pounding dream, probably needed to rearrange his facial expression, as well. He dimly recalled taking a noisy, sweaty tumble- and hadn't he fallen hard for a girl with powder-blue eyes? Mmm, all very enticing, but the critical details had dissipated like a cloud of steam.

"It's only a one-way, Benn: good news from the academy. I'll read it to you, all right?" The creamy voice, which Benn had named Wila many years ago- after his late mother- now reverberated within the Sonicspray stall as he began his dry shower: "The counselor is delighted to inform you that you achieved perfect scores in the series of three examinations given this winter by the Mars Wellness Institute. Way to go, Benn! A fine achievement, he says-how's that for an understatement! The academy takes pride, and so on; let's see... he goes on: the next-highest score was twelve percentage points below yours- that's huge - and the third-highest was well below that, etcetera... let's see, skip that... ah. Supported by your superb essay entitled "The Vanishing Role of Humans in Medical Practice," as well as enthusiastic faculty recommendations, your application for medical internship on Earth has been unanimously approved. Wow! High five, Benn!" Benn had never figured out the meaning of that curious metric, high five, but had programmed it into Wila's Casual Phrases anyway.

"Of course, the counselor adds his heartiest congratulations."

Of course. Still wearing his dingy self-laundering undergarments, Benn stepped out of the Sonicspray, peered in the mirror, and carelessly combed his straight black hair with his fingers. He yawned again and padded into the kitchen area, just a few steps to the south; Wila's voice, pausing momentarily to let the momentous news sink in, followed him.

"This year's interns will gather on the twentieth of April-say, that's only three weeks from now, Benn- at the Mars Wellness Institute in Highland City, for briefing prior to departure for Earth." Wila was now addressing him from the steel countertop. Crumbs and half-eaten packets of variously-flavored Vitacubes lay strewn around a large plastic bag, which had been ripped open through its Synthedible Corp logo. Benn helped himself to the leftovers, and then emptied out the bag in search of his favorite flavors, as Wila kept reading. "They'll supply you with seasonal clothing suitable for the northeastern quadrant of the American Zone, as your medical training at the YaleConn University campus will last a full year. I guess you'll have to leave your ecosuit behind," she pointed out, and Benn feigned disappointment. "Also, you won't need monetary credits: it says here that MWI will pay for travel, tuition, room and board, as well as entertainment and all related expenses." Benn dropped his Vitacube.

"Such a deal, Benn! Such-a-deal!" That was another quaint twentieth-century expression Benn had discovered at the Tharsis Library, while poring through reams of kitsch from his father's current home, New York Metropol. Ha! Such a deal: perfect for

Wila's Casual Phrases, programmed so many years ago that it took a long moment to recall the correct response: "Oh yes. A bargain at twice the price."

"Thank you, Benn. There's also a nice view attachment, showing you the whereabouts of MWI in Highland City. Would you like to take a look? It's quite an eyeful!" Benn smiled; he had completely forgotten that one.

"Yes, an eyeful, I'm sure. Smashing. A beaut, right? A knockout. Um, anything else, Wila?" asked Benn expectantly.

"Yes, dear. Not too bad, for a ten-year-old." Wila's voice resonated with pride.

This last bit was actually a message from Benn to himself, programmed along with Wila's other casual phrases. On Earth, Benn would have been, what, nineteen, almost twenty? But he preferred to think of himself in terms of Mars years, so he was just ten. Not too bad, indeed: and yet oddly unexciting, considering what this meant for his future. Not for the first time, he wondered at how blandly this type of news impacted him- had for his whole life, really. Where was the Q? He tried giving himself a kick-start: Did you hear, Benn, you're going to medical school on Earth! Benn? Earth? Nothing. He shook his head, perplexed. Great news, just wonderful.

Especially considering his fatal handicap: growing up Martian.

Seriously, he reflected, outperforming those kids from the New Colonies was a coup. They were mostly recent settlers from Earth, with easy access to resources Benn could only dream of. The New Colonies enjoyed active commerce with Earth, attracting an influx of capital, space-struck tourists, and ultimately new waves of settlers. There was quite a real-estate boom going on over there, providing a huge flow of credits to a number of Earth-based interplanetary corporations, as well as a steady tax base for the government space agency. On the other hand, Benn's home city, Tharsis One, and its small satellite, Tharsis Two- the original colonies on Mars- had as much influence these days as the extinct volcanoes in whose shadows they had been constructed.

Benn knew the year, like all Tharsis schoolchildren: in 2072, the first American settlers had established Tharsis Colony just north of the equator, at the eastern foot of Olympus Mons. How ironic, that citizens of the three New Colonies, 124 years later, would refer to the American descendants as Martians, usually in the context of an ethnic joke! But it's not just contempt, thought Benn: it's their fear of Tharsis. Fear had led to the New Colonies snuggling together, no more than a hundred kilometers apart, in the lofty highlands of the South, a safe distance from the Martians on the canyon-crossed plain.

When had Tharsis One and Two dropped off the map? Shortly after the Great War of Unification. Mr. Otis Walker, Benn's second-grade teacher, had explained it many times- often in heatedly emotional terms- to his young, impressionable students. From the Martian (that is, Tharsis) viewpoint, the centralization of Earth's government in 2096 marked the beginning of the end: birth of the Pan-World Electorate. What was it like, his teacher wondered, receiving the news that your home government no longer existed; that your country had been all but destroyed in a cataclysmic global war? That NASA, an agency of the former United States of America and your lifeline to Earth, had suddenly vanished?

At other times, Mr. Walker suggested that the colony's downfall actually preceded the PWE, that the slow death- he termed it the "apoptosis"- of Tharsis Colony was encoded in its DNA at the very moment it was conceived. To explain this apoptosis, Mr. Walker would use his guiding principle: follow the water. The second manned mission to Mars, launched in 2049 (thus nicknamed "The New Forty-Niners") discovered significant quantities of liquid underground water, which had only to be mined in order to allow large-scale colonization. Of course, water was necessary for supporting life, but beyond that, water was found in perchlorates, hydrated salts which could be converted to solid rocket fuel (this was before the harnessing of nuclear fusion, Mr. Walker reminded them). The seminal discovery of water, he said, sweeping both arms dramatically to his left, then to his right, essentially divided the history of humanity on Mars into the pre- and post-Forty-Niner eras.

Regarding the former, Mr. Walker reviewed for his class: in 2030, Orion, the first manned mission, capped decades of exploration by unmanned probes which had revealed the intricacies of Martian geology. As early as 1976, the two Viking landers spotted streaks running down the sides of craters, known as recurrent slope lineae. In addition to gathering evidence of sub-surface frozen

10

water within the northern polar ice cap, as suggested by Mars Odyssey in 2002, the Phoenix mission of 2008 detected perchlorates. These findings were confirmed in recurring slope lineae a decade later by the Curiosity rover, as well as by Orion. Many other missions contributing to the ultimate colonization of Mars, such as Mariner, Pathfinder, the Mars Reconnaissance Orbiter, Opportunity and Spirit, were never forgotten by history.

Also never forgotten: the fact that the United States agency NASA had been responsible for all of these missions. Sure, Mr. Walker allowed, successful probes were launched by Russia, Europe, China, India, Brazil, New Zealand, and even private enterprises. But only the United States had the means to access the water- to monopolize this most vital of natural resources- and establish a full-fledged colony. Tharsis was a triumph for the United States, but to the rest of the world, it was only the latest example of American empire-building and colonialism. Resentment among the nations of the Third World (a Eurocentric term, to be sure) had already reached a boiling point at the end of the most tumultuous century in human history, and Tharsis was merely the last straw; it provided a nidus around which the global revolution subsequently grew. As regional conflicts in the Third World coalesced, "developing" nations which had once been fierce rivals pooled their armies and forged previously unimagined political alliances. Eventually, an increasing number of "developed" nations, such as France, Belgium and Switzerland- sensing a profound change in the wind- jumped on board. The aftermath of the decade-long Great War, as surprising to the Third World as it was to the United States, was the elimination of all national governments. Drawn from a global population reduced by ten percent- literally decimated by war- thousands of representatives from newly-defined geopolitical zones gathered in Beijing to form the Pan-World Electorate (an awkward name translated from the original Mandarin). This was initially just a voting group, but eventually grew to encompass all the far-reaching functions of the world government, including its powerful military-industrial complex. The PWE wasted no time at all in stamping out all traces of national ego. And what was the most vivid symbol of the old world order? That's right, class, Mr. Walker almost laughed at his own rhetorical question: the American colony on Mars! So it came as no surprise that Tharsis Colony headed the list of targets for elimination. At this juncture, Mr. Walker would stop for a moment of respectful silence (and to catch his breath, calm himself down) before pressing on.

The PWE- give them due credit- did not outright dismantle Tharsis and cast its colonists adrift into deep space. Nothing quite so obvious. Rather, they promoted the rapid development of three New Colonies, far to the south, with the help of the giant space-tech corporations, using faster supply lines, improved building materials and close attention to lifestyle and fashion, in order to attract an upwardly-mobile generation of immigrants to Mars. All in stark contrast to the Martian descendants isolated at Tharsis, many of whom even saw themselves as backward and uncultured. Mr. Walker clearly shared the deep resentment felt by all of Tharsis toward the New Colonies, and to Benn, this attitude was understandable- but he rejected their generations-old inferiority complex.

"All right, please show me the visual, Wila. Let's take a look at this eyeful," Benn sighed, stepping carefully around the counter which separated his cluttered kitchenette from his even more cluttered bedroom. He had never ventured beyond Tharsis One and Two, but had seen far too many advertisements and newscasts depicting the Utopian life at the New Colonies. And Utopia, southern-style, was clearly centered on massive consumerism.

On the blank wall facing his bed, a floor-to-ceiling image of the Mars Wellness Institute flickered to life, accompanied by swells of grandiose martial music. The five-story MWI seemed relatively nondescript, especially as the view expanded to include extravagantly stylish apartment fronts; towering, elegant spires topped by colorful flags which fluttered in a non-existent wind; bustling parks lush with faux-vegetation; and graceful pedestrian arches (look at all those graceful pedestrians, Benn marveled) in the background. The Highland City Compliance Center came into view, above its imposing stone entrance an engraved quote from J. P. McGrew, the first mayor of Highland City: To Each New Generation on Mars, Greater Wealth and Status.

Rolling his eyes, Benn pictured the buildings and grounds of Tharsis One, which consisted of dull metal sheds of all sizes, lumped together in seemingly haphazard fashion, and often resting on bare soil, with a rudimentary first-generation terrasphere arching over all.

J. P. McGrew must not have meant each new generation at Tharsis. No elegant spires, graceful pedestrians or colorful flourishes here. No grand public projects of any kind. In fact, over ninety percent of the habitable structures in Tharsis One were hidden beneath the planet's surface, in case of a breach in the terrasphere. We live like moles, safe only underground, thought Benn with a shudder.

In contrast, the metrospheres of the New Colonies, built out of new/improved "chain-link" metallopolymers and lined with stout plasma shields, allowed the raising of cities a hundred times the size of Tharsis One. These materials admirably resisted gamma rays, meteorites, the extreme seasonal temperature variations in the South, the six-month long winters, and the horrifically violent dust storms that returned each spring. Not to mention the occasional Marsquake. No, the new colonists had no need to cower underground as the Martians did. They breathed purified, odorless air; their children played in bright, radiation-free sunlight filtered by translucent domes high overhead; they engaged in professional and social lives approximating those they had left back on Earth. Benn struggled simultaneously to imagine the Utopian life, and to resist even thinking of it, as he stared at the visual on his narrow bedroom wall.

Not that Benn had ever coveted such a glorious lifestyle. Instead, he regarded the New Colonies as sadistic social experiments gone terribly wrong. The new colonists were like lab rats scurrying about their cages, desperately amassing material belongings, along with bleeding gastric ulcers. Or he could interpret the New Colonies as three gigantic culture plates, whose jelly surfaces grew out virulent new strains of microbes. He grinned at the image: the new colonists were opportunistic fungal spores, settling between the sweaty toes of Mars. Ha-HAH!

"What's so funny, Benn?" asked Wila.

"Nothing, Wila- nothing at all," Benn replied, feeling somehow chastened. Of course, Wila's maternal persona went only as far as he himself had programmed it, but she did represent authority, which Benn had previously decided was badly lacking. He had never actually known his mother, who had died in childbirth at Tharsis Med. The official cause of death, astonishing to learn, was toxemia of pregnancy- an extremely rare diagnosis, given modern obstetrical management. Still, in dear old Tharsis Colony, anything was possible.

"Music please, Wila?" Benn diverted his stream of thought. "Beethoven, oh, maybe... Opus 111?"

"Certainly, Benn- it's your favorite."

As the pensive opening notes of Beethoven's final piano sonata filled the room, Benn distracted himself by picking up clothing and stuffing it into an old military-green filing cabinet next to the bed. His ecosuit remained crumpled where he had tossed it on the bedroom floor; he would soon wear it back to work, anyway.

On top of the cabinet, next to a scuffed baseball and a modest rock collection, stood a dusty holograph of Benn's father, posed stiffly with his hands in the pockets of a long white lab coat, his feet planted on a grassy island which floated in the center of a transparent pyramid. Although the resolution was poor, one could tell his Asian origins from the eyes and jet-black hair. His down-turned mouth expressed disappointment, regret. Or maybe that's anxiety- who knows, thought Benn. In any case, despite his well-known achievements in the pharmaceutical industry, Owen Marr did not appear a happy man.

Benn didn't think of his father often, but just recently had been reminded of him at the holoplay "Measure for Measure," put on by Tharsis-on-Avon, the community Shakespeare company. His best friend, the irrepressible Jace Cohn, had played the Duke. Addressing the Friar in one scene, Jace might have been describing Owen Marr when he said: "...precise, stands at a guard with envy; scarce confesses that his blood flows, or that his appetite is more to bread than stone." This had stuck Benn with a familiar hollow feeling for the duration of the play.

Maybe if Father had been around to watch The Game, Benn thought, he might have been less disappointed, or regretful, or whatever the hell Father was. He rolled the baseball- still stained with red Martian dirt- in his hand, recalling the gritty thrill of that moment. It was the greatest highlight of Benn's sports life- all right, of life in general. A game in which he had not only hit a two-run homer, but had also made "the biggest play of the season," according to the announcer- that impossible double-play which had won the pennant for his team, the Hydra Giants! The game ball now sat on Benn's bedside cabinet. I'll bring it with me to Earth, he decided.

But not the holograph of Father, or the rock collection; most likely there would be weight restrictions. Staring at the ball brought it all back: bottom of the tenth, the screaming crowd, his teammates surging at him with fists pumping in triumph... and there (again!) was the sudden burn in his nose, and the unexplained appearance of moisture at the corners of his eyes. Benn blinked and forced his gaze back over to the holograph.

Doctor Owen Marr. Project Director for the giant pharmaceutical company Eunigen. A native of Tharsis One, Owen had become a local legend simply by breaking free of the old colony- a very rare occurrence. As a student he must have been extraordinarily brilliant, to attract the attention of faraway Eunigen, which had plucked him out of Tharsis Academy (who knew that any Earth-based corporation, let alone one as prominent as Eunigen, would even look at Tharsis for young talent?) and whisked him off to Earth for completion of his formal education. Their prescience had been rewarded by over two decades of breakthrough discoveries in the highly lucrative field of theragenomics, and over a decade ago, Eunigen had promoted Owen to the lofty position of Project Director.

Owen had met Wila at Eunigen Center New York, married, and brought her to Tharsis to raise their future family. However, duties at Eunigen pulled him back for long stints on Earth: two or three Earth-years at a time. These absences comprised the majority of Benn's boyhood. His mother had died in childbirth, and as Benn was progressing well in school- despite a few minor episodes of adolescent misbehavior- Owen's visits became more infrequent. Honestly, his long absences were a relief to Benn, as Owen's oppressive approach to child-rearing (traditional among the Chinese, Benn had learned from a library book on psychosocial development) included caning his son when he broke the rules, or slapping him for asking impertinent questions. Benn rubbed the back of his head, imagining a dent where Father had once applied his shoe. The effect, however, was the diametric opposite of what Owen intended: as a child, Benn reacted to physical punishment by further rejecting the rules, his impertinence growing with every blow. Eventually resigning himself to the fact that Father was not providing the constructive authority he needed, Benn programmed Wila to be a rational, self-imposed limit on his own behavior. Father's last visit

15

was over two- no, three- years ago, counted Benn with mixed feelings. His recollection of the details of Father's face was not much better than the faded holograph. No compelling reason to make the long trip from Earth, he supposed.

Nor were there other relatives or friends to justify the time and expense. Owen's parents, Leong and Lucy Marr, had perished in a water-mining accident sometime during his teens, over thirty years ago. Father would never discuss the details, and that day's Tharsis Chronicle contained barely more than a headline. Except for his prodigal son, Owen had left no-one on Mars: loneliness, it seemed, was the price of his professional success. Sensing the onset of that familiar, enervating gloom which would sometimes incapacitate him for many hours, Benn reflexively shifted his thoughts to a brighter subject- his rock collection.

Not a grand one, by any means. But it did boast several nodules of hematite collected from Reinfeld Crater, as well as two handsomely symmetric, bright-red pieces of pure crystalline Aresite- rare buried treasure, discovered deep in basaltic sand- and a half-dozen excellent examples of local obsidian, all carefully polished. In contrast, next to these eye-catching products of ancient volcanic eruptions sat a large, speckled lump of conglomerate Movais rock, totally undistinguished to the casual observer, but which, on close inspection, was seen to incorporate round pebbles created by the flow of a river on the planet's surface. That river had now been dry for over two billion years, but had bequeathed Benn this deceptively dull piece of Movais rock, the prize of Benn's collection. Like a straight-faced poker player casually holding four aces to his chest, this stone carried some profound implications. Similar stones- from small clumps to some the size of a house- piled at the bases of exposed canyon walls not far from Tharsis One, had ignited a frenzy of prospecting and water mining, giving fresh meaning to the term "New Forty-Niners" almost a century and a half ago. Tharsis Two, which had started out as a mobile base for exploration of those canyons, planted permanent roots at the foot of the Movais Cliffs, and thus became the gateway to the water mines. The ubiquitous Hydra, a water-mining company which now had interests in nuclear fusion plants, New Colony construction, and even polar exploration, owed its very existence to the discovery of those cliffs.

The sonata's second movement, Arietta, commenced in its stately fashion as Benn turned to scan the room. It began to sink in: his apartment would be converted to storage, given the declining population of Tharsis One. Its built-in Household Program would be deactivated.

"Wila? It just occurred to me- your cognitive functions are directly built and programmed into..."

"Into this apartment. Of course, I am available in a portable version."

"Yes, I've tried bringing that program with me to the water mine, but it's just not the same, Wila. Responses and vocabulary are so limited. It's like talking to a cartoon version of you."

"I agree," replied Wila with sudden enthusiasm. "She's nothing at all like me, so there's not much point, is there? It looks like I won't be coming along for the ride, Benn. This will be your first time away...from me."

There was a sort of tightness in Wila's voice, almost as though she was struggling with emotion- but no, he must have imagined that. After all, Quasi-human Intelligence, or QI, had its limits.

Benn's survey paused at the two narrow wall shelves which, along with his old-fashioned metal desk, filled the entire northwestern quarter of his apartment. What a terrific waste of space, thought Benn: old school projects falling apart; his first-grade datadisc, more like a toy than the real item; forgotten school awards, tarnished and piled with dust; all arranged indifferently on the top shelf. In contrast, the lower shelf was reserved for one large trophy: last year's prize for Hydra's Top Employee of 2195. The corporate logo, a four-headed rampant dragon molded of titanium, wrapped its long body around Benn's name. And Hydra's imperative to employees- Be Content In Your Good Fortune- was etched just below the dragon's tail. Benn squinted. Now that he looked at it more closely- could it be a subliminal statement by some disgruntled employee?- the rounded letters looked like a trail of dragon droppings!

To Benn's chagrin, he took perverse pride in the award- but kept it in perspective. After all, who else would ever care about this achievement? Father was certainly unaware, and his envious co-workers would hardly celebrate him for it. At the award presentation, only his friend Jace Cohn had come over to congratulate him, but that had quickly degenerated into mutual ribbing over Hydra's shady business and political practices, which provided such an easy target for Jace's cynical brand of humor.

Don't be disrespectful, he rebuked himself.. Be Content In Your Good Fortune. After all, Hydra had provided him with cramped but adequate living quarters, Vitacubes for three meals a day, schooling at Tharsis Academy, and now gainful employment. Weren't those the important things in life? Owen Marr had made all the arrangements years ago, and for that at least, Benn should be a little more grateful.

And more punctual as well! Benn spotted the spherical white clock at the far end of the shelf: a homemade gift from Jace, on his ninth birthday. Cunningly fashioned to resemble an oversized baseball- complete with red stitching and a forged autograph of Babe Ruth- the clock urgently flashed a message that he was already half an hour late for work.

Chapter Two

"I know exactly what you're thinking," said Benn, as the elevator continued its rumbling descent into Hydra Mine Three. Slack-jawed, Jace Cohn stared as though mesmerized by the glowing numbers above the door: two hundred, two-fifty, then three hundred meters beneath the planet's surface. The Eye to the left of the numbers stared back. Those ubiquitous Eyes: yet another of Orbitvision's inestimable contributions to modern living. Etched on the wall behind Jace, in flame-red lettering against a backdrop depicting heroically-proportioned miners gazing with determination into a radiant future, was Hydra's original company mission: To Hydrate Mars!

"You're thinking I'll love it so much on Earth that I won't come back. You think I've been dying to leave Tharsis all these years, don't you. Believe me, Jace; I can't say I'm jammed about going to Earth, even for medical school."

Jace considered this for a long moment, then nodded earnestly. "It's true, you don't get Q over much, do you, Benn." They had been friends since early childhood, when the school principal, Mr. Bry Yelic- with Benn's father Owen standing close behind him- had practically roped the two of them together. Over the years, Jace could almost count the times when Benn's impassive nature had yielded to anything resembling emotion, let alone Q. And come to think of it, most of those rare occasions had involved nothing more than baseball.

He recalled vividly- two years ago- a league championship game, his Hydra Giants leading six to five, with one out in the bottom-tenth and Meteor Dodgers standing on first and third. The Dodger batter slapped a grounder sharply toward left field. The ball bounced on uneven ground and took a high, crooked hop. Benn, at shortstop, had already leapt for it- but somehow changed direction in mid-air to make an absolutely miraculous flying catch! Nobody else on the team could have even come close. Jace, at second, yelled for the throw as the runner fast approached. The boy at third was now racing toward home, and a tied game. But Benn, lying on the base-path with his face turned into the dirt, goggles caked with choking red dust, still managed to snap the ball to second (how had he not dislocated his elbow?). Jace received the ball and tapped his foot on second for the out, but then, transferring it from his glove, let it slip! The crowd moaned as the ball traced a high, leisurely arc toward shallow center field. Benn had scrambled to his feet, and, evidently lacking faith in Jace's ability to execute the double play, was already sprinting in that direction. Reaching up, he seized the ball with his free hand, spun around, and hurled it to first, just in time! The announcer screamed, "Got 'im! Did you see that? Marr turns an amazing, uh, an amazing six-four-six-three double-play to end the game! That was unbelievable! The biggest play of the season! Benn Marr and the Hydra Giants win the Tharsis League championship!" It was one of the most thrilling moments in Jace's memory.

But was it as thrilling for Benn? Amidst the ecstatic whoops and yells of his surging teammates, Benn made a vague (happy?) noise before bending over to clap the red dirt off his pants. That was as Q as Benn ever got. For his euphoric teammates, any impulse to rush over and hoist him onto their shoulders came to the sort of screeching stop that can cause severe whiplash. Still, Jace realized, it was mainly on that dirt field at the outskirts of town, where the terrasphere rose from the dusty plain, that Benn leaked any emotions- however subtly. In the long hours spent in classrooms or meetings at work, Benn's face remained always a blank mask: he was a two-dimensional portrait of the diligent student, fully-contributing worker, and well-behaved citizen.

Jace remembered that Mr. Yelic had debriefed him at length on that particular game, taking even more detailed notes than at other interviews regarding Benn's attitudes and daily activities. Despite vague misgivings about the arrangement, Jace knew that the monthly meetings with the school principal were a critical source of extra monetary credits for his parents, who made sure of his regular attendance.

"Q? No, I guess not." Benn removed his hands from his pockets and began to fidget. Here we go again, thought Jace. At four hundred fifty meters, the elevator jerked to a halt, and the doors hissed open. Jace winked at the Eye as they stepped out of the elevator into the vast, brightly-lit cavern where the Worm silently awaited them.

As he had dutifully reported to the principal, the only other setting where Jace felt any deeper currents flowing in Benn, was undeniably the bi-weekly Waterhunt. Even as they exited the elevator, Jace could sense an instant change in his friend's demeanor: a quickening of his step, a stiffening of his usual lax attitude. According to Jace's Theorem, Benn's intensity level was inversely proportional to the square of his distance from the cockpit of the Worm. It wasn't so much a burst of excitement as a snapping to attention. The base foreman, seated behind a greasy desk near the elevator, mumbled warily, "Cohn, Marr," and tossed a starter key toward Benn, who snatched it out of the air without even a glance in his direction. The foreman grunted and made a notation on his datadisc. He supervised a team of twenty dedicated water-miners; theirs was a highly dangerous occupation, and in a coach-like, paternal way he felt very close to all his boys (he had even playfully coined their nickname, the Hydrants). Close to all his boys, that is, except Benn Marr, whose intense manner- especially at the beginning of a Waterhunt- might generously be described as intimidating.

Benn's long strides brought him quickly to the front end of the Worm. Awkward in his ecosuit, Jace ran the last dozen steps to catch up, while Benn opened the cockpit and climbed straight in. He barely waited for Jace to seal the chamber before starting up the massive quad engines. And Jace was still fumbling with his safety harness at the echo station when Benn pulled off his helmet and tapped the control screen, abruptly throwing the Worm into its ponderous forward crawl.

Formally known as a Water Exploration and Retrieval Machine, the Worm was essentially a sixty-meter-long drill-bit on tracks, with five interlocking "splitters" at the nose end and spiral-grooved sides which spun the entire vehicle into the relatively soft sedimentary rock enclosing the deep cavern. Inside, Benn and Jace felt no hint of the spinning motion, indeed had no view of the exterior, and were guided only by Jace's station, which periodically emitted an amplified microwave pulse and analyzed its complex echo. The resulting image, consisting of red and green flashes of varying duration and intensity, when translated by the skilled navigator, enabled them to drill through the planet's crust, much as a spaceship might find its way safely through an asteroid belt. It also provided a hint at the location of underground collections of precious water: a rather crude aid they would actually have relied on, if not for Benn's inexplicable ability in that area.

How had Benn Marr won his trophy the previous year for Hydra Top Employee? Simply by finding water: copious amounts of it. Water was worth a veritable fortune on Mars, especially to those in the New Colonies, who paid extravagantly to keep pets and the occasional live houseplant. In contrast, anyone at Tharsis owning so much as a tiny cactus could expect a sobering visit from the Resource Committee. Even among the new colonists, few households could afford more than two or three hundred liters a week- added to the recycled water, this was barely enough to cook, wash (although the Sonicspray did most of that) and still maintain renal blood flow. It was said that Hydra would never offer a discount- not even to a man dying of thirst- but would accept his vote in lieu of monetary credits. Wealth and power on Mars flowed from water, and Benn, to the extreme envy of his fellow Hydrants (how he disliked that silly nickname), had an uncanny talent for locating it.

Grasping the steering handle like a divining rod, Benn guided the Worm toward water in a trance-like state, with eyes locked shut and a fierce facial expression which Jace found both inspirational and frightening. It's like he's possessed, Jace had once told Mr. Yelic; I think he hears voices. Sometimes he had to shake Benn by the shoulder to warn him of an impending collision with a large boulder. Except for those minor deviations, their journey followed a straight path to the water site, which was usually a zone of moist gravel or clay, with an occasional small pocket of standing water, located in the midst of volcanic rock. These zones were the remains of vast underground aquifers which, in the first half of the planet's existence, had fed bubbling, methanous hot springs on the surface. The discovery of water was momentous enough, but the large reservoirs of methane contained in the volcanic rock- methane which, in theory, could serve as a food source for underground microbes- were nearly as exciting to the early explorers.

Without any indication from his navigator, Benn simply knew when they finally arrived at the target site. He slammed the

Worm into park, flopped his arms to his sides, then leaned back, completely exhausted. As usual, it was left to Jace to operate the giant vacuum which, over the next hour, noisily slurped any water in the vicinity into the Worm's holding tanks. During that hour, Benn's eyes stayed shut, his jaws clenched. An occasional wisp of vapor rose from his shiny forehead into the cold chamber, reminding Jace of the holograph of a hardboiled egg he and Benn had once gawked at, in nutrition class. As he gawked even now: like the base foreman, Jace was too interested in self-preservation to disturb his eccentric friend before the job was finished. Watching the blue bar slowly rise on his intake monitor was probably safer than attempting conversation with Benn during that endless hour.

"Benn, we're almost done here. Benn? I said we're done, and I have a rehearsal for Hamlet tonight. Let's repair to the cave." Although Jace did look forward to the Waterhunt, if only for the chance to watch Benn at his mysterious work, confinement in the Worm, with infinite tons of rock extending in all directions, had limited appeal.

"Just a little longer." There was a rasp of irritation in Benn's voice.

"Tanks are full, Benn. Yup, another successful outing for Hydra's number one team, so… time to head home, all right?" Jace had to reach over Benn to turn off the vacuum and seal the holding tanks.

"What's the hurry? You're always in a rush to start back. In fact, Jace, I think you're nervous about coming out here to look for water. I bet you're claustrophobic."

"Not at all: finding water is Q!" Jace tugged at his collar. "'Tis a consummation devoutly to be wished."

Benn rolled his eyes; it seemed Jace's inner thespian wasted no opportunity. Jace, striking a princely attitude, continued in a quavering voice: "To drill no more- and by a drill to say we end the heartache and dessication which flesh is heir to. Ay there's the rub, for on that Waterhunt, what thousand natural shocks may come from being buried alive! Hold, hold, my heart. Must give us pause." As in previous outings, Jace now slid onto the floor, hands clasped around his throat, his face turning the deep red of a Tharsis sunset. Jace took the act further each time: both feet kicked upwards, his tongue protruded, his eyes bulged with disapproval.

"Enough already, I'll start the Worm!" Benn responded. He had witnessed this too many times: a protracted death scene, concluding with a strangled accusation, "Et tu, Benne?" Jace showed no sign of letting up.

"I said I'll start the Worm!" Benn laughed. "Stop acting like a Martian! Or better yet, stop over-acting as a martyr!"

Jace struggled to his feet, shook his fist at the slings and arrows of outrageous fortune, and then, without further opposing them, shuffled off to his echo station.

On the long return trip to the cavern, Benn was relaxed and talkative, as usual. His astonishing success in collecting water was the obvious explanation, but strangely, Benn regarded the water with complete indifference back at the base, ignoring the paperwork by which he would receive credit for productivity. It was Jace who handled the mundane details, such as setting up the re-powering of the Worm, while the foreman, goggle-eyed at their Water Yield-to-Worm Time Ratio (emphatically noted on his datadisc), lavished praise on Jace, with an occasional sideways glance at his partner. Benn stood alone by the elevator, humming tunelessly to himself as his mind wandered in some uncharted place.

It was not until they were almost back to the surface that Benn finally broke the silence.

"Jace. I'm leaving next week for Earth, you know. That was my last Waterhunt for a very long time, and I've got a feeling I'll miss it."

"Miss it? Yeah- as much as you'd miss one of your lungs! You live and breathe the Waterhunt. But I still don't get it, Benn: how on Mars do you keep finding the water? Even with eyes open, your success rate would be considered a miracle." Jace stopped pressing: never got a satisfactory answer anyway, and his initial astonishment had by now faded to mere curiosity. Benn's explanation only managed to compound the mystery.

"It's no miracle. Like I've said before, it's a feeling that comes over me, Jace. A huge wave of sensations… like music rising up. Or wonderful aromas. Sensations that come from distant memory, or maybe never even existed…"

Not again. Jace wrinkled his nose, as Benn dreamily continued, "…a comforting feeling, I guess- new every time, yet familiar. Pretty weird, right?"

You have no idea just how weird, thought Jace, nodding vigorously. A comforting feeling, indeed!

"It's all rolled into one giant, how to describe it...a giant sphere that wraps completely around me. It's like hearing your mother's heartbeat or voice- and when we're near water, the voice sings to me." So it was a siren song that pulled Benn through the depths like a man possessed: maybe we should install a mast on top of the Worm and tie him to it, thought Jace, puffing out his cheeks.

"Don't tell me you've never felt that, Jace." A condescending tone. As though any normal person should enjoy such a cornucopia of the senses- a circus of aural, olfactory and tactile pleasures- while blindly drilling his way through the dirt and rocks! Jace had experimented with a few entry-level psychopeptides during his elementary school years, but he had never experienced anything close to what Benn was describing.

"No wave of sensations for me, thank you- unless you count bladder spasms." He twisted his face, in between a wink and a wince. "Oh yes, I also experience belching and flatulence. In fact, all those wonderful aromas roll into 'a giant, round sphere that wraps completely around me.'" It was simply in Jace's nature to mock, but a fleeting frown crossed Benn's face.

"But Benn, 'comforting' is not the word for a Waterhunt. 'Terrifying' is more like it! I prefer your version, the image of your loving old grandma, humming a lullaby while she bakes a batch of fresh Vitacubes. Such wonderful aromas."

"That's pathetic, Jace. And I never had a grandma, as you know. When I was an infant, it was my father who hummed the lullabies."

Jace knew very well that was a lie, but made no comment. Their long farewell was becoming increasingly uncomfortable, and Jace caught himself thinking, Come on, elevator! To his relief, Benn returned to his original point. "I am definitely going to miss this. Imagine a Waterhunt on Earth? I'd stumble onto that little patch of moisture they call the Atlantic Ocean, while drilling through New York City in my Earthworm. Then, after filtering billions of liters of water, my pumps would clog up, with those- what are they, Jace- you know, those animals?"

"Animals? What animals? You mean, *fish*?" They both erupted in laughter, and Jace was grateful for the brief release of tension.

Then a sudden pang of... probably acid reflux... grabbed Benn, who strained to make his awkward smile look authentic. For an entire year he would be cut off from the two people (well, one person and Wila) who came close to understanding his attitudes and actions. Who could possibly take their place? His narrowed eyes glistened. On the upper half of his face, he struggled to erase a deep frown, while stretching the lower half tightly in a grin. Jace, gaping at the battlefield of Benn's facial expression, tried to bring back the jovial mood, without success: the image of fish no longer amused. In any case, his effort was short-lived. Their ascent slowed to a grinding stop at the surface of Tharsis Two, and even before the elevator doors had fully opened onto the shadowy canyon floor, Benn's face was already wearing its customary blank expression.

Chapter Three

The ME120 Glidebus, Mars-Elegna's oldest model, emerged from South Tunnel and adjusted its course five degrees to the west. Despite its light load of only three passengers (Benn counted a total capacity of ninety-six), the automated bus took longer than he expected to accelerate to a modest cruising speed about twenty meters above ground.

It would be a twelve-hour journey to Highland City, so Benn made himself comfortable. Finding his safety harness malfunctioning (just how well did they maintain these old buses?), he fully disengaged it, allowing him to tilt his seat back and turn sideways to look through the dusty porthole at the Martian countryside. The sight of massive boulders passing by, like a herd of elephants charging on an endless red plain rimmed by distant mountains, was interesting enough to hold his attention for the first couple of hours. After that, it no longer served to distract him from his growing feeling of isolation.

It was completely novel to Benn, the wrenching sensation just as the Glidebus lifted off the ground: a painful separation, as though those twenty meters of altitude had torn him away from his previous life. Through the years of living alone in his father's absence, and having only one human friend on the planet, Benn had never felt such a dense isolation as he did now. There was an undeniable sense of finality about it. Perhaps some dark intuition, he mused, was telling him that he would never return to Tharsis.

Even deactivating Wila that morning, while closing up his tiny apartment, had not left him with such a profound emptiness:

"Your bus leaves in twenty-seven minutes, Benn. You don't want to be late. And don't forget to bring along some extra Vitacubes- you'll get hungry on the long flight to Highland City," Wila had fussed.

"Don't worry, Wila. I'm all packed. And yes, I did remember to leave my ecosuit behind. Thanks for reminding me. Uh, Wila?"

"Yes, dear?"

"It's time for me to go. I think I have to... to switch you off now."

"Yes, Benn- it certainly looks that way."

"I just didn't think it would be like this, Wila. It feels so strange, you know, to be turning you off like a...."

"A Household Program with Quasi-Human Intelligence? Don't worry, Benn. You know what they say: not about me, babe; it's all about you."

"They" hadn't said that for a hundred and fifty years, but Benn thought that line from an old folk song was perfect for Wila. Yes, it's all about me.

"Listen- go have a wonderful time on Earth, Benn. I'll just sit here alone, in the dark." Another hilarious, long-forgotten line from the New York cultural archives which Benn had programmed for just such an occasion. Piling guilt on someone was funny, right? But now, in actual application, it wasn't that amusing. He grinned, despite the burning sensation in his chest.

"Don't be like that, Wila. Now look, I'll be back before you know it."

"In one-and-a-quarter Earth-years, that's counting travel. You know, Benn, it wouldn't hurt to call home, once in a while."

Another good line: this flurry was like the climax at the end of a fireworks show.

"All right, already- I'll call! And I'll see you very soon, Wila." A promise made to be broken, he realized sadly. Then, holding his breath, Benn had touched the All-Off command, sending his apartment and its cybernetic functions into a state of hibernation.

Now over a quarter of the way into his journey, Benn realized that Wila had been right about being hungry; he pushed himself upright and reached into his backpack for a Vitacube. In doing so, he saw the passenger seated across the aisle quickly turn away. The man, in his mid-forties and heavyset in a muscular way, had sandy hair sparsely covering a bullet-shaped head. Heavy eyebrows crossed his low-lying forehead, and his hard, steel-gray eyes reminded Benn of primitive ball bearings. The man cleared his throat fitfully while brushing some invisible debris off his lap. He glanced back at Benn, and then began to show a mysterious, intense interest in the small clumps of lint dotting the seatback in front of him. He studiously picked off a few specks and flicked them into the aisle, as Benn openly continued to observe.

The Lint Man, thought Benn, now becoming mildly amused. Lint Man was painfully self-conscious, and justifiably so: he looked distinctly uncomfortable in his glossy blue one-piece business suit, stretched tightly across his broad shoulders; crimson boots made of some scaly, faux-reptilian skin reaching mid-calf; several multi-colored rings forced onto large, spade-like fingers. An expensive-looking metallopolymer briefcase stood solidly on the floor beside him. Must be some Hydra executive returning to Highland City-certainly no native of Tharsis would ever be caught dressing like that! An odd thought crossed Benn's mind: this costume is so outlandish, it must surely be a disguise. And why would such a successful person be obsessed about cleaning the furniture of lint? Most suspicious, indeed!

Eventually the seat in front of him was immaculate, and Lint Man, following another sidelong glance at Benn, leaned his head back, and within a few seconds, appeared to be fast asleep. Too bad, thought Benn, Lint Man was getting to be quite entertaining, and would have helped to pass the time.

The only other passenger on the bus, a woman Benn estimated to be in her early twenties by Earth-years, was sitting twelve rows ahead. Benn had watched her climb aboard, glance nervously at the Eye located at the front of the bus, and then haul her enormous black duffel bag down the aisle, carefully checking the seat numbers against her ticket. Really she could have taken any of several dozen empty places, but was apparently determined to find the precise assigned seat. Once there, she showed the same determination in hoisting her duffel bag, with great difficulty, into the overhead storage compartment. Could've just left it on the seat across the aisle, thought Benn.

She had to be Level Two. Not Level Three- they weren't allowed to travel outside the old colony. Level Two workers were raised with her sort of regimented behavior; their biggest fear was of getting into trouble. Benn felt privileged indeed to be Level One, his rank determined by school performance and, of course, his unique talent for the Waterhunt. Had he been stuck at Level Two, Benn wouldn't have lasted long: their lives were much too orderly, their rules too restrictive. He managed to play the model citizen, not only because Wila had raised him right, but because of his high degree of freedom; at Level Two he would soon have ended up in PsySoc Rehab, if not permanent quarantine.

Benn's mind began to wander even farther afield. Had this woman, Level Two, ever been subjected to PsySoc Rehab for breaking the rules- maybe just once? Why else would she be so fearful of getting caught in the wrong seat? And the way she hauled that huge duffel bag around- it was a sort of symbolic baggage, wasn't it: the crushing suppression of her true nature. Had she been locked up at Tharsis Med and given forced infusions of Tabulon, in order to help her see the dangers of independent thinking?

Tabulon was only the latest in the series of PsySoc regulators shipped from Earth, by way of the New Colonies and MWI. First had come a disappointingly weak pair of drugs- Parvan and Orthonil- and then the infamously more powerful Ordrax, which earned well its odious nickname: Bottled Lobotomy. It was rumored that over forty percent of Level Two- and essentially all Level Three- workers at Tharsis had received PsySoc therapy: for the common good, as explained by the authorities. Only the unfortunate ones suffering permanent dementia or psychosis as a side-effect of Ordrax had reason to protest; but they were also the least able to raise their voices or mount a cohesive argument- how very convenient for said authorities! Benn's second-grade teacher, Mr. Otis Walker, was the sole Level One worker ever to receive Ordrax, and he had never returned to the classroom from his PsySoc "retreat." Tabulon, on the other hand, was touted for its high degree of specificity in correcting anti-social behavior; that is, workers could have their aberrant thoughts re-aligned without any loss of productivity.

Judging by the tilt of her head, Level Two had also fallen asleep. Probably a PsySoc side-effect, Benn guessed. If so, he owed her an apology: how ironic, after all, that her somnolence may in fact be caused by a PsySoc regulator developed for Eunigen by Benn's father, Dr. Owen Marr.

Benn felt his own eyes closing. The hum of the Glidebus filled his mind, then faded gradually over a long, unmeasured stretch of time. He waited expectantly for the familiar holostage scene to open: the snowy mountaintop beneath two glowing moons, the blue-gray valley, the freezing wind. His Dream Sequins. But nothing appeared to him this time, just random thoughts of Wila, Jace, the Worm. And then came a distinct feeling that he was being watched.

With some difficulty, Benn forced his eyelids open and shot a look across the aisle. Lint Man, staring back, appeared flustered, then began to fuss with the seatback again. What was that clown doing now, returning the lint to its original location? No longer amusing. Benn snorted, shut his eyes, and turned to face the porthole.

He must have remained in that position for an hour or two, he later reasoned, because of the crick in his neck, when he was awakened by the vibration of the headrest against his left ear, and in his right ear, a loud mechanical voice:

"...in your seats with restraints securely fastened. We are experiencing severe turbulence due to a dust storm from the north. Caution: please keep the aisle clear at all times. Food service and entertainment will be temporarily interrupted. Elegna Transcorp thanks you for your understanding."

Thus far there had been no sign of either food service or entertainment (except for Lint Man), so Benn was not unduly disappointed. And the announcer's caution was well-taken. There had been dust storms forceful enough to flip larger vehicles over and spread their wreckage over dozens of square kilometers. Of course, Orbitvision's satellite network would have detected these storms, but somehow that information did not translate to greater safety for travelers between Tharsis and the New Colonies. A dust storm from the north: violent katabatic winds sent rushing down the southern slope of Olympus Mons to scoot Benn along on his journey. Outside his porthole, he could see nothing but a horizontal brown streak, broken by red swarms exploding against the window. The bus, flying an erratic course, began to shake and sway, its computer unable to respond with sufficient speed to the sudden gusts now buffeting its port side.

Benn reached up to reactivate his safety harness, but then, with a sinking feeling, he remembered: it was malfunctioning!

The overhead voice gave an update: "Wind velocity from the north now exceeds 180 kilometers per hour. Extreme caution. Please keep the aisle clear at all times. Food service and entertainment will resume at the earliest opportunity." In case you were either hungry or bored, thought Benn grimly.

31

The risk of getting up from my chair is much greater than staying seated, where at least I can grab onto the armrests. I'm all right here. No, I'm not. That's insane. Better get into a harness, before it's too late.

Suppressing a fleeting sense of panic, he stood up but had to lean heavily on the chair with his right arm. The bus gained altitude, swept upward by the storm. Lint Man had jerked sideways, knocking his briefcase over, his ball-bearing eyes riveted on Benn, his thick eyebrows arched in disbelief. Although the floor rocked back and forth, tilting sharply down toward the stern, Benn thought that he could, by clinging to his seatback, swing quickly around into the chair behind. It would be much easier than some of the plays he had made on the baseball diamond. He pressed his right leg firmly against the aisle side of the chair, bracing himself, getting ready.

What happened next would never be entirely clear to Benn: he felt like a fastball slammed right out of the park, with no memory of either the pitch or the mighty swing. Just as he began his lunge into the aisle, the wind changed direction, and the bus was suddenly thrown down thirty meters. Benn left his feet, and in a split-second would have snapped his neck against the ceiling. He remembered flying upwards, then came a sudden shock in his left shoulder as something very heavy flashed between him and the ceiling, spinning him back onto the aisle. The heavy object crashed loudly into a porthole and slid onto the floor between two seats. Lying prone on the carpet, Benn lifted his head, sending a sharp pain through his neck and back. His vision blurred, but beneath the seats he recognized the shiny blue fabric, the crimson faux-reptilian boots. The floor continued to sway, or the movement may have been in Benn's head. He shut his eyes tightly and listened, through the floor, to the Glidebus engines struggling valiantly to compensate and adjust to the whims of the storm.

Wila…

The grinding of the engines gradually subsided. The swaying eased, and then mercifully stopped.

"Are you all right?" A woman's voice, urgent. Wila? No, it was the female passenger, Level Two, who was now stabilizing his neck and cautiously helping him to sit up.

"Yes, I think so," Benn replied slowly, although he didn't quite believe it. His entire left side seemed to be numb and immobile.

"Your left shoulder is dislocated. Hold on- I'll reset it." She ran forward to her seat, returned with a Dermamist cannister, and injected something painlessly into his neck. After a few seconds, she placed one hand on his chest, the other on his elbow.

"Here we go. Ready?" Before Benn could say no, he felt a tug here, a pressure there, an easy pop, and his shoulder was back in place. The woman, although young, was evidently experienced: no wasted movement, all efficiency. She knelt back on the floor and regarded Benn with concern, some checklist almost visibly running through her mind. A wisp of auburn hair had fallen across her face.

A highly attractive face, thought Benn- under other circumstances.

"You're extremely lucky," she said when the checklist was apparently complete. "The other fellow was killed instantly, probably right when he hit the wall. There was nothing I could do for him." She wondered, but did not ask, how the two men happened to be out of their harnesses during the peak of the storm.

"Yes, very fortunate you were here. My shoulder- thanks. Are you a… a doctor?"

"No, a paramedic." She flashed a bright but incongruous grin, given their situation. "But I'm about to start a year of medical school. In fact, that's why I'm traveling to Highland City."

Benn let this sink in, while slowly pushing himself to a more upright position, favoring his left shoulder. She was a paramedic, and therefore a Level One- and just like him, she was heading for Earth. He said nothing, but craned his neck to look at Lint Man, who had been pulled into the aisle, the front of his blue suit opened, his chest attached by several cords to a small red box on the floor.

The woman followed his gaze, then resumed her focused observation of Benn. Why is she staring at me like that? Is my behavior unusual? Maybe it's the absence of behavior that's unusual- shouldn't I be a little upset at this point, with my shoulder dislocation, and Lint Man lying dead over there? Where's the Q? Hope she doesn't check my pulse: she may not find one.

"Extreme head and neck trauma, two displaced skull fractures with massive subdural hemorrhage, atlanto-axial subluxation caused by impact of a seatback to the throat, followed by respiratory and cardiac arrest," she coolly recited.

Maybe she's talking about me, thought Benn, still marveling at his own unnatural poise. No, that sequence was the direct cause of Lint Man's death. But her basic diagnostic tools, effective as they were, would never explain why Lint Man had purposely removed his harness and leapt up to save Benn's life, at the cost of his own.

"I'm very lucky indeed," he repeated. "And very grateful to you. My name is Benn, by the way. Benn Marr." He extended his right hand, palm forward.

The woman smiled again, a gentle and sympathetic smile this time. "Good to meet you, Benn Marr. I'm Lora Wheeler." She placed her palm on his, he thought, for just a shade longer than was customary. There was an awkward silence. Then she re-gathered her professional demeanor: "Excuse me now, Benn. I have to file a report on this incident."

Followed closely by Benn's unabashed stare, Lora retreated to her seat and opened her black duffel bag, which now lay in the aisle. She took out her trusty handheld ResQDisc-ES- indispensable to paramedics- and conversed with it in a hushed tone. Whatever she had given him in the Dermamist was already wearing off, and a dull pain was creeping back. Benn carefully pulled himself up, let the gray fuzz in his head clear, and staggered into the seat across from Lora. Ignoring the ache in his neck and shoulder, he immediately fastened his safety harness.

The mechanical voice overhead gave another update. "Your attention, please, passengers. The dust storm has passed to the south. Our cruising altitude is once again twenty meters, and no further turbulence is anticipated. However, it is advised that you remain in your seats with restraints securely fastened. Attention: the passenger lying in the aisle at Row 23, please return to your seat at this time. Arrival at Highland City will be in thirty-nine minutes; enjoy the remainder of your journey. And thank you for flying with Mars-Elegna, a subsidiary of Elegna Transcorp."

With a grateful sigh, Benn noted that the announcer had omitted any mention of food service and entertainment.

Chapter Four

The Mars Wellness Institute was much grander than Benn had expected, consisting of five floors above, and nine below, ground level. He had left Lora at the bus terminal- where the Highland City compliance officer detained her regarding Lint Man's demise- and had taken a taxi to MWI, vaguely requesting a circuitous route through the tourist attractions. Still slightly groggy from the anesthetic, he had paid little notice to the streets and buildings passing by, and his first impression of that trip was of MWI's enormous stone lobby. The matronly receptionist, fussing over his look of utter exhaustion, had personally led him past the clinic offices, now closed for the day, to the cafeteria. The meal consisted of unfamiliar, mostly gelatinous or foamy substances, but still tasted far better than his usual Vitacubes. The room she assigned him on the dormitory level was luxuriously appointed by his standards, easily twice the size of the apartment at Tharsis One. Although it was early in the evening, Benn collapsed into bed and passed a dreamless night.

The next morning, his entire body ached as he reported ten minutes late to the main auditorium, picked up his assigned datadisc at the door, activated it by peering into its scanner, and then sat toward the rear of the room. A half-dozen people were already seated in the front row, and Benn recognized Lora Wheeler by the now-familiar back of her head. A tall, middle-aged man in a black business suit, who had been closely studying the screen on top of the podium, looked up sharply at Benn.

"Mr. Benn Marr, is it? Please, come down to the front- this room is, ah, actually much larger than we need."

Lora turned and stared in surprise at the mention of Benn's name. Sauntering- he hoped in a confident but casual way- down to the second row, Benn felt his heart pounding and his eyes straining to avoid Lora's.

"You see, it's just the six of you here, and you will all need to become better acquainted," the man in black continued. From

35

closer up, Benn saw a graying goatee under primly pursed lips. The suit was not glossy like Lint Man's, and of a much more conservative color and style. If Lint Man was a wealthy executive hoping for a bit of fun on his business trip, this fellow was a colorless bureaucrat who followed protocol to the letter.

"I am Rion Salkend. Welcome to you all." His eyes remained fixed on Benn as he spoke. "I serve as Terran Liaison for the Mars Wellness Institute. First, I congratulate you on being selected for this highly competitive program. For diverse reasons, you six are the top examples of your generation. Three of you live right here in Highland City, and I believe you already know one another." There was an exchange of nods and winks at the end of the front row. "You come from the, ah, wealthiest and most powerful social circle at Highland, and we expect that you will have a great impact on healthcare on Mars in the future." One of the three, an extremely pale fellow with silvery hair- almost an albino, thought Benn- shrugged indifferently.

"Sool Tamura is from the South Beach area of our neighbor city, New Miami. She is a martial arts champion, as well as a robotics engineer." No-one showed any reaction at all. New Miami had long ago settled into the role of Second City, the gritty, industrial cousin of Highland City. The three Highlanders regarded Sool as a nonentity; nor would she have fared better if she had come from Utopia South, the oldest and least fashionable of the New Colonies.

"And two of you have come all the way from Tharsis Colony." There was a collective gasp from the front row. *Tharsis*? Not Utopia South? The *Martians* are coming? Martians, at the top of *our* generation? Benn shifted uncomfortably in his chair, as he and Lora had already been identified as outsiders- most obviously by their outdated clothing and conspicuous lack of decorative facial hardware. And of course, he thought, our hair colors clearly set us apart, not being close to either end of the visible spectrum.

"Yes," said Rion Salkend, indicating Benn and Lora, "Tharsis Colony. In fact, you ought to know that the highest test scores of all, by, ah, quite a considerable margin, belong to Benn Marr, there in the second row. Lora Wheeler, who is, by the way, an accomplished paramedic, scored second-highest."

When the murmuring had died down, he continued. "Because of, ah, space limitations, you will be divided into two groups: those from Highland City will spend their year of training at MassMed, while the remaining three will intern at YaleConn."

At this excellent piece of news, the Highlanders wiped their brows, thanked their deities loudly, then broke into an outburst of giggles.

Salkend chose to ignore their antics. "Both are campuses of the, ah, Eunigen Institute, so curricula will be identical. I'm beaming detailed information now to each of your da-discs, including all the course materials you'll be studying this year. Please take advantage of the four weeks of travel time to Earth by getting a head start; mastering such a tremendous amount of material in one year will not be a picnic in Highland Park!"

He touched the podium, and six da-discs received huge boluses of data with simultaneous hiccups.

"I will personally escort you to your respective campuses." Salkend suddenly paused to stroke his goatee. "Now, ah, please excuse me if, at times, I appear overly, ah, cautious- but it's my duty to ensure your safety. You may be aware that this year is the centennial of the Pan-World Electorate, and quite predictably, passions are running high in certain quarters." He lowered his voice. "Terran politics are complex- hardly my area of expertise- but I predict an increased level of, ah, unrest this year. We will see violent demonstrations in the cities. And large regional uprisings would not, ah, lie beyond the imagination. Even with the aid of PsySoc regulators, it has not been easy to suppress reactionaries, those who conspire to restore the, ah, separate nations of Earth."

Salkend paused dramatically, then continued in an even more ominous tone: "There is another, ah, matter of grave concern. Over the past decade, a major problem has emerged, involving the illicit trafficking of, ah, what we might call, ah, recreational psychopeptides: a problem that spans all strata of society, from the Quarantined Class up to the Level Zero administrators. These illegal peptides, just like the PsySoc regulators, are genetically tailored products which profoundly impact one's thought processes. But, whereas the PsySoc regulators suppress one's consciousness, these illegal products are designed to do the opposite: to expand awareness of one's surroundings.

"Until recently, recreational drugs have been, ah, mere hallucinogens, inducing false visions. In contrast, it is claimed that the current drugs actually enhance one's knowledge of real events (and even thoughts?) taking place in the next room or building, for example. This, ah, hyper-awareness is accompanied by an extreme sense of euphoria, which ultimately leads to addiction."

Benn took in a sharp breath. Salkend might just as well have been describing the hyper-awareness that enabled him to find water, and the intense pleasure he felt on every Waterhunt!

A drug-like effect of the Waterhunt was intriguing, but it was Salkend's next statement that really grabbed Benn's attention: "It is further claimed that, at the height of this euphoric reaction, there is the ability to *project* one's own thoughts out of body- although personally, I find that concept quite preposterous."

At the mention of projecting out of body, one of the Highlanders, a tall blond man, whispered lewdly to another, a red-haired woman whose shoulders shook with suppressed laughter. Salkend frowned, without looking up from his datadisc.

"The inevitable, ah, withdrawal from this euphoric experience is harsh: one might say its mirror image. There is extreme, ah, dysphoria- even severe pain- and the user's hyper-awareness decays, ironically, to its opposite: a temporary non-awareness which, with repeated use of the drugs, eventually becomes permanent.

"How apropos, that the, ah, foremost of these peptides now beginning to appear on the underground market is named Deep Coma: some drug trafficker's idea of a cruel joke! Deep Coma is reputedly ten times more powerful than its predecessors, and presumably the, ah, withdrawal and eventual brain damage are ten times as severe! But as a group, all of these peptides are very dangerous indeed: do not approach them, ah, at any cost!"

Salkend, whose voice had become quite strident, suddenly paused. Clearing his throat, he visibly gathered himself, then dispatched with the rest of his agenda in a pro forma monotone: rapid instructions on the next morning's departure, cabin assignments on board the Elegna Transcruiser, regulations governing space travel, importation of soil samples (a good thing Benn had left his rock collection behind), decontamination procedures, and a long list of minutiae, before concluding the meeting with a perfunctory reminder to concentrate on studying their texts during the long flight.

Upon Salkend's exit, the three Highland City chums stood up in unison and, without acknowledging the others, swept pointedly out of the auditorium in a cloud of smirks and laughter. Lora smiled tentatively at Benn, then introduced herself to Sool Tamura, a broad-faced woman with prominent silver cheek studs, hard narrow eyes, and violet-colored hair with a metallic sheen: a robotics engineer- and apparently a martial-arts expert- who lived in South Beach, the factory district of New Miami. What an odd group of people they had assembled for this internship. Benn stayed seated in the second row, staring blankly ahead for several minutes before finally getting up and slowly heading toward the back door.

"Benn!" called Lora. "Can we talk later?"

Benn nodded distractedly, his mind swirling with competing thoughts. First was the previous day's catastrophe en route. Then there was Salkend's dark and dramatic warning about Terran politics and uprisings on Earth: would that really be an issue for them, as medical students? And then there was the hostility shown by those snobbish Highlanders- perhaps he should have expected prejudice from the "wealthiest and most powerful social circle at Highland City" toward Tharsis colonists. Also, what was that awkward feeling- like appearing naked in public- on seeing Lora again? The avalanche of new input since leaving Tharsis was quite overwhelming. But at the heart of that avalanche, Benn found his thoughts riveted on illegal psychopeptides. Why? He had never used or cared about drugs before. Was he experiencing withdrawal from Tharsis and the Waterhunt? Particularly captivating was the idea of perceiving distant events, and even projecting his own thoughts! He finally had to admit to himself: although it was regrettably illegal, he would not pass up a chance to try the psychopeptide known as Deep Coma.

The Elegna Transcruiser, accelerated by Flowsorb (cyclic particle absorptive hypervelocity) technology, would take only a fraction of the time required by conventional spacecraft to complete the flight to Earth. The lesser of two reasons was the incorporation of its modified nuclear fusion reactor, which provided a limitless source of power, without the nasty problem of radioactive waste. Safely containing a fusion reaction within the small dimensions of a spacecraft, as noted in Benn's fourth-grade engineering text, counted among the great advances in space travel of the past half-century.

In terms of significant milestones, though, it paled next to Flowsorb itself, which had allowed its patent-holder, Elegna Transcorp, to dominate space travel for thirty years. After all, the fusion reactor didn't create the ship's astonishing velocity. Benn knew that Flowsorb sequentially accelerated subatomic particles, working like a series of super slingshots- that was the extent of his passing knowledge of the process- and he was therefore shocked at the modest size of the engine room and its silent machinery. After hanging around the engine room aimlessly for a couple of days, Benn finally asked a sympathetic engineer for a tour.

"All right, Benn, I'll give you a simplified version. To start with, let's consider these subatomic particles as such, although we analyze them as waves. Flowsorb takes a variety of hyped-up particles, by-products harvested from the fusion reactor (efficient, right?) and fires these particles from the central initiator, where they first enter the cyclic countercurrent mechanism. Meanwhile, at the terminal emitter, each compatible, or what we call candidate, particle degrades to a capacitron: you remember that's a cousin of the anti-proton, capable of absorbing energy like a sponge, storing that energy until a specific threshold is exceeded, then discharging it. Following me so far?"

Benn nodded uncertainly.

"See, the Flowsorb mechanism exploits the power of the Almighty Exponential," said the engineer, bowing his head only half in jest. "Changes in particle direction are forced by plasma nano-platforms, which are folded by powerful magnetic fields. These folds are embedded in thousands of larger platforms which fold into larger convolutions, and they, in turn, fold upon themselves- and so it goes, over and over.

"The repeated folding forces streams of energized particles to pass streams of capacitrons traveling in the opposite direction, millions of times over, each time transferring a portion of energy back toward the center. Finally, a new cycle begins- but with their energy multiplied in each cycle, these exponentially-accelerated particles asymptotically approach the speed of light. You see?"

The engineer, now multiplying his own energy level, waved his hands in the air. "Particle velocities literally explode by orders of magnitude! Then we eject these particles into space, and the rest relies on Newton's Third Law: you know, action and equal-slash-opposite reaction. *Major thrust* is what I'm talking about! And that enables us to reach Earth in only four weeks, a journey that used to take more than seven months!"

For the first week of the flight, Benn was too distracted by the ship around him- its command chamber, the spectacular viewing decks, and above all its amazing engine room- to focus on the course materials in his da-disc. Lora was initially willing to explore the ship with him, but soon showed signs of restlessness. She reminded Benn that Rion (already on a first-name basis!) had said this year would not be a Martian picnic.

On one of the view-decks, while pensively watching the stars, Lora explained that she was the only child in a Level Two family; that her parents had high hopes for her future- their own future- and that there was just too much at stake to waste any time. Of course, she had already over-achieved by attaining Level One, and even there she had excelled; Lora had been recognized as one of the top three paramedics at Tharsis Colony. Her parents, however, had minimized her success: a paramedic is not a doctor, they had actually complained, on the day she received her award! Sure, they had pointed out, she could pursue that career path- but *at what cost?*

"At what cost, Benn!" The pain on Lora's face, as she poured her heart out to Benn, appeared to pass completely unnoticed.

There was also the chance to rebuild the fallen family name: Lora confessed that she was the great-great-granddaughter of the legendary Captain Scott Wheeler, who, as a young man, had led the original colonists to the barely-established Tharsis Base and been the guiding hand in its expansion. Unanimously elected the first Governor, Scott Wheeler had served Tharsis Colony faithfully for four decades- including the painful transition from being a colony of the United States to one of the PWE- and his only son had succeeded him. However, after only a few months in office, corrupt Scott Junior had been impeached for crimes involving the fledgling water-mining company, Hydra (Benn could hear himself and Jace Cohn sharing a good chortle at this point). Thus had begun the great decline in the long arc of Wheeler family history. Through successive generations, various character flaws, poor investments, lapses in judgment, and plain bad luck had steadily degraded the Wheeler name, and now Lora was the first to rise up against that trend. Benn could see that her parents' rigid attitude was merely the tip of the huge, multi-generational burden she carried. Suddenly reminded of the heavy black duffel bag Lora had dragged aboard the Glidebus, he watched the strain building in her face, her head tilting forward, her shoulders raised stiffly. Lora's unyielding sense of duty in the face of her parents' opposition and her family's shady reputation- the ferocious headwind against which she struggled- was quite a novel concept to Benn, one which he found intimidating, but at the same time slightly ludicrous.

Lora, too, felt the strain in her neck and shoulders, but to be honest, by the second day of the journey, she had already begun to feel a more subtle strain: that of opening up to Benn Marr. Nonchalant, uncaring Benn. He-of-no-visible-reaction. Benn to whom she had so naively displayed her painful wounds, her most profound fears, and then received absolutely nothing in return. It's as though he's hollow- devoid of feelings, she thought. Was his flat affect a sign of depression, or was he consciously denying his emotions? Perhaps there was a degree of narcissism too. Well before entering medical school, Lora's nascent, inner diagnostician was already starting to blossom.

One day on the viewing deck: "Have you even peeked at the sheer volume of material we have to learn?" Lora interrupted Benn's monologue regarding the difference between the elliptical orbits of Mars and Earth around the sun. The challenge of grasping Benn's babble about the variance in distance between Mars and Earth- and its obvious impact on the very journey they were now taking as well as the return flight, the ideal launch interval coming every eighteen to twenty-six months, how that was shortened by the Flowsorb engine, and so on and on interminably- triggered a furious sort of panic in Lora, who promptly detached herself to an elliptical orbit of her own.

Eventually, even Benn had to pay some attention to the mountainous reams of text crammed into his innocuous-looking da-disc. Although thrilled at the prospect of attacking the task ahead, he

42

made a rule of spending six hours a day- no more- on his studies. Benn imagined reading eight hundred and seventy-four dense chapters not as a daunting challenge, but rather as a magnificent buffet, spread out on a gigantic groaning table; it was a Lucullean task, certainly, but once he saw the basic pattern underlying all chapters, he was able to chew and digest large chunks at a time. Nevertheless, proper digestion required adequate time between meals, and eating too quickly would diminish the pleasure, the savoring of it.

Perhaps the fact that the massive text had been written by a network of medical supercomputers, collectively named Osler IV, centered at a place in the American Zone called Bethesda Institutes of Health, explained its logical teaching strategy. After a brief introduction to genetic tailoring, the text expanded rapidly on theragenomics (recombinant gene templates), then correlated with theraproteomics (peptide products translated from those templates). The genetic codes of billions of organisms had been deconstructed, and the resulting Complete Earth Biogenome, referred to as a "menu" by those in the trade, provided a staggering multispecies array of sub-genes, building blocks of infinite variety, for the construction of complex new templates and thereby, the production of individually-tailored therapeptides. As Benn progressed through the first hundred chapters, he saw that even the most minute alteration in therapeptide structure would produce a strikingly different end-result.

The medical field essentially consisted of tailoring and applying these peptides in clinical situations. Diagnostics had long ago been relegated to machines, which scanned, analyzed, and diagnosed the patient. They even prescribed the appropriate therapeutic plan. Frankly, the production of theragenomic peptides could also easily have been taken over by- and, in fact, seemed particularly suited to- the medical computers. What remained were the sensitive tasks- acknowledged haltingly by the most advanced teaching hospitals- of deciphering patients' wishes and guiding them through the pitfalls of treatment.

"Wishes" meant the patients' attitudes toward both disease and treatment, resulting from a global summation of their personalities, prejudices, neuroses, education, religious beliefs, family dynamics, and a host of other factors not amenable to analysis by computers. After all, physicians had to balance the purely technical or algorithm-driven approach with personalization of care. Didn't they? Wasn't the admirable desire to *do something* for the patient best complemented by a healthy skepticism and sensitivity to the patient's wishes? In Benn's application essay, "The Vanishing Role of Humans in Medical Practice," he had pointed out that technology did not supply social awareness, creativity, or idealism. Wasn't the physician also a humanist? he had asked. A historian, digging out, interpreting and telling individual stories? The essay had focused on this tiny corner of the field of medicine, and while conceding the value of face-to-face human interaction, had also predicted that it would continue to fade away.

The six-hour study limit gave Benn a much-needed break from a growing sense of futility. He took a brisk walk every afternoon around the ship, mainly to shake off the disquieting knowledge that he would ultimately be irrelevant to medical practice. Twice he spotted one of the other interns- the albino-like Highlander with his silver chin cup, matching nose ring, and shiny white hair tied back in a short ponytail- vanishing from the hallway outside his room as he set out on his walk. On a different day, Sool Tamura silently departed the view-deck as soon as he arrived. Were these people avoiding him, and why? Benn found himself thinking of Wila; he felt again that sense of utter isolation which had struck him as the Glidebus departed Tharsis. Was this how Father had felt when leaving for Earth the first time? Benn saw no sign of Lora or Rion Salkend, and, once the novelty of the engine room had worn off, there was little to distract him from returning to his cabin, and to his heavily-loaded da-disc.

Benn's medical studies, he soon realized, might just as well have been named, in their entirety, "The Age of Therapeptides." It seemed that, whatever the nature of the disease, somewhere there was an actual or hypothetical therapeptide to counter it. Day by day, chapter by chapter, Benn developed an intimate knowledge of each theragenomic template, exactly where its various genetic building blocks had originated (for example, one segment of DNA from a Bethesda lab mouse, another piece from a stuffed tiger at the Washington zoo, and yet another from an extinct canine species, the wolf, whose DNA had been preserved at the Smithsonian Museum), the process of stitching thousands of DNA pieces in sequence to form a template, and the translation of the final product- the therapeptide- from that template.

To Benn, the effect of therapeptides on humans was actually the least interesting part of the story. What truly fascinated him was the way these fragments of disparate life forms related to each other in their forced coexistence, and how that symbiosis mirrored the macrocosmic relationship between their parent organisms in nature: a murine, a feline and a canine: a mouse, a cat and a dog, all stitched together! But, coming from a world without predators and prey (not counting the predatory practices of his former employer, Hydra), Benn missed the irony and the intrinsic violence built into that arrangement, concluding only that the combination within a single gene yielded a sum greater than its parts.

At the end of the fourth week, Benn marked his da-disc at Chapter Two Hundred Ninety-Five and set it to Rest mode. He made his daily rounds of the vacant observation decks on his way to the mess hall, a cozy compartment with capacity for only six diners (each allotted thirty minutes per meal), near the stern of the ship. In the tight corridor outside the mess hall, he nearly collided with the three interns from Highland City, who were just emerging from their supper, tensely discussing that evening's workload. One of them referred to Chapter Thirty-Eight: was that as far as they'd gotten?

All talk suddenly stopped. The Highlanders gawked at Benn, as though he had turned bright green and sprouted a couple of long, waving antennae from his forehead. They stood awkwardly by the narrow entrance to the mess hall, unable to pass without pressing their bodies together in a humiliating, if not hazardous, maneuver. Such close contact was to be avoided at any cost: who knew what contagious disease the Martian might be carrying? Benn recognized the ghostlike fellow with the white ponytail, who quickly averted his eyes. Up close, his pale skin appeared almost transparent, and a blood vessel throbbed visibly at his temple. With nothing else to do, Benn silently counted the pulsations: six, seven, eight. One of the Highlanders finally spoke:

"So here's the high-scorer from Tharsis. Say me, Nema, what again's his grip? Rion tagged him Benn, am I off? Benn Marr-*tian*?" The young man snickered at his own lame humor.

He was tall, broad-shouldered, impossibly handsome in a Nordic way, sporting waves of waxy, platinum-blond hair streaked with bright green highlights; a polished golden chin cup with matching nostril ring; arched, perfectly-trimmed eyebrows; an aquiline nose, down which gem-like blue eyes stared without a hint of self-doubt. Except for (or perhaps because of) the obvious contempt and hostility flashing from those eyes, he possessed what Benn had always imagined to be aristocratic features. So that makes this fellow a high-class bigot, thought Benn. More a caricature of one. It's amazing that these people haven't outgrown their prejudices by now- wake up, it's the end of the twenty-second century!

Nema, equally tall and statuesque, a striking redhead (the red so emphatically vivid that Benn had to avert his eyes before long) with green-tinted irises- an unnatural beauty who could have starred in one of those New Colony advertisements touting the Utopian Lifestyle- placed her heavily ring-laden hand on the blond's elbow.

"Trip! You know that's high-low: 'Benn Martian.' Add, your grip misleads." She looked genuinely concerned- but, it turned out, not a whit about Benn's feelings. "He's a preemer and is sure leading in the now, by high yield. Say, Benn Marr, am I off? We anxed only the face of tight study, while you had your eye on speed?" She looked at Benn appraisingly, a subtle upward curl at one corner of her mouth. She had never before met anyone of pure Chinese descent (such beautifully shiny black hair, maybe she'd try it someday); most of them lived and worked in Utopia South, and there were quite a few in New Miami, but, to Nema's regret, almost none were to be found in Highland City. Their industriousness and value as Level Two and Three workers was well-known.

Benn hesitated, thrown off by her peculiar manner of speech, and no less distracted by her glowing twin Aresite cheek studs- one on each cheek- which highlighted her vibrant red hair perfectly. What had she asked him? Angst? High yield? What was that about "ion speed"? Maybe she was referring to the Flowsorb engine?

"Oh," he replied. "Ion speed... is that what you said? No, no- I haven't gotten very far in my studies, if that's what you mean by ion speed. It's pretty dense stuff, isn't it- I can't seem to get jammed about it." In truth, far more than jammed, Benn had devoured the fascinating material with the enthusiasm of a gourmand, whereas these Highlanders appeared to have no appetite for it. Perhaps intentionally, drawing on an unrecognized mean streak within himself, he allowed the barest hint of jamminess to leak out. Just enough to exceed the threshold of detection, a few parts per million to stir their angst. To Nema and Trip, Benn's reply seemed implausible, more like camouflage than modesty.

"Yes, the da-disc load sure tightens the reading," admitted Nema coolly. "But by my guess, Benn Marr stands far under it, by the time- more even than you, Trip." Her eyes stayed wide and innocent. "Say me, Benn- your guess- need we mind so many gene templates and therapeptides, so many detailed hundred-thousands? Won't the med-comps just outpick the combine for us?" Her thumbnail-sized cheek studs, jiggling suggestively as she spoke, continued to fascinate Benn. She noticed this and tossed her head slightly.

In the corner of his eye, Benn could see that Trip had become increasingly agitated at the direction of their conversation. What surprised him was that he was enjoying (to the point of relishing) Trip's simmering anger, which now threatened to boil over. Was he, then, just as competitive and insecure, just as prone to Schadenfreude, as these pathetic Highlanders? What else would he call the pleasure he was feeling at their discomfort?

"How will this Martian stand under much ahead of us, reading three together?" Trip interrupted Nema, his voice almost a growl. "Why attend him, Nema? The study's same-tight for him, so how can this preemer help us?"

Ignoring Trip's question- nearly incomprehensible, in any case- Benn replied in his most earnest and soothing voice, "Don't worry- Nema, is it? Nema, I doubt we'll need to memorize the exact multispecies origins of every single gene template.

"It's impossible!" he continued with an insouciant shrug- although he was already well on his way to achieving just that. "You're right- computers will design the peptides for us anyway. It's not each peptide in itself, but rather the effect of the peptide on our patients' health: that's what's relevant to our future practices."

Benn, who could not have disagreed more with what he heard himself saying, kept a straight face. The bigger picture, the interdependence of so many separate species on one peptide, was what really mattered. But he persisted, "You know what I mean: the risks and benefits of treatment, and so on. That should be easy enough to learn." Even for the three of you, Benn left unspoken.

Nema, now eager to believe him, purred at his reassurance, but Benn could see that all three Highlanders were at least somewhat relieved: here was the preemer, down-playing the huge challenge ahead. Trip, nonetheless, interjected, "Easy claim from Marr of Mars! My guess, he mistargets us. Enough study loss! There's long tight reading in time, so come away, Nema. And you, Foye." So that was the ghost's name.

Trip scowled at Benn, seized each of his companions by the arm and steered them roughly down the corridor, pushing Benn hard against the wall. Foye clearly resented his role as Trip's battering ram, but offered no resistance. And neither did Nema; the subtle curl of her lip had blossomed into a wide grin. Benn and Trip had each delivered what she so wholeheartedly desired: from the preemer-freak Benn, reassurance about the impossible academic workload; and from her forlorn lover Trip, a declaration of his subservience and jealousy (but then again, a loyal pet-dog could have same-louded his bark). Sadly, Nema's hard-won victory quickly evaporated, as she turned to see Lora Wheeler rounding the corner, chatting in an overly-intimate manner with Rion Salkend. They were completely absorbed in conversation, and even Benn noticed that their heads were inappropriately close together, almost touching.

Benn had not encountered either of them for well over three weeks. Had Lora been studying in her room the entire time? She held the same determined expression as always, but apparently had allowed herself enough time to become friendly with Rion Salkend. Startled by the unusual gathering up ahead, Lora took a quick step away from Salkend and cast a sheepish glance at Benn. Salkend was taken aback as well; he had not seen Benn- or Sool Tamura, for that matter- at all during the entire flight.

"Well! Mr. Marr, at last. On the very eve of our arrival. I trust you have been well? Ah, will you join Lora and me for dinner, or have you already..." he inquired, gesturing vaguely at the three Highlanders.

"No, I'll join you, thanks. We were just parting ways."

Nema was visibly upset. "Rion! We mis-met you tonight, at our steady meal." She threw a piercing look at Lora, who appeared not to notice. "Can we quest you in the time? Trip and I have unknowns on those MassMed regulations, and same..."

"No, I'm afraid not, Nema. Perhaps after breakfast tomorrow- and, ah, I'll have a week in Boston after we arrive at your campus." He waved her off, not completely disguising his distaste. Although a Highland City resident himself, Salkend had only transferred from Earth a year ago; he still struggled with the strange patois of the colony's younger generation, and quickly found it tiresome. He would also be glad to escape their thinly-veiled, competitive anxiety, if only for an evening.

Over dinner, Salkend read off a checklist from his da-disc: tomorrow morning, arrival at Queens ElegnaPort, a meeting to be held at MWI's Manhattan office, then a short journey by Glidebus to the YaleConn campus in New Haven. With a sudden pang (one of disappointment, naturally), Benn realized their bus would be passing close by his father's lab at Eunigen. No doubt an opportunity to visit New York would come, once he had settled in at school.

"Speaking of the Glidebus," Lora spoke up suddenly, "did you hear what happened to Benn and me on the way to Highland City?" Salkend shook his head absently, still organizing the next day's schedule. But his concern quickly escalated as Lora's story unfolded; before long, he was interrupting her repeatedly: But hadn't the orbiting satellites predicted the storm? And why would a Glidebus, even an outdated one- specifically designed to handle such a situation- fail just at that moment? He was especially baffled by their account of the third passenger, whom Benn still thought of as Lint Man.

"Who was this passenger, and what was he doing on that bus?"

"Maybe he was an executive," Benn suggested, describing Lint Man's expensive clothing and briefcase.

Salkend was incredulous- and so was Lora, hearing the details for the first time- when Benn told them of his disabled restraint and recounted Lint Man's sudden leap to save him from being crushed against the ceiling. "But why would anyone do that?" Salkend demanded. "Why would this... *businessman*, you say, sacrifice himself...." He suddenly fell silent, playing the scene over in his mind. Benn and Lora stared at Salkend awhile, then, unsure whether to continue, picked at their meals through an awkward silence of several minutes. At long last, when Salkend spoke again, he offered a non-sequitur, as though nothing at all had derailed their conversation.

"Well then, ah- tell me, ah, how have your studies been coming along, Lora?" Salkend seemed to be addressing Lora's blurry reflection on the steel tabletop. He was still adding up all the pieces of the puzzle.

"My studies? Well, my studies are coming along just fine- as you know, Rion. You've been helping me for weeks, after all." She dutifully began to discuss the chapter just completed, Forty-One. Salkend nodded encouragingly, but his thoughts were clearly elsewhere.

"I've really made progress with the Biogenome Menu." Lora cleared her throat. "But the fact is: if this were a restaurant menu, I would still be stuck in the Appetizer section!" To Benn's amazement, Lora snorted as she inhaled sharply, and then recovered, "The Appetizer section, Rion! You see..."

Lora had made a joke! Caught off guard, Benn felt no spontaneous reaction at all, but knew that in this context he should somehow appear amused. But how? Should he tell her that he was well into the Entree section? Dessert? Quickly now, he nudged himself, but could summon up nothing verbal that would do- so he settled for a modest outburst: "Ha-HAH!"

"Fine. Fine," Salkend looked up from the table, his additions complete. "Well, ah, Lora, there are many, ah, preparations I must make for tomorrow, so I will have to cut short this, ah, pleasant evening." He continued to talk to the air. "The interns will gather at, ah, eleven hundred New York time, in the debarcation chamber. I'll see you then." He rose abruptly and started to leave, then turned back as an afterthought and gave Lora's shoulder an apologetic squeeze. With a curt nod to Benn, Salkend hurried off.

Lora, nonplussed, shot a puzzled look at Benn, who- following his seemingly successful response to Lora's joke- pondered how he ought to react now: there were so many options, and it never occurred to him that saying nothing was one of them. The correct reaction, a quick analysis revealed, would depend on Lora's feelings toward Salkend. And what was their relationship: how had it developed, the weeks of assistance he had provided her, that intimate conversation he had witnessed in the hallway, and just now his hand squeezing her shoulder? Complicated.

"You're wondering what suddenly got into Salkend?" Benn began, deciding that perhaps staying with levity would be safest. After all, her attempt at a joke showed she had a sense of humor, didn't it?

"We already know that Salkend is extremely, ah, concerned. Remember?" Benn stroked an imaginary goatee and stretched his face into a starchy, portentous expression.

"There is, ah, another matter of grave concern. Ah, please excuse me if, at times, I appear overly, ah, cautious." Oh no, maybe this wasn't the best approach after all, it suddenly dawned on him.

Lora reddened. "Benn! That's so heartless of you! He's concerned for our safety, that's why he had to rush off. Rion's really wonderful. Besides helping me study during these past weeks, he's been constantly in touch with MWI, checking our security arrangements at YaleConn. And – I might as well say this- at least Rion cares a bit about people- I mean, other than himself."

She poked pointedly at her food and, eyes downcast, waited for Benn to say something, anything. The sharp metallic sound of her fork striking the plate was nearly deafening in the silence between them. Benn, baffled at first, slowly realized the full extent of his faux pas. He sighed softly, turned away from Lora, and spent the rest of his allotted mealtime in penitent contemplation of the mysteries of human relations.

Chapter Five

Earth!

Benn stepped eagerly through the doorway of the MWI shuttle, which had carried Rion Salkend and his group of expectant interns directly from the debarcation chamber of the transcruiser, through the tangled network of underground passages permeating New York Metropol, to the MWI offices in what was still quaintly termed "midtown Manhattan." He ceremoniously placed his right foot, for the first time ever, on Earth soil- terra firma, at long last! Polyfoam carpeting, actually, but that was beside the point. He imagined a distant fanfare of trumpets, a voice echoing: "One small step for man...." But certainly a giant leap for Benn Marr.

Except for the very brief transit across Queens ElegnaPort (itself nondescript, but oh, that sudden flash of brilliant blue sky appearing overhead! He had never imagined such a beautiful, blinding blue!) into the blackness of the Long Island Tunnel, and then the momentary glimpse of a bottomless gray steel and concrete canyon as the shuttle crossed from the Av5 Exit to the modest MWI building, Benn had seen little of the outdoors. And now he found himself confined in a stuffy, windowless meeting room, seated with Lora, Salkend, Sool and the three Highlanders around a smoked-glass table, listening to the MWI Vice President of Colonial Affairs- a pale, overweight bureaucrat named Dmitri Lezhev- drone on in a thick Russian accent.

The V.P. served on the Board of the Mars Wellness Institute, but his full-time job was with the PWE, where he held the title Associate Secretary of Security for the American Zone. Lezhev was baffled: why in the world had MWI assigned him to deliver this welcome speech, apparently unwelcome at best? In the manner all too typical of today's youth, his audience looked completely apathetic. Still, they must have their reasons; he had long recognized that MWI had an agenda quite separate from its outward, corporate mission of supporting the PWE in health-related matters through research, education (hence his wasted speech to these students), drug development and healthcare administration. Even as a Board member, he felt shielded from the opaque inner workings of MWI. Maybe these young people had something to do with his role in American Zone Security. Not very likely; Lezhev pressed on with his speech.

Benn paid little attention; he thought longingly of the bright blue sky just outside. At the same time, he had become aware of an aching pressure behind his eyes, and a low humming noise had been growing steadily over the past hour. Was there some machinery laboring behind the wall? Nobody else seemed to hear it. Benn rubbed his temples and tried blocking his ears. The nagging sound persisted, but by focusing intently on it, he found that he could suppress its volume.

Then Lezhev said something about an assassination attempt, which, to his satisfaction, got everyone's attention. Just the day before, a powerful bomb had exploded at PWE Center in Beijing, killing four. Two members of the Central Council of the Pan-World Electorate had been wounded. So even Level Zero bureaucrats were not immune. A week ago, a dozen masked gunmen waving an outlawed French flag and chanting slogans had attacked a Vitacube factory on the outskirts of Paris Metropol. Those French and their hatred of Synthedible Corp! The gunmen had been arrested and dispatched to the Louis Pasteur Institute for Psychosocial Rehabilitation. Could anti-societal thoughts be pasteurized? wondered Benn.

In the Mideast Zone, where there remained inexplicably strong sentiment in favor of returning to the ethnically-defined political boundaries of the nineteenth century, agitators had torched a PWE branch in Beirut. Thirteen employees had perished in the flames, while demonstrators outside chanted *Death to the PWE*, said Lezhev, shaking his head gravely. And all because a recent PWE journal had included a satirical column denouncing the Mideast agitation as "Ottomania"! Worldwide, neo-nationalists and other reactionaries had become ever more violent during the centennial year of the PWE. In the American Zone, the number of rebels banished to the Quarantine Zone had doubled in the past nine months. With each bit of alarming news, Rion Salkend blanched; the situation was even worse than he had imagined.

53

But for the young interns, this news was merely abstract, not of immediate concern. Foye fidgeted idly with his da-disc, while next to him, Trip slowly inched his chair around to ogle Nema, who winked back at him and shifted her legs in a suggestive manner. Two seats over, Sool was either praying or fast asleep, her hands folded in front of her on the table. Lora put down her da-disc and peeked out the corner of her eye at Benn, who, in turn, had gone back to rubbing his temples while staring fixedly at the glass tabletop. He was trying very hard not to envision the pasteurization of anti-societal thoughts, which conjured an image of a large blue-veined cheese, floating like a brain in a bell-jar. Slowly, another image began to form in his thoughts: a dog, a cat and a mouse, all stitched together in forced co-existence by the PWE.

Dmitri Lezhev, chagrined by the group's lack of attention, their frank indifference to his message, cleared his throat pointedly. He skipped forward to his concluding remarks- the usual congratulations and generic encouragements- delivered at an accelerated pace. Then, with a dismissive wave of his hand, he signaled Rion Salkend to lead his undisciplined charges back to the shuttle port, and on to their final destinations.

Greater Haven, to Benn's continuing disappointment (now becoming a daylong affair), turned out to be a dreary wasteland, all the way from its western limit at the Bridgeport Gate to what little of Greater Branford he could see in the distance from the shuttle window. They flew at low altitude a few kilometers inland, beyond sight of the shore. A vast expanse of heavily industrialized neighborhoods, formerly separate townships which had grown confluent over the past century, gave way to residential zones comprised of row after endless row of faceless apartment buildings, stacked one upon another. To make matters worse, the heavy sky, looming with dark clouds, lent a dense gray cast to the entire city.

Benn searched in vain for a hint of that electric blue, which he knew lay hidden just behind the towering clouds; but it soon dawned on him that these clouds themselves were the main attraction. Huge accumulations of water vapor, weighing tons yet magically defying gravity, just hanging up there in the sky! Quite dreamlike- he had seen pictures of clouds, which didn't come close to the real thing. But amazing as they were, clouds were nothing, compared to rain.

Slowly and subtly it began: just a slight haziness at first appearing on his window- was he imagining it? Then unmistakably, *water*, actual drops of water, began to strike the outside of the pane! The pulsing, murmuring noise in Benn's head, which he had finally managed to eliminate by concentrating his will and mentally shoving it aside, was soon replaced by a loud drumming of heavy rain on the metal roof of the bus. The disappointment which had been piling up all day now promptly vanished. Even the jaded Highlanders were soon screaming like monkeys in a cage. They leapt from window to window, gawking, pointing, grinning foolishly at one another, barely noticing when the bus finally landed at Phelps Shuttleport. There the Highlanders stayed on board, mesmerized by the novelty of water falling from the sky, while the rest jumped off without any farewell and stood, in varying degrees of astonishment, on the Old Campus of YCU: ancient, storied YaleConn University.

Despite the rain, Benn found himself immediately distracted by the Old Campus itself. Had he not been exposed in elementary school to examples of old Earth architecture, the surrounding buildings would have appeared bizarre, at best. He was familiar with sandstone and other ancient building materials (an experimental dome built of Martian sandstone sat broken and abandoned on the outskirts of Tharsis Two, too fragile to withstand Marsquakes), but these jutting ledges and bulky columns served no discernible purpose whatsoever. And what were these horned creatures with protruding tongues- gargoyles, he seemed to recall. What was the point of those? And to his left! Why were those two crumbling red-brick buildings still left standing? Their dangerously leaning chimneys, slanted windows and crooked shutters flaking off green paint would have been laughable, if not for the sadness of their decayed state.

At the top of Harkness Tower- an imposing medieval structure which directly faced the shuttleport- a large glowing screen broadcast their arrival in real time, beneath the logo of the YaleConn Daily News, "Oldest College Daily By Far." Benn watched himself, Lora, and Sool up on the screen, staggering in the rain with palms and faces uplifted in wonderment. Even one as devoid of religion as

Benn could recognize the ritual of baptism represented by this watery scene; by sheer coincidence, a bold headline high overhead compounded the symbolism: "Rainfall As Miracle of the Heavens: Martian Pilgrims Discover Water on Earth!" The heavy raindrops, miraculous indeed, continued to pelt their tingling foreheads and stream down their cheeks. Benn and Lora grinned at one another as they watched Sool breathlessly whirl around, oblivious to all but the rain.

Rion Salkend, completely unimpressed by the rainfall and shading himself as best he could with his da-disc, darted into a nearby archway. Since his young charges showed no sign of following him to shelter, he soon returned with a reluctant-looking security officer in a dark blue uniform which, although neatly pressed, failed to disguise his slovenly nature. Unshaven, hair shaggy and randomly arranged, clearly annoyed by the fact that his uniform was getting soaked, the officer stood deferentially a few steps behind Salkend.

"Please, if I can have your attention," Salkend interrupted Sool's dance. "This is, ah, Torch Halsey, head of, ah, University Security." Halsey, who seemed young for someone with such a serious title, jumped a little at the mention of his name.

"He will show you to your dormitory and make sure all the necessary procedures for enrollment are taken care of." Salkend frowned at Halsey. "As for me, ah, I will take my leave now, to bring the other three, ah, interns to Boston, and then I shall return to New York. Should you need me for any reason, I can be reached at MWI for the next two months."

A look of panic slipped across Lora's face.

Salkend noticed, and his official tone softened. "Ah, the moment of truth, Lora! The first of many! You'll do well, after the initial jitters pass; remember, Lora- and I mean you as well, Benn, and, ah, Sool- you are at the top of your generation! Just stay clear of any, ah, political unrest, but more importantly those, ah, recreational psychopeptides, and I'm sure you'll be fine." Sool, who had paused momentarily, started again to twirl in the rain.

"Ah. Well, then." Salkend hesitated for a long moment, then, with a look of dread on his face, climbed reluctantly back aboard the shuttle, where he was immediately accosted by Nema and Trip.

                                    * * *

    Behind a locked steel door at the end of a long, well-lit corridor, two men faced each other in a darkened room, surrounded by a network of machines: biometers blinking and ticking rhythmically; a Hyper-Probot and its linked monitors; nano-surgical equipment of various kinds; all connected to a slim bank of supercomputers which, if not for subatomic transistor technology, would have filled half the room. At the back wall, a polished black cylinder three meters long lay on its side, atop a large and complex control panel. No fewer than three glowing red Eyes surveyed the room: one on each end of the control panel, and one in the center of the ceiling.

    The room was kept uncomfortably cold. A white-haired man in his late fifties, wrapped in a white lab coat, sat stiffly behind a wheeled, rectangular bio-transport table with his arms folded, while the other stood on the opposite side, leaning forward with his hands spread on the table. They had reached the end of a long conversation which, at several points, had erupted into argument.

    "I feel strongly that we should commence," said the man standing. "As I keep telling you, we must move ahead with the project- now. Bring him in..."

    "No! Haven't you been listening?" came the exasperated reply. "He is nowhere near ready. We have to consider the possibility of another severe backlash, until he's been thoroughly prepared."

    "Again. There isn't the time for all that. Read my updated report, will you: some unexplained events have come to light, which may indicate that opposing interests are already at work. While we are painstakingly preparing him, as you suggest, we may end up losing the project altogether."

    "I did read your report. Despite your... in my opinion, paranoid imaginings, we have no proof of any actual immediate danger, of any interference with our plans for the project, so I really must insist that we wait. It will take at least a month to adjust to his new environment; before that, there is no way he could survive the trial. Besides, there is Phase Two yet to go, have you forgotten that? We need to calibrate the scale, before committing everything.

Making a precipitous move now... well, judging from previous experience, that could be totally disastrous, wouldn't you agree?"

A third voice suddenly cut in, soft and breathy, originating somewhere above them. "YES. BEAME IS RIGHT. PRECI... CIPITOUS. DISASTROUS. NOT YET READY. SURVIVE THE TRIAL. BEA... BEAME IS RIGHT. DON'T. LET. HIM. COME."

"You see? I have the support of the OMC! The OMC, himself." Beame smiled crookedly, in that patronizing way he had. "We wait for now. Any more objections? Or can you possibly be questioning not only my judgment, but even that of the OMC?" He had played his trump card with a flourish.

"No...all right, we'll wait for now. The OMC has more insight than we BOTH do, and we'll follow his advice. But, Dr. Beame, you'd better make sure the project is secure. Paranoid imaginings, you say? Paranoid or not, I'm warning you again: unexpected events have already occurred, and if something goes wrong with the project, you will be the one held responsible."

"YES. UNEXPECTED. DISAS... DISASTROUS. BEAME. DON'T. LET. INTER...FERE."

The seated man, having exploited the overhead voice sufficiently to his advantage, now chose to ignore it. "Warning me, are you? Don't forget- you are working for me, and not the reverse. I am fully aware of possible dangers, and hardly need your... warning to keep things in line. And you know there are security measures in place- we've hardly left this to chance!

"There is one thing you got right," admitted Dr. Beame, attempting a more conciliatory tone. "I will indeed be the one responsible. After all, this has become my project now, hasn't it? And I plan to do a better job than the previous Project Director, who, shall we say, paid the price for his imprudence."

"YES. BEAME. CAU... CAUTION."

"Yes, yes, caution." He waved a hand at the darkness. "Now, if there's nothing further, I have to finish a few things in here...." He turned his back on the other, who, after two hours of exhaustive discussion, could think of nothing further to add.

Only the ceaseless ticking of the biometers could be heard. Seated at the Dataframe, Project Director Walther Beame lightly touched its controls, tinkering with a minor subroutine. He was grateful that the OMC, who had the annoying habit of constantly interrupting, had decided to shut up.

Finally breaking the intransigent silence, the standing man turned abruptly on his heel, let out a painfully stretched sigh of resignation (how typically over-reacting and theatrical, thought Beame) and waved the door open. He paused a few seconds for his eyes to adjust to the light before exiting into the warm and humid corridor. Then, as required by strict corporate protocol, Rion Salkend remembered to watch the heavy steel door close and re-lock firmly behind him.

Chapter Six

Slope-shouldered, plump Torch Halsey, long underestimated by his peers, now considered himself a top success. At age thirty-six, he was already Chief of Security at YCU, transferred from outside the YaleConn system, right over the startled heads of his current Sub-chiefs. In his previous job at the Eunigen Institute, he had been merely one of two dozen Policy Enforcers, but had clearly distinguished himself in the eyes of his bosses. As a result, he no longer toiled in the fields of mediocrity.

Eunigen Policy Enforcer: basically a snoop or spy, charged with the tedious task of "scrubbing" endless hours of records from the company's Eye network, monitoring all communications for the slightest irregularities, even trailing the occasional employee out in the field. Halsey made a mental note to meet with his network of informers this week, to discuss the negative attitudes of his Sub-chiefs, as well as the rank and file. Was there resentment at being passed over for promotion? Undoubtedly- in fact, some of the Sub-chiefs had been openly sharpening their blades since his appointment. Not to worry, though: no insurrection could succeed, as long as Eunigen supported him.

Would he uncover any disloyalty to Eunigen? Very likely he would. Not from the Security Department, but from the faculty and administration of the university. Yale had once been a great private institution, forced after the War of Unification to make a "donation" of itself to the State of Connecticut and to change its name to YaleConn. After the dissolution of the states less than a decade later, YaleConn had fallen into a tug-of-war between corporate bidders. Eunigen had prevailed and, for the past eighty years, had held the controlling interest in the university. Torch knew that many on campus still resented Eunigen as a corporate pirate looting their ivory tower for its inventions, research, influence in academia and prestige. Disloyalty to Eunigen would be widespread.

And finally- on a much brighter note- would he discover the illegal sale or use of recreational therapeptides on campus? Oh yes, most definitely, he would! This sin he could forgive, Halsey conceded, since he himself was an occasional user- but only of the entry-level drugs. Insight Out. JAMpot. Common Scents. These were all fairly benign, easily self-injected by Dermamist. Despite the painfully ugly- but mercifully brief- withdrawals, they relieved stress, improved self-esteem and helped him focus his thoughts: three areas in which he had lately been experiencing an ever-growing need. Better yet, they gave him an idea of what mischief his subordinates were up to. It was a dose-dependent response: just one vial of Insight Out, and he could clearly sense the hatred directed at him, down at the Security building. Two vials, and he knew from which floors, which cubicles, the hostility radiated. It was palpable and specific. Three vials, and he knew just where to find that incriminating memo, unauthorized weapon, or- best of all- the illegal therapeptide stash of another user, which of course he would promptly confiscate!

Insight Out was Halsey's favorite; the others gave him more pleasure and excitement, but not much useful information. Of course he had heard of Deep Coma, supposedly the ultimate mind-expander, but had not been able to find a supplier- it was still under development, he supposed. Even the new arrival, Roving Eye, which lay secure in his office safe waiting for just the right moment, was an experimental sample. According to rumor, Roving Eye would enable him to leave his body and travel about undetected! All right, he had stolen the sample, but Torch was more than happy to participate in market research: the spirit of unsolicited volunteerism was what made the drug economy great. He could already imagine an advertisement for Roving Eye: *"Enter* faraway, secret places! *See* behind locked doors! *Feel* the hidden passions!" Oh, Torch could hardly wait.

Now returning to the Security Office from Edward S. Harkness medical dormitory, Halsey made another mental note: there was something special about the latest arrivals on campus. For one thing, they came from Mars. Eunigen was paying them extra attention, so he'd better do likewise: what with the hyper-encrypted memos coming from New York two months ago, the unannounced inspection of the campus by Eunigen agents last week, and today this pushy fellow Rion Salkend, fussing and hovering over his three interns like a freak on JAMpot, Halsey resolved to scrub the Eyes a little more closely for the next few weeks.

In addition to the guard, there was an Eye at the medical dorm entrance, two in every hallway, and, unbeknownst to the occupants, one concealed in each apartment, in a location which allowed privacy only in the bathroom (the designers had reluctantly agreed to that one concession). Halsey had no qualms about the ethics of spying on interns; it was established practice. He passed quickly through his untidy office within the archway at Phelps Gate, and into the circular View Room- it was so much more stimulating in there, compared to filling out endless forms at his desk. After a quick glance around, he excitedly activated the three new screens. This would be almost as good as Roving Eye!

Torch just couldn't help himself: the first room he peered into had to be Lora Wheeler's. To his great disappointment, she was already fast asleep, and she was sharing her bed with... who, or what, was that? It looked like that huge duffel bag she had dragged around earlier- thank goodness. The lights were off, but to the hidden Eye, Lora's room appeared as in daylight, with a yellowish cast. Strange that she was in bed so early, thought Halsey, as she hadn't seemed at all tired an hour ago.

Hadn't Lora just been teasing and flirting with him, over in the Harkness lobby? Although a little cautious and confused at first, she had quickly warmed to him, hadn't she? She called him Torch- not Halsey, like everyone else. When he distributed the registration form to their da-discs, that coy look she gave him carried volumes of unspoken meaning- plain as a printed invitation. And he would even call it brazen, the way she so casually took the stylus right out of his breast pocket, without even asking: wasn't she signaling a desire for intimacy? She signed her form, glancing at him in that suggestive way, then tucked the stylus back into his pocket, and patted it! Wait, did she? Yes, definitely, I remember her touching me right on the chest. Torch, he thought, women sense your special qualities right away. They get you. Too bad Lora was already asleep: well, there was always tomorrow, not to mention the rest of the year.

Now Sool Tamura, she was a different type altogether. He moved eagerly to the next screen and watched Sool get up from her desk and disappear into the bathroom. She had addressed him as Halsey- all business, cold and aloof, demanding answers. Still, the mere fact that she came from Mars made her, well, a little exotic, right? Torch suspected that Sool had been surreptitiously shadowing him all afternoon. Yes, she couldn't take her eyes off him either. She was attractive too, in her own way. But all that shiny facial hardware and wild hair coloring that Sool favored had long since gone out of fashion on Earth. You couldn't blame an outlander for being out-of-step, but somehow Lora had managed to overcome her Martian handicap.

For a moment he glanced hopefully back at Lora (still clinging to her duffel bag), then moved on to Benn's screen. Here was an odd one, that Asian fellow Benn Marr. Stone-silent all afternoon; couldn't tell what he was thinking about. Marr was a Chinese name, right? So that would explain it: he was *inscrutable*. Marr was not at all bewildered like Lora, or uptight and watchful like Sool- even though all three of them had literally entered a whole new world. Marr seemed able to adjust very quickly to his surroundings, but his confident manner was a big bluff. Not for one moment did Halsey accept that Marr belonged on his campus.

There was something, well, alien about his intensity. On the way to Harkness, he had sat in a trance, staring hard out the window of the squad car at the falling rain. Some internal conversation seemed to be going on: he would frown, then chuckle, then rub his temples, chuckle again, then go back into his trance. After Torch delivered the orientation talk- to which Benn paid no attention, it was quite obvious- he simply stuffed the da-disc into his backpack and vanished straight up to his room without even saying goodnight to Lora (I know I would have, thought Torch with a shiver).

Now onscreen, Benn sat sideways to his desk, on which lay his open da-disc; a handful of squashed Vitacubes (in unpopular flavors they didn't even make anymore, Torch sniffed); the YaleConn ID/credit badge issued to each of the interns; and- no mistaking it- there was a baseball, badly scuffed-up. That's very strange, Torch wondered: where did it come from? Did they play baseball on Mars? It didn't seem likely. But even stranger, Benn seemed to be looking straight at Torch, even though the Eye in his room was well-disguised. The longer Torch stared at the screen, the stronger his feeling that Benn was staring right back at him; badly unnerved, Torch was forced to turn away. No need to be paranoid, he reassured himself- he can't possibly know about the Eye!

Nevertheless, after distractedly rounding on the rest of the screens in the View Room, Torch Halsey made a rapid bee-line to his outer office, without once looking back- not even at the tantalizing image of Lora Wheeler.

Lora stepped out of the Pan-Bio Analyzer, commonly known as the Probot, and reached for her paper robe. Her skin was flushed and tingling- it felt like a Sonicspray, she thought, only without the blowing sensation. The Probot scan, which produced a detailed analysis of anatomy and organ function- it would have detected a gastric ulcer, sinus infection or brain tumor, for example- was the final part of the physical evaluation required of all students, and she had passed without a hitch. So had Benn and Sool, who were already on their way to the first formal lecture for the incoming class of interns, scheduled to begin in Cushing Hall in just a few minutes. After a week of organizational meetings and introductory talks, it was a much-anticipated moment.

Lora nodded to the technician seated at a control panel, hurriedly crossed the cold Probot Chamber to the adjacent dressing room, and exchanged the robe for her standard-issue orange bodysuit. Almost everyone attending YaleConn Med- not only the lowly interns- wore those bodysuits to class, so Lora shrugged off their resemblance to the prison uniforms worn by PsySoc reformees back at Tharsis One. In a way, Lora was disappointed that the computer hadn't found anything wrong with her: no explanation for the distracting noise, that persistent insect buzz that had kept her up for part of the night. It was faint, but intermittently took on a pronounced throbbing pattern- quite annoying. Neither Benn nor Sool seemed to hear that noise, whatever it was: A blood clot? Eustachian tube dysfunction? Seizure activity? The Probot said no, no and no. Meaning that there wouldn't be an easy remedy.

Clutching a da-disc to her stomach, which gurgled audibly as she hurried down the broad, wood-paneled corridor toward Cushing Hall, she thought of another disappointment: the Probot had also ignored her abdominal upset. Maybe the gastrointestinal symptoms and the buzzing noise were merely "endo-cranial," a word she had heard a resident use pejoratively in discussing a patient's symptoms.

Medical school introduced many unsanctioned terms to students; in this case, the dismissive term meant "supra-tentorial" or, in plain language, "imaginary." Lora had to admit, she was anxious about starting medical school- who wouldn't be a little nervous?- but this was definitely not the time for any weakness or dependency. No imaginary symptoms, please!

Maybe Benn could help. Quite unexpectedly, since arriving on Earth over a week ago, the maddening frustration Lora felt in Benn's company had faded away, as though their two disparate orbits had somehow mysteriously aligned.

"You know, Benn," Lora had pronounced at dinner the previous evening, "I used to see your lack of expression and response as a disregard of others' concerns, but I've changed my mind; I think you don't react to every little concern because of your emotional depth and stability." Benn shrugged carelessly; as far as he knew, she had gotten it right the first time.

Lora now saw Benn as solid and unflappable, not callous and self-absorbed as she had so unfairly thought. Emotionally, his center of gravity was extremely low, and that's why he didn't engage well with others- such as those three arrogant, insecure interns from Highland City. Their egos rode high. They were so top-heavy emotionally that the slightest breeze could tilt them over. Lora kicked herself for misjudging Benn: it was understandable that he kept to himself. But couldn't he understand that Lora, too, was different from the others?

Lora had decided to test Benn's boundaries gingerly, that first evening at Harkness dorm. It was after the rambling disorientation speech by that awful Torch Halsey. Chief of Security, ha! Halsey, who had been eyeing Lora in an obvious way all afternoon, had finally approached her and stammered some inarticulate remark, maybe a joke, about her being a Martian. She had ignored him and pointedly walked over to Benn- sitting by himself, as usual. Fully aware of Halsey's persistent stare, she had casually removed the stylus from Benn's breast pocket and completed her form. Then, with an ostentatious wink visible to the Security Chief, she had tucked the stylus into Benn's pocket and patted it back in place- all without a word. Benn had nodded absently and certainly not objected. Didn't that demonstrate Benn's tacit acceptance, an unspoken intimacy they already shared? And then to see the crestfallen look on Halsey's face- that alone was worth the effort. The churning in her stomach began to subside.

Rushing down a long corridor lined with portraits, barely glancing at their brass labels- Galen Vesalius Hippocrates Da Vinci-Lora reached a wooden double-door marked with gold lettering: Cushing Hall. She read this name slowly, with a measure of awe. One evening on the Transcruiser, Benn had told her about Harvey Cushing- YaleConn Class of 1891 (it was known as Yale College in those days, he had pointed out). Cushing had described the medical syndrome later named after him, along with the corresponding dopaminergic therapeptides. But more significantly, said Benn, Cushing was once captain of the Yale baseball team! Inscribed above the door: "Inspiring Teacher, Pathfinder in Neurosurgery, Master of the Science and Art of Healing." All admirable- but, Benn had wondered facetiously, what position did he play? Pitcher? Or had Cushing been good enough to play shortstop? Ha-HAH! Poor Benn and his goofy sense of humor.

Now late for her first lecture, Lora threw the door open, rushed forward, and squeaked to a sudden halt before the first in a long series of steps descending to a stage at the bottom of a deep, cone-shaped auditorium. At the center of the circular stage, gazing up at his orange-clad audience, stood a gray-bearded professor in his late sixties, dressed in a long white lab coat, white Oxford shirt, pin-striped gray slacks and red paisley bow tie: right out of a History of Medicine text. He turned slowly as he spoke, to address his entire audience, but it was hardly necessary, as his replicated image, magnified five times, rotated in a three-dimensional display just a short distance above his head. The professor was already well into his lecture.

Not seeing Benn or Sool anywhere, Lora took a seat on the aisle and focused on the scene below. Next to the lecturer stood a tall, elderly man, completely naked and looking quite disgruntled. Lora gasped, not because the man was completely naked or quite disgruntled, but because she realized the man was also quite deceased. Whatever was holding this person- this cadaver- in an upright position evidently included a complex hinge mechanism running the length of his spine; the lecturer, with a theatrically jaded expression, rapped unceremoniously on the corpse's forehead, and the entire body split and swung wide open from scalp to groin, revealing the entire, bulging contents of its head, thorax and abdomen. To the crowd's huge relief- especially those in the front row, who had reflexively leaned back- all of these bodily contents, though threatening, did not spill out onto the stage.

A loud murmuring rose up in the cone room. Lora's neighbor said to no-one in particular, "Dr. Neelin loves hauling out that antique, just for shock value." So that was Dr. Nestor Neelin, the infamous Professor of Recombinant Anatomy. Beyond his brusque, aggressive style of teaching, Neelin was known for his tireless efforts to expose fakery, exploitation and deliberate malpractice in the medical profession. Between lectures, he could be found testifying in court, or giving an interview to the media, in which he would rail against "quacks and quasi-sequencers."

Dr. Neelin introduced the subject with a wave of his arm. "Ladies and gentlemen, say hello to Bob." A titter and several hellos swept through the audience. "Bob comes to you from the Gates-Smithsonian Institution, where he has enjoyed a distinguished career in educating generations of health workers, such as yourselves, about the pitfalls of early, primitive genetic engineering. Although silent by nature, Bob still manages to speak volumes."

Neelin dived in quickly: "Now if you'll observe: here in Bob's brain, there sit not one, not two, but look- three temporal lobes! Bob, you see, suffered a devastating stroke in his sixties, and in those early days of therapeutic stem cell infusions, an effort was made to replace the lost brain tissue. This effort marked a step forward in stem cell technology, prior to which most tissue types, such as brain, liver, eyes and so on, required engineering in vitro, then transplantation of the developed tissue to the patient. The new targeted stem cells, in contrast, could be infused intravenously, and would find their way to their appropriate location, guided by seeker molecules implanted in their membranes. There they would differentiate to the desired organ, thus obviating the need for a transplant procedure. In Bob's case, the infused stem cells did develop into a temporal lobe as planned, but unfortunately, growth stimulators infused at the same time caused the partially necrotic lobe to regenerate within his already-crowded skull- leaving him, quite literally, with not enough room to change his mind!"

Many in the audience, confused by this last phrase- was it meant to be funny?- consulted their da-discs only to find their

67

screens blank. Only one laugh could be heard, a loud "HA!" coming from the opposite side of the hall, some twenty rows below Lora. "Ha-HAH!" the same voice persisted. And that was how Lora finally located Benn.

Dr. Neelin glanced at Benn, then went on, "Now we enter the thorax. We see Bob's lungs, his heart, an atrophied thymus gland. And here is the esophagus... the hilum... some rather enlarged lymph nodes... ah. Can anyone tell me what this is?" He was holding the heart, in its glistening gray pericardium, off to one side- and there, in the back of the chest cavity, continuous with the left lung, was a kidney!

"Come now, speak up- it's just what it looks like. That's right- a kidney, in Bob's chest! Poor old Bob also suffered from hypertensive renal failure, and this was an attempt to generate a new kidney for him. But given the early stage of technology, there was no guaranteeing where those wandering stem cells- those naughty rascals- would end up, was there? Searching for their home in the retro-peritoneum, they settled and vascularized instead at the back of the thorax- which, by the way, looks remarkably similar, to a seeker molecule. In this case, to Bob's extreme chagrin, the little kidney actually put out a small daily amount of urine into Bob's lung! This gave him a productive cough, confused his doctors, and ..."- Neelin threw another quick glance in Benn's direction- "...probably didn't help with Bob's halitosis, either!"

"Ha! HahahHAH!" came Benn's anticipated response. The intern sitting in front of him spun around, scowled at Benn, and pinched her lips tightly between her thumb and index finger.

"That's all right," said Neelin. "Viewing these terrible errors and outcomes with humor, after all, is a healthy way of rejecting them. How else can we propel ourselves out of the dark days of Medicine, into the modern age? Admittedly, such examples of misguided recombinant anatomy are now quite irrelevant, since we hardly ever manipulate anatomy anymore...ever since the advent of theraproteomics." There was a hint of wistful regret in his voice. "But occasionally it is still necessary to alter a physical structure, and not just supply a curative therapeptide. Our techniques are far more precise now, of course, and we're only likely to see rogue stem cells and these sorts of bizarre results when *quacks* and *quasi-*

sequencers are involved." The audience broke out in polite applause.

Neelin held his right hand up. "I have one more example of quackery to show you. Bob, you see, was a victim not only of technical incompetence, but of outright fraud. Late in his life, he fell out of a Banyan tree while bird-watching in the district then known as Australia. He sustained a pelvic fracture and had to enlist the help of a migrant clinic in the back country, in order to regenerate the broken bone. They infused him with an unidentified stem cell, his diary shows, but the end result was only discovered at Bob's post-mortem." Neelin appeared to be rummaging around in Bob's intestines. He finally pushed them toward the back with outstretched fingers, exposing two thin bony structures pointing upward from the pelvis. Puzzled interns frantically interrogated their da-discs, again without success.

"Their treatment provided Bob, bless his original heart, with these two extraneous bones, which you see protruding here. These bones did nothing to help Bob with his pelvic fracture, but he would have found them useful- very useful indeed- had he... been... born... a..." Neelin paused expectantly.

"A kangaroo!" shouted Benn triumphantly.

Neelin released Bob's intestines with a loud flop and whirled around to face Benn. "A kangaroo or any marsupial- excellent! Young man, you are the first intern in over two decades to recognize these as epipubic bones: their function is to support a marsupial's pouch. Excellent! Your name, please?"

"Benn Marr, sir. I'm one of the new interns." The entire class turned to stare.

"So you're one of the three from Mars colony? But how would someone from Mars know anything about kangaroos? Curious. Well, no matter." Neelin returned to his subject, rapped its shoulder, and waited in respectful silence as the body slowly resealed itself. "That's all for today, ladies and gentlemen. Please read the supplemental material on recombinant anatomy which I have transferred to your da-discs. I will see you all in one week."

Amidst the noisy shuffling as the class began to empty out, Neelin quickly crossed the room and gestured to Benn to come down to the stage level. "Mr. Marr," he announced loudly as Benn approached, "you've impressed me with your quick eye today. Also, you seem to have a *sense of humor*." He took a meaningful, sweeping look around the room. "I wonder if you'd care to attend a small function I am hosting at the Great Hall of Mellon College next Friday evening at eight."

A dozen stragglers had turned to overhear the conversation, and they regarded Benn warily. From her distant seat near the top of the cone, Lora could hear every word clearly, including some biting comments among the remaining interns; the hall had obviously been designed with acoustics in mind.

"Sir?" Even at close proximity, Benn wondered if he had heard correctly. Attend a small function, with Dr. Neelin? Was he looking for a waiter? A dishwasher?

"Just an informal social gathering- about twenty faculty members, a couple of undergraduates and interns. Perhaps you know that Mellon College is one of the eighteen residential colleges of YaleConn. It's the one shaped like two overlapping pyramids."

"Yes sir- I know where it is. Between Brewster College and Jonathan Edwards."

"Good- you've familiarized yourself with the undergraduate campus. So you'll be there on Friday, Mr. Marr?"

"Uh, yes sir. I'll be there. Do I need to bring anything, Dr. Neelin?"

"Not at all. I'll supply the glasses." Benn looked puzzled. "Oh, did I mention that it's a wine tasting?"

"Wine tasting?" Benn had no idea what that was.

"Yes," said Neelin, turning toward Benn on his way out the door. "We'll be tasting a few special wines. But don't look so worried, Mr. Marr- you have a whole four days to practice the fine art of spitting."

Benn and Lora were able to sit together at their next class, Gene PerMutations, taught by Dr. Cira Vincent, who was quick to point out to the small group of interns in her seminar that she had a PhD, and not a medical degree. This conferred on her a higher level of prestige and authority, since it took at least two years of research after the three traditional college years to attain the PhD, whereas medical doctors attained their status by completing the equivalent of

70

only one year of college (and Benn's education on Mars would be considered a very questionable equivalent), followed by one year of internship. Physicians were, after all, mere technicians, applying the new concepts and technologies created by the true doctors, the PhD scientists.

Dr. Vincent, in her mid-thirties, fashionably dressed and full of cheerful energy, was a smooth lecturer, delivering her material at the maximal speed that could be absorbed by the average intern. Several, in fact, appeared to be struggling to keep up, their heads rapidly bobbing up and down as they tried to correlate her lecture to their da-disc chapters. One word that occurred to Benn was "chirpy"; another was "slick". Both were pejorative, he noted; something about Dr. Vincent rubbed him the wrong way. Lora, on the other hand, was completely taken with her crisp, no-nonsense style. She listened intently with both elbows on the circular wooden table, chin resting on her palms.

Gene PerMutations covered the principles of theragenomics, against the larger backdrop of non-therapeutic gene manipulations, with its applications in every field from food production to clothing manufacture. Dr. Vincent served as a consultant in many sectors of industry. Of course, this being a medical school course, her emphasis would be the combination of subgenes selected from the complete Earth Biogenome menu, then shuffled and re-shuffled into a set of PerMutations, in order to generate the desired theraproteomic products.

Her first challenge to the class: why use the trillions upon trillions of subgenes derived from chopping up existing genes, rather than simply design and construct new genes? Certainly the technology had long existed- for about two centuries- to dictate a sequence of nucleotides and then assemble them de novo. But countless efforts to produce any but the most rudimentary therapeptides from these built-from-scratch sequences had failed: among many reasons, one of the most important was that gene-associated proteins affecting conformation and expression were necessary as well, and these did not result from de novo synthesis. And so the lengthier and more complex gene sequences, along with their associated proteins, had to be harvested from natural sources.

Within the allotted two hours, Dr. Vincent managed to distill the essence of chapters twenty through fifty of their texts, which dealt with Deficiency States; even Benn had to be impressed. As she prepared to move on to States of Excess, a question was timidly raised by one of the interns who had been struggling to keep pace: a lost-looking fellow sitting apart from the main table, near the back of the room.

"Dr. Vincent?" the intern ventured. "I understand why you would combine the gene fragments from the biogenome menu to make therapeptides? And how the therapeptides correct the deficiency state? But you would have to keep administering the peptide indefinitely, right? Because it wears off?"

Dr. Vincent, unaccustomed to interruptions, stared at him with eyebrows raised. "Yes, of course, there is a finite half-life for every therapeptide," she replied warily, sensing the question to follow. "They have to be administered periodically. But they can be engineered to have extremely long half-lives, as you know."

"Yes? But wouldn't a better solution be to transfer the PerMutation into a stem cell? Then introduce the stem cell into the host, you know, to grow actual tissue? Once the genetically modified tissue took hold? The patient could then, you know, make his own permanent supply of the therapeptide?"

Vincent's face reddened as she consulted the seating register at her lectern.

"No... Mr. Messler." Her smooth delivery had been brought to a sudden halt by his naïve- no, appalling- question. "That would not be a better solution. Not at all! You haven't studied medical history much, have you, Mr. Messler. The PerMutations obviously consist of multispecies DNA. Multispecies Proteomics- and subsequently the use of the protein products as pharmaceutical products- is a well-developed field. But not the incorporation of PerMutations themselves into human beings. It has been over ninety years since the first attempt at introducing multi-species DNA into humans. Can anyone here please tell us what the consequences were?"

Benn and Lora looked at each other blankly.

An intern sitting across from them, a bearded black man a few years older than his peers, spoke up: "I believe you're referring to the Boston Gene Project. In one experiment, chimeric DNA, part mouse (from a strain of New Zealand mice with hyper-immune traits) and part human, was inserted via stem cells into patients

72

suffering from a variety of immune deficiencies. Balancing deficiency with excess: it seemed a straightforward idea. But there were nucleotide sequences in the DNA, previously considered 'junk' or nonsense, and even some non-genetic material, such as the associated proteins you mentioned earlier, which turned out to be important. Ninety percent of DNA doesn't code for proteins, yet remains biochemically active: for example, directly regulating- or coding for RNA which regulates- gene expression. The 'junk" interacted in unpredictable ways with the patients' genes, sometimes destroying them, or worse yet, re-sequencing them and changing the end-products. In the Boston experiment, subjects developed unexpected consequences: aggressive auto-immune diseases, multiple cancers, and even bizarre body changes involving... non-human tissue."

"Yes! And therefore, in vivo application of multi-species DNA became illegal, Mr. Messler- it's a major violation of the genetic engineering code. In fact, the law forbidding this application is second only to the universal ban on human cloning! Does that answer your question?"

Messler, whose jaw had dropped open, quickly nodded. Dr. Vincent, again checking her seating chart, said appreciatively, "Thank you for that excellent summary, Mr. Coffin. And Mr. Messler, you would do well to review the Three Laws of Theragenomics: The First Law, as I said, bans all human cloning, including the transfer of life from dying subjects. The Second bans in vivo application of multi-species DNA- what you so disingenuously proposed, Mr. Messler. Those are fairly straightforward, but the Third Law, more nuanced and what critics have called a slippery slope, followed centuries of debate. You may be aware that supporters of eugenics at the turn of the twentieth century advocated selective breeding of optimal human specimens, as well as the prevention of procreation among "low" types, such as criminals, the insane, and the poor. No? Well, Mr. Messler, do look into it. You'll find that such crude approaches to eugenics carried too high a societal cost, for example giving the state too much control over individuals. The advent of gene therapy and editing supplanted those approaches, but failed to resolve many ethical issues: the criteria used in selecting "desirable" traits, the potential to create a superhuman ruling class by the wealthiest one percent of the population, and so on. The Third Law of Theragenomics, Mr. Messler, addresses the marketing of "desirable" genomes. It limits gene-editing at birth to a maximum number of actionable genes, and is directed generally at disease-associated genes. The current limit is 200 genes, which is an arbitrary number, of course. But you do have to draw the line somewhere on the spectrum of eugenics, to preserve the conventional definition of what it is to be human." She paused to gather her thoughts, took in a sharp breath, and, as though Messler's interruption had never occurred, launched briskly into the second half of her rapid-fire lecture.

Chapter Seven

The following days were crammed with a quick succession of MedTech seminars, covering medical computer functions, from initial diagnosis to the prescription of specific therapeptides. Benn found these classes painfully dull, although he noticed Sool Tamura perking up as the topics became increasingly technical and obscure. Sool had appeared quite subdued- even depressed- in their other classes, but here in MedTech, she was in her element. As a robotics engineer, she knew QI, or Quasi-human Intelligence, inside and out. Her highly-specialized questions often left the unfortunate lecturer- a different technician rotating in each week- either stammering a hand-waving explanation, or else parrying with the classic defense, "Good question. Why don't you look it up and give us a talk on it tomorrow." To which Sool would promptly riposte with an immediate mini-lecture on the very topic- touché! Her skill at martial arts appeared to be paying off in medical school.

Sool had literally distanced herself from her fellow Martians, always choosing a place on the opposite side of the lecture hall. Sensing Sool's disdain for Benn and Lora, the class had essentially ostracized the two of them since the first day in MedTech class. At the moment, Benn and Lora found themselves surrounded by empty seats, whereas about twenty interns were grouped around Sool like petitioners before a queen, seeking her advice on complex QI concepts or approaches to difficult diagnostic algorithms. Whenever the instructor failed to answer- or, often, even to comprehend- her question, Sool's cadre of admirers would begin to hoot and shout. Thus encouraged, Sool would condescend to answer her own question. It's appalling, thought Benn: they're like sharks in a feeding frenzy. But feeding on small fry. After all, the pathetic lecturer was merely a technical post-doc, not one of the distinguished faculty for which the university was renowned.

To make matters worse, his headaches had returned in earnest, and whenever Sool stirred up the class, the dull pain behind his eyes sharpened, accompanied by waves of nausea and a harsh pulsating sound which required an ever-greater strain to will away. He became aware of Lora, watching him with concern as he leaned over his desk, hands cupped over his ears. The image of Lora running through her mental checklist on the Glidebus came back to him. But, unlike that first encounter, Lora's attention this time seemed less clinical and more empathetic, as though she felt his pain. And indeed she did.

"Benn, it's that noise, isn't it?" she finally asked.

Benn looked up sharply. "You hear it too? That repeating sound?"

Lora nodded; a look of relief washed across her face.

"You have a headache too, Lora?"

"A little. But mainly it's that noise. Sometimes it sounds like gears grinding. It kept me awake a couple of nights ago and came back just now."

"I wonder why just now, and to both of us simultaneously. It has to be something we're both being exposed to, right now. Maybe it's Sool! She's hard to take, like some noxious irritant that reaches a toxic level." Of course Lora dismissed the idea out of hand, but Sool's scolding of the instructor did seem to punctuate the throbbing in his head. Feeling a sudden strong craving for fresh air and open space, Benn stood up abruptly and lurched for the exit. Half the class turned to watch, and Sool stopped pontificating in mid-sentence to squint suspiciously at Lora as she followed Benn out the door.

"Benn, wait- please," Lora called, but Benn was already well ahead of her.

Not until they reached the Sterling Memorial Rotunda, a substantial jog farther along, did Lora finally catch up. Benn consciously slowed his pace as they crossed the busy quadrangle in front of the dormitory building. The shouts of children playing at war echoed off the old brick walls and flagstone paving. Some fresh air this is, thought Benn: thick and humid, smelling of sea salt and smoke. Rain was expected again that afternoon.

"You see? It's better already. The Sool Effect is fading."

"I don't think that's it," said Lora, still catching her breath. "Since we're the only ones who hear that noise, it's caused by something the both of us, and nobody else, were exposed to. Probably our space travel affected us, for example...in the sinuses?

That could cause an inner ear problem, although the Probot didn't detect it. Sool might be affected too, but she's so carried away with MedTech that she doesn't notice."

"No, Sool is insensitive to pain, among other things. She acts like a machine. In fact, I have a nasty suspicion that Sool is actually a humanoid robot... a CyberSool, ha! Her metallic hair and all that hardware on her face and hands are just the uncovered parts."

The image was so apt that Lora couldn't quite stifle a grin. But that was all she allowed herself; it wouldn't do, to participate in this sort of sniping. "I'm going on to our next class, though it's a little early. I guess you'll head back to the dorm?"

Benn closed his eyes and pinched the bridge of his nose. "Right. I'm going to lie down awhile and try to lose this awful headache. Then I've got that thing tonight- the wine tasting?- with Dr. Neelin."

"Oh, the wine tasting! I didn't have a chance to tell you before- Dr. Vincent, from PerMutations, is going to the tasting, and she asked me to come as her guest."

"Good for her! To be honest, I was dreading it, not knowing anyone there, and not seeing any point in 'wine tasting' anyway. But now it might even be enjoyable."

As he entered Harkness, Benn managed to flash a weak smile at the Eye overhead. Lora, at Dr. Neelin's party: excellent. Whenever he felt unsettled, her presence was calming. He had been wrong about Lora. What he had first derided as a vise-like Level Two mentality, driven mostly by an abject fear of punishment, he now recognized as her moral backbone: an unswerving desire to do the right thing guided her actions, simple as that! And she also tolerated Benn's quirky nature as so few did. Only Lora and Jace understood Benn. Waiting for the elevator, he mused about Lora's admirable qualities- an adequate distraction from his persistent headache- until the dormitory guard approached with a brown mailing box tucked under his arm.

"Benn Marr? This package came for you today." The box was imprinted with a bold return address: EUNIGEN CENTER NEW YORK. All quite confusing, thought the guard: Torch Halsey, his boss, had brought the box to the front desk at Harkness, staring at it jealously the whole time. He had even held it next to his ear and shaken it, like a child with a birthday present. And now

Halsey was sitting on a sofa at the back of the lobby, sneaking peeks around an upside-down copy of a journal, YaleConn Medicine. Very puzzling, all of it.

"I think it's from Eunigen Center in New York," the guard pointed out needlessly, mild awe in his voice. The package was less puzzling to Benn: there was no doubt his father had sent it. The real mystery: why was Torch Halsey hiding over there behind the magazine? Just as the elevator door closed, Benn saw Halsey leap off the sofa and sprint out the front door.

Benn aimed the package sensor at his right eye, touched the Open tab, and set the box on his bed. Its lid and sides retracted, revealing a single message orb, tucked next to a Dermamist injector. Beneath those items, he discovered three loaded injection canisters, labeled in numerical order. He first had to find the message reader, which turned out to be an older model, attached to the inside of his desk drawer. He pulled up a chair, hesitated for a second, then finally dropped the shiny black ball into the reader. Immediately the Eunigen logo, a golden caduceus with double-helical nucleic acid sequences in lieu of the traditional pair of snakes- basically a DNA molecule with wings- appeared silently on the wall facing the desk.

After a few seconds, the logo faded away, and the image of Owen Marr took its place. The projection was of surprisingly poor quality- grainy, unfocused and interrupted by frequent dots and flashes. Owen wore the white lab coat with which Benn was so familiar, the one in his hologram back home. However, his hair, no longer jet black, was now salt-and-pepper, and definitely on the saltier side. The face- ageless, dissatisfied, anxious, disapproving- had not changed at all. Owen's voice, which Benn had last heard over three years ago, floated softly across the room.

"Hello, son." Owen paused, and his image flickered. "I'm glad that you are now here, on Earth. I can't get away at the moment, to welcome you in person. Soon enough, though- soon enough. You have completed several weeks of studies, and I've heard that you're doing exceptionally well, as I expected. So it won't be long before you come to New York for a visit. In the meantime, I am sending you something in this package to help you along.

"By now you have experienced the same thing I did, when coming from Mars: severe headaches, a constant drumming noise in your head- have you, Benn? You've wondered what causes these symptoms? It will surprise you to learn that they are caused by a change in your brain activity."

Brain activity? Not sinuses? Benn felt a sudden foreboding.

"You see, Benn, it was discovered decades ago that there is an extremely weak electromagnetic field surrounding Mars- so faint that it could not be detected until improved sensors were developed. The magnetic field did not completely disappear with the cooling of the Martian core, as you and I were taught in school."

That's what I learned in first grade, Benn recalled. The core of the planet cooled, the protective EM field disappeared, and then solar winds stripped away the atmosphere.

"Much later, scientists found that prolonged exposure to this residual EM field slowly altered the electrochemical brain activity of Mars colonists, who gradually adapted to it. Much more importantly, Benn, the adaptation is heritable, passing genetically from one generation to the next! Of course, you see the implication right away."

I do?

"A rapid evolution of the brain occurs! It's a genetic change, not just a transient environmental effect. By the way, the same effect on evolution applies on this planet: the Earth's encircling energy field also shapes the life-energy within it, impacting everything from the migration of birds to communication between insects.

"Your arrival on Earth was painful, Benn, because your brain's electrochemical activity is simply incompatible with the EM field of this planet. And, worse yet, because your ancestors have lived on Mars for many generations, you have evolved further than most of the present colonists. Your symptoms, I would expect, are much more severe than those of the classmates who came with you.

"Years ago, I experienced the same problem when I first came to Earth. But, as part of my work at Eunigen, I was able to design a series of therapeptides which helped me adjust to the energy field here. That's why my visits to Mars became less frequent over the years: once I became acclimated to Earth, it was increasingly difficult to go back and forth. Do you see?"

Benn was still puzzled. The "extremely weak" EM field of Mars should pose no greater challenge to his father than it did to any other traveler from Earth. But there was no Question and Answer period.

"Here in this package are vials containing the three therapeptides I designed for myself. Use the Dermamist injector to administer one vial per week, and your discomfort will soon resolve. It is critically important to use the vials in the numbered order, one to three. It is also critical that you avoid exposure to any of the illegal therapeptides circulating on campus, as they can interact with the treatment."

He must have been talking to Rion Salkend, thought Benn.

"And Benn- don't tell your classmates anything about this. Their symptoms are nothing compared to yours, and there is only enough for you. By the end of a month, you should be adequately adjusted to Earth- enough, at least, for one year of internship. When you are feeling better, I will send for you."

Owen's image faded out, and the message orb popped out of the reader. Benn tried to rub the throbbing pain out of his eyes while sitting at the desk for several minutes, then sighed with frustration and walked over to his bed. His hands trembled slightly as he picked up the Dermamist injector and inserted the first vial. The headache and thumping noise had worsened considerably- he would be willing to try anything, at this point.

Benn chose a site on his left forearm for the injection, which snapped in painlessly and left a barely perceptible tingling at the skin. Almost immediately, the headache vanished- but as the annoying sound gradually ebbed, Benn began to feel a spinning sensation, although nothing within his view was actually moving. His father had said nothing about vertigo: well, each individual was bound to have his own side-effects. He flopped onto the bed, knocking over the remaining vials, and closed his eyes tightly.

Then he closed them again. And once more. It made no difference; somehow, Benn could still see.

Not perfectly well, granted, but he was definitely staring at his ceiling, right through his eyelids, which were tightly shut. Weren't they? He checked with a brush of his finger- yes, his eyes were closed. The ceiling pulsed and wobbled, sending waves down the adjacent walls, and every few seconds, the floor wobbled in sympathy with the ceiling. After some tenuous experimentation, Benn found that he was able to rise and propel himself forward haltingly. His furniture appeared hazy as he swayed and staggered past it. Vaguely aware of something amiss, Benn stopped halfway across the room, turned, and only then did he see himself- or at least his body- still lying on his bed! Although the vertigo had begun to resolve, he had to wheel back around, fighting down a sudden panic. At the shock of seeing his lifeless body a few meters away, he felt a strong aversion, an urgent need to leave the room. The closed door was merely a blur as he approached and- bracing for impact- passed smoothly through it, into the long hallway. He then drifted ahead a short distance, wondering: how was he doing this? He knew his body had not moved an inch- it was still back in the room- but his consciousness was definitely outside. Could he go further? On an impulse, Benn willed himself forward and entered another apartment, directly across the hall.

Benn's neighbor, a darkly tanned twenty-year-old wearing an Ocean College heliosurfing T-shirt, sat slouched over his desk, frowning as he studied a complicated diagram on his da-disc. His name was Kai, and all Benn knew was that he came from an island in the Caribbean Zone. In contrast to the darkly shimmering room around him, Kai appeared in unnaturally sharp focus, surrounded by a greenish halo that shimmered about a decimeter beyond his physical boundary. There was an unpleasant sickly-sweet floral aroma in the air, which soon gave way to a pungent odor of rotten fruit (closer to the smell of durian than peaches, but Benn knew neither one). As the green halo flared, the sulfurous stench increased.

Kai had become hopelessly lost in his da-disc! Looking over his shoulder, Benn recognized a diagram he had encountered during the second week of his flight from Mars: admittedly the diagram made for tough chewing, but was still digestible. Kai was frustrated in his struggle to build even a rudimentary understanding of it. In Benn's new perception, Kai's mental state looked like an unsupervised construction site: here a flimsy beam splitting from the strain; there a cracked brick sitting on watery cement; over that, switches disconnected from their primitive wires. Surrounding the

81

entire construction, the potent vacuum in Kai's thoughts, like a black hole, threatened to suck its fragile components into oblivion. How could Kai even begin to master the enormous amount of material that lay ahead this year? Then it became clear: the remainder of the year was irrelevant; Kai's meager goal was somehow to develop the *appearance* of understanding. Just for this one diagram, and just for today. On the table next to the da-disc, Benn noticed a glass of water, which, to his surprise, seemed to be emitting its own sort of aura, a powerful impression of fear and anger. This was novel and fascinating: somehow, the water mirrored Kai's mood.

Making matters much worse, Kai's QI lab partner, that timid fellow Messler- probably upset by his poor showing in PerMutations class- had failed to complete his half of this week's important QI programming project. The green halo flared widely, and Benn gagged at the smell and the accompanying thoughts: *why* had Kai agreed to take Messler as a partner! This time, Kai would be unable to bluff his way through. In class discussions, he was adept at picking up key phrases, and even body language, from the faculty and other interns, and then strategically recycling those phrases as his own. Even Kai was amazed at how well it worked: he would simply pronounce these sentence fragments or incomplete ideas in an authoritative manner, adding a confident nod, you-know-what-I-mean, or an explicatory wave of his hand, and-so-on-and-so-forth. His audience would unconsciously fill in the missing pieces. A semblance of knowledge seemed to suffice. Kai's perceptiveness and confident style had carried him all the way to his prestigious internship. But this time? Benn stared at Kai's turbulent aura. This time, style was even more devoid of substance than usual.

Benn watched the aura decay from a light green to brown, imitating the process of rotting in nature. He sensed that what Kai thought of as justified frustration was actually an angry mix of self-pity and envy, and the water in the glass echoed in complete agreement. Kai's thoughts sounded clearly: *why* did he have to struggle, when things came so easily to others clearly less deserving? It wasn't fair! All these other people had an unfair advantage! The floral/fruity odor now turned frankly fecal. Reflexively Benn tried to clamp both hands over his nose and mouth- in vain, as he remembered too late that his hands, nose and mouth had stayed behind in the room across the hall. At that

82

moment, he was merely a shapeless blob. Although it was possible to withdraw his vantage point to the farthest corner of the room, Benn found that, as long as he faced Kai's anger, waves of the foul odor continued to assault him.

He finally had to retreat into the hallway. To his relief, the air here was clear and odorless, without any trace of the turmoil erupting in Kai's apartment. He turned and wandered down the empty corridor, desperate to shake off the whole disturbing encounter. Most of the apartments in this wing of Harkness would be unoccupied for the next several hours, until classes ended for the day. And yet Benn now felt the strong presence of someone else in the corridor. It felt like a hostile, threatening heaviness which permeated the air. It crackled in his senses like a thunderstorm gathering directly behind him.

Benn spun around. The ominous being flickered at the far end of the corridor, then vanished. Had someone rounded the corner just then? He hadn't actually seen anyone. Benn had to pause and consider carefully: in this new drug-induced, hyper-perceptive state, how far could he trust his senses? How much of what he saw was real, how much imaginary? The hallway was certainly real, despite its strange, shimmering appearance, and Kai's apartment had been all too pungently real. But what about that hostile presence? Drug-induced paranoia? As if to underline the question, Benn now spotted, at the opposite end of the hall, a faint, disembodied aura drifting through the air: a light-green orb outwardly resembling Kai, before his rapid decay to brown. This aura was barely visible, stealthily silent- and mercifully, odorless. Was this vision real?

Benn leaned back as it flitted past him, first in one direction, then another, seeming vague and indecisive. Eventually it paused outside Kai's door and hovered awhile, its color darkening to a grayish green. Then, without warning, it zipped across the corridor and disappeared through the wall- into Benn's room! Hey, that's my room! Alarmed by this sudden move, Benn hurried to catch up, and discovered- wasn't it fun, learning the rules of this new dimension- that he was not limited to running speed; he could project himself to a distant point, simply by thinking of it.

Thus he was instantaneously back in his own room. Benn saw himself- at least his physical self- lying motionless on the bed, eyes still shut, and the mysterious stranger positioned less than a meter above him. It had now darkened to gray-brown, resembling a dirty snowball, or a puff of smoke. The puff was closely observing (if something without eyes can be said to observe) Benn's face; his right hand, which tightly clutched a Dermamist injector; and especially the three vials- one discharged- strewn on the bed. It appeared completely oblivious to the other Benn hovering in the room.

I might look like a blob too, thought Benn, but for some reason, that thing can't see me at all.

The aura appeared to be waiting for Benn to wake up, but soon gave up its watch and wandered aimlessly from the bed to the bathroom, to the front door, back to the bed, then over to the desk, where it settled in front of Benn's baseball. It was the ball that Benn had carried from Mars. Tentatively, the aura zigzagged closer and closer to the object of its curiosity, examining it from different angles. Its nosiness was becoming quite annoying.

Hey, leave that alone, protested Benn- and to his surprise, the puff tumbled a short distance away from the desk. How had that happened? Did I do that? From its erratic movements, Benn could see that the puff- whatever its consciousness entailed- was frightened, dashing first for the door, suddenly turning back to the bed, standing absolutely still awhile, then warily circling the desk. Once again, it began to inch slowly toward the baseball. What possible interest could this thing have in the game ball from the Greatest Play of the Season? Its unwanted attention was not only annoying, but also somehow disrespectful.

Get away from there, thought Benn much more forcefully. And this time, the puff was blown all the way through the building's exterior wall and out of view.

Benn rushed to the window. What exactly had just happened, how had he ejected it from his room? From his vantage point, four stories above the courtyard in front of Harkness, he was looking down on a dozen people, and saw that each person was outlined in a light-green aura. They were crossing the courtyard, alone or in pairs, walking in all directions. Of course they were unaware of their surrounding auras, Benn realized, but notably, whenever two auras overlapped, they would immediately recoil, like electrons repelling one another. This prevented the auras, and their

84

owners, from coming too close together: unconscious "personal space" took on a new meaning for Benn.

He finally spotted the gray-brown puff clambering out of the bushes opposite the dorm. Ragged and disoriented, it stood and rotated on a tilted axis, then inched along the edge of the quadrangle to a clear area, withdrawing from anyone who stepped in its direction, clearly avoiding contact with other auras. Then, for an amorphous object, the puff gave a remarkable impression of straightening up, dusting itself off, and limping away in the direction of the Old Campus.

Benn suddenly felt a great hollowness, a need for solidity. He turned from the window and floated reluctantly to the bed, where he wrestled momentarily with the tempting notion of staying a little longer outside of his physical form. After all, his body was so severely confining, wasn't it, lying there, inertia-bound in its pitiful dimensions. But the choice was not his: time was up, the injection had worn off, and he had to return to his body.

With that thought, Benn immediately plunged into darkness. It was simply the darkness behind his closed eyelids, and he promptly opened them to the familiar view of the ceiling, which was now flat, no longer wobbling. Taking careful inventory of his surroundings, he could feel a slight draft in the room, the firm pressure of the bed beneath him, the metal surface of the Dermamist in his clammy right hand. He heard a faint humming sound, but thankfully, the headache was gone.

Shortly afterwards, Torch Halsey also opened his eyes, but to a completely different experience. There was PAIN! No, AGONY, OH! POKING him HERE, and THERE! The pain was MERCILESS, stabbing DEEP in his ORGANS. His EYEBALLS felt as if, as if, they'd been NAILED onto the DESK! And the HAMMER that NAILED them was now POUNDING away in his GUT! The room swirled blood-red, then blinding white. Torch grabbed his head and rocked violently back and forth. Back and forth, gasping to suck air around the choking spasm in his throat. A vision of large shadowy figures began to form in the air, their bony arms reaching for him. THEY HATE ME! ALL AROUND...

Staggering to his feet, he swung his fists feebly at the vision, as the HAMMER POUNDED ON. THEY HATE ME! Torch thought he recognized one of the figures, and swung his fists again. HATE clawed at his tearful, contorted face, his nailed eyes, his hammered gut. Doubling over, Torch vomited copiously onto his desktop.

With a hiss, the vision dissipated. It took an eternity for the hammering pain to subside, as he stood trembling and hunched over, staring at the large pool of pink slime on his desk. Oh, this was much, *much* worse than Insight Out, he groaned, wiping his tears and mouth with the sleeve of his uniform. Infinitely worse than any other drug he had ever tried- and there had been many. Insight Out and JAMpot were nothing like this.

Torch felt as if he'd been in an all-night brawl: bruised all over, completely drained, unable to keep his feet. And it wasn't over yet: collapsing into his chair, he smacked the desk sharply with his elbow. The objects on his desk jumped. AH-AHH! His small Dermamist injector rolled off the edge and bounced on the tile floor. Torch grabbed at his elbow with one hand and wiped the tears off his face with the other. He fought the urge to vomit again.

The sudden agony at his elbow did, at least for a moment, get his mind off all the other competing agonies. Got to focus, Torch. Before I forget, as usual. Focus! AHH, my elbow.... *focus*! All right, Roving Eye... focus. I've got to remember everything: that's the whole point. First the injection... oh, my elbow. All right, I separated from my body; that was bizarre... finally figured out how to move around... practiced steering around the Old Campus, then headed over to the Med School... I remember that hallway at Harkness, then Benn Marr's room. Him, lying there on the bed, without a clue that I was in the room! But he didn't move at all- not even breathing- such a long time, I wondered if he was dead. Pretty boring, if he was dead. Went and checked out the bathroom, the medicine cabinet- too obvious. Not surprising, he wouldn't keep his stash there. Then back to the desk, and- hey, that's right- there was a baseball sitting on his desk! That's strange- they don't play baseball on Mars, do they? Martians playing baseball? Doubt it- sounds stupid. Oh, my elbow. Wait: didn't I see that baseball before? Can't remember, exactly.

Anyway, next thing I knew, something shoved me hard- right out of the room! And then I was lying on the ground, way over on the other side of Harkness courtyard. Had to scramble out of the bushes. Lucky so few people were around. Stumbling around, felt like a drunk... made it harder to avoid contact. That's important with Roving Eye: you have got to avoid touching other people.

On my way to Harkness, I bumped into that guy on High Street. Passed right through him! Didn't I? Yes I did, and he acted like he was having a heart attack. That was a creepy feeling, like someone's hands groping around your insides. Not something I ever want to repeat. And when it was over, there was the horrible PAIN, and the HATE! One of those giant shadows: it looked just like one of my sub-chiefs! Harrison, up on the second floor! But the hate, the bony hands, all that, Torch- it was just a hallucination. Don't forget the thrill you enjoyed. Passing right through walls without being seen... Roving Eye is definitely light-years beyond the others: it was worth a try, even considering the horrible withdrawal. Thanks to my source at Eunigen: it was so easy to intercept the sample meant for Boston. And that means I was the first in the world to use Roving Eye! Goal, Torch, goal! It was worth trying, but no, I can't imagine going through that withdrawal again.

Shuddering at the thought of it, Torch made as (relatively) firm a decision as he ever could, concerning psychopeptides: the first use of Roving Eye would also be his last. Coming to such a blessedly sensible conclusion, however, did nothing to extinguish his burning desire to get hold of that other drug, the brand-new one: Deep Coma! It was supposed to be the ultimate mind-blower; even Roving Eye would be like child's play, compared to Deep Coma. That was his new goal. Oh, to try it once, he begged himself- just once!

Chapter Eight

Benn studied the row of eight stemmed glasses, each containing a small quantity of red liquid, varying in darkness and clarity, neatly arranged on a white tablecloth before him. The cloth covered a very long wooden table, on either side of which stood similar groups of eight glasses, interspersed with silver buckets- enough for roughly twenty participants. Benn sat with his back to the main common room entrance. Dr. Neelin was occupied with the task of carefully distributing the wine, then placing the empty bottles, each wrapped in a plain brown bag, on the side-table.

The Great Hall was quite typical of the YaleConn colleges: a cavernous, yet inviting, chamber made warmer by dark walnut paneling and two enormous stone fireplaces. The high arched ceiling appeared to be held up by a combination of exposed wooden beams and copious cobwebs. Thirty gilt-framed portraits of historic Masters of the College hung at regular intervals along the walls, alternating with flags and banners representing various aspects of College life. Dim evening light barely penetrated the stained-glass windows encircling the room, just below the ceiling and too high up for Benn to make out details of their design. Ancient sconces provided the main wall lighting, just sufficient for Benn to examine the portrait hanging directly in front of him: that of a thin, silver-haired man in a black scholar's robe with green hood signifying his medical degree. He sat facing slightly to his left and held on his lap a closed book, apparently taken from the library depicted behind him. Deep in thought, he appeared, at the same time, somehow distracted. There were three inscriptions in the portrait: first, the name Andreas Vesalius, prominent on the spine of the book; then above the studious Master, against the bookshelves in the background- Benn could barely make it out- "Here Silent Speak the Great of Other Years;" and on the tarnished brass plaque at the bottom, "Dr. Alan Goodrow, Master of Mellon College, 2141-2159."

Only one other guest had arrived: a smug-looking man in his late thirties, dressed in dapper evening wear. Benn recognized him as a junior faculty member named Lou Hunter, an obscure instructor at the medical school specializing in- was it Medical Economics? His memory proved correct, as Hunter took the seat facing Benn and, studiously looking at something over Benn's shoulder, extended his palm casually. In a lazy drawl, he said, "I'm Professor Hunter, Med Econ. Fellow of Mellon College." He eyed Benn's orange bodysuit with obvious distaste. A spontaneous insight regarding his tablemate popped into his mind, catching even Benn by surprise: Make that Assistant Professor and Junior Fellow. Hunter had inherited high social status, but was weak academically and frustrated by his lack of career advancement: a poor combination, accounting for the condescending attitude. Where was this analysis coming from? Had some sort of hyper-awareness lingered from this afternoon's out-of-body experience?

Mistaking Benn's scrutiny for interest, Hunter continued. "Parents were both chaired faculty, and Daddy was Dean of Mellon for years. I, myself? Born and raised right here in this college." He tried to read Benn's expression, but found nothing legible. So he took a different tack: "In fact," he threw out carelessly, "growing up here, my nickname among the undergraduates was Mellon College Baby."

They touched palms in a perfunctory manner, as Hunter, his eyebrows raised, waited in vain for an amused reaction from Benn.

"I'm Benn Marr. Sorry, Mr. Hunter, but- Mellon College...Baby?"

"That's right. Melancholy. Never mind. And that's *Doctor* Hunter." He looked around unsuccessfully for someone, anyone, else to talk to, then added in an even lazier drawl, "This your first time in Mellon College, Benn?"

Before Benn could answer, Hunter's face suddenly brightened. He stood and waved vigorously at the small group now gathering in the common room, where they had paused to shake the water off their coats before entering the Great Hall. It was still raining lightly outside.

"Cira! Over here! Cira!" He flapped both arms- hardly necessary, thought Benn, since the long table was otherwise unoccupied.

Dr. Cira Vincent hesitated as she acknowledged Hunter's calisthenics with the barest nod of her head. She smoothed her damp hair back, searched around the room, then apparently decided there was no polite alternative: she promptly claimed the seat to Benn's right, and, at her direction, Lora walked down the opposite side of the table and sat facing her, to the left of the visibly-disappointed Lou Hunter. Several other new arrivals began to take their seats, and Dr. Neelin seemed to notice for the first time that he was not alone.

"Hello, Dr. Vincent," said Benn. He nodded silently at Lora, who was examining the array of glasses before her with a puzzled look.

"Outside the classroom, please call me Cira. I remember you from my PerMutations class, Benn." She smiled warmly at him, and Hunter shifted impatiently in his seat before speaking up.

"Evening, Cira. Been too long, hasn't it? Never mind. Didn't know you were interested in wine at all. Good of Nes to put on a tasting."

"Yes, Lou, wine is not new to me, although it's hard to come across any real wine, these days. I believe these bottles are from Dr. Neelin's private collection, which has largely been handed down in his family for generations. It's truly a privilege to be invited- and especially so for Lora and you, Benn. When Nestor told me I could bring a guest, I thought, 'who would benefit more from the experience than one of the interns from Mars?' I asked Lora to come, but I understand you were invited by Nestor himself! That's impressive, Benn- it doesn't happen very often, at least for interns."

"Did you say Mars? You're from Mars Colony? Good Lord! Martians! Never mind your first time in Mellon College- it's your first time anywhere, in fact!" Hunter was interrupted by a clinking noise coming from the head of the table. It was Dr. Neelin, rapping on an empty glass with his pen. He beamed at his assembled guests as the final arrival sat down at the far end.

"Welcome, all, to Mellon College- where I proudly serve as Most Senior Fellow- and also welcome to my biennial tasting of Great Wines of the Past Century." The guests applauded enthusiastically- Lou Hunter less so, as he watched Benn warily out of the corner of his eye. Neelin had donned a gray jacket matching his pin-striped pants, and, with his red paisley tie, reminded Benn of the prosperous banker or stockbroker pictured in a political-history text he had once read, in a chapter decrying the pre-Universal Credit days of opportunistic capitalism.

"For this tasting, I have gathered a fascinating group of tasters, and- apologies where due- an even more fascinating group of wines. This will be a 'blind tasting': to eliminate prejudice, the wines are identified only after you render your opinions as to the quality and origins of the wines. After all, a great wine will speak of time and place, from its inception through its lifelong evolution. But I will provide some hints as we go along, which may enable the more experienced tasters to name the wines." Lou Hunter perked up.

Benn focused on the eight pools of red liquid, and immediately began to sense that they were very different from one another. Perhaps there was an after-effect from the first vial, thought Benn. The wines seemed to vibrate, like bells freshly struck and issuing their pure, unique tones. The question rose again: was it real, or was it hallucination? But there was no mistaking the seven different characters, or signatures, emanating from the eight wines; surprisingly, two of them had identical signatures: so there must be a duplicate wine, some sort of trick to fool the tasters! Benn knew instinctively that these signatures had to do with the water content of the wines: the very structure of the water, which was the dominant component. The strong emotional vibrations emitted by the glass of water in Kai's room immediately came to mind. Could the water's structure- probably at its micro-crystalline, or even molecular, level- have been impacted by the thousands of dissolved organic compounds present at the time and place of origin, then influenced or shaped over the years by surrounding events? The longer Benn studied his eight glasses, the more the seven distinct signatures boggled his mind. Each wine did speak of a time and a place, as Dr. Neelin had promised, but he had been referring to actually tasting the wines, not just sitting nearby them!

"One of the wines comes from the Quarantine Zone," Dr. Neelin began. "Specifically, the Northern California sector, near the Pacific Ocean. The vines were planted forty years before that harvest, in well-drained volcanic soil, in the vicinity of their famous eucalyptus trees- very few will recognize that distinctive aroma, I expect." Indeed, the wine's water content had recorded that constellation of characteristics- and Benn, in his hyper-aware state,

91

was able to read that recording. He tapped the lip of one of the glasses with his finger, and Lou Hunter, who had been systematically swirling and sniffing the wines in the proper order from left to right, looked up briefly. What was the Martian tapping his glass for?

"Another is from Bordeaux, in France. It was made in the legendary wartime year, 2093." The guests collectively gasped; the credit-value of such a rare and old wine would be stratospheric! Benn noticed that Dr. Neelin had used the country's original name, rather than its designation under the PWE, the French District of the Eurozone. "2093 was an unusually hot, dry year," he continued. "Towards the end of the Great War, no pesticides or chemical preservatives were available, and there was a severe shortage of manpower and equipment. The resulting wines were powerful and the most natural-tasting ever made, being hand-harvested and unadulterated, in the vineyard and in the winery." Benn immediately tapped the fourth glass from the left. Lou Hunter, just now sipping from his first glass, glanced at Benn and frowned, then returned distractedly to wine number two.

"Another is from Australia. This is a relatively young wine, only fifteen years old, produced in the Barossa Valley, in a secret facility hidden from the PWE. It has a cult-like following, both for its rarity and for its unusually intense concentration of flavors; note the eucalyptus, as well as black currants and cherries." Benn had no idea what these fruits tasted like, but he could sense a variety of primary flavor compounds in one wine in particular, as well as a distinctive compound already described in the California wine-eucalyptus. "Perhaps Mr. Marr can identify it, given his familiarity with Australian marsupials." Dr. Neelin winked at Benn and noticed that he was now tapping his finger on the sixth glass, to the further consternation of Lou Hunter.

And so it went, for four other wines. Dr. Neelin described esthetic and geologic elements: earthy forest or mushroom; the smell of rain falling on hot stones; delicate floral scents; the tang of iron, like a bloody nose; roasted coffee beans, licorice, chocolate, berries of various colors; the mineral effect of a steep, rocky slope; a summer plagued by hailstorms; or a long hot spell before harvest. And, though it seemed far-fetched, even as Dr. Neelin described the historical context of each wine- the influence of an ancient monastic order, or the personality of an eccentric winemaker- Benn detected traces of each element. He imagined some sort of ambient energy field interacting with the water content, imprinting all of this data into the structure- the hexagonal, square and triangular formations- of each wine. It was like the electronic translation of sound or sight into a recording (not so different from the volumes of data previously recorded in ancient tapes, plastic phonograph records, or metal discs; and now the micro-crystalline core of his datadisc) which could be heard or seen again, and replayed endlessly, if only one had the diamond-tipped needle, the laser, the ability to translate the data in reverse. Apparently the therapeptide had temporarily given Benn the ability to read the recording: after listening to each description, Benn would, without hesitation, tap on a different glass.

By the seventh wine, Lou Hunter was glaring hard at Benn. Cira and Lora, and several guests on Benn's other side, were also regarding him with curiosity.

"Really think that's the Burgundy?" challenged Hunter, setting down his sixth glass with a firmness that said, Enough is enough. He shook his head. What could this, this Martian bumpkin possible know about wine, coming from that red dustball in the sky?

"Sorry?" Benn looked up.

"You're pointing at that glass, number three. Really think that's the Burgundy? Tasted a lot of Burgundy back on Mars, have you? Well, Benn, I am what you would call a serious Burgundy taster, and I totally disagree with you." Benn thought, No, that isn't close to what I would call you; but yes, you are totally disagreeable to me.

Demonstrating his utter seriousness as a taster, Hunter picked up the third glass, swirled it grandly, stuck in his nose and sniffed sharply, then took a large sip of the pale-red liquid, gargled loudly for a full five seconds, and spat aggressively into the silver bucket on the table between him and Benn. From the splash, a small drop landed on Cira's elegant left sleeve, and she quickly withdrew her arm.

"Three's not Burgundy, it's a Rhone!" Hunter railed. "An old Rhone. The faded dried-fruit flavors. Earth and truffle in the nose. Black pepper in the finish. Get all that, Marr? Any serious taster can tell it's a Rhone."

"I don't know it by that name," replied Benn evenly, "just by the description Dr. Neelin gave us. Number three fits his description of Burgundy better than any other wine. It's number eight, I believe, that fits his description of the Rhone."

"But... but what do you taste in this wine that makes you think Burgundy, for God's sake?" Hunter sputtered.

"Well... actually, I haven't tasted any of the wines yet," admitted Benn.

Hunter's face reddened, his eyes bulged. "You haven't... you haven't *tasted*? But you're going on as though you've already identified all the wines! You mean you can tell which wine is which, just by *looking* at them? Never mind! According to you, let's see, number two is Californian; four is Bordeaux, specifically the famous 2093. How's this for sheer blind luck on your part: I actually agree with you there; even a grubby Martian wouldn't mistake such a great wine for anything else! You claim that number six is an Australian, hah! Number three, you've just wrongly informed us, is a Burgundy; I think you've drunk too much Martian swill for your own good. It's definitely a Rhone, but you think the Rhone is number *eight*? What about one, five and seven? Have you identified them as well, without actually tasting any of the wines? Good Lord!"

"Well... I can't be sure, of course," said Benn, wading into ever deeper water.

Hunter snorted and folded his arms. He would not be placated by any show of modesty. He was going for Benn's jugular vein.

"I think number one is from Argentina. Dr. Neelin described vines with original rootstock which escaped Phylloxera three times, once in the late nineteenth century and twice again in the twenty-first...."

Hunter looked like he was about to explode. "You can taste that? Oh, I forgot- you haven't even tasted yet! Never mind!"

Benn debated briefly whether to push on, but finally he couldn't resist. Maybe he did have that cruel streak, after all.

"Number five is another Bordeaux, but it comes from the opposite side of that estuary which Dr. Neelin mentioned- the Gironde? He told us there's more clay in the soil, and the water doesn't drain as readily there. The retention of water balanced the excess concentration of the drought year, which was lucky for that estate."

"I'd say you're the lucky one, Marr. All right, I'm shocked, but once again we agree- another coincidence! Number five tastes like a Pomerol to me, and 2166, as Nes said, was a drought year." Hunter frowned again. "What about seven?" he muttered, picking up his glass and sniffing it absently, his eyes riveted on Benn.

"It's from the same vineyard as the Burgundy, same vintage year, made by the same winemaker using identical methods, but the grapes came from much younger vines than number three."

"What? Really? Young-vines Burgundy, you're saying... now, that's interesting." Hunter held up numbers three and seven, and went back and forth, sniff, sip, sniff, sip. In his zeal, he had forgotten to spit. "May have something there, Marr. There's a family resemblance, though seven is certainly the pale sibling- the melancholy baby, right? Never mind. Don't think seven was ever meant to age this long. It's too old and faded."

But still echoing its gentle song, thought Benn. The signature was frail indeed- in a way neither decrepit nor stingy, but tender and yielding. Staring at the tawny liquid, Benn could feel its harmonious balance, captured in microcrystals of water.

"Seven is lovely," murmured Cira, her nose in the glass.

Lora remained reticent as she swallowed a small sip from her eighth glass. She knew, somehow, that Benn was right. The wines were so distinctive in their aromas and flavors, and in yet another parameter- something abstract and undefinable. They each had their individual... essence.

She came out of her reverie. Neelin was clinking his glass again.

"Has everyone finished? Good. You've all formed your opinions as to the quality of the wines, and perhaps even their identities?" Nods and smiles around the table. "Good. Now, rather than embarrass ourselves- no changing your opinion *after* the unveiling, now- let's reveal the wines and see if we can tell a Cote-Rotie from a Richebourg." Hunter raised an eyebrow at the mention of Cote-Rotie, in the northern Rhone, and Richebourg, the famous Burgundian vineyard. Cote-Rotie and Richebourg: the first two specific clues.

Neelin stood by the side-table and began to remove the bags, naming each wine as he went down the row. "Number one, Bodega Alta 2155, from Argentina! Two, Maya's Vineyard 2139, California! Number three, from Burgundy! We'll discuss the vineyard in a bit." Hunter studiously avoided looking at Benn, who was right about the Burgundy after all. Neelin paused after unwrapping the next bottle, then with a slight gasp and tremor in his voice, announced: "Number four is a Bordeaux, the legendary Lafite of 2093. From my great-grandfather's collection. My, what a wine!" Loud, sustained applause filled the room. "And here, next to it, the famous L'Eglise de Petrus, of the drought year 2166. I hope you can detect in this wine, compared to the previous, the difference between Right and Left Bank Bordeaux." Hunter was once again glaring at Benn, who had so far been completely correct.

"Next, Australia! Let's hear from someone who can recognize epipubic bones when he sees them. Any comments for us, Mr. Marr? Did you prefer the Australian, or the Californian, each with its hot climate and eucalyptus notes?"

Surprised to be called on, Benn could only voice what was uppermost in his mind. "There's no comparison, Dr. Neelin. I mean, it's like apples and oranges," he recalled the old Earth expression. "Or rather, it's like grapes- and different grapes. The Australian wine comes from the same type of grape as number eight, the Rhone wine. So it can't really be compared to the Californian."

"Quite right!" said Neelin, astonished. "The Australian was made from Syrah, the same varietal as in the Cote-Rotie." So number eight WAS the Cote-Rotie, thought Hunter. And that meant that number seven had to be...

Neelin eyed Benn appraisingly. "And what of number seven? What do you think of that wine, Mr. Marr?"

Lou Hunter blurted out, "It's a young-vines Burgundy, Nes! Clearly it comes from the same vineyard as number three!" Isn't that what Marr had said? A young-vines version of number three? The room fell silent. Hunter thought of the clue Neelin had leaked: let's see if we can tell a Cote-Rotie from a Richebourg. He had the answer, but had spoken much too quickly. Reel it in slowly, he told himself. Now with exquisite care- as though dissecting the wings of a butterfly- Hunter continued, "Its aromatic profile suggests, hmmm..." All eyes were on him and he found that even more delectable than the wines themselves. Hunter stretched the moment by swirling and sniffing pensively, "This is typical of the commune of Vosne-Romanee...it's certainly not a Romanee-St. Vivant or, heaven forbid, an Echezeaux...let me see now... yes, I do believe... wine number seven has the telltale characteristics of a Richebourg!"

"Bravo, Lou- well done! Young-vines Richebourg it is indeed, from the same vintage and producer as wine number three. Both are the 2141 Domaine de Beaucoup Richebourg, but number seven was produced from ten-year-old vines. But how on Earth did you know? That's an amazingly perceptive feat of wine-tasting!" There was scattered applause. Looking straight at Benn with his eyes narrowed, Neelin muttered, "Simply amazing, Lou."

Several of Hunter's friends came down the table to clap him on the shoulder. In parallel with Lou Hunter's sudden celebrity, the noise level now increased rapidly. Also rising rapidly were the blood alcohol levels of most attendees, their token efforts to use the spit buckets long abandoned. Dr. Neelin and May Acheson, the current Master of Mellon College, were engaged in intense conversation, gesturing occasionally, for some reason, at Benn's wine glasses, which still remained pristine. Master Acheson seemed particularly agitated, and Benn guessed correctly that he had been swallowing his wine all evening long.

Generous refills were poured (from duplicate bottles of some wines, certainly not the Lafite). The formal tasting had turned into a full-blown party. Four guests at the far end of the table started to sing in wavering harmony: "Bright college years, with pleasures rife, the shortest, gladdest years of life..." Before long, Cira and Lora could hardly hear one another discuss the wines.

Cira turned to Benn, who was dreamily watching Lora swirl the Richebourg in her glass. "Well, you've certainly distinguished yourself tonight, at least in our immediate circle," she almost had to shout. "You've had no previous exposure to wine? No? Then I suppose it's simply a talent that some have, and some don't." She looked pointedly at Lou Hunter, who cupped a hand next to his ear and struggled to hear her.

"Benn, it's gotten so noisy, I think Lora and I will be going now. Will you share a cab with us back to the medical school?"

Nothing could have appealed more to Benn at that moment. Too eagerly, he jumped to his feet- followed by Lou Hunter, who immediately began to stammer and gesture at Cira. Dr. Neelin noticed Benn standing and tried to summon him, but only managed to give a vigorous wave before being pulled back to his debate with the insistent May Acheson- a wave and its undertow. Acheson, whose face, by now, glowed frighteningly crimson, was not to be denied.

Using a variety of hand signals, Benn offered all of his wines- as yet untouched- to the clearly-disgruntled Lou Hunter. But Hunter sneered and rejected the offer with several dismissive flicks of his fingers. Never mind, thought Benn, as yet another novel emotion began to rise in his chest: something tinged with sadness.

"Come on, Benn, let's go," shouted Lora, now standing beside him.

Lou Hunter tried to cajole Cira back to the table, but his distressed mating calls went unheard in the din, and his shoulders slumped as Cira escaped into the anteroom. From the darkness of that room, Benn looked back at the Mellon College Baby with- was it contempt? No, despite his opportunism and self-promotion, Hunter was not contemptible, just rather pitiful. Benn regarded with fascination the raucous society of swirlers, sniffers, sippers, spitters and songsters; Orpheus and Bacchus would certainly be pleased. Lou Hunter, freshly revived, had flung himself with a roar back into the midst of an admiring crowd. Benn observed the luminous liquid spilling from a glass Hunter clutched greedily in his right hand. Checking his own row of glasses, Benn now noticed a conspicuous gap which, just seconds earlier, had been occupied by the legendary Lafite of 2093.

Chapter Nine

As the following weeks rolled by, Benn noticed a puzzling change in his status at the medical school. Since the beginning of classes, the other interns had treated Benn as though he carried Martian typhoid, and had dismissed his answers in class as naive, provincial, typical for an ignorant outlander. They had considered it freakish when his insights seemed to satisfy the faculty, and made no effort to conceal their outrage. To his own chagrin, Benn had found himself clinging to slim threads: he had been the top student at the Tharsis Academy; he had been Hydra Employee of the Year; he kept thinking, "In my own country I am a king." None of that had made the slightest difference. Now, for some unknown reason, a few of the interns episodically approached him with questions on class work, looking for the sort of help that Sool Tamura provided in MedTech class. They awaited his answers with taut anticipation- as though he were stringing together pearls of wisdom behind his teeth. Most of the class still shunned him as a pariah, so these episodes stood out all the more in contrast. Perhaps they had gotten word of his performance at the wine tasting, he wondered. But it wasn't his tasting notes they wanted, was it: they just wanted to use his ideas for their own advancement. Still, the sudden shift in attitude was striking and, Benn decided, must be inspired by the changed manner in which the professors now received him.

The change was obvious to everyone. Whenever class discussions were stalled by tangled arguments, professors Neelin and Vincent, and several other members of the faculty, would call on Benn before anyone else. No one- including Benn himself- understood how, but his responses would immediately settle the issue at hand. His terse answers, consisting of one or two sentences- or sometimes even a single word- would break through the blockage and release the free flow of discussion, much to the relief of his classmates. It was like inserting a urinary catheter into their collective distended bladder; he laughed aloud at the crude image. For Benn, it was quite simple: he said the most obvious thing, whatever thought came first, without pausing for any internal struggle or debate- to be honest, he had no idea where the answers came from. And without fail, his answers would be correct.

Although success was trivial to Benn, his uncanny insights filled his classmates more with apprehension- fear over their own relative standing in class- than with admiration. It reminded him of his friend Jace Cohn, when returning from a Waterhunt: similarly alarmed by Benn's success, Jace would pull at his already-sparse hair and ask, just how *did* he manage to find so much water every time? These demonstrations of Benn's magically effortless problem-solving, which had inspired Dr. Neelin several times to label him "a true natural" in class, culminated in a major announcement one Friday in Recombinant Anatomy. Benn had just made another of his modest suggestions, thereby unraveling a particularly knotted debate: a heated argument over the application of recombinant anatomy technology for purely cosmetic purposes.

When the crowd noise had settled, Neelin shook his head and said, "I confess, I would never have thought of applying the principle of Natural Selection." He sighed at the sea of vacant faces and added, "For those unfamiliar, it's the passing down of genes which increase survivability, for the good of the species. For a thousand years, outward appearance has replaced survivability as the driving criterion in choosing a mate, has it not? What did you so aptly call it, Benn- "*Un*natural *De*-selection"? Thanks to cosmetic procedures, Mr. Marr is telling us, genes that weaken the species are just as likely to be passed along as genes that promote survival of the fittest. It's hardly better for the human species than, say, choosing mates by the attractiveness of their clothing!

"How typical, Mr. Marr- applying concepts three centuries old, to help decide a modern question." Before continuing, Neelin glanced momentarily at Sool Tamura. Sool had not particularly distinguished herself in his class. In fact, she appeared to be fast asleep- as she often did- so not all Martians were created equal. "Your education on Mars- particularly at Tharsis Colony- appears to have covered the Classics, Benn. Perhaps you share my distrust of modernity. Here on Earth, our students are completely consumed with the Modern: with Tech for the sake of novelty, with today's fashions, with the pointless accumulation of credits, the politics and machinations of the Pan-World Electorate- in my opinion, they are

100

educated to the point of getting a job and living in the world, but fail to learn the more important aspects of attaining a full life." A few interns shifted uncomfortably in their seats- but only because their tight orange bodysuits pinched in the narrower places.

"They have received a trade-school education, nothing more." Dr. Neelin seemed determined to push the point further, but his effort to shame his students was futile; none of them even realized he was being critical. Some even nodded earnestly and emphatically in agreement. Benn spotted Sool across the room; she still appeared to be asleep, but then he caught a sudden smirk crossing her face.

"I feel it would help this class greatly if you played a more formal role in future presentations and discussions, Mr. Marr. To that end, I wish to make an announcement now, regarding your promotion." Benn's face remained blank, as the classroom fell tensely silent. "I'm going to promote you, Mr. Marr, to a rank above teaching assistant... but not quite an Assistant Professor (for that you would need a higher degree, and research)... let's make you Assistant *to* the Professor, shall we?" All around the room, grumbling broke out in opposition to Neelin's proposal. But the professor continued undeterred.

"Yes, that's perfect- your title is now Assistant to the Professor. How does that sound? Of course, Mr. Marr, you have no right of refusal: 'unto some, greatness is thrust,' eh? And greatness is certainly what lies ahead for you." Greatness! That's the word he had used. Benn was speechless; Dr. Neelin was the first person to predict greatness in his future- not his father or his teachers at the Tharsis Academy. Not Jace, or even Wila.

"The great Benn Marr!" came a disembodied shout, clearly sarcastic. But Dr. Neelin mistook it for adulation and grinned broadly- and so the matter was settled. Trying to ignore his classmates' negative reaction as well as the moist fullness burning both his eyes and nose, Benn stared blankly ahead.

Lora, seated next to Benn, was also beside herself. "*Benn!* Do you realize... do you know what an honor...Benn!" She hugged him, then kissed his temples, right then left- this was customary in offering congratulations- but Benn noticed, with a tingle of pleasure, that her hands still clasped the back of his neck, and was quite sure that the firm pressure of her lips, and her warm breath on his ear, had lingered significantly longer than was considered proper. Hadn't he felt the same tingle when they pressed palms on the Martian Glidebus?

"Lora, I... I've been meaning to talk with you...."

"Mr. Marr, I think we'll need you down in front, from now on." Neelin waved excitedly at the first row of seats, which, as far back in his long career as he could recall, had always been entirely unoccupied. As engaging a lecturer as Neelin was, it spoke volumes about his abrasive personality that the closest intern today was sitting in the fourth row. Reluctantly, Benn left Lora's side and, paying no attention to the hostile stares of his classmates, made his way down to the front row- he chose the seat nearest the lower exit.

Despite this tactic, Dr. Neelin still managed to collar him at the end of class, before he could make his escape. There was so much to go over, he told Benn, so many plans to draw, what with multifunctional recombinant anatomy coming up, and midterm exams in only two weeks.

"The patient, W.P., is a 64-year-old transportation executive who complains of severe, sharp pains and tightness in all of his muscles, of eight months duration." Kai began his presentation, reading from his open da-disc to the small group of interns, who were supervised that Friday by Dr. Hol Chan. W.P. was sitting hunched over on the hard examining table, wrapped in a short white cellulose gown, hands spread on his exposed knees. He had been through this ritual ordeal so many times before. Less than a meter away, his wife sat stiffly upright on a short metal step stool. Standing just to her left, Benn observed her jaw muscles, clenching and unclenching. A state of agitation. Her middle and distal knuckles showed the bony enlargement of mild osteoarthritis. There was a tiny growth on her forehead, which he diagnosed as a seborrheic keratosis; the Probot would have concurred. Because the room had been designed to accommodate only the patient and one physician, Dr. Chan and her interns were forced to crowd around.

"He is previously healthy, except for a very brief period of PsySoc rehab in his twenties, and his social and family histories are non-contributory." Kai glanced nervously at Dr. Chan, who, having heard Kai's presentations before, watched him with an expression of deep concern as she activated the wall projection. Kai continued, "I have put W.P. through the Probot twice, and both times the results were identical: signals of tissue injury or regeneration, inflammation, pre-mutagenesis and metabolic derangement are completely absent. Epigenetic expression, including at the micro-RNA level, is normal. Risk loci mapping and haplotype structure are unremarkable. You can see on the next screen that the central and peripheral chi are not in any way obstructed. I entered the patient's history, systems review, family history, physical exam and lab data into the analyzer and found no matching diagnosis. And so, without a suitable coding of his diagnosis, there is no way to initiate the billing process."

Dr. Chan, studying the wall screen, nodded in agreement.

Kai looked up from his da-disc and shrugged. "In fact, W.P. is perfectly healthy, even though obviously he is persisting in his illness behavior."

W.P. stared fixedly downward at his legs, now pale and mottled in the cold room. Unsure what "illness behavior" implied, at least he knew that his pain was very real. It was excruciating, every minute of every day; the sleepless hours of each night passed exquisitely slowly; previously athletic, he had lost the ability to exercise for pleasure; and the pain had ultimately broken his marriage, as he knew full well that his wife's fierce protectiveness came purely out of guilt. Long-suffering to the point of sainthood (at least that was how she put it), she had long ago given up on relating to him in any normal fashion, but did possess an undying sense of obligation. His wife finally shattered the silence: "*Healthy? Perfectly healthy?* What are you talking about? Can't you see he's in pain? What's perfectly healthy about that? Can't you just rearrange his genes and end this once and for all, instead of giving him all those… those therapeptides to control pain but only make him more lethargic than he already is? You doctors and your damned machines: scanning and probing here and there, coming up with nothing. Epigenetic expression is normal. Oh, so everything's just fine then, is it? Well it's not, and I am at the *end of the line*, people! I can't stand it anymore- you find the problem, and you find the solution…you find it." She suddenly began to sob, her shoulders shaking, her arms folded tightly across her chest.

Kai had panic scrawled on his face. "But the Probot is accurate within ten-to-the-minus-seven-percent! As I said, there's nothing wrong with your..." Dr. Chan cut in abruptly: "Kai. Excuse me." Then, addressing everyone in the room, she said in her most calming voice, "I think we'd better break here, and collect our thoughts. Why don't we go to the conference room and review our findings?

"If you don't mind," she said to the patient's wife, who had just as suddenly stopped her crying but shook her head slowly back and forth, unwilling to accept that she and her husband were going through this yet again. Averting his eyes even from his wife, W.P. slowly rose to his feet, wincing with every movement. Benn regarded him closely as he wavered slightly on the cold floor; he gathered the inadequate gown tightly around himself, Benn saw, in the same way he clung onto his tattered dignity and his fatalism, his intractable pain and bitterness. His hands had assumed the same pale and mottled appearance as his exposed legs, and Benn wondered momentarily whether this was a relevant physical finding. Before he could ask aloud, the patient spoke.

"Not at all, doctor." His voice brimmed with anger. "I know this act of yours very well. Now go off and discuss my case, as though you're really trying to help." He took a deep breath. "But I'm sure nothing will ever come of it." W.P. reached out, and his wife immediately took his hand. Benn decided that it was an inopportune moment to point out the mottling, especially in light of all the normal test results.

The team shuffled out of the room and headed down the hall in contrite silence, like misbehaving schoolchildren sent to the principal's office. As soon as they had seated themselves around the conference table, Kai spoke up, his tone already defensive: "I'm sure there's nothing wrong with that patient. The pain is endo-cranial: maybe his previous PsySoc rehab caused some permanent damage, like a late-emerging delusional state ..."

"A delusional state? And yet you believe there is nothing wrong with the patient?" Dr. Chan challenged.

"Well, I wasn't serious. I didn't really mean delusional." He glanced down at his da-disc, hoping for some supporting evidence.

"And Kai, please don't use that term, 'endo-cranial,' in my presence. It's really demeaning. So if there's nothing wrong with him- as you just said, Kai- then what do you suppose compels this patient to return, time and again, to this clinic, where we have done nothing to help him?"

"I have no idea, Dr. Chan. Maybe there are monetary credits at stake- a disability subsidy from the district, for example."

"Doubtful. Everyone, since the inception of Universal Credits, is guaranteed an income far above subsistence-level, so there is no need for supplemental income in cases of illness. A disability subsidy would be awarded only in a case of personal injury, where the State is at fault. So the prospect of getting rich does not motivate your patient in his sick role. What else? Anybody?"

Two other interns raised their hands, and Hol Chan nodded at them.

"Power over others, or control, can be a strong motivator," suggested one. "He impacts the medical system, and keeps us- the doctors, the authority figures- running around helpless."

The other intern agreed, "Yes! It's about control. Dr. Chan, I think you're incorrect in saying that we haven't helped him at all in this clinic- in a twisted way, he has actually achieved his goal, by frustrating, and therefore, controlling us- at least that's how he might feel, on some deep level. And you can also see the tremendous power the patient holds over his wife. The poor woman wants us to change his DNA: in other words, she wants a different husband. His pain keeps her on a very short leash; she even said it herself: she's 'at the end of the line!' And as long as the pain can't be cured, he owns a steady source of ego gratifica... "

Kai interrupted, calculating quickly, "And I'm sure that, uh, gratifies his ego. My own theory is that he gets a sense of control from, you know..." he faded out.

The first intern ventured softly, "How about gaining self-knowledge? Couldn't the patient be testing his own limits in some way?"

Pretending he hadn't heard, Kai said, "I wonder if the patient is somehow testing his own limits, you know, in order to have...uh...better self-knowledge, or..."

Dr. Chan nodded, but was unconvinced. "Ego, influence, control over others: these remain powerful motives in a society where gaining wealth has lost relevance. But is it really that simple? What else could our patient possibly seek, by clinging so stubbornly to his sick role- by holding so tightly onto his pain? Kai?"

Kai mumbled a few words which failed to elicit any response- no partial credit this time. An uncomfortable silence followed. And then the interns- all ideas exhausted- turned toward Benn, as they had been doing in other classes all month long. This was Hol Chan's first personal encounter with Benn, but she knew of his reputation, and now regarded him with great curiosity. Actually Benn had not been paying attention, instead wondering about Lora's first day at the Gene-Frame Nano-construction lab.

So- quickly, now- what did the patient W.P. seek, if not wealth, ego, power, control, or- what had that intern suggested- self-knowledge? What did anybody really seek, or need, these days? The team was staring at him expectantly, as though he might produce a coin from behind his ear. Better say something, and soon- so Benn wasted no time struggling for an insight. As Dr. Neelin's "true natural," Benn merely said the first thing that came to mind. His thoughts at that moment consisted largely of Lora in her Nano-construction lab, and he blurted out the answer, much to everyone's amusement:

"Is he looking for love?"

Chapter Ten

The ceiling was wobbling again. Although better prepared for the experience than the previous week, Benn did not feel sanguine about projecting himself, an invisible trespasser, into his neighbors' rooms. But at least there wouldn't be many people to intrude upon, he rationalized. It was Friday evening, a popular time for sporting events, and most of the dorm rooms were unoccupied. Lora and Akili, a transfer intern from the Kenya District, had gone to a cliff-hockey match in Danbury. Sool was at her favorite weekly event, the No Haven Robo-Combat Challenge. Earlier in the evening, he had watched Messler and Kai depart in a celebratory mood, to catch some High-a-Lie in Bridgeport. Benn himself was alone as usual, lying prone on his bed, clutching a Dermamist injector in one hand and an empty vial in the other.

The experience was different this time. Benn, with his eyes closed, could make out nebulous shapes beyond his ceiling, and for a while was content to watch them move about like clouds in the sky. But then, just focusing his thoughts on the room above his own, he suddenly found himself drifting in an upper corner of that room. There he saw Theo Coffin, the older intern from Dr. Vincent's class, standing stiffly at attention next to his desk. The door was slowly closing. Someone had just left in a hurry, and Theo looked distinctly worried. Like Kai, Theo was enveloped in an aura which projected about a decimeter beyond his physical outline, but Theo's aura had a dense crimson hue, and to Benn's relief there was none of the rancid odor that had clung to Kai's foul mood.

Theo Coffin's walls were plastered with colorful old posters, some creased and torn, representing famous musical performances, classic plays on Broadway (with live actors, imagine that!), and major political events. Il Trovatore, at the NeoMet, 2114. The Ring Cycle at Bayreuth, summer of 2135. An advertisement for the Fourth Worldwide Jazz Festival, in Las Vegas Metropol, 2129- obviously before the western quarantine. A circular flyer touted the infamous 2077 debate held at the Geneva Convention Center in

Upstate New York: Bradlee vs. Xu, entitled "Who's The Fittest of Them All: the Ethics of Class Eugenics." On the desk stood a small figurine of a portly black man dressed in early twentieth-century clothing, eyes squeezed shut and cheeks distended, blowing on a golden trumpet.

Coffin's da-disc lay open on his bed, displaying a diagram of extensive underground passages superimposed on a map of the YaleConn campus. Benn peered at the label at the bottom; apparently the passages were steam tunnels, installed in the early twentieth century. What did steam have to do with tunnels, and what did either have to do with Theo Coffin, Benn wondered.

The door clicked shut, and Coffin visibly relaxed. Still, to Benn he appeared flustered, as he sat down on the bed to study his da-disc. His reddish aura flared, then subsided, then suddenly flared again, with greater intensity. Who, or what, could have triggered Theo's agitation? Speaking with him between classes, Benn had been impressed by his self-assuredness; it would take a lot to upset this man. Theo was one of a handful of outstanding children of the Quarantined Class permitted to attend school outside the western Quarantine Zone, thanks to the efforts of several Eastern universities- in his case, YaleConn, which had petitioned the PWE's Department of Rehabilitation on his behalf. Leaving his parents behind in Portland Metropol, Theophilus Coffin had arrived at YaleConn at the tender age of fourteen, excelled in his field of study- Medical History and Anthropology- then graduated three years later at the top of his class. The YaleConn Faculty had offered him an assistant professorship after the usual two-year proofing period during which his publications, specializing in Medicine after the Great War of Unification, established him as a major authority in that field. Now in his late twenties, Theo saw internship in the medical school as the logical next step in his career, and had already distinguished himself in that role. So who could intimidate the supremely confident Theo Coffin: who had just walked out the door?

As soon as the question arose in his mind, Benn involuntarily flashed through the door and found himself floating in the corridor. This means of transport, he could see, was much too sensitive: thought-controlled steering! Upward through his ceiling earlier, and now into the hallway, the moment the thoughts crossed his mind!

He would have to figure out the brakes before long. He almost considered going back into Theo's room, but managed to suppress that impulse long enough to scan the corridor. The elevator had just left, and Benn knew that it would be discharging its anonymous passenger a few seconds later. In fact, just having thought of it- the brakes, Benn, the brakes!- he was instantly there in the lobby, watching the elevator arrive.

Dr. Nestor Neelin stepped out of the elevator and strode briskly toward the main Harkness entrance, without looking to either side, despite the obvious attention he had stirred among the few interns milling about the lobby. Sighing, he pulled a heavy black overcoat over his shoulders as he exited the building. Nightfall had brought an onshore wind accompanied by a sudden drop in temperature, and it was beginning to rain once again. His thoughts turned to an early retirement; after all, he was fully eligible under University policy, and that twinge of guilt that he felt about jumping ship was irrelevant. YaleConn was hardly the grand institution Neelin had conquered first as an undergraduate, then as an MD/PhD candidate. The curriculum, the quality of students, the condition of the campus: none of these were at all comparable to their heyday. Early retirement may be self-indulgent, he admitted, but oh, for glorious sunsets at a beach-house in the California sector- south of the quarantined part, of course. Santa Barbara seemed an attractive spot. Or, he mused- if not for that quarantine- he might prefer to view the setting sun from Mt. Shasta, where he could tend a few vines and even produce a modest cabernet.... The Quarantine Act of 2144: passed by the PWE in order to contain those rebels who had failed Psychosocial Rehabilitation, restricting them to an area consisting of the former Northern California, Oregon and Nevada. How ironic that the Act had rewarded the most recalcitrant rebels- the Quarantined Class- with some of the most glorious sunsets in the West. Neelin hailed a passing taxi.

Coincidentally, Benn was also picturing a sunset, as he observed Neelin's surrounding aura change from a gold-tinged blue to a deep, reddish purple. What was Neelin doing on this part of campus, this late in the evening? And what was his interest in Theo Coffin? Benn decided to follow the taxi, and for the next ten minutes he stayed a prudent distance behind, experimenting with raising and lowering his mind-controlled speed. In fact, he could have occupied the front seat, right next to the robotic driver, without ever being detected.

As the taxi cruised through the wet and desolate neighborhoods, crossing several bridges along the way and turning off the main boulevard onto increasingly narrower and darker streets, Benn soon realized that they were passing over the enormous twenty-first century landfill project which constituted Greater Branford. Buried in the clay and sand beneath these streets were ancient marinas, fishing piers, bait shops, and seaside cottages.

There had been water here, once upon a time- lots of water, he could tell, even while sensing a *whole lot more* of it, just a kilometer to the east. That mind-boggling sensation of water, which was Benn's strongest perception thus far of the nearby Long Island Sound, distracted Benn so acutely that he failed to notice when the taxi stopped abruptly on a back alley, in front of a large, nondescript brick warehouse building. Still lacking firm control of his "brakes," Benn passed right through the bumper, the trunk, and then the back seat of the taxi; in doing so, he momentarily shared the same physical space with Dr. Neelin, who was still sitting by the open taxi door.

The resulting explosion of vertigo, disorientation, and personal violation (Torch Halsey, while transported by Roving Eye, had experienced the same gut-grabbing feeling) shocked them both, but the sensation passed instantly for Benn. Neelin grunted sharply and toppled out of the car onto his knees, as though he had been punched in the solar plexus. Rising uncertainly, he stumbled to the front of the warehouse, where he stood clutching his waist and furiously searching the darkness in every direction. The taxi moved off despite Neelin's frantic attempts to get the robotic driver to wait. He groaned and fumbled with trembling fingers along the rough brick wall. Finally locating the hidden panel, he stooped to position his right eye in front of its enclosed scanner, and with a soft click, the metal door swung open. Someone was standing just behind it: a man dressed in black mechanic's overalls, his face obscured by deep shadow. Benn could tell that he was short in stature, but his large hands and threatening, combat-ready posture projected a looming presence.

His voice, however, was almost childlike. "Dr. Neelin! Oh, I'm really glad to see you," he gushed. "There was another search today, just three blocks over that way. So noisy, with sirens and shouting. Did you hear anything about it downtown, Doc? They sure left a mess. I think it was PWE enforcers, but I don't know what they were looking for."

"What are they always looking for, Zak?" Neelin snapped. "Us! You, me, and the others: that's what they're looking for." He pushed the other man back from the doorway, took another long look down the street, then reached into his overcoat and pulled out a small yellow envelope.

"Listen, Zak. I don't have time to waste. Take this packet, will you, and keep it

locked up- whatever you do, don't lose it! When the messenger comes tomorrow, have him bring it back to the lab in Virginia. Tell him it's for sequencing and proteomic analysis. Have you got that, Zak? Sequencing and proteomic analysis. All right?"

Zak answered sullenly: "Yes, I can handle that, Professor. And no, I won't lose it." Benn still couldn't see Zak's face; from the voice he imagined a childish pout, but the large, rough hand that accepted the yellow envelope from Neelin suggested a Neanderthal face.

Neelin immediately regretted his impatience. "Good. Listen, Zak, I may seem out of sorts. I've just had an awful experience, right out here- but don't worry, it's getting better now. So I'm returning to Mellon, all right? Lock up behind me. And don't forget to tell the messenger, sequencing..."

"Yes, Professor, I won't forget!"

Neelin stepped back from the entrance and headed down the alley toward the main boulevard, where perhaps he could catch another taxi. Behind him, Zak slammed the door a bit more loudly than he had intended. Neelin paused with a sigh, muttered something about a child doing a man's job, then set out again. What was he up to next? Benn had to decide quickly: follow the professor back to Mellon College, or investigate this warehouse?

He settled on the latter: there was a great mystery about the warehouse and that fellow Zak. Benn held himself mentally on guard as he passed slowly, in a tensely controlled manner, through the thick stone inner wall. Good! I've found my brakes, he congratulated himself. He emerged into a cavernous garage illuminated by blue-filtered lamps high overhead, its wide concrete floor parked with vehicles of all sorts: some for single riders, several similar to the common Elegna Glidebus, and many others of an obvious military nature, equipped with armor and weapons turrets.

Zak descended a narrow staircase just to the right, and Benn followed a few steps behind. He felt a sudden flash of familiarity: had he seen Zak before, maybe somewhere on campus? The way he walked, leading with his wide shoulders, legs striding so smoothly- like a tiger- reminded Benn of someone, but he couldn't place him. They passed the first landing, continued downward to the third level underground, then angled off to the left, entering a long tunnel. Zak walked briskly toward a brightly-lit chamber at the far end, in which Benn could already make out several self-mobile QI units roaming the floor, banks of viewing screens, and a large number of computers grouped along the back wall. There was a distant humming noise. He sensed that someone else- someone as vaguely familiar as Zak- was in that chamber, but saw only shadows moving about. In the tunnel, a glistening, viscous liquid carrying a foul vegetal aroma dripped from the black, mold-encrusted ceiling: this seemed not to bother Zak, who either had a poor sense of smell or a high tolerance for the disgusting. To Benn, the physical surroundings were mildly offensive, but his physical body (that poor thing, so susceptible to the senses) would have found it unbearably dank. At this depth below street level, in the middle of the Branford landfill zone, the seepage of water through the old stone walls was not at all surprising.

What did surprise Benn were the sounds he now began to hear, originating somewhere behind the damp walls: they were unmistakably human voices, filled with anguish. The voices came softly at first, then quickly grew louder and closer, soon surrounding him with a tumultuous clamor which echoed off the tunnel walls. Benn glanced at Zak, who showed no sign of hearing anything unusual. The din was punctuated by muffled explosions, and Benn began to isolate individual voices: some clearly calling out names, commands, prayers and curses; others simply screamed. His senses expanded. There was the pungent ferrous aroma of blood, mixed with acrid smoke- then came the actual sight of billowing black smoke, flashing red and yellow amidst deafening explosions. Benn made out indistinct shapes of men running through the thick smoke,

112

some carrying others in their sagging arms; several were ablaze, he was shocked to see, and many collapsed as they ran. The carnage and the smell of burning flesh were overwhelming, but just beyond the melee, Zak continued walking at his brisk pace, placidly unaware that Armageddon filled the tunnel all around him.

Alan Goodrow held his younger sister's hand as tightly as he could. At first Katie had objected to the crush of his grip, but now found it reassuring. The young captain- only a few years older than Alan- had just departed, leaving them in a stuffy underground room with only one exit. The room was crowded with children, ranging from toddlers, most of them sobbing uncontrollably, to teenagers trying in vain to keep everyone- including themselves- from breaking down in panic. All the adults had run off, back up the winding stairs, and Alan guessed correctly that they were out in the street by now, taking with them the few weapons remaining. He took a deep breath, fighting back a wave of nausea.

"Gather around, everyone!" Alan shouted. "Come on down to this end!"

As the group- he counted twenty of them- shuffled uncertainly toward the doorway at his corner of the room, Alan continued in a voice which he hoped sounded authoritative, "The captain has instructed me to lead you all to an emergency exit about fifteen blocks away. He says it won't be long before the enemy troops find their way down here, and we'd better be gone by then. The enemy will never take us alive." Immediately Alan regretted his choice of words.

"Never-ever?" piped up a five-year-old boy with a profusely runny nose. He was on the verge of tears.

"Well, we don't want to find out, do we? I've got a map and instructions," he continued, holding up a data-pad. "So follow me. Bigger kids, ten and older, hold onto one or two of the young kids. Take a lamp if you have a free hand, and don't fall behind- we've got to stay together."

Fortunately, he realized, most of the kids knew him and would obey without question; the others would have no choice. These were the children of his neighbors. Their parents-

schoolteachers, businessmen, researchers at the university- were now engaged in a deadly firefight in the streets above them, and Alan recognized the kids' confusion and terror as a reflection of his own distress. They badly needed someone older to lock onto, so he had to bury that distress deep down. He knew they would follow him. Still- at age fifteen- Alan had no idea whether he was saying all the right things.

"Stay together," he repeated, then took another deep breath and moved decisively to the door. The children jostled each other trying to leave the room, but eventually lined up in twos and threes, half-running down the dim corridor with their lamps swinging beams of light in random directions. Katie had taken the hand of a small toddler, whose short stumbling steps caused her to drop back in the group. From time to time, Alan turned to look for her: a glimpse of her reddish-brown hair, caught in a sudden dart of light, would have to do.

After two hundred meters, Alan raised his hand and halted in front of the doorway indicated on his map. Behind it lay a musty storage room cluttered with boxes of spare machine parts and tools. Consulting his data-pad, Alan reached upward and felt carefully along the narrow ledge above the door; there, under a layer of dust and sticky grime, he could barely feel the switch, almost flush with the ledge.

"Stay back," he warned, depressing the switch then stepping back out into the corridor. A low noise rumbled beneath them, and several of the children in front aimed their lamps at the floor of the storage room. Or, rather, where the floor had been: there was now a stairway dropping steeply to another dark corridor below.

Alan went down first, shouting back cautions: the steps were narrow and a little slippery; it was dark and the ceiling was low; they had to stay together- don't fall behind! Just as the storage room floor slid closed behind the last of the children descending the steps, he touched a switch on the wall, and the corridor, which stretched for hundreds of meters (westward, Alan guessed), was bathed in the soft glow of dozens of light panels mounted along the walls on either side.

There was a sudden collective gasp, and many of the children started to cry again: these light panels were nothing like the plain and sturdy industrial-military lighting they had become so

114

accustomed to, over the past weeks. These panels were of the sort used in private homes, with soft decorative frames and ornate three-dimensional images: the closest one showed Trampus the Pirate on the deck of his ship, pointing his cutlass at the Jolly Roger. In another panel, a dozen woodland fairies watched a donkey-headed man sleep in a clearing. Were these panels a message left as a final farewell from their parents? The wailing crescendoed as the group proceeded haltingly along the corridor. Even Alan, struggling in vain to control his emotions, pictured his parents bringing these panels out of their home supplies- probably not very long ago- and carefully installing them here in this gloomy tunnel, in order to light their children's path to safety. He turned and looked again for Katie, who spotted him first and waved with her free hand, before wiping off her cheeks.

A loud explosion sounded somewhere not far above them, and the children began to run. A few of the light panels flickered. Another explosion sounded- much closer and louder this time- as they passed by a red vertical stripe on the wall to their left. The third explosion was very nearly on top of them, making the floor jump. Instinctively, Alan ducked his head, then shouted out, "We're almost there!" Now he kept his eyes trained on the low ceiling, searching for the sign. According to the instructions, there would be a star on the ceiling. But there was nothing. "Look for a blue star," he asked the teenage boy running alongside him for help. The girl just behind them, six years old at most, softly volunteered, "I thaw a blue thtar."

"You saw a star? Where was it?"

"Back there," she said, pointing. Then, suddenly shy, the girl looked at her feet in silence.

Alan brushed past her, reached back to take her hand, and then waded back through the group. He must have missed it when the third explosion went off. And there it was: faint against the dingy white ceiling, a light blue star- he had ducked his head just past the red stripe on the wall.

"All right, everyone, step back," he warned again, checking with the data-pad. Standing on the tips of his toes, Alan was just able to reach and press hard on the star. Immediately a meter-wide hole slid open in the ceiling, and then a ladder rattled downward into the crowd of children, who stepped back and stared.

"Now follow me!"

The sight of Alan climbing boldly up the ladder gave the children the focus they needed: this was the way out! Even the youngest ones visibly gathered themselves and mounted the ladder in a semi-orderly fashion, with the awkward assistance of the teenagers. No-one could see anything in the dark hole above, but they could hear Alan's voice echoing down to them.

"There's a latch up here... I'm sliding it over... all right, here it goes."

A light suddenly appeared high up in the darkness, partially obscured by Alan as he climbed out into the street, followed by the proud six-year-old who had spotted the blue star. They climbed on, drawn by a rising sense of hope. One by one, the children finally emerged from the escape shaft and then huddled closely together in a cold evening drizzle, slowly taking in their unfamiliar surroundings.

As children of a privileged social class, none of them had ever seen a slum before; the neighborhood they now found themselves in, identified on Alan's map as the Greater Branford Projects, would certainly qualify as such. Unlit four-story apartment buildings stretched from one empty street to another, their worn faces featureless except for tiny barred windows which dotted the upper apartment fronts, and the occasional random obscene phrase or image, or call to violence, lasered indelibly into concrete walls. Even though abandoned, these buildings exuded generations of pent-up resentment and frustration, which only the youngest of the children failed to sense immediately. Still, some of the graphic designs on the walls flew in the face of the neighborhood's grim destitution. Particularly striking was a detailed self-portrait of a laser-painter with rays of light beaming out of his forehead into a starry night sky, which drew Alan's attention despite himself. Beneath the portrait, in golden capital letters, ART STARS; below that, POETRY IN POVERTY; and finally, GRAFFITI GRATIFY!

Even a momentary diversion was therapeutic, relieving the heavy tension. But respite was all too brief: walls collapsing with a loud rumble only a block or two away, the shriek of shattering glass, an overpowering smell of fuel burning, and the furious flashes of rapid-alternating-pulse lasers, known in the military as Razers, illuminating the clouds overhead, quickly brought Alan back to the immediate danger.

"This way! Follow me!" Alan pointed toward the northwest and began to jog. The children moved surprisingly quickly for the first leg of their journey through Greater Branford, pausing only when the explosions seemed safely distant.

"Keep holding hands! Never get separated!" Alan shouted back over his shoulder.

"Never-ever," the boy with the faucet nose shouted back. He had stayed glued to Alan's heels the entire way.

Directed by his data-pad, Alan led his group of twenty toward the old city center. But he was also instinctively heading home- back to the university, where he had grown up as a faculty child. Block by block, he gradually began to recognize the streets, which were subtly but surely climbing to a higher altitude as they made their way into New Haven proper. One more bridge to cross, a slight rise around a deserted office building, and the children could finally stop to catch their breaths, and to look back upon the Greater Branford Projects.

What they saw forced most of the children to turn away: towering plumes of black smoke rose from the very place where, just an hour before, they had climbed out of a hole in the street; small patrol-craft circled above the ruined area, sending an occasional Razer burst into a back alley, onto a flaming rooftop, wherever pockets of resistance remained; and high above them, a command ship of the Pan-World Electorate hovered, its massive underbelly dipping beneath the clouds. It was then that the utter hopelessness of resistance sank in, and Alan Goodrow- not much older, after all, than his tear-stained band of followers- became overwhelmed by the certainty that they would never- ever- see their parents again.

Chapter Eleven

The lab technician, identified only by the number 0749 on his lapel badge, held no illusions about the coldly impersonal nature of his job. In fact, when working on secret research projects within the laboratories of Eunigen Boston, he would even try to forget his own name, to cast himself as a mere cog in a very large machine. As one of a thousand anonymous technicians, his actions carried little significance: they didn't imply anything, did they, about his values, ethics, upbringing... who he really was.

Still, it would bother him considerably if the subjects suffered pain, or even died, as the result of an infusion or other procedure in which he was personally involved. Maybe if he transferred out of Repro (after only three months!), to some other division which didn't deal with live subjects, such as Sequence Control or Protanalysis. Or maybe out of the lab altogether, to Public Relations? But that wouldn't be stress-free either: imagine how the public would relate, if they gleaned any idea of the activities going on behind the innocent façade of the Eunigen building, an architectural gem on the bucolic south bank of the Charles River!

0749 sighed, touched a control which regulated the concentration of a solution inside a labeled white vial, waited for the sequalyzer to rate the solution, then carefully detached the vial from its clamp and tubing. He placed it in a purification chamber and made a lengthy entry in his da-disc. That done, there was nothing left but the interview- no more reason to delay. 0749 turned to face the subject, who was strapped into a reclining chair on the opposite side of the room.

A young man, nineteen, almost twenty. Not unusual; so many drug addicts he had seen were around this age. Just as they entered their vocational years, that's when they needed the additional help of the mind-expanders. What had surprised 0749 was the fact that this young man had come from a colony on Mars- now that was funny! A hick from the Martian colonies, ending up here in a Eunigen lab! They probably couldn't get hold of any Deep Coma on

Mars, so this poor fellow may have over-indulged, given the chance. Or maybe he was more sensitive to Deep Coma, not having built up a tolerance by using the weaker therapeptides first. In any case, he was in pathetic shape: his mind had melted badly, but he was still able to communicate a little- that was a relief to 0749, who had the interview in mind- but undoubtedly they would have to label him a "poor historian."

Another surprise was that Director Walther Beame was going to run this experiment himself. It was not unusual for Beame to come up from New York to get an overview of lab projects, but this time he would be in the room with the subject himself. The Grand Poobah would actually be pushing the buttons- highly unusual. 0749 did not look forward to meeting Beame, who was reputed to be aggressive and bull-headed. He looked down at the subject's face: skin clammy, eyes unfocused, mouth hanging dumbly open. The last withdrawal had taken a particularly heavy toll.

"Can you answer a few questions for me?"

The young man raised his eyebrows and looked vaguely in the direction of 0749.

"You can? Yes? Then tell me, which of the following drugs have you tried within the past year: Insight Out? Common Scents? Yes? And how about JAMpot? Yes? Roving Eye? It was unlikely, but maybe this junkie was the one who stole the sample coming up from New York. No? All right then."

So he had actually used a couple of the weaker therapeptides. He marked the boxes next to Common Scents and JAMpot on his da-disc, and then continued.

"And how many times have you used Common Scents and JAMpot? One to five times? Six to ten? Eleven to twenty? More than twenty?" 0749 waited, but the subject ignored the question. Perhaps it was a little too wordy for his present state of mind.

"After using Common Scents and JAMpot, did you experience a painful withdrawal?" The subject slowly shook his head.

"Did you feel confused? Disoriented?" A frown, then a slow nod.

"Confusion. Disorientation," read 0749 as he carefully marked two boxes.

"And tell me, when using those two drugs, did you at any time have an out-of body experience?"

"No. Same." The young man's voice was grainy, almost cracking.

"Would you like some water? No? Sure? Then let's go on: with Common Scents and JAMpot, were you able to read the thoughts of anyone around you?"

"No. Same. Thoughts."

"Very good. Now, as you know, you are here today because you agreed to participate in a study on the new drug, Deep Coma. We provided you with a small supply of Deep Coma, three days ago. Tell me, in those three days, how many times did you use Deep Coma? One to five times? Six to ten? Eleven to…"

"SIX. No. Eight. Nine."

"Six to ten." Another marked box.

"When using Deep Coma, did you at any time have…"

"Yes. Out. Of body."

"An out-of-body experience, very good. And when using Deep Coma, were you able to…"

"Read thoughts."

"Good. But let me finish the question before you answer, all right? Let me see: Yes to reading thoughts. Tell me, after using Deep Coma, did you experience a painful withdrawal?"

The subject faced away and shifted uncomfortably in his chair.

"Pain. But Q!"

"Cue?" What was cue? Probably a Martian expression, not on the da-disc index, so 0749 moved on.

"When using Deep Coma, did you at any time co-occupy a physical space with another individual?" The subject shifted again, but otherwise ignored the question.

"On a scale from one to ten- one being the worst, and ten being the best- how would you rate your experience with Deep Coma?"

"Q."

"No, no- on a scale from one to ten…"

"Q."

"Again. On a scale… "

"Having some trouble, 0749?"

120

0749 whirled around and faced a tall, stocky man in his fifties, with prematurely white hair thinning at the crown, a broad impassive face, large hands hanging casually at the sides of his white lab coat. Despite his relaxed appearance, Director Walther Beame projected a sense of tension, like a spring tightly wound. How long had he been standing there? And who was the pale, skinny fellow standing in the doorway? Such an odd, outdated look: silver hair in a ponytail, of all things!

"Dr. Beame! I'm sorry- I didn't hear the door open. I was just concluding my interview with the subject."

"Good- that's fine. Now, is the new dose ready?" Beame brushed past 0749 on his way to the purification chamber.

"Yes, Dr. Beame. I raised the concentration by five percent, as directed. The sequalyzer shows a sequence integrity of over ninety-eight point nine, so..."

"Excellent. Let's proceed." Beame removed the white vial from the chamber, then quickly crossed the cluttered room, at the same time attaching the vial to a Dermamist injector, with the smooth motion of one well-practiced in such procedures. He showed no interest at all in the results of the preceding interview.

Beame leaned closely over the subject and examined his face. The subject had drifted off to sleep.

"Can you hear me?" Beame shouted.

The young man, startled, looked up in a daze.

"You can hear me? What is your name?"

No answer. He tried to go back to sleep.

"Is your name Ibsen? Are you Thor Ibsen? Tell me!" No need to shout, thought 0749, who was also perturbed by Beame's use of the subject's actual name. It was definitely a major breach of lab protocol.

The young man replied hoarsely, "Yes. Trip." The subject squinted in recognition at the thin fellow, now standing behind Beame with a smug smile on his face. "F- Foye?"

"Thor Ibsen, my name is Dr. Walther Beame." He was speaking more rapidly now. "I am about to give you a higher dosage of a drug very similar to Deep Coma. Is that all right with you? I should tell you that there may be a substantial risk of serious side-effects at this high a dosage, including rash, headache, fever, abdominal pain, death, incontinence, loss of taste, and loosening of the nails. All right then?" Beame smiled thinly at Trip and nodded encouragingly as he spoke.

"Yes. Q."

"Note that informed consent was obtained," Beame murmured to 0749, who duly marked a box on his da-disc. Without further ado (except for an audible gasp from 0749), Beame then applied the Dermamist injector and emptied the entire contents of the white vial into the subject's carotid artery.

It took only a few seconds for the effects to begin. Trip's eyes slammed shut, his jaw clenched, his lips pulled tightly back in a grimace reaching almost ear-to-ear and revealing gold-capped molars on either side. Nice, thought 0749: designed to match his gold chin cup and nostril ring. Trip's tremulous hands grabbed onto the seat, knuckles white; his back arched against the plastic restraints pinning down both shoulders; his feet kicked violently against securely tightened leg straps.

But from the subject's perspective, there were no plastic restraints, no leg straps, no arching or kicking. Trip was not even in the room. He was passing, disembodied, through the walls of the building, outside at the speed of thought, into the frigid night air, then plunging straight into the black, churning river below. The water was freezing, yet it burned! A hot primordial soup, it dissolved him as it would a tiny grain of salt. Trip found himself coursing through a blood-red sea, saturated with vibrations of the past, events and lives of people all appearing as pure energy, bright blue spots and flashes stretching and crisscrossing in fantastic patterns. A dazzling light poured straight through him, searing him with intense pain and pleasure. He heard voices (singing?) against a droning, chanting sound which grew louder by stages; he marveled at overlapping clouds of memories; in the chaos he could make out luminous circles, squares, symbols of meaning, logic, ideas. They were stacked in massive parallel piles- crystalline arrays of thoughts, rigid and impenetrable. He approached cautiously, brushed against them, and soared upward, away from the agony of contact. Then, frantically seeking answers, he drilled downward, further and further, unable to stop even when the immense pressure began to crush him. He felt himself suddenly expanding, then inverting, wrenched inside-out. For a tiny moment, before all emotion vanished, he recognized and welcomed joy, fear, rage, Q: the last traces of his own world. The merciless river now stretched, and he stretched with it; as it widened, he widened. The torrent swept him, along with mountains of memories and events, into a turbulent, bottomless ocean, where they fell from the heights and shattered into innumerable spinning points of light. The ocean roared with delight. Despite his feeble attempts to hold together, Trip exploded like a nova but only reached the size of an infinitesimal drop in the ocean's vast, saturated memory currents. At the Eunigen lab several kilometers upstream, his physical body responded by kicking hard again at the straps.

That wasn't quite a seizure, thought 0749, but it was close. He searched his data-disc. Seizures were not listed among the side-effects.

"Dr. Beame, just what are we observing here? I mean, what are we expecting to happen to the subject? Do you think the higher dose of drug will result in a more prolonged extracorporeal experience? And will the withdrawal therefore be more painful than the previous?" 0749 tried to suppress the rising anger so familiar by this point in his short career at the Repro Division. He really should get around to filling out a transfer application, and soon.

Beame continued to stare at Trip's contorted face, as he considered the question. 0749 was struck by the resemblance between Beame's face and that of the subject: the tightness of its expression, the mouth drawn back, the look of one greedily searching for something in the obscure distance. Finally, the director explained matter-of-factly to his conscience-plagued lab technician, "Don't worry yourself, 0749; he will not experience any painful withdrawal this time. Extrapolating from results so far in our titration protocol, you can rest assured that this time the subject will successfully expire."

Benn discovered, in addition to his "brakes," a more crucial technique: how to disengage his awareness/perception/presence from the powerful stream of recorded events, the water-etched memory. If he stayed, the stream would undoubtedly overwhelm him with its massive waves of chaotic energy, slashed by intrusions of myriad long-ago thoughts and voices. The story unfolding before him in the dripping tunnel was incredible, but he knew he could not continue to follow it. Forcing himself to disconnect from the stream by a certain twist of his mind, Benn found himself now at the end of the long tunnel, peering through a low archway into the brightly-lit chamber, at its banks of computers, its roving QI units, and its two human occupants.

Lou Hunter stood with his feet planted apart, suggesting authority, hands on hips, impatiently watching as Zak, in a painstakingly careful manner clearly designed to infuriate Hunter, tucked the yellow envelope into an open wall safe. "You say Dr. Neelin left that package with you, for the Virginia courier?" Benn felt the jealousy and hatred flowing between the two men, equally potent in both directions.

"Yes, Dr. Hunter." Benn could clearly read Zak's unspoken afterthought: *Don't sound so amazed, that he trusted me with something important.* Zak re-arranged the contents of the safe, then suddenly closed it with a sharp snap and turned around to confront Lou Hunter.

At his first sight of Zak's face, Benn recoiled in shock. The sandy hair he had seen clearly from the back, but not the thick eyebrows crossing his low forehead. The emptiness behind his close-set eyes, hard as ball-bearings. The last place Benn had seen Zak's face was above the same broad shoulders and compact, muscular body, but that body had squeezed into a glossy blue one-piece business suit. Zak was the Lint Man.

Lint Man had somehow survived the crash! But Lora, who certainly knew her business as a paramedic, had pronounced him dead, and Benn had seen it himself- Lint Man had definitely met his demise aboard the Glidebus. Could someone have reversed his death, and the laws of nature? Had someone restored Lint Man's brain, heart and other bodily functions, after many hours of decomposition? It was a miracle! Thrilling, Q, like something out of the Frankenstein story, one of Benn's favorites from school days.

"Too bad Dr. Neelin didn't come in, because I need to talk to him, and he would have given me the sample, I'm sure. Never mind. Did you even mention to him that I was here?" Benn read Hunter's afterthought: *Neelin took a real gamble, leaving the DNA sample with this dimwit Zak.*

"No, Dr. Hunter- he was in a rush. There wasn't time for him to come into the warehouse," Zak explained. *Dr. Neelin wouldn't want to see you anyway. And why would it be better for him to give you the sample?*

"You didn't open the envelope, did you?" Hunter asked sharply. *Not beyond Zak to touch something with his filthy hands and completely ruin the sample.*

"No, Dr. Hunter. I didn't. I wouldn't do anything so... stupid." *Insulting me again. One day you'll be sorry.*

"Never mind," said Hunter. Then, muttering to himself: "It was a real challenge to get this off the rim of the glass, where he tapped with his finger. He never even picked up the glass- good Lord! We had to amplify the few strands we got, and that's all there is." *You don't have a clue what I'm talking about, do you? Dimwit. Neelin's taking too many chances these days; maybe we need a change of leadership.*

Benn saw the aura emitted by Lou Hunter turn slowly from dark green to a gray-brown, just like that puff of smoke he had blown out of his dorm room, the previous week. That's when he noticed something strikingly different about Zak: he had no surrounding aura. He was the first person Benn had seen, while out-of-body, who did not emit that glowing color which seemed to reflect not only the person's mood, but his essential character. His soul, Benn supposed. So why was Lint Man different? Well, for one thing, death caused profound changes, didn't it? It was wild speculation, but maybe death separated bodies from their auras. Didn't the old superstitions say that the soul left the body when someone died? When Lint Man was killed on that bus, he must have lost his aura, his soul, and whoever brought him back to life couldn't restore it. But that would make Zak some sort of zombie- a soulless, re-animated body walking the earth. Even wilder speculation, Benn admonished himself. And even more Q!

"And when the lab courier comes tomorrow, Zak, don't forget to check his identity markers. Good Lord! I can just see you handing the package over to some PWE goon..." *One goon handing over to another.*

The resulting surge of rage hit Benn with a shock: outwardly civil to this point, Zak suddenly seized a handful of discs and slammed them onto the floor. He ignored Lou Hunter's startled glare as he stalked out of the chamber and back into the long, foul tunnel.

There it was again: the hollow feeling. The need for solidity, impossible to resist. Benn no sooner knew he would have to return to his physical form, back at the dormitory, than he found himself once again plunged into pitch darkness- the Dark of Harkness, his fellow interns called it- reluctantly re-united with his physical self. He opened his eyes, focused for a second, and looked at his clock: there was an hour before dawn. Too late to sleep; he found no reason to sleep much anyway. Benn contented himself with lying comfortably in bed, listening to the rain clatter against his window. Somewhere far beyond the rain, he also heard faint sighs and whispers.

An occasional image flashed through his mind: frightened children hurrying down a trembling corridor; a determined Alan Goodrow searching for a stripe, a star; then Goodrow again, in later years- now Benn remembered- the same face as in the portrait; Goodrow had grown up to become a physician, a professor, then Master of Mellon College. He had become an accomplished scholar and leader- but Benn finally understood the distraction painted indelibly into his portrait: the look of a man haunted by devastating memories.

And then, unsummoned, the face of his fellow intern inexplicably appeared, the arrogant one from Highland City- what was his name? Trip. He and Nema, and also Foye, were up at MassMed. But what was happening to Trip? Clearly he was in agony, his staring eyes hollowed out, his shocked pupils constricted to tiny points, his Nordic features distorted in a silent scream. Trip's face elongated grotesquely, then widened like a piece of rubber stretched to the point of snapping: soon unrecognizable as Trip, or even as a human face, it continued to spread quickly in every direction, fading into the darkness of Benn's room.

126

Chapter Twelve

His eager anticipation of the third and final vial made the week pass quickly for Benn. On Monday, Dr. Neelin showed unfettered enthusiasm for Benn's new role as Assistant to the Professor in Recombinant Anatomy, which Benn himself saw as that of teacher's pet. Dr. Cira Vincent invited Benn, Lora, Theo Coffin and a few of the more outspoken interns, to a Tuesday afternoon tea at her house on tree-lined Bradburn Street, at the eastern edge of the undergraduate campus. Wednesday morning's gene-frame nano-construction lab offered new insights into the complex interactions between genetic building blocks once they were locked into sequence. And on Thursday, Benn attended another group session with Hol Chan and patient W.P., who reported a worsening of his unbearable symptoms; the previous mottling of his hands and legs could no longer be seen.

Benn found himself grinding robotically through the week like a Worm set on automatic navigation, with very few deviations along the way. One such was a midweek encounter with Lora, in front of Harkness. Benn stood in the courtyard admiring the elms with their fall foliage. He had wrapped himself warmly in an old-fashioned greatcoat, which was a heavy, thigh-length waterproof jacket with a hood and large front pockets, its interior lined with recombinant fur, phenotypically somewhere between alpaca and corn silk. Lora had one too; probably all the interns had been issued a greatcoat by MWI- although Benn could not imagine stylish Nema wearing one: its military-green color was typical of Army Surplus. He sensed Lora's presence behind him, just as she reached out to tap on his shoulder. Gently: it was the shoulder he had dislocated on the Glidebus.

"Hey there. That's a great coat you've got on, Benn."

"Ha-HAH. Good one, Lora. I like yours too."

She wore an identical jacket, zipped up to her chin. Fall had commenced in earnest, and the air, so recently humid and sticky, had suddenly turned brisk- almost overnight, the leaves had turned as well, their bright red-gold hues highlighted by a brilliant blue sky.

"They do look a bit ungainly, don't they?" Lora rotated slowly around with her arms extended. "MWI must have gotten a cheap deal on a bulk purchase."

"No, no. First class all the way, Lora. This must be what they mean by 'deep pockets.'" He waved his hands around in the front pockets, but Lora missed the connection. "The real source of funding may be Eunigen, though- I suspect there's a strong link between the two corporations." His mailings from MWI, he had noticed, were printed with the same twenty-digit Sender's Permit Number as the package he had received from his father.

"Really? I had a feeling about that too. Whether it's MWI or Eunigen, they're paying for everything: even tickets to holoplays, concerts, sports, you name it."

"Concerts?" Benn had received a small catalog of events he could choose from, but skimming quickly through it, had missed the concerts. It was those baseball playoffs down at Yanqui Stadium, scheduled to start in the next few weeks, which had caught his eye. "What sort of concerts?"

"Oh, mostly synthesized music by QI units, with junky light shows, that sort of thing. But last week I attended a special concert held at Sprague Hall, near the Old Campus- a group called the Juilliard, I think- they've been around a long time. It was Q, listening to Beethoven's late string quartets, which I just love, performed on original period instruments! And the musicians looked like they may have been the original owners!"

Benn laughed, picturing an ancient foursome clutching centuries-old string instruments with skeletal hands. And this was surprising: not only was Lora amusing, she was a fan of Beethoven. The wild, impulsive idea of inviting her up to his room that evening, to listen to Opus 111 together, suddenly entered his head, but exited just as rapidly.

"You're right, Benn," Lora continued. "MWI is a first-class operation. Which makes it all the more puzzling, about Torch Halsey."

"That guy from Security? What about him?"

"Well, he's YaleConn Security Chief. But it's quite clear that he really works for Eunigen- or MWI- right?"

"Sure. It struck me that Rion Salkend, who's a deputy of MWI, treated Halsey like a mere underling."

"That's true. But I was thinking of the orientation speech that Halsey gave us, the day we arrived on campus- remember? It was basically a pile of propaganda about MWI and Eunigen!"

"You're right. He practically stood up to salute, when he read the part about Eunigen making life better for all of mankind..."

Lora remembered. "For all mankind, as it reaches into the distant galaxy. Blah-blah-blah! Honestly, Benn, would you consider Torch Halsey to be an example of – you know that old YaleConn expression- the Best and Brightest?"

"No, he's pretty low in the wattage department, I suppose. So you're surprised, that MWI would actually hire someone..."

"He's come by my dorm room twice, since we first arrived. Once, to inspect the walls and ceiling, or so he let on- tapping here and there, looking at the light panels. What a suspicious character. The second visit was more disturbing: he asked me for details about what I had done that week- where I had gone, anybody I had spoken with."

"Outrageous! And let me guess: he claimed it was part of his duties as Chief of Security? Insecurity, rather?"

"Yes, to both. But I don't see how that information has any bearing on university security. It's almost as though...he has a personal interest, or expects something. As though I've promised him..."

A group of interns came out of Harkness, chattering and laughing loudly as they passed behind Benn, who frowned as he waited, then shook his head impatiently. He took Lora's arm and steered her toward the outpatient clinic building.

"Promised him...what? You said..."

"I said 'as though' I promised. Who knows what random act he interpreted as a sign of friendship, that first day? He was crowding me quite a bit that afternoon, I remember- but I purposely ignored him. And when he came over, supposedly to inspect my room, I left to visit Akili until he was finished."

Benn nodded uncertainly. "Maybe Halsey's just doing his job."

"You're probably right, Benn. Torch Halsey doesn't have designs on me; I'm over-interpreting." She feels the need to reassure me about this, thought Benn.

"Besides, he did ask a lot of questions about you, as well."

They were now standing by themselves, in front of Sterling Memorial's looming central tower, which appeared to be leaning forward to catch their conversation.

"He asked about me?"

"He wanted to know how long we've known each other. And whether we've ever gone out, you know, for fun. None of his business, but he was so officious about it that I told him about Dr. Neelin's wine tasting. He asked if we usually sit together in class..."

Benn exploded. "Lora! Those are still questions about you! Halsey is fixated on you."

"...OR, whether *you* sit with others, such as Theo Coffin. He wanted to know who joins you at meals. What you do in your free time. Whether I've noticed anything weird about your behavior. To that one, of course, I answered YES!"

Benn snorted. "You know, I do try awfully hard to keep the weird behavior to myself."

Lora spotted a segue opportunity. "Actually, you might rephrase that: trying so hard to keep to yourself *is* your weird behavior." Lora took a deep breath- it was as good a time as any to say it. "This has been bothering me since Highland City. Benn: you are, without doubt, an extremely difficult person to read."

Benn, who had a history of stumbling badly where Lora was concerned, thought she was still teasing. "You mean difficult to read, as in a boring novel? I'll try to spice up my plot." She met his grin with a blank look.

"Difficult because I'm written in a foreign language?" he tried again.

"Come on, Benn." Lora rolled her eyes. "Not a foreign language. But you do act like a foreigner. I always get the feeling that you're holding back, standing apart and watching, as though you don't belong."

"That's because I don't belong. And you do? I admit, you fit in much better than I do, what with having social skills and all. I'll be forever an outsider, Lora: the colonial subject visiting the imperial capital, tolerated only as long as I have something to contribute. Otherwise it's 'Back to the colony, boy, your permit's been canceled.'"

"You don't need to feel that way, Benn. You see yourself as more of an outsider than others do."

"Do you really suppose these folks consider us Martians their equals? Back to the original subject, do you think Torch Halsey thinks of us as neighbors or alien freaks?"

"Halsey's not a valid example; to him, everyone is a potential terrorist. I'm talking about Cira, or Dr. Neelin, or Theo. Akili, too. You're not an alien to them. You're the one who's built a barrier around yourself. I know, engaging with others can be rough, sometimes brutal. But Benn, even I can't get through your barrier, though I'm a Martian just like you!"

"So you're saying it's not Mars- I am the problem."

"I'm saying if you just loosen up the defenses… you've got great qualities, Benn. You don't need to protect yourself constantly against getting hurt."

Benn puzzled over this last concept. He knew Lora meant well, and that she sincerely believed her explanation of his "barrier". But she was quite wrong: the barrier was not there to protect his feelings from being hurt.

"Benn? You're staring."

"Oh. Right. Sorry. I was just trying to remember…"

Unconsciously, Benn took Lora's arm again and led her down the street, past Sterling Memorial, toward the Brady Hospital Building. They paused to watch an ambulance glide by, lights and sirens pulsing until it turned into the Emergency entrance. Benn stared at the ground as they walked on.

"When I was, I think, an infant… but how could I remember that far back? Do you ever wonder if your memories are imagined?"

"Not if I can help it- I'd go insane. What do you remember, Benn?"

"I remember…a lot of pain. And rage. Sadness. And Q! But also emptiness. Boredom. Fear! Joy! Sure, people feel these things, but I felt them all at the same time, Lora. All jangling together, the volume turned up to maximum and beyond. A roaring noise in my head, every second of every day. At first I couldn't shut it off- I remember rolling around in bed, trying to stop the terrible noise."

"Benn…"

"But then I found a way. I learned how to block it out; it took a certain turn of thought, like closing a fist, and the flood of …" he stopped. "Lora, now you're staring."

"I remember something like that too! Well, not nearly what you're describing, but much milder: there was this rush of feelings- I think of it as a noise too- that goes back as far as I can remember. At some point, though, like you, I was able to control it. You know that noise we were both hearing, our first week here on Earth? That reminded me…"

"The thumping noise- and the headache? I think I can explain all that now." Benn decided to tell Lora about his father's message, and, omitting any mention of the three Dermamist injections, he carefully related his father's explanation for the headaches and noise.

She was incredulous. "Incompatible with…the Earth's energy field? That's a fair theory, I suppose- especially coming from the Research Director at Eunigen- but how would that explain our childhood symptoms, back on Mars?"

Benn shrugged, and they continued in silence. Some things simply could not be explained, as they had both learned early in their medical training. Whatever had affected Lora as a child, his experience had been a thousand times worse. The barrier he had thrown around himself at a young age had shielded him from exposure to the extremely weak electromagnetic field of Mars, but was insufficient to protect him here on Earth. Admittedly, his initial discomfort had ebbed over the past two weeks, but still, Benn could hardly wait for that third injection.

Even as Benn was looking forward to that Friday's injection, trembling hands were taking the third vial out of its Eunigen mailing package, which Benn had carelessly crammed into the top drawer of his desk. The same eager hands transferred the vial's contents to a smaller vacuum container, luckily managing not to spill any, and replaced the precious liquid with an identical-looking, dilute salt solution. The vial and mailing package were then carefully returned to the top drawer.

After making certain he had not disturbed anything else in the room, Torch Halsey shut the door and hurried to the elevator. Marr would probably be back very soon, as he had no classes scheduled that morning. He had gone out for a long walk with Lora, and that bugged Halsey, but right now, much more important things were on his mind. He remembered Marr's first injection: with the help of Roving Eye, Halsey had visited Marr personally in his dorm room that time. Then there was the second injection. From the View Room at his office, he had watched Marr take a vial out of that box last Friday, then use the Dermamist to inject himself. That time Marr had lain motionless in bed until nearly dawn, and Halsey had a pretty clear idea what the vial had contained: judging by the duration of its effect, it was certainly one of the stronger recreational psychopeptides. There was a good chance that the third vial would be stronger yet: it might even contain Deep Coma. And he, Torch, had switched it out for a vial of salt water! On the drive back to Phelps Gate, Torch could hardly contain himself: Deep Coma! Why not? At the first opportunity, he would give it a try!

Chapter Thirteen

Another Friday evening on the quiet YaleConn campus. Two young men, waiting in high anticipation: one lying on a sweat-stained foldout cot in his littered office, the other on a disheveled dormitory bed. The two men were separated by barely a kilometer, and yet, in many ways, were light-years apart. Seconds before, almost simultaneously, each man had applied a loaded Dermamist injector to his skin: one to his left forearm, the other to the right side of his neck. The liquid contents had snapped through their porous skin, and then the two men had forced themselves to relax. And wait.

Torch Halsey felt his first misgivings about the injection: after the horrendous, painful withdrawal he had so recently gone through with Roving Eye, how could he take such a huge risk? What if he didn't come out alive from this one? Why did they call it Deep Coma, after all? Well, it was too late now- he had gambled and was committed (good!), so let the fun begin; whatever came, he would just have to ride it out.

Not having experienced any withdrawals so far, Benn Marr had no misgivings at all. He felt only an intense curiosity, an irresistible urge to ascend to the next level. With the initial injection, he had traveled out of his body for the first time; had perceived the auras surrounding others; and had directly impacted that floating aura trespassing in his dorm room. The second injection had freed him of his body for a much longer time, so that he could travel farther afield. He'd discovered he could read the inner thoughts of Lou Hunter and Zak, or Lint Man. Reading anyone's thoughts, let alone those of a dead man- amazing! But most astonishing was his ability to read the century-old record of children fleeing the PWE, etched in the micro-structure of underground water. Apparently Owen Marr had mapped out an escalating series of extracorporeal experiences for Benn, applying therapeptides of increasing potency. He couldn't wait to see what this third one would unveil.

Benn closed his eyes as he felt the familiar sensation of lifting out of his body and hovering in the space above it. He immediately applied the brakes by that turn of thought he had mastered the previous week; he had no plan to pass upward into Theo Coffin's room this time. Rather, he steered himself to the floor below and drifted slowly through a half-dozen rooms, not fully aware of any particular destination. The first room he came to was occupied by Sil Vargas, a highly diligent intern Benn had met briefly, now studying Chapter 109 of the Biogenome Menu with his feet propped up on his desk. With the possible exception of Lora, Sil was likely the only one studying on a Friday night. Loud music with syncopated rhythms, dominated by brass instruments, filled the room, and Sil's aura pulsed red in time with the musical beat.

The next four rooms, although cluttered with the detritus of student life, were unoccupied, probably because of the usual sporting events around town. The sixth room Benn entered, in contrast, was strikingly well-ordered: desktop clear, da-disc primly shut on a side-counter, bed folded back into a reading chair. A small holograph stood next to the da-disc, showing a rather stern-looking older couple, each with one hand on a shoulder of a fresh-faced teenage girl standing between them. She had a hopeful, innocent look, but the eyes captured her drive and intelligence. Benn turned to the front door and recognized the green greatcoat hanging on its hook, just as Lora entered the room.

She came in behind Benn, from the bathroom, dressed in white multipurpose underwear of a type found these days only on Luna or Mars. Clothing suitable for the rustic life, extreme durability being its chief, or sole, merit. Despite her lack of, well, style, Benn thought that Lora had never looked more attractive. She was surrounded by a deep yellow aura, close to gold, which extended at least a meter beyond her physical border- farther than others he had seen. The aura flared slightly as Lora suddenly stopped, frowned, and then slowly scanned the room. Q! She sensed his presence, Benn understood with a silent yelp and the panicked thrill of being caught red-handed. Benn, you voyeur, you!

Seeing nobody in the room, Lora brought her da-disc to the desk, opened it and began to read. Benn could see that she was studying what little was known about the Martian electromagnetic or E.M. field- so faint it was practically nonexistent, according to this

135

article- and judging by the numerous annotations, punctuated with exclamation points, in the margins of the text, Lora had made significant progress over the past two days. She read intently, her aura flaring at moments of discovery, for the next hour. Over her shoulder, Benn read along.

It seemed that the weak E.M. field of Mars was not purely electromagnetic, but was intermingled with a secondary energy field, one termed by its discoverers a "bio-wave field." This secondary field, significantly stronger than the E.M. field, could not have been generated simply by the movement of the planet's barely molten core, but rather, had characteristics consistent with the more complex and delicate forms of energy known to be generated by life on Earth. The implication was that there had once been life on Mars, life which had projected a planet-wide web of bio-wave energy. Despite its eventual extinction, Martian life must have left behind fossils, whose crystalline cellular structures continued to emit energy, enabling the bio-wave field to persist. In fact, the article speculated, a very similar bioweb may also exist on Earth but was undetectable, being swamped by the strong electromagnetic field of Earth.

So Benn's incompatibility was not with the E.M. field, as his father had claimed, but with the bioweb! That would explain his childhood symptoms, wouldn't it? Owen Marr had mentioned gene-based changes in brain activity, passed from one generation to the next: sensitivity to the bio-energy field was the result of a rapid evolution. But why was Benn so much more sensitive to it? Lora's family tree stretched back to the very first settlers on Mars, whereas Benn's family, as far as he knew, had appeared de novo, only two generations ago. And why hadn't Owen mentioned this phenomenon? The journal on Lora's da-disc was very specialized and esoteric, granted, but surely Owen was aware of it.

There was much left to explain. Benn edged closer, reading so intently that he failed to notice how close he was to Lora. When she suddenly scribbled another notation in the margin, and he leaned in to read it, he overlapped her aura- unintentionally, and for the briefest of moments, but her reaction was instantaneous.

"Benn!" she gasped. "I knew it!" Wide-eyed, Lora pushed herself back from the desk and looked quickly around the room, recalling Dr. Neelin's startled response outside the warehouse. But not quite: she was startled, certainly, but showed none of Neelin's visceral reaction; Lora appeared more intrigued than frightened. As for Benn, who was equally intrigued, the sensation of overlap had been completely different this time: no personal violation or disorientation, but rather a powerful sense of harmony. And melody, it occurred to him: the touching of their auras had the effect of striking a musical cord.

"Benn?" Lora whispered, then closed her eyes to regroup her thoughts. Was extreme lack of sleep causing her to imagine outlandish things? This was no time to let the imagination take over. It served her right, for pushing herself so compulsively for the past several days. Just in case, she checked the room once more, then sighed at her own foibles and resolved to try and get more rest. Nevertheless, she promptly resumed her reading of the da-disc. Benn, who had withdrawn instantly to a corner of the ceiling, now gazed upon her with a newfound appreciation. He had caught- or stolen, really- a glimpse of a completely different Lora, an impression of her myriad unseen layers. His thoughts returned to the musical analogy: it was as though she were a harmonious composition consisting of separate melodic lines, intertwined in a complicated yet orderly fashion. He perceived a steady internal rhythm. A high note imparted a sense of tension, while emerging contrapuntal themes contributed a fascinating complexity and the promise- the anticipation- of surprise. Lora had immediately known that Benn was in her room: she was separate, yet intimately connected to him through the bio-energy field. There was a lot for Benn to absorb.

He reviewed what he knew about the life-generated energy fields on Mars and Earth. He had connected as a child on Mars, and that was painful. The therapeptides sent by Father linked him to the field on Earth. Lora had her own native ability to connect, whereas his connection needed an artificial boost from synthetic peptides. But why would Owen Marr send the three injections? Not simply as a cure for headaches, or a way to "acclimate to Earth," as he had claimed. Benn felt like a chemistry experiment, a solution undergoing a drop-by-drop titration. Each drop increased Benn's abilities, his range. With this thought, his foot off the brakes, Benn began to drift slowly out of Lora's room, and he made no effort to stop himself from backing through the wall and descending to the

Harkness courtyard. There he found himself surrounded by students returning from their Friday entertainments. The air was filled with laughter and excitement. An intern suddenly approached from behind, and Benn's reaction was reflexive; he willed the intern's aura, and thus the intern herself, to steer widely clear of him.

He could move the auras! Q! The dimensions of his interaction with the bioweb were expanding. He could hear its stories and travel along its invisible pathways, but with this third vial, he discovered that he could also push back at it. What should he do with this newfound ability; where should he go, while the effect of the peptide lasted? The choices before him were limitless, but one towered above all others. The ocean! It called again to him; perhaps he'd been avoiding it. The cold black ocean was unfathomably deep, and even at some distance, he felt hollow, transparent, minuscule, as if peering down into the deepest part of a bottomless well. But the pull of eons upon eons of life-memories etched in an infinity of water was a siren song impossible to resist, and all he had to do was take the big leap. What would the little voice of his recurrent dreams, his Under Mind, have said? Go on, take a chance for once! Do it- now! Benn decided to go for a swim.

Torch Halsey braced himself for the wild ride of his life. Deep Coma! More than likely, anyway- Deep Coma was the only logical step, to follow Marr's second injection. And wouldn't Marr be disappointed, when he injected the saline solution that Torch had substituted for the real thing. You could only go so far with the placebo effect, after all- an out-of-body experience was simply not going to happen tonight for Benn Marr.

"Poor Benn Marr!" Torch said aloud, and he began to laugh at the irony. Poor, poor Benn Marr. He'll never know what went wrong. He'll never experience what I'm about to: I'll go anywhere I want, see and do anything I desire. Read thoughts. With Deep Coma, they say you can project your own thoughts, maybe even...maybe even make others do your bidding. Torch immediately thought of Lora and Sool, and a cold thrill shivered his spine.

138

He shook his arms, tried to relax his neck, kept his eyes shut tight. It was taking a little longer than the others, but it would be worth it. Be patient, he told himself. The minutes- five, then ten- went by, and still nothing happened. Fifteen minutes. Oh no! It sadly began to dawn on him, the amazing wild ride he was expecting would not happen after all. It's not poor Benn at all: it's poor Torch, his mind wailed. What "poor Torch" failed to appreciate was that he was actually the extremely fortunate, and insufficiently thankful, Torch: had the vial actually contained the Deep Coma which he so fervently desired, Torch Halsey's extracorporeal journey might have mimicked that of poor Thor Ibsen, who had vanished into the Charles River. The immense pull of the bioweb would have dragged him southward, silently screaming, into the churning waters of Long Island Sound. He would have plunged straight down into its bottomless depths. Torch Halsey, caught like driftwood in a giant whirlpool, would very quickly have been smashed to bits by its centripetal force.

As it happened, both Torch and Benn had administered themselves harmless injections of saline solution, and neither had realized it. While Benn immersed himself joyously, swooping like a dolphin through swirling memories in the warm and welcoming sea, Torch rose stiffly from his cot, stared at the floor for a sullen moment, then kicked his Dermamist injector hard across the room.

Chapter Fourteen

Benn emerged from his long swim, thoroughly refreshed. His time limit would probably come soon, he realized. Rather than will himself directly back to the dorm room, he decided to pay a visit to the warehouse in the Greater Branford District. He was still curious about Zak, and of course the others as well. There must be quite a few people involved in this clandestine operation, whatever it was: Neelin, Hunter and Zak could not possibly maintain the warehouse and the network which undoubtedly extended well beyond the city. Was Theo Coffin involved? And what about all the computers and military equipment? Benn couldn't be sure yet, but he had an inkling about the group's purpose. To his disappointment, the warehouse was unoccupied, not even guarded by Zak; the group must be engaged in some special activity tonight.

He headed back to his room at a running pace, slow enough to take in the neighborhood, which had changed little since the day Alan Goodrow led his small band of children through its streets. The same faceless apartment buildings stretched for block after block, but they were now spotless and orderly, completely devoid of graffiti. Gone was the sense of oppression and anger; in its place stood the security promised by the Pan-World Electorate- security smothered by a heavy, bland conformity. Maybe he'd come back here one day and laser GRAFFITI GRATIFY on the same wall. Benn crossed several bridges on his way home, stopping at each to gaze downward at the dark water streaming underneath, to listen to its whispered stories. He followed other voices to the high ground where Alan Goodrow's young charges had turned to survey the PWE's systematic destruction of the lives they had known.

Benn pressed on, his thoughts dark-edged as he crossed empty streets and squares, passed an abandoned train station, and climbed up the hill to the medical school. He slowed his pace and allowed the gloom to dissipate by the time he reached Harkness. When Benn finally passed through the wall into his own room, two very important observations struck him in quick succession. The first was that he had not been drawn back to his body by that unpleasant, hollow-feeling need for solidity which he had felt the two previous times; this time, he had been free for a much longer period, and still felt no compulsion to return. The second observation, even more intriguing, was that his physical body was nowhere to be seen: it had left the room!

Benn stared at his vacant bed, the bedsheet strewn on the floor. He searched the bathroom (call of Nature?)- but no, it couldn't have gotten up...without him. Couldn't have wandered off on its own, could it? Someone must have removed it... but who? Other questions followed: could they have gotten it out without being observed by those ubiquitous Eyes? And more importantly, what if the body was harmed in some way, or even killed? Maybe it was already dead, and that was why he didn't feel drawn back to it. With this alarming thought came a brief stab of panic. Could he survive for long in this disembodied state? And even if his body was unharmed, how would he find and rejoin it?

All excellent questions, he allowed, but first things first. Benn concentrated. His perception widened. He felt the brakes come on, unbidden. Don't panic- must go slowly. And be careful, he warned himself, not to attach fully to the bioweb; the explosive flood of data could kill him. But even loosely engaged, he could already piece out of the loud background noise a faint signature belonging to his physical body, located somewhere to the east. Relieved that he had not been harmed after all, Benn stayed focused on not losing the distant signal. He experimented by expanding the image of the two previous rejoinings. His aura was an energy signature, recorded in the water within his cells, his bloodstream: energy which had simply departed for a ride on planet-wide filaments of bio-energy. Now the big question was, how would he get off the ride?

As he methodically recreated the feeling of joining- fitting in a piece at a time, like a jigsaw puzzle, or hooking up the two sides of a zipper- Benn felt himself being pulled stepwise, first across the room, then through the wall into the cold New Haven night. But now he actually felt a distinct chill, and the feathery touch of fog on his face. He had regained some of his normal senses; the closer he got to his inert body, the more clearly he could feel its physical surroundings. Piece by piece, he continued to stitch himself together. Further to the east, his body was lying on some sort of carpet. There was a pain at his waist, perhaps from a strap holding him down. He felt a strain in his neck... was he leaning backward? Then thick fog again brushed his cheek, carrying with it a tang of sea salt. No, it wasn't salt that he smelled: it was the heavy sweet aroma of burning wax. Uncomfortable within the confines of an overheated, heavily paneled room, he was also floating slowly alongside unoccupied university buildings lining a damp, empty street. On that street, it was darker than midnight, and yet he saw himself in a large hall illuminated by hundreds of candles. As he finally arrived at the silent and forbidding High Street gate to Mellon College, Benn felt very much alone in the world- but at the same time realized that he was surrounded by a large, noisy and inquisitive crowd.

A series of sharp raps on the door: not wondering whether anyone was home, but rather demanding explanations *now*. It was past midnight. Lora, bleary-eyed from hours of dense reading (a highly complicated diagram of a proposed mechanism for the projection of bio-wave energy by plant life, including a novel role for the Higgs boson, now occupied the screen of her da-disc), stumbled to her door just as another series of raps began, even more insistent this time. Alarmed, Lora threw open the door.

"Sool! What are you...?"

"Lora, where is he? Where's Benn?"

Sool Tamura, standing in the doorway with the hallway light behind her, violet hair aglow and silver cheek studs glimmering in the shadow, was clearly agitated. Her fists were clenched, her broad face even more fiercely intense than usual. She seemed to be out of breath.

"Benn? I haven't seen him since Gene Ethics this afternoon." Lora thought of her vivid feeling- her momentary certainty- of Benn's presence in her room earlier that evening. "I think he was planning to sleep early tonight."

"He's not in his room, I checked." Sool was peering over Lora's shoulder, searching the room, her gaze settling on the da-

142

disc. "Can I come in," she said; like her knock on the door, this was not a question.

"It's quite late…" Lora began, but then stepped aside as Sool pushed forward.

"So you haven't seen him this evening?" Sool's tone was edged with doubt.

"Like I said…"

Sool stopped in front of the da-disc and studied the diagram on display.

"Sool, what is this about? You can't just…" Lora sputtered. Especially considering the distance Sool had created between herself and her fellow Martians, barging in like this was presumptuous.

"I need to talk to Benn. It's personal." She was still staring at the diagram.

Lora felt her cheeks flush, a faint prickling at the back of her neck. What does she mean, it's personal? What could be personal, between Benn and Sool?

"When you saw Benn today, did he mention anything about Theo Coffin?"

"Theo? No, he didn't say anything about…"

"*Look*, Lora," Sool snapped. She turned from the da-disc, eyes ablaze, voice lowered like the growl of a bloodhound about to attack. "You're hiding something. Benn's missing, and I think you know where he is. Now *tell me*."

"This is insane. I don't know where Benn is; why would you think that I know; what business is it of yours anyway, where Benn is; and how dare you come into my room and accuse me of… whatever it is?"

Sool leaned forward menacingly, then appeared to reconsider. Her breathing slowed. Lora watched, fascinated, as Sool's tense face began to adjust, one piece at a time. The eyebrows slowly descended; one corner of the mouth twitched, then the other; the flaring nostrils pinched, flared again, and finally relaxed. Lora was reminded of Benn's remark, that Sool was some kind of robot- what had he called her?- a Cyber-Intern, or Cyber-Sool, either way.

"I'm not accusing you of anything. Sorry. Lora. You and Benn. You two are working on something, and I… I wanted to get involved. To help, Lora. It's the bioweb, isn't it? I can see by this diagram…"

"No, we're not really working on anything, just curious. What's your interest in this theory about the bioweb?" Lora suddenly remembered: "Sool, have you been hearing a sort of humming, pulsing noise, or getting headaches, since we arrived on Earth?"

Sool stared at Lora, uncomprehending. "What humming noise?"

"When you said you wanted to help, I thought you had been experiencing the same discomfort that Benn and I have. Isn't that what you meant?"

"I don't know what you're talking about," said Sool, who had experienced nothing of the sort. But she thought, So it's true- they do have some sort of sensitivity to Earth's bio-wave field.

The urgency in her voice rose again. "Benn's missing. And Theo Coffin's not in his room either." How does she know, wondered Lora- has she been pounding on everyone's doors tonight? Sool scanned the room again, but this time, her gaze rested an extra moment or two on the light panel above the desk, where she knew the Eye was hidden. She would have to be more direct.

"Theo and another person were seen helping Benn down the hallway. Benn appeared to be ill."

"Benn's ill? Sool, why didn't you mention this earlier?"

Sool ignored the question. "They were carrying him along, as though he was asleep."

They? "Who was the other person?"

"A short fellow, looked like a wrestler." Sool watched Lora's face closely. "We don't know who he is."

We? "Sool, what's going on?"

"They somehow disappeared from the lobby."

"How do you know all this?"

"There's no way to get past the front entrance without being seen…" Sool was speaking more to herself now, as she mentally reviewed her thorough search of Theo Coffin's room- especially the odd display on his da-disc. Then, suddenly locking eyes with Lora, she demanded, "Did Theo ever say anything to you about steam tunnels?"

"Steam tunnels? What do you mean? What are steam…?" Lora began to shake her head, but Sool had pushed past her without a word and was already well out the door.

144

Chapter Fifteen

The capacious hall, reverberating with a monotony of low chanting voices, appeared upside-down: there was an inverted human skull attached to the under-surface of a broad marble mantelpiece; dozens of white candles stood above their flickering flames; bluish smoke drifted downward, past a flag with red stripes and a cluster of stars at the right lower corner, which Benn recognized as that of the former United States of America. But below the flag, or rather above it- as Benn realized his head was tilted backwards and he was viewing the room upside-down- the words E Pluribus Unum somehow appeared upright and perfectly legible.

"Good, you're coming to. I apologize, Benn. When I came to your room, I found you unconscious, and your Dermamist injector made it obvious why. We had to carry you here." It was the voice of Theo Coffin. "I didn't want to put you on the floor, so I hope the table isn't too uncomfortable."

Slowly bringing his head forward and fighting a mild vertigo, Benn took in the high arched ceiling, wooden chandeliers holding more lit candles, dark paneled walls to either side lined with 19th-century tapestries, wall sconces in the shape of skulls and crossbones. He was lying on a Persian rug which Theo had thoughtfully thrown on the table. Oddly, Theo was wearing a long black gown with a hood pulled over his head. Slowly circling the chamber, which was about half the size of the Great Hall, were at least two dozen people dressed in similar hooded gowns, just concluding some sort of ritual in Latin: perhaps reciting an oath of allegiance, or a call to worship, or even a magical incantation.

"...DIGNIUS BONOS MORES SERVEMUS, STUDIA UTILIA EXERCEAMUS, PATRIAM AMEMUS."

As the echoing voices faded out, several of them began to uncover their heads. Beyond the main crowd, two of the monkish figures stood forbiddingly in front of sealed double doors.

There were no restraints around his waist after all, just acid burning in the pit of his stomach. Benn stared briefly at his presumed captors, then craned his neck to look again at the flag, which was now behind him. The skull sat on top of the mantelpiece, the American flag was upright, the flickering candles trailed smoke upward- everything was properly oriented, except that the dark blue banner, with E Pluribus Unum emblazoned in white, was now upside-down.

"We've turned the old E Pluribus Unum on its head. Ironic, isn't it?" A heavy, forceful voice echoed in Benn's mind. *On its head. Ironic, isn't it.* Behind his usual expressionless face, Benn could feel his mind racing: whose voice was that? He flinched as a large cloaked figure lunged forward in an aggressive manner, throwing back his hood. It was the plethoric Master of Mellon College, May Acheson.

Nonplussed after an awkward silence, Acheson glanced over his shoulder at a second, less imposing, figure, who stepped up and removed his hood. It was Dr. Neelin- no surprise there, thought Benn. Lou Hunter's probably here too, and Zak. So that's why the warehouse was vacant tonight. Neelin beamed a welcoming smile at Benn, as though this were just another social event at Mellon College.

"Don't mistake his expression for lack of comprehension, May. I have no doubt that our Mr. Marr fully understands the symbolism. Am I right, Mr. Marr? The original goal of uniting the states into a single nation- 'one, out of many'- is now..."

"The reverse: to split Earth's one world government back into many individual nations. Many, out of one," Benn completed Neelin's statement. Not much of a feat, really, since he could hear the words in Neelin's mind.

"Bravo, Mr. Marr, as always. You see, May? He's a very quick study- a true natural! But," he added, now looking darkly at Benn, "he's actually much, much more than that."

Benn felt a tingle at the back of his neck. What did he mean, much more than that? The words throbbed in Benn's head: *much more than that.* Probably a residual effect of the therapeptides from this afternoon, he decided: after each of his out-of-body travels, he had continued to read thoughts or hear echoes for several hours afterwards.

"But we'll get to that soon enough. First, let me introduce you to our group: they already know who you are, but you'll be more comfortable once you know them. Come, ladies and gentlemen, we've said our grace, so let's not remain so formal with Mr. Marr- or rather, Benn."

One by one, the hoods came off: There was the smirking Lou Hunter, as expected. Theo Coffin, looking quite chagrined. Mostly men and women he did not recognize, and a few he had seen around the medical school. Benn recognized Alden Hayes, the president of YaleConn, from a recent YaleConn Daily News article. Clustered together near the back of the room, a dozen youthful faces, about Benn's age- probably undergraduates. The two men guarding the entrance were the last to unhood, and Benn gasped when he saw they were identical: both had Zak's face. There were two Zaks! And possibly a third? Zak was also the Lint Man- or was he?

"Our society has its origins in one of YaleConn's ancient organizations, the secret society Skull and Bones, which has been located in this very spot for over three hundred and fifty years. Over the past century, our building was incorporated, along with several adjacent art museums, into the large dipyramidal structure you know as Mellon College. And our society- which, I might add, is even more secret than Skull and Bones- has been renamed Star and Stripe."

"Star and Stripe. That must have been Alan Goodrow's idea," ventured Benn, thinking of the escape tunnel and the signals on the wall and ceiling that had guided the young Goodrow a century ago.

"Yes, it was!" exclaimed Neelin, astonished. "When Alan Goodrow was Master of Mellon College- the fourth Master in the Age of the PWE- he coined the name Star and Stripe! He never explained why he chose that name, but Star and Stripe did seem symbolically more appropriate for our cause. But how on Earth..." *How on Earth...*

May Acheson interrupted.

"How could he possibly know about Star and Stripe, Nes, unless...?" *He's a PWE spy.* It was unsaid, but Benn perceived the accusation as if Acheson, his face redder than ever, had shouted it out. An angry murmuring picked up among the undergraduates, who relished the idea of conspiracy and lacked the restraint of their elders. For Benn, the violent thoughts and images jabbing at him from the poorly-controlled minds of these immature college students- *hold him down, string him up, fight, fight, fight*- were far more disconcerting than the actual noise.

To Benn's great surprise, Lou Hunter was the first to rise to his defense- although protecting Benn from a potential lynch mob was clearly not his purpose. "Never mind, all of you. There's nothing threatening about Benn's knowledge. For example, what he just said about Alan Goodrow and Star and Stripe. He just knows, that's all. As Nes said, there's more to Benn Marr than meets the eye. He has a special way of...knowing things." *Knowing things*, came the echo.

Hunter, relishing center stage, cleared his throat importantly and continued: "For months now, we've received intelligence reports of a secret Eunigen project involving mind-expanding therapeptides, and Marr is probably one of Eunigen's unwitting subjects. Mind expansion! That would explain his ability to, to, to know all sorts of things." *No wonder he could identify all those wines that night, without even tasting. Never mind- it was completely unfair.*

That's incredible, thought Benn- Hunter's still resentful about the wine tasting.

"That's what this is all about," said Neelin, his voice rising above the commotion. "That's why we've brought you here, Benn." *Brought you here, Benn.*

Neelin turned to face the group, and raised his arms to signal for silence.

"Many of you already know what Lou is referring to. The Eunigen project has gone forward, with the support of the PWE. As best we can tell, their goal is to develop therapeptides which will give their users expanded vision, with a likely goal of spying on groups such as ours. The biggest obstacle has been that users of their experimental peptides quickly degenerate, and in most cases they die. Our information has been fragmented, but we gathered, some time ago, that Eunigen had discovered something special about families living on Mars for many generations: perhaps that these people have genetically evolved an ability to survive use of the peptides. Are you aware of any of this, Benn?" *Any of this, Benn?*

148

Half-truthfully, Benn shook his head. Neelin nodded sympathetically.

"The PWE is manipulating you, in order to get to us. They want to use you because, as a descendant of colonists, you are more likely to survive their peptide experiments. And, assuming you do survive, they will use your abilities to fight the resistance movement." The angry murmurs resumed, and Neelin raised his hand again.

"Please! Benn is not yet a tool of the PWE. We may be able turn the tables on them, and here's what I mean. When Benn first demonstrated some of his abilities, we suspected that there was indeed a genetic difference between us and the Martian colonists. That would be consistent with what we had learned from our sources in Eunigen. Well, it was a simple matter to obtain a DNA sample- my apologies, Benn, but it was necessary- for analysis at our lab in Virginia." *Lab in Virginia.*

Neelin pointed to Lou Hunter, who brought a da-disc to the front and eagerly opened it. A section of the side wall, previously blank, flickered to life; a complex diagram of DNA base pairs, colored red, crowded into view. Several segments, colored yellow, stood out from the rest.

"I have something amazing to show you all- no doubt this is new to you as well, Benn. The sample was scant and somewhat degraded, but we have detected, mixed in with the normal human genome, several dozen anomalous alleles. They are definitely alien- in fact, one of the nucleotides is foreign to us. I have never, in my long career, encountered anything like this!

"It's not a new concept, of course: we routinely deal with the microbiome, a host of other species living within our bodies, without which we could not survive. It's well-known that, of more than five hundred chemicals found in blood plasma, thirty percent are actually bacterial proteins. Also recognized is the phenomenon of micro-chimerism, which is probably more relevant than the microbiome, in Benn's case. The trace incorporation of DNA sequences from one individual into another, or micro-chimerism, occurs naturally over time. But certainly we've never before encountered your alien nucleotide! Could this be Martian DNA interspersed with your own genes? It's mind-boggling: micro-chimerism involving Martian DNA! Astounding for several reasons, not least of which is that there have been no reports of DNA on Mars- unless we're talking about the best-kept secret in the history of space exploration.

"Don't worry, Benn," Neelin continued. "You are undoubtedly human. But following generations of your family living and evolving on Mars, you have taken on, shall we say, some of the local flavor." *Local flavor.*

Through his shock, Benn could see that this news fit perfectly with his father's message. Owen Marr had mentioned a gene-based, heritable change in the brain activities of Martian colonists. And Father's working for Eunigen meant that Dr. Neelin was right- there was a connection to the giant pharmaceutical company.

"When we heard that Eunigen- through the Mars Wellness Institute- was bringing six students to Earth, we realized their project was moving ahead. We were blocked from learning more about you- even your names were unknown to us- and this cloak of secrecy further convinced us of your importance, not only to the PWE/Eunigen project, but potentially to our resistance movement."

"So you sent Zak, or rather..." As the truth fell together quickly, Benn's words seemed to pour forth on their own. "...you sent a *clone* of Zak, to ensure my safe arrival."

Neelin appeared even more astonished than before, if that were possible; Acheson and Hunter were equally dumbfounded. At the back of the room, the Zaks, two mirror images, looked blankly at one another, then shrugged.

Neelin composed himself. "Outstanding! Such quick insight. Yes, we did send an agent- a clone of Zak, as you said- to watch over you and Lora. We felt it was more likely that colonists from an older settlement would have the genetic characteristics desired by Eunigen." His unspoken thought: *amazing- so quick! He's truly a natural. But ironically, he's just as truly UNnatural.*

"But what about Sool, and the others from Highland City? Don't they have what you called that 'local flavor' of Mars?"

"It's not likely," replied Neelin, "for two reasons: one, our intelligence from Eunigen indicated no special interest in Sool, or in the three interns who went to MassMed. And second, their families were relatively recent arrivals on Mars, and would not have had the exposure over generations required to evolve to your degree. We guessed that they were a sort of camouflage, to obscure your central role in all this."

"I see. So Lora and I…"

Hunter interrupted. "Lora hasn't demonstrated your special qualities. You're the one, Benn." *He's the one- it's so unfair.* "Not only because you can potentially survive Eunigen's experiments, but because it seems that you may be genetically endowed with the ability to expand your own consciousness. That's how you 'know' things so easily!" *That's how he knew the Cote Rotie from the Richebourg.*

Hunter gathered steam: "Imagine your potential usefulness to Star and Stripe! Eunigen controls the therapeptides, but never mind! You may not need the therapeptides at all!" Among the echoes and the jabbing thoughts of the undergraduates, Benn heard: *Eunigen controls the therapeptides, but we control Benn Marr!* Hunter's face glowed disturbingly with the zeal of the power-hungry, but his speech drew only sneers from the twin Zaks at the back of the hall.

Neelin raised his hand again. "Thank you, Lou- well put." *But quite premature. Don't jump the gun, Lou- you'll spook him.*

He cleared his throat and addressed the entire group. "Before going any further, I propose we now move into the dining room. I always find that difficult talks proceed better over a meal and a glass of good wine, don't you?" *A glass of wine. I could use a drink right about now.*

The members of Star and Stripe- overheated, famished, having already said their grace, and in no mood for more lectures on genomics- voiced its hearty approval and immediately began to shuffle toward the double doors. The Zaks passed their large hands over I.D. scanners positioned on either side of the doors, which slid open to admit a welcome wave of cool, humid night air.

It was long after midnight, around the time Sool first banged on Lora's door. Most of the society's members, in various stages of inebriation, had already retired to their rooms several floors above, in the residential portion of Mellon College. Dr. Neelin gazed thoughtfully at the dark wine in his glass as he swirled it to release the bouquet.

"We are truly privileged, you know, to have this Tuscan red with our dinner. So little wine is made nowadays, and most of it synthesized in factories, from vats of chemicals. To share the product of real grapes- in this case, Sangiovese grapes- with thirty people, over a meal of vegetables grown in our own garden, and not a Vitacube in sight, is virtually unheard of, in this day and age!

"That's what the wonderful Pan-World Electorate has brought us, Benn: a great equalization. Uniformity of resources, laws, influence, power- of course some of that is desirable. Elimination of hunger and poverty. Aiding of justice. No more exploitation of the disenfranchised by an elite minority." Neelin raised his glass high. "The end of war, for heaven's sake! After the Great War of Unification, all war ended! Of course we want that, who wouldn't? Am I right, May?"

May Acheson merely grunted, his chin resting on his chest.

Alden Hayes, a prim and disciplined administrator, had sipped sparingly from his glass throughout the meal. He answered for Acheson: "Obviously, those are desirable goals, Nes. A rhetorical question, meant for Benn's consumption. The flip side is that individual freedom has been sacrificed; the PWE watches our every move, provides (and limits) our resources, dictates university policy, sends enforcers if we stray off the path." Hayes warmed to the subject, shifting forward in his chair. "And that's just the small picture, Benn. After all, what's the difference between the PWE and other empires of the past? Star and Stripe is part of a much larger movement here and abroad, and what this movement most strenuously opposes is- well, putting it simply- the erasure of history. The loss of culture. Ancient traditions, developed over millennia. Values embedded in groups of like-minded people; tribal values if you will. *National* values, Benn! We want to preserve our national values, to restore the United States of America. An independent nation in a multinational world. Needless to say, the Electorate takes a very dim view of that agenda."

Neelin jumped back in. "And what do they have to show for one hundred years of rule? Regional conflicts still erupt: neo-Balkanization, saber-rattling in the Korean District, crimes committed under the guise of holy wars." With a wink, he added,

"Prophet-mongering, eh, Alden?" A few chuckles followed, among those still awake.

Lou Hunter, well into his sixth glass of Sangiovese, spoke up: "It's the centennial of our resistance movement, Benn! Born at the very moment that the charter of the PWE was signed in Beijing, one hundred years ago. Great leaders have come and gone. Alan Goodrow was well before my time, of course. Never mind. The Masters of Mellon College have always played a big role; May Acheson- are you awake?- May was extremely active, even as an undergraduate. I heard that at graduation he was voted by his classmates 'Most Likely to Secede!'"

Ba-da-Boom, thought Benn.

"Ha! I'd forgotten that," exclaimed Neelin. "And I was a voter!"

Hayes smiled benignly, but Benn caught a glimmer of impatience in his eyes. He was thinking, *Stay on point, gentlemen; we haven't got all night.*

"As I was saying, the PWE takes a dim view of our movement. They have devoted vast resources to rooting us out; we're fortunate to be able to maintain an active cell here in New Haven, so close to their American Zone headquarters."

"If this is only one cell, where is the rest of the movement?"

Hayes paused and looked hard at Benn. "We're scattered around the world..." Another pause. *Should I tell him?* Yes, let's see which way he leans. "But the center of operations lies in the Quarantine Zone, out on the West Coast. Propaganda campaigns, public demonstrations, bombings at factories and government offices, even local armed rebellions worldwide: they're all planned and coordinated in an underground location out west." Faintly, Hayes formed a name in his thoughts: was it *Maggie Sullivan*? Benn also caught part of another name: (Somebody) *Protem*?

"It's quite ironic, actually." Hayes smiled at the thought: "In the early days of the PsySoc regulators, PWE used Parvan, and then Orthonil, on anyone they suspected of belonging to the nationalist movement. But these regulators didn't always work. There were so many failures, in fact, that the government was forced to create a large sealed-off area to relocate these people- essentially to imprison them.

"Later on, when Ordrax was released, they were able to suppress rebellion more effectively, but rebellious thoughts were replaced by psychotic thoughts- and often by no thoughts at all. Those people had to be removed as well, and so they were shipped out west, away from the public eye. You see the irony, Benn: first, the PWE concentrated the manpower and a cadre of leaders for an anti-PWE movement, by banishing them all to the same area. Then they sent out all those Ordrax victims, who served as a constant reminder of the Electorate's abuse of power- and that spurred the movement on!

"The Quarantine Zone consists of regions once known as Northern California, Oregon, and Nevada; it's sparsely populated, with few cities remaining, such as Berkeley, Portland and Las Vegas. No doubt the Electorate is sorely tempted to simply wipe out the entire Zone with a nuclear bombardment, but even they realize the negative impact such an action would have on their support worldwide."

"The Quarantine Zone is completely cut off?"

"Not quite. There is traffic back and forth, but only for those on government business, the military, and the few locals allowed to exit are monitored very closely." *Why does he ask?*

"How do you communicate with leaders in the Quarantine Zone?"

Hayes made no reply; a troubled look crossed his face.

"You've said too much," growled Acheson, eyes shut and chin still resting on his chest. There was a hard, black line in his thoughts, and beyond the line lay the words *Betray, Coerce, Eliminate.* "What if Benn doesn't..."

"May! You're awake!" Neelin cut in. "What a relief. I thought I'd have to carry you up to your apartment."

Acheson opened his eyes narrowly and pushed himself upright. "No, I've been listening, Nes, and I think we've had enough discussion for tonight." He shot a stern look at Hayes, who winced slightly.

"Yes, I agree," said Neelin, draining the last drops from his glass and staggering to his feet. "Given the late hour, Benn, we've prepared a room for you upstairs; I don't think you should return to Harkness tonight. Zak will show you the way."

* * *

A mere four hours later, as Benn descended a flight of worn marble stairs through a narrow arched entryway to the Mellon College greensward, the disconcerting thought crossed his mind: would they let him leave? The large courtyard appeared gloomy and deserted; despite his greatcoat, Benn shivered slightly in the chill autumn dawn. He was in the South Wing, the pyramid abutting High Street, and the blue-gray early morning light, filtered through its glass apex, allowed only a vague impression of the courtyard, the windows overlooking it, and a wider archway leading out to the street. And there, barely discernible in the shadows, was the silhouette of Zak (Clone One or Two?) sitting motionless by the main gate.

Was Zak there to prevent Benn from leaving? Surely they wouldn't gamble on his co-operation, having revealed so much about their society and its operations. May Acheson certainly doubted Benn's reliability, and Alden Hayes didn't quite trust him either. But, in that case, why not simply lock his door? No, Zak must have another purpose.

The sound of Benn's approaching footsteps triggered a startled reaction from Zak, who had fallen asleep. Seeing Benn, he jumped to his feet in an agile feline motion, instantly alert. Just like his duplicate, Lint Man, Zak was apparently cloned for his physical qualities: resilience, strength, quick reactions, and coordination. Maybe not so much for his mental attributes, conceded Benn; how unfortunate for Zak, to be created according to someone else's ideal image.

"Mr. Marr? Are you going back to the Med School now?"

"Yes- Zak, is it?" He added optimistically, "I'm heading back to Harkness Dorm."

"No, I'm Abe, not Zak." He drew himself up to his full height of almost five and a half feet, and all his muscles suddenly tensed, giving Benn the impression that he was, after all, here to prevent Benn's departure. But then Abe visibly relaxed.

"People sometimes call me Zak. But I'm Abe, really." His forehead crinkled in a deep frown.

155

"Sorry, Abe, but you look just like him, and I hadn't met you before. I'm sorry. Are you here to... accompany me back to Harkness?"

"Dr. Neelin wants me to make sure you get back all right." Abe cheered up at the thought of an important assignment from Neelin.

As they walked down High Street together in silence, Benn admired Abe's smooth and coordinated gait, his extreme vigilance and uncanny awareness of his surroundings. The slightest movement, such as the flutter of pigeon wings on a window ledge, drew his keen eye. Recalling the way Lint Man had leapt through the air, Benn knew that Abe's physical strength posed a real threat. But finally his curiosity overcame caution.

"Abe. You must be...related to Zak, right?"

"Zak's my brother."

"I thought so. And do you have other brothers?"

"Lots." Abe knew that there were twenty-two in all. Twenty-one now. "But they don't all live here."

"Where do they live?"

"Mostly out west. I'm not sure." Benn looked thoughtfully at Abe for a moment.

"Did you come from the Quarantine Zone?" It was just a guess on Benn's part. Abe was more difficult to read than his brother Zak, his thoughts and intentions appearing much more opaque. He also didn't respond to the question.

"You're not supposed to discuss that, are you?"

"I was born here. We were all born in New Haven." Abe scanned the rooftops as they neared the southwest corner of Mellon College and turned onto York Street, toward the medical school. Something had caught his attention. Benn looked around and noticed nothing unusual: to their right, a pair of pigeons landed on the roof of the YaleConn Daily News Building; farther down York Street, a robotic sweeper made its swooshing way along the curb; an unoccupied, off-duty taxi was parked opposite the New Pierce Foundation, a research and development facility belonging to Synthedible Corp. The cool morning breeze carried with it the pleasant yeasty aroma of Vitacubes.

A moment later, Abe's attention was drawn back to the corner of the Pierce building, where two large panes of smoke-gray glass met at an acute angle. To the normal human eye, only the reflections of the street scene and glare of the rising sun would have been visible; to Abe's eye, a silhouette crouched behind the glass. Someone is there watching us, Abe thought. Following us since the corner of High Street, and now hiding behind that building: definitely hostile, but keeping enough distance that I don't have to do anything- not yet. Any closer to Benn Marr, and I will have to eliminate... her! Abe relaxed and continued toward Harkness without any perceptible break in the rhythm of his cat-like stride.

Chapter Sixteen

Director Walther Beame was not at all happy with the reports coming from New Haven. In fact, he was furious, as his unfortunate assistant was now quickly discovering.

"He went missing for almost twelve hours!"

"Yes sir. I'm afraid he did."

"That's unbelievable! What about all the measures we've taken? How can someone simply disappear for twelve hours under that sort of scrutiny?" Beame was doubly- no, triply- livid. Why triply? First of all, Benn Marr had gone missing (even though he was now back on screen, heads would roll); second, Beame had been awakened from a perfectly sound sleep in his East Hampton home and dragged back to the city; and third, it was inevitable that the annoying, over-anxious Rion Salkend would seize on this opportunity to prove that he had been right all along.

Beame, still dressed in a silk night robe, had flown straight to Eunigen Center, and now sat in the same darkened room where he had last argued with Salkend. His assistant stood wilting before him, nervously clutching his da-disc to his chest.

"What about Halsey? Wasn't he watching Marr?"

"He claims that Marr simply disappeared from the Eyes."

"There is no way to disappear from the Eyes! Halsey dropped the ball. We'll skin him for this. And aren't you the one who recommended him for the position?"

"No sir, it was Simmons who…"

"SIMMONS. LIED. TO HELP HALSEY."

The assistant reflexively looked upwards. Of course he heard the OMC's voice before- usually interrupting whatever discussion was ongoing- but was still unaccustomed to the bluntness with which he spoke. And how did the OMC know that Simmons had lied to get Halsey his job as Chief of Security at YaleConn?

"SIMMONS. LIED."

All right, so you know, thought the assistant. But beyond that, there was a rumor that Simmons had tipped him off to a shipment of psychopeptides intended for the Boston lab- a shipment that had mysteriously vanished en route. Halsey was widely known to use recreational psychopeptides, so he was the prime suspect. Also, because of his drug use, Halsey was prone to forgetfulness, imagined memories, or worse. Someone with poor mental health, who had probably stolen Eunigen property, would hardly be the best candidate for the position...

"HARDLY."

"Hardly what?" said Beame, even angrier now that the OMC had butted in. "Yes, it's obvious now that Halsey's the wrong man for the job, but as you know, he's only one of the many security measures we had in place. How could we have lost track of him?"

"STEAM."

"What? Did you say steam?" Here we go again, thought Beame.

"TUNNEL. STAR. STRIPE." More incomprehensible gibberish. The OMC had really become so difficult to understand, he was almost useless. There had been a time when the OMC's insights were invaluable, but his decay was accelerating. A major change in direction was needed... Beame was distracted by a red light blinking on the panel in front of him, and poked the screen rather forcefully. "What is it?" he demanded, rubbing his painfully sprained index finger.

"It's Security in the lobby, sir. Sorry to interrupt you, but Mr. Rion Salkend is here. We're holding him pending further instruction, because he seems, well, a little upset, sir. What should we do with him?"

Damn. Beame forced himself to calm down, to gather his thoughts. That sure didn't take long for Salkend to show up. It figures that he'd hear about it right away; he has his own spies in the company. And he'll crow about this- I told you something would go wrong! Paranoid imaginings you said! You'll be the one responsible! That's his style. He has no idea how difficult and complex this project really is. With a sigh of resignation so vocal that even Salkend could hear it on the other end, Beame said, "All right, bring him in." Then, after a long, reflective pause, Beame muttered, more to himself than anyone else, "Yes, it looks like we'll have to bring him in after all."

* * *

From across the large oak table in Gene PerMutations class, Lora watched Benn closely, searching for any signs to support Sool's wild story: if he had really been carried unconscious from his room and smuggled out of Harkness two nights ago, wouldn't he at least look more disheveled than he normally did, or act differently somehow? Clearly he didn't want to discuss it, and Lora had stayed clear for the past two days. True, he had appeared a bit distracted yesterday afternoon in Recombinant Anatomy, sitting down there in the front row, lost in thought- and was he avoiding eye contact with Dr. Neelin? But today he had already produced one of those instant, cut-to-the-core analyses that left everyone in class, including Dr. Vincent, impressed, if not intimidated.

"I quite agree, Mr. Marr," said Dr. Vincent with a broad smile. "Multi-species DNA might truly be considered a microcosm of our worldwide ecosystem. A fascinating insight. Does anyone have anything to add? Mr. Messler, perhaps?"

"Oh, uh. No. When you put DNA from many species together in one template, uh, they probably interact like the original sources. So when the two species are compatible..."

Benn stopped listening: as usual, nothing original from Mr. Messler. He glanced over at Theo Coffin, who kept studiously focused on his da-disc. Theo had said nothing to Benn in their classes together. There's no need to be embarrassed, Theo. You're only following your sense of justice. You have a wide view of history, especially of the former United States of America: certainly a much more complex and nuanced view than I have, thought Benn. But my brief encounter with that one slice of history- the children escaping from the PWE- was so traumatic that I can easily see what drove you to join the ranks of Star and Stripe.

Cira Vincent interrupted Messler's monologue, which in any case had drifted tangentially; he was now muttering about the genetic compatibility between both ends of a horse. "The point we should take away is that multi-species DNA is more likely to yield a stable and productive peptide if the originating species related in an organic way- a way that made sense in nature. Do you see that, Mr. Messler?" asked Vincent, suppressing her thoughts about the back end of a horse.

160

Cira was not a member of Star and Stripe, Benn realized; she knew nothing of the secret society based near her office and run by some of her closest associates. No, her passions had nothing to do with injustice, nationalism or world government. He narrowed his focus from the content of Cira's lecture to the quality of her voice, which at one moment burned with her desire to score a key teaching point, and at the next moment sang as perkily as a well-rehearsed sales pitch. Benn pictured Cira laboring at a lab bench, advancing her science- but at the same time honing her marketing strategy. He examined her well-composed face and hair, the stylish outfit she wore with natural ease, and saw, in one person, the whole spectrum of the pharmaceutical industry: a successful researcher/developer, a prolific manufacturer of product, and a highly convincing sales rep.

A different aspect of Cira Vincent, to her credit, was her strong concern for Lora- almost a personal feeling of responsibility. They had connected early in the year, when sheltering occasionally under Cira's wing had helped Lora tremendously in adjusting to her new world. To be honest, Benn found Cira's protective attitude intrusive and annoying, but then had to remind himself of Lora's admonition to let down his self-imposed barrier. Why did he reflexively take others' good intentions in such a negative way? Also burning in the back of his mind: hadn't Rion Salkend, back on the ship, helped Lora with her studies- with good intentions? And Benn had made a joke out of Salkend's, ah, concerns! There was no way to erase the humiliating silence which had ensued, but he would go to great lengths now, to avoid any recurrence.

With these countervailing thoughts already in mind, Benn gave himself a mental kick to banish that automatic annoyance when Cira Vincent approached him after class and asked, "Is everything all right with you, Benn? You seemed distracted today, although your comment on multi-species DNA was really very astute. Is something going on with you and Lora? I noticed you weren't sitting together as usual."

Since class was over, he felt free to speak informally. "Everything's fine, Cira. Nothing's wrong: Lora and I are in so many different classes now, we often arrive separately." Why was he explaining this to her?

"That's a shame, when the demands of school split up a pair; I always picture the two of you belonging, you know, together."

Intrusive and annoying. Benn felt the blood rise to his cheeks, but before he could respond, Cira continued, "I've got an idea. As it happens, I have four tickets to a baseball game in New York this weekend. It's the playoffs: first round, Yanquis against the Fidels- should be a great game, Benn!"

"At Yanqui Stadium?" Benn was incredulous. Cira Vincent was a baseball fan?

"Yes, Benn, Yanqui Stadium, in the Bronx. Do you know baseball at all?" she asked, regarding the Martian with a curious look.

"Well, yes. We do play it on Mars, and I follow the league standings..."

"Great! I'll invite Lora. Oh, and also the other intern from Mars. She's not in any of my classes."

"You mean Sool Tamura? Somehow I can't picture Sool at a baseball game, cheering and getting Q. Unless they have cybernetic players who can rip each other to pieces, I doubt she'd even be interested, let alone Q."

Queue? Why wouldn't Sool queue up, like everyone else: there would be no getting around the line at the gate. She shrugged it off. "Oh, I wouldn't judge her so quickly, Benn. She might enjoy baseball. After all, you never know what someone like Sool is capable of." So true. With that, Cira turned and hurried after Lora, waving at Benn with the back of her hand.

Three days later, at the game, Benn vividly recalled Cira's parting remark. He and Lora watched with revulsion as Sool consumed her sixth so-called "hot dog" (a misnomer, as the recombinant DNA used to generate the pink polymeric substance contained only one or two canine sequences). Cira had bought each of them a program at the stadium entrance, and Sool was using hers to protect her lap from drips of genetically-engineered mustard. Benn turned away to take in the scene. They had excellent seats in the second balcony, with sweeping views of fabled Yanqui Stadium, home of "beisbol" legends, such as Babe Ruth, whose counterfeit autograph graced Benn's digital clock! Benn imagined himself on the field, ranging between second and third base, and wondered who was playing shortstop with his friend Jace these days.

Benn thought back to the Yanquis of legend: Ruth, Gehrig, DiMaggio, Rodriguez, Clemente, and so many others; but those were the ancient days. After the Great War of Unification, the stadium and team had passed from the ownership of despised capitalist exploiters into the hands of El Mercado, a Mexican District conglomerate. And the new owners had promptly renamed the team, much to the delight of New York Metropol's dominant ethnic group, and to the resentment of everyone else. The "House that Ruth Built" became "Casa al Mercado". More universally well-received in New York was the Yanquis' continued domination of the World Series, a contest more aptly named in recent times: a round-robin tournament in which teams from all over the world competed for the championship. The team closest to the Yanquis, in terms of their daunting winning record year after year, their image of invincibility, was the Caribbean District Fidels. Although this was only a first-round playoff game in which the two rival teams, like wolves circling warily before a fight, would each test the other's skills, the tension in the air was as heady and dense as the aromatic smoke billowing upwards from dozens of hot dog stands into the hazy blue October sky.

The number of visits that Sool had paid to the nearest of these stands was all the more remarkable because the game had only reached the bottom of the fourth inning. The Yanquis had men on first and third, with two outs, and their cleanup hitter, Max Quintero, was at bat. Benn asked, "Hey Program. What's the count?"

"One ball, two strikes," replied the program in a hearty male voice. The pitcher, who had "great stuff," according to the program, nodded to his catcher, then took a quick look at first base. From the stretch, he threw a breaking ball which Benn's program later said "hung just a mite too long over the plate." CRACK! The sound of the ball embarking on its towering journey out of Yanqui Stadium sent Benn instinctively to his feet, as though he might sprint to the outfield and attempt a leaping catch at the wall. A program somewhere in the next row down excitedly announced, "He hits it *hard*... he hits it *deep*... it is *outta here*! Adios Pelota!"

Cira, who was sitting to Benn's left at the end of the row, joined the crowd in standing and applauding the Quintero three-run homer, but then looked over at Benn and Lora. She had on the requisite Yanquis baseball cap (and even that plebeian item of clothing looked stylish on her), but to Benn, Cira seemed distracted, not totally engaged in the boisterous scene around her. Now, as he returned Cira's look, she quickly flashed a smile at him and shouted, with a thumbs-up gesture, "Go Yanquis! Six to four!"

The Yanquis had indeed taken the lead, Benn's program was quick to confirm. Lora, seated between Cira and Benn, hadn't moved at all, except for a brief glance at the field when the roar of the crowd made it impossible to continue listening to her program. She had turned off its play-by-play analysis of the game, selecting instead a lengthy article on the history of performance-enhancing substances in the game of baseball. When the commotion following the Quintero homerun interrupted her program, she had just gotten to the heated debate over the illicit use of multi-species therapeptides which gave players amazing visual acuity, spatial judgment, strength, speed and agility- albeit only a transient boost. Ultimately the peptides had been banned, but many players (including the great Max Quintero) were still rumored to be users. Lora frowned, pulled her baseball cap- also kindly provided by Cira- lower over her forehead, and returned to her reading.

"Say, Lora. You can stop studying now. Take a break and watch the game," Benn pulled her cap back up with a grin.

"That's all right. This is really interesting, multi-species therapeptides boosting athletic performance." She read in silence for several seconds, then smiled and pointed at the program screen. "Say, you should enjoy this, Benn- there's a quote from Lupe Rincon- you know, the retired first baseman who became a comedian? He admits to using illegal peptides and signing up for a detox program: 'No twelve-step program for me: I joined a *thirty-six* step program to quit drugs!' Then he says, 'One step forward, two steps back!'"

"Ha! Hahah! Ba-da-Boom!"

Badaboom? A crash of drums, Lora supposed: a theatrical sound from twentieth-century vaudeville. Poor Benn. He really loves these corny, old-fashioned jokes, thought Lora, a feeling of warmth touching her cheeks.

See, she really does have a sense of humor after all, thought Benn with equal affection.

When the game finally ended (the Fidels won, twelve to seven, amidst much booing by the home fans), Cira shepherded her interns out of the stadium, to a black limousine waiting a block away. The robotic driver raised the car to an open lane and steered through crowded rush-hour, post-game traffic to the Lower East Side of Manhattan, an area slowly recovering from decades of repeated flooding due to global climate change. Here the darkening streets were nearly deserted; the few remaining shops were closed two days before the weekend. As the limousine descended to the curb, a lone police rover flitted silently overhead, and an Eye blinked indifferently from the top of a nearby lamppost. They climbed out in front of an anonymous-looking restaurant whose entrance was marked simply with the letter H.

Cira paused at the entrance and announced a bit coyly, "Tonight I have two surprises for you. Menu?" Posted behind a glass plate by the door, a menu with a fleur-de-lys design began to emit spirited Pre-War Continental tunes- old-fashioned music familiar to Cira and Benn- played on a simulated accordion. Da-da-da-DA…. Da-da-da-da-DA: the menu's voice sang along. Benn recognized Cole Porter's Begin the Beguine, and the menu sounded a bit like Jacques Brel! Oh, this was going to be good.

"The first surprise," Cira beamed, "is the extraordinary meal we are about to enjoy. This restaurant, which I discovered years ago through a rave review in Inner Circle Magazine, specializes in Eurozone cooking. It's my personal favorite, especially the cuisine of the French District. They use only fresh, organic ingredients, without any bio-engineered products…"

The music suddenly stopped. "Well, actually, we do have some recombinant ingredients," the menu corrected her in a tone more critical than apologetic. It spoke with an exotic but nonspecific Eurozone accent. "A policy change forced upon us, too bad. The cost of organics has simply, how to say, gone through the stratosphere."

Cira reddened slightly, then regained her positive attitude. "The chef is originally from Paris Metropol, where he earned ninety-one Michelin stars (out of one hundred) and a reputation for innovative combinations and techniques."

"Yes," agreed the menu, "Chef Hubert is really at the cutting edge, if you'll pardon the…"

"Menu! Read only!" Cira nearly barked.

"Certainly." The menu shut down with a loud, disapproving *click*, and the bouncy accordion music resumed.

Undaunted, Cira ushered her interns into the darkness of the restaurant and seated them at a polished zinc table illuminated by a softly glowing four-sided pyramid at the center. The same fleur-de-lys menu now appeared on each face of the pyramid.

"Welcome to H," said the menu, pronouncing the letter "ahhhsh" in a langorous, caressing way. "Tonight's special is the 'Tout Not Sashimi', a crudo mousse translated from the recombined genes of three extinct species: Pacific tuna, Monterey cypress, and arctic walrus. We are also featuring the rare Atlantic codling, where Chef Hubert cooks a recently living fish. Farmed off the low-mercury coastline of the Greenland District, our codling is spin-poached in a bold, yet contemplative, bath of piscine neurotransmitters and herbal amino acids, garnished with just a soupcon of white Eurovin foam."

"Eurovin foam?" Cira was aghast. "But Eurovin's not even made from grapes! It's a fermentation product of recombinant seaweed."

"So? Seaweed goes with fish." The menu had dropped its accent, and now sounded like someone from New Jersey. "You want wine made from grapes? Try the Quarantine Zone!"

"Menu, read only."

"Certainly." *Click.*

Without the aid of their irate menu, the interns had no clue as to the arcane items listed, so Cira, who had frequented the restaurant years ago, took the liberty of ordering for the table. H was a great stabilizer for her when times got tough, during her post-doctoral fellowship years in New York Metropol, Cira explained; without H as a high point, she had found the confounding city both manic and depressive. Benn wondered whether a mood-stabilizing psychopeptide could be added to the water supply, but wisely said nothing.

Despite her sentimental fondness for H, Cira couldn't disguise her disappointment later, as the four of them struggled through their entrees: on each plate sat a purplish, homogeneous block of chewy "braised bovine blend" which was surprisingly tasty-but the strong sweet-and-sour flavor quickly grew tiresome. The surrounding soft, green gelatinous dice offered essential amino acids, but no additional flavor.

"This isn't much more than a giant Vitacube with jelly," commented Cira drily, not realizing just how close she was to the mark. "I'm afraid H has really gone downhill since my day. I apologize for the poor quality of this meal."

Lora was the first to reassure her. "Apologize? But this is really delicious, Cira. For example, the combination of sweet and sour tastes: how original!"

"Yes," added Benn. "Like you said, it's innovative. And I find the, uh, the, uh, the, uh, texture of the bovine blend to be a brilliant contrast with the soft green jelly. The two flavors also contrast..."

Sool snorted loudly and continued chewing without any sign of pleasure. Her appetite's probably been ruined by all those hot dogs, thought Benn.

"That's all right," said Cira. "Thanks for trying to enjoy the meal anyway; it's edible but really, the ingredients available these days are atrocious. As they say so proudly in the ads, they use only the finest edible food-like substances!"

"That's what the wonderful Pan-World Electorate has brought us," Benn quoted Dr. Neelin's remarks at the Star and Stripe dinner. Cira looked quickly at Benn.

"So you think the PWE is responsible for the restaurant's decline, Benn?" She looked quickly around the room, which was devoid of waiters or other customers.

"Well, yes, indirectly. The great equalization," Benn recalled Neelin's words. "Elimination of hunger and poverty. All that's good, of course, but the re-distribution of resources to the former 'third world' takes certain items off the menus of New York restaurants. Instead of the great organic food you expected, we find these synthetic 'edible food-like substances' on our plates. Coming from Mars, I don't find this meal objectionable at all, honestly- to me it's delicious- but clearly you see a huge drop in quality."

"You're right, I suppose," replied Cira. "But I've lived my whole life under the PWE, and I don't blame its policies for the decline in quality of food... or in fashion... or general lifestyle. I blame the failure of technology. For example, we're not being aggressive enough in applying Multispecies Proteomics to create new resources, better products. The potential is limitless, if we would just push the boundaries..."

Lora, who had been picking quietly at her entrée, suddenly spoke up. "Like the Boston Gene Project? Weren't they pushing the boundaries, and weren't the results disastrous? Non-human tissue growing unpredictably..."

"No, Lora- I'm not advocating that sort of reckless experimentation," Cira countered quickly. "The genetic engineering code must be observed. I'm suggesting a more aggressive search for PerMutations in order to generate new therapeptides, better food products and materials for clothing, even construction materials that can..."

"But why?" Sool interrupted. They all turned to her, surprised that she had been paying attention, after all.

"Why improve proteomics?" Cira frowned.

"Why observe the genetic engineering code. So there were some bad results in the Boston Gene Project; haven't all great advances come at some expense?" Sool leaned back in her chair and waited, her lips pursed. Cira's frown deepened.

Lora finally broke the silence. "Is that what you would call it, Sool? 'Some expense' doesn't capture the horrible suffering those poor experimental subjects must have gone through. I can't believe you, or anyone, would find that an acceptable price to pay- even for scientific progress!"

Sool said coldly, "Your problem, Lora, is that you're not willing to take risks."

Lora began to rise, but Cira placed a restraining hand on her shoulder. "Well, this has certainly developed into a thorny discussion. To be honest, I can see both sides of this argument. How far to push the boundaries: that's the eternal question." She turned to Benn. "It's a perfect segue, because it brings up the second surprise that I promised you earlier. We have the opportunity tonight to consult one of the most prominent researchers in Multispecies Proteomics, to ask him how far he would push the boundaries. This person has contributed to the development of therapeptides used in treating many diseases- he's considered a giant in the pharmaceutical industry."

Benn felt his pulse quicken.

"He was recently promoted to the position of Project Director at Eunigen," Cira continued. Recently? Now puzzled, Benn thought, Father has been Project Director for years.

"Dr. Walther Beame has graciously agreed to give us a tour of the Eunigen labs this evening, taking time out of his very busy schedule." Walther Beame? What's happened to Father?

Lora could barely contain her thrill at the thought of a private tour of Eunigen's inner sanctum- such a rare privilege! Sool merely nodded slowly, her eyes locked on Lora.

"And Benn," Cira said, nodding with excitement, "Dr. Beame has promised that sometime tonight you will have an opportunity to visit your (famous!) father."

Chapter Seventeen

Dr. Walther Beame, recently-appointed Project Director at Eunigen. Scion of a distinguished medical family, graduate of a prestigious internship and post-doctoral fellowship at MassMed. Developer of numerous theraproteomic patents, holder of top industry awards. He was even listed, in a recent issue of Inner Circle Magazine, among New York Metropol's most-eligible bachelors. Ha! White-haired and balding on top, in his late fifties, still most eligible!

Yet never had he possessed the same *gravitas* as on this particular evening. It was the culmination of years of work, and the potential for a major scientific advance could be compared to... well, there was simply no precedent! Not the first multi-species gene created; not the first stem cell injected into a lab animal; not even the discovery, over two centuries ago, that DNA could be snipped apart and recombined. But it wasn't over yet- Beame glanced back at the two security men following him at a discreet distance, slowed his pace and forced himself to take a deep breath as he rounded the corner to enter the main lobby, where his guests were waiting.

Beame stopped abruptly and stared. What he saw under the five-story-high ceiling looked distinctly like a religious tableau: two women sat to the right side, heads bowed slightly in quiet conversation. By the entrance on the left, a third woman had the vigilant stance of a sentry. And alone in the center of the dome-shaped lobby stood Benn Marr, looking so innocent and vulnerable (appearances certainly can be deceiving, thought Beame). Looming high in the air directly above Benn was a huge glowing holographic projection of Eunigen's symbol, the caduceus entwined with a double-helix of nucleic acid sequences in lieu of snakes. The caduceus rotated slowly on its axis, creating the effect of a giant drill pointing downward right at Benn Marr. It was one of those unplanned moments rich with symbolic meaning: He is the One. The message would hardly have been clearer if a golden halo borne

170

by cherubs had suddenly been placed on top of Benn's head. Flushing with pride, Walther Beame felt a justification- some might have said exoneration- of his entire life's work, implicit in the surreal vision.

"Dr. Beame!" called Cira Vincent excitedly, ruining the illusion.

"Ah, Dr. Vincent- welcome back to Eunigen." Beame stepped forward. "And this is, undoubtedly, Benn Marr? Welcome, young man! I must say, you certainly look a lot like your father." The slightest smile crinkled the corners of his mouth.

Beame nodded at Lora and Sool in a rather perfunctory way (much to Lora's disappointment) and gestured with a sweeping motion of his arm that the group was to follow him into the main hallway, which, even at this late hour, was fairly crowded with people in white lab coats or other uniforms, hurrying crisply about, their purposeful footsteps echoing off the marble walls and ceiling.

"As you see, the business of Eunigen never slows down! I'm afraid that we have a number of ongoing projects which put me on a tight schedule tonight," Beame explained to Cira, "so I thought it might be more efficient for your interns to split up, each to focus on one particular area of interest. For example, I'm sure that Benn would be most interested in seeing his father and learning about his work."

"Yes. I would," agreed Benn. It seemed an obvious choice, but there was something about Beame's voice, the intensity of it, and the unblinking stare of his eyes, which caused the back of Benn's neck to tingle.

"And we can show the two of you..." Beame turned toward the others.

"I'm Lora Wheeler." Lora raised her right hand.

"...our latest project on a new generation of PsySoc regulators." Beame turned away, ignoring Lora's proffered palm. He signaled for one of the security men to accompany Lora and Sool. Lora, hand still outstretched and hiding her chagrin, waved instead at Benn and Cira, and then hurried to catch up with Sool, who was following the security man down a perpendicular hallway.

"Wait. Lora..." said Benn, but she had already turned the corner.

"We'll catch up with you later," Cira called after her. She looked at Beame inquiringly, nonplussed.

"Dr. Vincent, you hardly need a tour of Eunigen, so I suggest you wait for me in the executive lounge, just here to the right; I'm going to deliver Benn to his father, and then I'll be back shortly. All right?" He smiled broadly, but again there was something in his affect that Benn found unsettling.

"Well..." Cira hesitated.

"Won't be long," Beame said with finality. He placed a large hand on Benn's shoulder and steered him toward another hallway, while pointing to the executive lounge with his other hand. Thus dismissed, Cira had no choice but to acquiesce; the second security man stayed with her in the lounge.

"Right this way, young man." Beame seemed to be in a hurry, impatiently entering a code and then placing his right eye next to a scanner which allowed them passage into a more highly secured area of the building. A uniformed guard seated behind a thick window nodded at Beame as they rushed past him and entered a waiting elevator. In an upper corner of the elevator, Benn noticed an Eye dimly glowing red.

"I'm sure you're looking forward to seeing your father. It's been a few years, hasn't it?" Beame, perspiring as he stared at the floor indicator above the door, didn't seem to expect an answer, so Benn offered none. Suddenly the elevator stopped; it was the 86th floor, and the ascent had taken a mere twelve seconds.

"Come along, Benn. Your father's waiting." Beame led the way down a long, brightly-lit corridor to a secured steel door, entered another code, and waved Benn forward even before the door had fully opened. "I'm glad you're wearing a coat- it's a little cold in here."

And why so dark, Benn wondered. He entered what was clearly a laboratory, judging by the impressive amount of scientific equipment present: biometers, a huge Dataframe ES standing next to an advanced-model Probot, nano-surgical machinery lined up by the back wall. A shiny black cylinder three meters long lay on its side, atop what appeared to be a control panel. The room was silent except for the soft ticking of the biometers.

Despite the cold ambient temperature, Beame took off his own jacket, then indicated a chair in the center of the room. "Might as well make yourself comfortable, Benn. We've got a lot to talk about."

Lora barely felt the tingle on the back of her hand. The security man had instructed her to place her palm on a square panel next to the lab entrance, presumably for an identification process. As soon as she had done so, Sool had quickly stepped forward and pressed a Dermamist to her hand, instantly snapping in its contents. Lora remembered expressing surprise, demanding an explanation- but now it all seemed distant, as if in a dream. They had pushed her forward into the lab, which she could tell was a small room with a table at the opposite wall, but otherwise appeared blurry and vague. The floor tilted one way, and then the other, as she stumbled toward the table, her shoulders in the strong grip of the security man.

"Go on. Up on the table. I'll help you. That's right, just relax. Now give me your other leg. That's it." He spoke softly, his voice smooth and reassuring, his hands and face as hard as stone.

"But why…"

"Relax, it's all right. Now we're just going to put on these straps, to make sure you don't fall off."

"I'm not…"

"All done. See? It's not so bad, is it?"

"I don't want…"

"It's not what you want at this point, don't you get it?" Sool's voice was harsh and impatient.

"Sool," another voice, quite familiar, interrupted. "That's enough. Why don't you, why don't the both of you, wait outside. Technician, ah, 0749 will help me with the rest of the procedure. All right? Sool?"

Reluctantly, Sool stalked out of the room, eyeing Lora with the hungry look of a jackal deprived of her prey. Lora watched the security man leave, then craned her neck to see who had spoken. His face appeared as blurry as the rest of the room, but Lora quickly recognized the gray goatee.

"Rion…"

"Yes, Lora. Are you comfortable?" Rion Salkend came closer and leaned over her. Although indistinct, she could make out the genuine concern, mixed with more than a little embarrassment, in his expression.

"Lora, I apologize, but things are moving along very quickly now, and I'm afraid we have had to, ah, accelerate the project."

"Project? What are you...?"

"No, of course you know nothing of the project. You see, Lora, you play a key role in one of the most important experiments in the history of both genetics and pharmaceuticals, ah, having to do with psychoactive peptides. You have a rare opportunity to help in the, ah, advancement of science- I hope you can appreciate that. Now, before we proceed, I want to know, Lora, have you used any of the, ah, recreational drugs I warned you about?"

"Drugs? Rion, I don't know what you..."

"Roving Eye, Deep Coma, Lora. Have you used anything like that?"

"No, of course not."

"Truthfully? Good, excellent. I didn't think you would. Now please don't struggle. It would be best for Technician 0749 to attach you to the biometers before the sedative completely wears off. It can be a little painful, I'm afraid."

0749, who had just transferred down from Eunigen Boston, cursed his bad luck as he sorted through the tubes and wires he would now have to plug into the subject. You're afraid? What about her? And how was it that his application to transfer out of the awful Repro division- to Protanalysis, Public Relations, anywhere- had resulted in a move to New York, into an even more horrendous job? Someone in H.R. must be having a good laugh right now, at his expense. He felt the old guilt begin to rise in his chest like a poorly digested meal, but then- applying a skill which, unfortunately, he had frequent opportunities to hone- managed to rally his professionalism and toggle over to a cold, objective evaluation of the experimental subject.

A female, age twenty-two. Salkend had addressed her by her real name, which- as with Dr. Beame and Thor Ibsen- was strictly forbidden. But 0749 could make himself forget that, as well as many other things. Next: the subject was naïve to psychoactive therapeptides, check. She would be administered the same extreme

174

dose of Deep Coma as the subject in Boston, who had unfortunately not survived that trial. Check. And the goal was to... was to discover... what, how quickly she would die? Next: the subject was a Martian, check. So was that other fellow, but he was from one of the New Colonies, whereas this one apparently came out of the old colony, Tharsis. That must be the variable in the experiment, check. Maybe they were expecting that a native of Tharsis would respond differently to Deep Coma? Who knew what Salkend and Beame hoped to learn from these experiments? Next.

One by one, hindered somewhat by his nagging empathy, 0749 attached skin-piercing electrodes and intravascular monitors to the subject, whose sensorium remained mercifully clouded; still, she moaned and squirmed uncomfortably, and 0749 felt himself distracted, not up to his usual efficiency. Salkend studiously faced the Protanalysis unit, twiddling with the dials and needlessly rechecking the sample purity. He's not at all like Beame, thought 0749: Salkend's got no stomach for this.

"Are you... are you going to..."

Salkend approached the table again, and Lora could now see his face clearly.

"We are going to administer a dose of Deep Coma, Lora. But not to worry: based on titration trials in, ah, other subjects, we have calculated a seventy-two percent probability of survival. Perhaps even higher: after all, the hypothesis is that lifelong exposure to the Martian environment imparts a greater tolerance for psychoactive therapeptides."

I was right about the variable, thought 0749. Must be gaining some insight into how people think around here. But it seemed to him that Salkend was talking too much, in a forced manner- not as much to educate the subject, as to assuage his own guilt. Without recognizing that he himself had done exactly the same thing, 0749 felt affronted by Salkend's dragging the whole grisly procedure back into a safe, and even noble, intellectual domain: that of an objective scientific experiment.

"You see, Lora, the Phase One trials, which measured the effects of drugs such as Ordrax on the population of Tharsis Colony, showed us that native Martians were more resistant to the side-effects of treatment than those who received PsySoc regulators on Earth. In Phase Two, we found that subjects with relatively recent exposure to the Mars environment, such as first- or second-generation colonists, are only weakly resistant."

"Recent exposure... you mean..."

"Yes, recent exposure would include your colleagues from Highland City. Nema first, and then Trip, helped us to determine the ratio of psychopeptide resistance to duration of Mars exposure. And now you, Lora, as a descendant of Mars colonists going all the way back to the original settlers, will give us an endpoint. You will, ah, 'zero' our scale, so to speak."

He felt no need to tell her about the additional psychopeptides in her injection. They were part of a separate, bonus experiment: assuming she survived, these additional peptides would allow Eunigen to control Lora's future actions, using certain visual triggers. A sort of delayed hypnotic effect. Salkend had pointed out to Eunigen project designers that they were introducing confounding variables, but his objection had been overruled. Since Lora was their final subject- except, of course, for Benn Marr himself- Director Beame had insisted on combining two experiments in one.

Lora, slowly coming out of her fog, struggled against the straps. "Zero your... you can't do this. Rion! I'm not a..."

"Years of work, Lora. No, ah, stopping now." He turned away. " 0749, if you're ready, you may proceed."

"What about Benn? Is he also..."

"Oh no, Lora. No, no, Benn is part of a much more important project. Much bigger than this simple titration study. Thanks to you, Phase Two ends tonight." Salkend paused to watch 0749 activate the injector, then quietly added, "Benn Marr is, ah, Phase Three."

Benn sat in the center of the room, where the lab equipment had been cleared away. A cold blue light overhead defined a circle around him. Seated in the dark periphery and peering upwards, Walther Beame touched a control pad in front of him and muttered:

"All right, Owen. Talk to him. Let's get this started." He leaned back and waited with his arms crossed, gaze fixed on the ceiling.

For almost a minute, nothing happened. Would his father enter the room? Benn listened for footsteps, but heard only the ticking of the biometers. Then, at the edge of the blue circle of light, the air began to shimmer faintly. Wondering whether it was his imagination, Benn watched, fascinated, as the vibrating air formed gray snow-like flecks, which swarmed momentarily before coalescing into a human shape: it was Owen Marr, dressed in his usual white lab coat, with his familiar graying hair and vaguely disgruntled expression. In fact, he looked the same as the image on the message orb Benn had received from Eunigen. Even the grainy quality of the hologram was the same. But why would they use a hologram- especially one of such poor quality- when Father himself was somewhere in this building?

"Hello, son." Benn, expecting that this was another read-only hologram, stared at his father's image without responding. But at the sound of Owen's voice, Beame stood up quickly, and his narrowed eyes swept the room. Strangely, he appeared not to see the hologram at all- which could only mean that it was actually something totally different.

"That's right, Benn. I am not a hologram. Beame cannot see me. He can only hear small parts of what I say. You can hear and see me, Benn, because of… what we both have in common."

Beame only heard: "NOT HOLLOW. CANNOT SEE. HEAR SMALL. IN COMMON." He rolled his eyes in frustration. How the hell was this going to work? He looked over at Benn, whose attention seemed to be fixed on an empty space in the darkness to his left.

"Why can't you be here in person?"

"I am, Benn. At least part of me is here. My physical form has greatly changed, degenerated- you would not recognize it. What remains of my body is contained in that cylinder where Beame is standing."

Benn searched in the darkness and again spotted the shiny black cylinder on the control panel. Beame alertly followed his gaze, then turned back to Benn with a smirk: so Benn Marr had learned the fate of his once-eminent father.

"You're inside that cylinder." On one level, it was almost laughable, and yet on another, it made perfect sense to Benn, whose thoughts constantly raced ahead of him, preparing his mind for even the most outrageous news.

"Yes. My physical degeneration resulted from a long-running project of which I was, for many years, the Director. Many years ago, non-human DNA was incorporated into my genome, and unfortunately there were... unforeseen consequences."

"Like the Boston Gene Project." Father's audacious experiment on himself did not surprise him at all, as though Benn had fully expected to learn this one day. He had always possessed a certain prescience. Hadn't Dr. Neelin called him a "true natural" for that reason? Answers just came to him automatically, and at this moment, the highest levels of his mind were already connecting the dots from Owen's story and extrapolating the story line forward. He could not yet see the logical conclusion forming in the hazy distance, but Benn knew he wasn't going to like it.

"Yes. Like the Boston Gene Project, but with a crucial difference." Was it pride that Benn sensed? "My non-human DNA came from extinct life on Mars! When water miners discovered fossils containing Martian DNA, Hydra sequenced the DNA, coded it digitally, and transmitted it via a pulsed magnetic wave decipherable only to Eunigen. This data was translated in our lab, where we assembled nucleotides to regenerate the original DNA."

Wait, thought Benn. Wouldn't that leave out the gene-associated proteins, restriction enzymes, and so on? And what about the difference between the nucleotides found on Earth and on Mars? Could the Martian DNA really be re-generated using building blocks available on Earth?

"Hydra kept the existence of Martian DNA secret, turning it over to Eunigen for great profit. Obviously, adding Martian DNA to the Earth Biogenome menu had enormous commercial potential, and Eunigen has exploited it well."

Walther Beame listened intently and glowered. What he heard was: "EXISTENCE OF MARTIAN. ENORMOUS. EXPLOITED IT WELL." Could Benn really understand this gibberish?

"It seems the primitive life on Mars was genetically enabled to project and to receive bio-energy, and each single-celled organism used this to link with all other Martian life. There was a planet-wide bioweb- of the sort we are now detecting around the Earth- covering

178

Mars before life there became extinct." That's what Lora was reading about, thought Benn.

"Eunigen recreated several variations of Martian DNA, translated them to therapeptides, and found that these therapeptides had powerful psychoactive properties. More than that, they enabled subjects to link temporarily with the Earth's bioweb."

"So that's what the three vials contained- therapeptides made from Martian DNA?"

"The first two did. And those injections enabled you to project your bio-energy, didn't they? Good. Now tell me, Benn, how did the third vial affect you?"

"It was the same as the others." Benn recalled his swim in the ocean, then returning to his dorm room, but suppressed any thought of his evening spent at Star and Stripe. "In fact, I traveled quite a distance that night."

"That third vial contained only sterile saline, Benn," announced his father triumphantly. "It was simple salt water."

This piece of news Benn had not expected. "Saline? So I injected a placebo? But that means... I can project without the help of therapeptides?"

"Yes, Benn. And so can I- this image of me is a projection of my mind- the aura, as you call it. My ability far exceeds that of Leong Marr, and your ability... will exceed mine." Benn caught a slight hesitation, and realized: he's not completely happy about my superiority- even though that's the stated goal of his project.

"Did you say Leong Marr? Grandfather?"

"Yes, Benn. Your grandfather, who grew up in Tharsis, did not die in a water-mining accident, as I led you to believe. At the time, Eunigen was seeking colonists for the early Martian therapeptide experiments; Leong volunteered, so Eunigen brought him to New York. They found that he reacted very differently from local subjects; he was able to project himself far better. He also resisted the damaging effects of the therapeptides, possibly due to living for years in the midst of a residual energy field on Mars. Because the therapeptides had very short half-lives, the idea of fusing the Martian DNA into a human genome was proposed, and Leong Marr was the natural candidate..."

Benn had heard this discussion before. Messler and Cira Vincent. Raising his hand as in class, he objected, "But the Second Law of Theragenomics..."

Owen ignored the interruption. "After a retrovirus introduced the Martian DNA into Leong's somatic cells, we used the "triple-stranded DNA" technique (you've learned about that in Nano-gene Construction) to trick the cells' repair mechanisms into incorporating Martian DNA into his chromosomes. Unfortunately the two types of DNA were not congruent with one another, proving rapidly fatal to the Leong Marr Chimera."

Benn shook his head. Talk about forced co-existence of species! A human being and a Martian protozoan- how organic was that? And how could Owen talk about his own father as a mere experimental subject- the Leong Marr Chimera?

"Before Leong's death," Owen continued dispassionately, "analysis of his genome revealed only a sixty-four percent fusion rate. The instability of his DNA led to the formation of anomalous proteins incompatible with survival, but did show Eunigen the next step: starting over again with a partially-fused genome, they could raise the fusion percentage in a second attempt. If only Leong's genome did not perish with him, it could be stabilized by methods already in use... "

It didn't take Benn long to grasp the logical conclusion.

"So they must have cloned him from a single germ cell to save the genome, as his body was dying! The Leong Marr Chimera lived on..."

"As the Owen Marr Chimera, or OMC, as they refer to me. However, as an identical clone of the LMC, it was only a matter of time before I, too, would degenerate and die. I was sent to Mars to spend the first sixteen years of my life, in hopes of stabilizing my chimeric genes in the residual Martian bio-energy field. It was simple to fabricate a story about my 'parents' dying in a mining accident to explain my presence there alone.

"And so I thrived, until the age of sixteen. Being linked to the residual Martian bioweb gave me insights that others lacked; my hunches always turned out to be correct, and I excelled in school- just as you did, after me. When I turned sixteen, Eunigen sent an agent to bring me to Earth- for advanced education, they said, and for a career in research. Eventually, they had to lay out the whole project and ask me to submit to the next step: a second attempt at fusion with the Martian genome."

"Why ask you to submit? Why couldn't they just force you to undergo the procedure?"

"Don't be naive, Benn. They could have forced me, but then coercion would have turned me against them. Remember, their goal was to create a superior being with the ability to link completely with the bioweb: that person would hold power over others-including Eunigen itself. Before giving me those abilities, they had to ensure my loyalty. Ironically, the prospect of success was more threatening than that of failure!"

They were afraid of creating a monster, Benn agreed. But their fear had been unfounded; Owen had eagerly consented to the fusion procedure. And look at him now: bits and pieces inside a black cylinder, locked inside this laboratory for the rest of his miserable life.

"I see the attempt didn't go too well." Benn regretted saying that, as his father's aura flared with anger. At the edges, the color of anger masked envy and self-pity, a combination recognized from his encounter with Kai.

"On the contrary! We started at sixty-four percent, and achieved ninety-two percent fusion," Owen declared proudly. "I could project myself at will. I could read others' thoughts, even affect their movements. The fusion provided me with my own endogenous production of the therapeptides." Benn noted that Father had not mentioned reading information recorded in water.

Owen continued, "Ninety-two percent was a resounding success. But after six months, I began to notice physical changes-progressive weakness and loss of tactile sense. Eventually I was completely unable to move or feel my extremities. Within eight months I lost my other senses: sight, hearing…"

"That's really sad," Benn tried to sound sympathetic, but Owen snapped back.

"It didn't matter, don't you see? I could project myself anywhere within a hundred kilometers. I didn't need eyesight, hearing or functioning limbs! When my lungs, heart and kidneys failed, Eunigen built the cylinder as a life-support system. But it's also a containment device; I began to put out highly caustic secretions hazardous to the lab workers…"

"That's all right, I don't need to know about that." Benn swallowed his rising nausea at the image of his father's withered thorax, an empty shell attached to vestigial limbs, continuously bathed in a harsh acid solution. Or did his disgust derive from the horrible conclusion which he now began to see more clearly?

"Oh, but you do need to know about that, Benn. You may think yourself clever, but don't assume you know everything. Even though the likelihood of your undergoing the same degeneration is small..." As Owen said this, Benn's racing thoughts connected the final dots, which now pointed to the staggering truth.

Somehow he had known it all along! The small thought steadily growing like a tumor in Benn's upper mind had proven malignant. He almost choked: "You cloned yourself! You knew you would die before long, didn't you? Your body began to fall apart, so you had to preserve the genome. Just like Leong, before you." As the logical implications tumbled forth, Benn felt a deep wound opening in his chest: a stab of loss, the crush of his entire life collapsing like a house of cards. His past, his identity, his whole being, it was all a fiction! His mother, Wila! Wila had not died in childbirth; she had never even existed.

"Yes, Benn. I created you by cloning myself: you are the Benn Marr Chimera, the BMC Project! So you see, this is not your first time on Earth: you were born in this lab. We set up a life for you on Mars, so that you would undergo the same stabilization process that I had. I fabricated a story about a mother dying of eclampsia- what name did I give her?"

"Wila." Benn answered flatly, although it felt as though a pound of flesh had been torn out of him.

"Ah, yes. Her name was Wila. I'm surprised you remember, after all these years. Given your ninety-two percent fusion, you demonstrated the same mental abilities as I did at school. My only disappointment is that you lack the creativity and drive that I developed at Tharsis, which led to my successful career. Why couldn't you be more inventive, and more entrepreneurial?"

"I got to be pretty good at sports, Father. My baseball team won the championship..."

Owen pressed on. "We allowed an extra three years on Mars for the ripening phase. When you turned nineteen, we felt it was time to bring you home, to make the third attempt at genomic

182

fusion. Through the Mars Wellness Institute, we dispatched an agent..."

"Rion Salkend."

"...to monitor your progress and to bring you safely..."

"To harvest me."

"If you must put it like that." Benn suddenly felt an angry surge from Owen's aura and realized that only a few years ago, his father would have slapped him across the face for putting it like that. "All right, then: we harvested your genome. And we prepared you with gradual therapeptide exposure, building up your tolerance, unlocking your potential with the first two vials, and then testing your native abilities with the third vial, the placebo. By passing all stages, you have arrived at the crossroads, Benn. Do you see how close we are to success? Starting at ninety-two percent, surely the third fusion will be complete."

Benn's mind raced on desperately, if only to obscure his pain and anger by intellectualizing Owen's horrible revelations: for example, wouldn't an alien nucleotide in the sequence transmitted by Hydra result in... translational errors? Did micro-chimerism play a role in, in stabilizing the partially-fused genes? But these wildly ranging thoughts failed to suppress childhood memories of his father's ambitious expectations, always couched in coldly impersonal terms and laced with the possibility that, if found lacking, Benn would be dropped like a failed project.

"But why should I co-operate with your project?" He tried to modulate the whiny quality that had crept involuntarily into his voice. In his dreams, he was the triumphant hero coming home, but in reality he was the pathetic prodigal son, returning sheepishly to face his father's stern disapproval.

"You were created for the BMC Project," Owen replied sharply. "The project is the only reason you exist."

Walther Beame, sitting on the edge of his chair while struggling to follow the conversation, heard Owen Marr say: "PROJECT. REASON YOU EXIST."

"That's right, Benn," he quickly cut in. "It's who you are-your role in life. Growing up, you must have wondered why you didn't fit into the community at Tharsis. And now, on Earth, you're even more of an outsider. To begin with, Martian colonials have second-class status, no matter what their accomplishments. But it's more than that, Benn. Your YaleConn classmates find your personality, behavior, and especially your insights in class, frankly scary. To them, you're nothing more than a freak.

"Don't turn this into a false dichotomy. Why go on trying to belong in a society that rejects you? Why, when you have the potential to rise far above them? You already possess great abilities, but after this fusion, Benn, they'll be like ants to you!" It was an old story, Benn thought: a quest for power, thinly disguised as one for knowledge.

Beame paused, but Benn could hear the thoughts which followed: *Of course we can't let him get that far, if he's not with us. We'll leverage Lora Wheeler to persuade him. If he still refuses, we'll terminate this arm of the project: force him to undergo fusion, and then clone him. He's dispensable once we have his clone. Start over again with the next generation. Such a waste, another twenty years...*

At this wave of unspoken threat, Benn rocked back in his seat. They would kill him after forcing the fusion. And Beame had mentioned Lora as well: why bring her into this? She's not one of your subjects! The threat to Lora triggered a strong protective instinct in Benn. Could he really project without a therapeptide? At the thought, he felt himself expanding outwards.

To Beame, the OMC warned, "FOOL. HEAR YOU. CONVINCE."

To Benn, Owen Marr said reassuringly, "Beame is a fool. We need you alive. Think of the power you'll have. The advance to medical science. Benn. Don't."

Benn rose out of his body and now perceived the chamber quite differently. His abilities were evolving: in the far corner Beame stood clenching his fists. He was surrounded by a dense greenish glow within which Benn could perceive individual components for the first time. It was as though Beame were wearing a coat of multicolored patches sewn together: brownish layers vibrant with fear and mistrust; hard yellow spikes of ambition; and a small bluish zone, where Beame's conscience resided. On the control panel, a pulsing blue aura stretched a thin tendril across the room to the image of Owen Marr, which now stood pleading with palms turned upward. Between Owen's grim expression and the accelerating pulsations of his aura, Benn sensed a mounting alarm-not out of concern for Benn, certainly. His father was alarmed because his project was teetering on the brink of failure. There was a familiar whiff of rotting vegetation in the air.

"NO, BENN. DON'T. LEAVE."

Walther Beame was suddenly on his feet. "Leave? Oh no, you don't! You're not leaving in the middle of the most important phase...." From the counter, he snatched up a Dermamist loaded with a powerful sedative and began to move toward Benn's body, still immobile in the chair. He took one step forward, then slammed hard into an invisible wall, which resulted from a soft blow Benn had directed at his vulnerable blue zone. Beame emitted a painful grunt as he tumbled backward.

Immediately the image of a frustrated and reluctant Owen Marr dissipated, and the blue tendril withdrew, like a retreating snake, into the black cylinder. Benn, confused at the rapid turn of events- his father's disappearance, Beame lying there on the floor, his own spontaneous projection out of body- forced himself to focus his thoughts, on Lora. She was in danger, that much was obvious. He could now see her, many floors below him, in another darkened room. A stranger, a technician, was bent over her, injecting something into her arm. She was tied to a table... but no, as he watched, she freed herself; now she was rising, turning toward the opposite wall, toward... Rion Salkend! A pale green aura shimmered over Salkend's taut, perspiring face. But what in the world was Rion Salkend doing there?

Benn realized suddenly- his brakes being fully disengaged- that he was already in the room with them. He recognized Lora's bright yellow projection, which, set free by the infusion of Deep Coma just received, had fully emerged from her body on the table. Lora now stood facing Salkend, who remained oblivious to everything but the fact that technician 0749 was, for some reason, stopping the infusion. If he had detected Benn's hovering presence in the corner of the ceiling; known of the catastrophic collapse of the BMC Project high up in the tower; and perceived Lora's looming projection and its impending collision with him, Salkend might have passed out, even without any encouragement on Lora's part. Lora, disoriented, furious and unaware of her devastating potential, was now raging blindly toward Salkend, like a bull with its horns lowered.

Benn knew the serious damage she could do in this state; despite mixed feelings about letting Lora have her way with Salkend, he staunchly positioned his aura between the two of them and braced himself for the impact.

"BENN!"

"HUH!" was all Benn could manage as their two auras met. It was not so much a physical joining of bodies- not the sensation he had hoped for, alas- but more like a merging of two liquids. Lora feels like oil, the odd thought came to him: he pictured a large drop of oil falling into a pool of water. As it splashed, the strong natural repulsion between auras took immediate effect: the drop embodying Lora displaced a smaller drop- a portion of Benn's aura- which rose straight upward. Then the Benn-drop fell back in and splashed up an even smaller droplet- Lora again- which in turn fell, and so on, until inevitably the last microsphere of Lora was captured by Benn's surface tension and could no longer escape. As separate liquids, the two of them had different viscosities: Benn flowed easily, whereas Lora's character was thicker, more unctuous. Their collision caused long, finger-like projections of Lora to penetrate into Benn's aura, causing it to blush red before snapping back to attention.

He recognized her myriad layers, those melodic strains, the steady internal rhythm he had so admired. With their thoughts so intermingled, mutual understanding arrived instantaneously, and no longer required the cumbersome verbal exchange of ideas expressed ploddingly one at a time, over periods measurable on a stopwatch. If their conversation had indeed taken place in that pedestrian way, it would have sounded something like:

"Huh."

"You said that before, Benn. This is amazing: so that's what you've been up to. Projecting out of body! I suspected something strange was going on, you know- I thought you were hiding somewhere in my bedroom the other night."

"Those therapeptides," replied Benn, quickly changing the subject, "they got me started in this out-of-body experience, as they just did for you. But Lora, I can project myself even without the help of therapeptides."

"Incredible." She discovered that she could read some of the recent events in his mind, to pull threads of thought out of the dense swirl of Benn's consciousness. "You don't need the therapeptides...

186

because your genetic makeup enables you to project out of body! You have... what, seriously? Martian DNA? Amazing! A chimera, isn't that what your father just called you?"

"I'm afraid he did. I'm a chimera, a fusion of two life-forms. But Lora... I hope you don't find that, you know, repulsive?"

"No, not repulsive... it helps me to understand, I suppose. Your conflicted nature, the essence of being a chimera! Your father's the repulsive one... I can't believe what you just went through, in his lab. Why would you even consider him your father?"

"Don't know. I guess growing up, like all children, I needed to believe that there was someone who could protect me. When he hit me or threatened me, I had to interpret that as a sign of his strength, and to... twist... my fear into a false sense of security. Lora, what we discussed earlier- all that noise and pain I experienced growing up; how I had to block it out..."

"Yes, I felt some of that too, but it wasn't a sad pain, like yours." Lora saw the psychic scar: constantly needing to twist his fear into something more reassuring had nearly destroyed Benn's will to engage with his world, his life. Suddenly feeling miserable, she shifted to a more technical issue, but her empathy had not escaped Benn's notice. "There's another big difference between us, Benn: obviously I can't project out of my body without the help of a therapeptide."

He'd been mistaken, thinking that Lora had the native ability to connect with the bioweb, whereas he needed the artificial boost: it was the other way around. Grateful for the segue, Benn replied, "That's a crucial point: the drug wears off. You may be pulled back into your body at any time, and that's actually a good thing." Benn knew from experience that the sense of unlimited freedom was illusory; their physical forms were actually exposed, vulnerable to physical harm. "We'd better get out of this building. Walther Beame is regaining consciousness upstairs. Try this, Lora: just imagine going back into your body, and I think it'll happen. I can take care of the restraints. Then head for the lobby- I'll meet you there in a few minutes."

Lora's separation from Benn was equivalent to a drug withdrawal, a wrenching mixture of pain and panic. Numbly, he watched her aura move away, then forced his attention over to the faint gray-green haze wrapped around Technician 0749. Influencing this weak aura would not be a problem. By simply thinking of the actions, he willed 0749 to raise his arm, flex and extend his fingers, and then unbuckle the straps which held Lora to the table.

To Rion Salkend's perception, the total time elapsed between the technician's injection of the psychopeptides into the subject, and now the baffling sight of 0749 undoing Lora's restraints, totaled just under four seconds. What the, ah, hell was he doing? There was not enough time for Salkend to confront the technician. Barely two seconds later, both he and 0749 (who would soon thereafter apply urgently for another job transfer) were sprawled, unconscious, on the floor.

Chapter Eighteen

The broad street bustled with hovering yellow taxis carrying gray-uniformed government bureaucrats to their tedious evening meetings; exhausted office workers on their way home to cubicle apartments in the crowded vertical neighborhoods of Midtown Manhattan; shoppers, some with disinterested children in tow, gazing at sparse window displays; and uninspired diners coming out of uninspiring restaurants. Cira Vincent stood back from the passers-by, shaded from the glare of a streetlight. Bored of waiting in the executive lounge, she had bundled up and told the security man that she was going out for a walk, to look around the old neighborhood. After an hour of waiting for she-knew-not-what, Cira reflected on the street scene. She was struck by the grim resignation on the faces of pedestrians pushing past her, their lack of expression. New Yorkers talked incessantly about what a great city they lived in; from the commercial and cultural viewpoints, it was a great city. But few of these people actually enjoyed living there, and it seemed to her that they were in denial about it. Forced to accept widespread Level One crime (at least Level Zero political corruption, which brought the death penalty, had vanished under the PWE), harsh weather, noise pollution, grime and trash, they faced each day with detached fatalism. To their credit, they had adapted to life in the City: bad weather engendered romance and drama, the unabating noise level ensured that the City Never Slept, and many had even come to see poetry in piles of trash. Such had been her life as a post-doctoral fellow. Now lost in thoughts of illusory romance in New York, Cira gazed across the avenue at the large reflective glass doors of the Eunigen building without any idea of what was transpiring at that very moment, behind those doors.

She did realize that something was terribly wrong. Walther Beame had acted so imperiously, splitting up her students without any discussion. When setting up this meeting, he had specifically asked Cira to bring Sool Tamura along- only to ignore Sool once they had arrived. And poor Lora, extending her hand in greeting, unanswered. That was embarrassing. But worst of all, he had tossed Cira aside, like a pair of old shoes! Cira Vincent, who had powerful connections to industry- his industry. And yes, who, along with the readers of Inner Circle Magazine, had thought of Beame as a most eligible bachelor- despite his oversized ego. He would regret his high-handed manner. And what was his interest in Benn? It was obvious that Benn was the only one in her group who mattered to Beame. True, Benn had demonstrated some remarkable abilities; no less, he was the son of their previous Director, Owen Marr. The great Owen Marr, trailblazer in therapeptides. And Walther was Owen's protégé- so, of course, the true "inner circle" had come together, leaving Cira Vincent out in the literal cold. But still, there was no reason for that arrogant....

Her bitter thoughts were cut off by a loud siren nearby, then flashing lights as a police rover rounded the corner to her far right. In the middle of the block, she spotted a short, broad-shouldered man standing oddly with knees flexed and arms extended to his sides: as tense as a cat preparing to pounce. Although everyone else on the street had turned toward the oncoming rover, the short man appeared calmly undistracted, his eyes focused on the same glass doors Cira had been watching. She felt sure she had seen him before: where? Not around this neighborhood, certainly; maybe back on campus.

Abe had immediately recognized the woman, Dr. Cira Vincent, lurking in the shadows on the opposite side of the street. She was watching the door too, but unlike Abe, had no sense that something explosive was about to happen. Not that Abe could see very far past the reflective surface, but his instincts told him there was a violent struggle taking place in the lobby, and he was waiting... any moment now...

Several things then occurred in such rapid succession that, to the normal observer, they were practically simultaneous; to Abe's special senses, they unfolded as if in slow motion.

The doors of Eunigen flew outwards, propelled by an immense shock wave launched by a security man crouched near the back of the lobby. The recoil had fractured the security man's right humerus and thrown him against the wall, so he now struggled bravely to re-position the shock cannon on his left side. He knew full well that the shock cannon was overkill- it was meant for crowd

190

control and was also meant to be held by a team of three- but he was alone, and it was the only weapon stored in the lobby.

Just behind him, a disheveled Dr. Walther Beame staggered out of the elevator with a look of sheer fury on his face and, lunging for the shock cannon, screamed "NO!" followed by a long string of obscenities.

Meanwhile, outside the building, two burly police officers jumped out of their rover at mid-block, weapons drawn: Abe saw that the officers were carrying handheld Razers, far more lethal than the shock cannon.

Another Eunigen security man, who had hurriedly positioned himself near the front entrance, crumpled slowly onto the lobby floor as Benn and Lora ran past him and through the blown-out doors, hand in hand. They paused briefly, then turned up the street- Benn with his eyes closed the entire time- directly away from Abe and the pursuing officers.

"Benn!" gasped Lora, winded by their escape through the lobby. "You knocked out that guard without projecting out of body!" She struggled to keep up, as Benn had quickened his pace.

"Yes, I just discovered I could do that- there's an effect that lingers after projecting, but only for a short time. As long as I can see their auras, I can influence them. But I have to stop and concentrate- so it isn't easy, when chased by armed men."

"Well, you influenced that last guard right off his feet."

"When we came outside, a couple of policemen were approaching quickly, but now I don't sense them anymore. Turn right here, Lora; there's nobody down this way."

A hundred meters behind them, Abe took note of the side-street Benn and Lora turned into. He allowed himself a moment to look around. On either side of him lay a motionless police officer: one had a broken neck, and the other lay in an expanding pool of blood, his back bent backward, his head tucked between his feet. The two had slowed Abe down a bit, but staying on Benn Marr's trail would present no challenge at all.

Cira Vincent instinctively dropped to a crouch and covered her eyes when the glass doors blew open, but quickly recovered when she saw Benn and Lora emerge from the building. As she crossed the street, pushing through the panicked crowd to keep them in sight, she noticed the short catlike man again. The officers were just passing next to him- their weapons aimed at Benn and Lora, for some reason- when he suddenly leapt upwards and spun around in a rapid blur. Too fast for Cira to see: but there was an unmistakable, sickening snap of bones fracturing, and now seeing the twisted shapes of the two bodies on the ground, Cira had to turn away, one hand covering her mouth.

How horrible! She searched for Benn and Lora; they had gone in this direction, but where were they now?

That's good: Dr. Vincent looked the other way and lost them; otherwise, if she managed to chase them down, he would have to deal with her as well. Abe ducked to his right and, keeping the crowd between himself and Cira, slipped past her unobserved. A few seconds later, he turned into the side-street and caught sight of the fleeing couple, who appeared to him as bright yellow human shapes in rapid motion within the still darkness of the alley. As he had expected: no challenge at all.

"Benn, what is it?" said Lora, glad for the chance to catch her breath as Benn stopped running and stood with his eyes closed again. He was scanning the alley for anyone following them. Although Benn's perceptions were far more effective, Lora searched as well, squinting into the shadows and upward at the silhouettes of ancient fire escapes rising to a narrow reddish strip of sky.

"I thought for a moment... no... no, there's nothing there." Benn opened his eyes but still felt that something was out of place. He had sensed something like a vibration, a subtle movement behind them, but his sweep of the alley had yielded nothing. Benn had forgotten, at least for the moment, that not everyone possessed an aura.

They were nearing an intersection with a major avenue, where traffic and pedestrians continued in their routine patterns, oblivious to the turmoil only two blocks away. Lora felt Benn's grip loosen as he turned again to check the alley behind them, something still nagging at him. She noticed that a long black sedan had separated from the flow of traffic and lowered itself to the intersection ahead, where it blocked their path. A door slid open, through which Lora saw only a black interior.

"Benn, who's in that…" Lora began.

Concentrating intently with his eyes shut, Benn replied slowly, "I'm afraid it's Lou Hunter. He's with a couple of men I don't recognize. None of them are in a friendly mood, Lora. I think we should run." His grip on her hand tightened as he took a step back.

And abruptly stopped again. Not more than an arm's length behind Benn and Lora stood Abe in a near-crouch with his arms partially extended: an odd stance, but clearly conveying a threat of physical conflict. The shock on both of their faces contrasted sharply with Abe's complete lack of expression: those lifeless ball-bearing eyes, the heavy eyebrows, his wax-figure head turning slowly from side to side, saying no, there was no possibility of escaping back into the alley.

"Zak!"

The low forehead, so familiar by now, crinkled in the center, the eyebrows drew together, and Benn perceived a sudden wave of resentment. "No, I'm Abe! Sometimes people think I'm Zak, but really I'm not."

"Oh, Abe, then- sorry. What are you doing here, Abe?" Benn was struggling to find a handle, some way of influencing Abe, but there was no aura he could read or manipulate. And it was already quite obvious what Abe was doing here.

"I'm here to protect you, Mr. Marr. To protect both of you. You have to get into that car. Mr. Hunter is waiting for…"

"Benn, do you know this person?" Lora asked innocently, finding Abe's appearance more fascinating than threatening. Clearly born with an abnormal body habitus- could he have some sort of medical syndrome?

Benn glanced at Lora with concern- driven by curiosity, she didn't realize what harm the object of that curiosity could inflict- then focused his attention back on Abe. He had to find a way into Abe's mind: just a tiny crevice to pry open. But his struggle was fruitless: Abe was impenetrable, like a perfectly smooth stone. Maybe if he upset him, a crevice might develop…

"Lora, this is Abe, Lou Hunter's… servant." No luck: the insult didn't crack the smooth surface at all, but Benn did sense a flutter of antipathy just beneath. He repeated it, more loudly, "Did you hear me, Lora: Abe is Lou Hunter's *servant*." There was a definite ripple of hatred, but that didn't lead to a sufficient meltdown; actually, mistaking Abe for Zak had hit closer to the mark.

"Come on then, get in," called Hunter's familiar voice, from inside the limousine. Such impatience in that lazy drawl, thought Benn, sliding into a seat opposite Hunter. Lora climbed in behind him and, seeing so many unfriendly faces crowding the compartment- particularly that of a large bald-shaven man with a purple bruise discoloring his entire left cheek- immediately reached for Benn's hand. It was a small gesture, but Lou Hunter raised a curious eyebrow.

"These men are bodyguards, here to protect you," he said unconvincingly, and Benn sighed: the insufferable Lou Hunter, Abe the zombie, and two musclemen spoiling for a fight: ideal traveling companions. Well, he consoled himself, at least the ride to New Haven would be a short one.

Moments after the limousine departed the northern outskirts of New York Metropol and made an unexpected turn to the west, Benn realized that they were not headed back to New Haven at all. He closed his eyes and directed his thoughts at Lou Hunter, who had kept uncharacteristically silent during the ten-minute trip. As time had passed since his last projection, Benn's ability to see auras was fading, but he sensed the familiar self-importance, layered with anxiety and something new which Hunter was trying hard to deny: he must have realized the implications of Benn's abilities, because there was now an additional layer of fear. It was fear of Benn! But really Hunter had no reason to worry about Benn. After all, he held the trump card: Abe, coiled and watchful as a rattlesnake, sat next to Lora, and Benn had no way of controlling him. Benn could not project again, leaving his body vulnerable. He was just thinking about ordering the two thugs to attack Abe- although his control would be weak now, and it was doubtful they could overcome Abe in any case- when the limousine, passing the border of a gritty factory town with the odd name of Poughkeepsie, swerved sharply off the highway. Had they been followed? The driver made a number of abrupt turns through a warren of narrow streets- so close to the ground that Benn thought he heard a scraping sound below them- and finally stopped at an abandoned service station.

"Where are we going, Dr. Hunter?" Benn asked, keeping his voice level.

"Never mind- it's time to get out. There's another vehicle waiting for you, behind that building." He indicated a two-story repair garage, long out of use.

"Why another vehicle, and why the big secrecy?" demanded Lora, but Hunter responded with the same dismissive flicks of his fingers Benn had seen once before. That first exposure to Lou Hunter- pathetic yet amusing- seemed so long ago now. Never mind, Mellon College Baby, thought Benn, and he nearly smiled as they climbed out of the limousine.

Playing his captive role, he complained loudly as the two bodyguards guided them toward the building. Hey, take it easy, Baldy, no need to shove, what's the rush. He stopped to adjust his shoe- anything to annoy the guards. But as they rounded the corner and looked up at the massive vehicle hovering a few meters off the ground, his complaints petered out. This was no passenger vehicle, but rather a robotically-driven toxic waste transport, designed to ferry deadly nuclear waste material! There was no passenger compartment, and not even a cockpit; the "driver" consisted of a QI unit built into the nose-cone and extending, like a long spinal cord, along the entire dorsal surface to the magnetic propellers located at the tail. On each side of the vehicle appeared the logo of its parent company: Brightlights Radio-Drayage: Our Business Is Glowing Steadily. Now Benn allowed himself a short guffaw; Lora, on the other hand, didn't seem to get it. As they approached, one of the men pointed a device, and the belly of the transport noisily slid open, a ramp dropping at an angle toward them.

"Where are you taking us, Abe?" Lora demanded.

"To a safer place."

"But Abe, that transport is not a safer place," Benn pointed out conversationally. "We will very likely be dead on arrival, if you stick us in there."

"Never mind," Hunter cut in. "You'll be tucked inside a heavily insulated tube right in the center, protected from the tons of radioactive waste all around you. No-one will look for you in there. But it's a long ride, so we have…"

"A long ride? But I have to get back for classes tomorrow," Lora's voice was desperate now. "Where are we going?"

"They're smuggling us into the Quarantine Zone, Lora- by way of Nevada, I would assume," Benn ventured. The two bodyguards shot quick glances at one another.

Baldy with the bruised face challenged Benn. "What makes you think you're going to Nevada?"

"Just a guess. I may be from Mars, but even Martians know that Nevada is the favorite dumping ground for nuclear waste on this continent."

"Mr. Marr, it's not safe for you here in the northeast- or anywhere in the American Zone."

"Thank you, Abe- I appreciate your concern, but I think we can handle…"

"Never mind, time to go," insisted Hunter. "As I was saying, it's a long ride, and you might get claustrophobic." Time to go? Claustrophobic? Benn was suddenly reminded of his impatient friend Jace. "You'll be more comfortable if we medicate you before loading you into the tube." Benn heard Hunter's afterthought clearly: a strong tranquilizer to block the therapeptide's effect, Neelin's idea. You can't read minds, not with this on board. Can't tell Burgundy from Rhone. It was just unfair.

Holding Lora firmly by her upper arm, Baldy reached into his coat pocket and brought out a Dermamist injector. In a well-practiced motion, he pressed it against Lora's neck. No, not twice in one night! she struggled, leaving Benn only a brief second to close his eyes and feel. He had to strain, as too much time had gone by, and the ability to control the bodyguard was almost gone. Feel for the man's aura: there it was: green, impatient, determined. But not determined enough: with his last ounce of energy, Benn froze the aura in place. Open your hand…. The man had lifted his thumb off the Dermamist, but Lora still squirmed uncomfortably in his strong grasp. Loosen your grip… Benn had just formed that thought when he felt the snap of a second Dermamist, this one held at his own neck by Abe's powerful hand. Desperately he thrust the command toward the bald man: loosen… your…. Then, like a velvet curtain, soothing darkness fell on all sides.

KIDNAP. QUARANTINE. ZONE. FOLLOW.

Owen Marr strained to project these few words to Walther Beame. He had felt a surprising, substantial drop in his energy level just as Benn emerged out of body, and so was forced to withdraw back into the cylinder. What could have drained his energy so rapidly? The degenerative process might be speeding up.

Beame was understandably furious: Owen should have crushed Benn when he had the chance! Why did he let him go? And what was he trying to say now? Benn Marr had been taken... to the Quarantine Zone? Owen could project out of body with a range of a hundred kilometers at most, and would not be able to follow. If Benn was headed to the Quarantine Zone, the most likely perpetrators would be found at Mellon College, where a cell of American nationalists was known to operate. The PWE had been monitoring that group for years, but for some reason was unwilling to intervene. When Owen had occasionally stretched his projection all the way to Harkness Dormitory, his capacity had been severely diminished. He had gathered only snatches of information- very little that had ever proven useful. Nothing specific to pass on to the PWE, who had shown an oddly laissez-faire attitude. Maybe it was time to start rounding up some of those people.

Beame tried to regain his calm. "We'll get him back. Just have to contact our people out west. They'll pick up his trail." Brightening at the thought, he decided to call in Dmitri Lezhev. "And who knows, with Benn Marr's appearance in the Quarantine Zone, all sorts of conspirators might come out of hiding. In recovering Benn, we might expose the core of the resistance movement. The PWE is bound to appreciate that!"

Chapter Nineteen

On an overcast afternoon in mid-November, a mixture of snow and sleet descended on Jack Folsom's upturned face, his parched mouth held open to catch the moisture. Jack loved the raw chill that November brought to his bones; discomfort heightened the pleasure of returning to the foothills from another expedition high in the Sierras. Not a successful expedition, even by Jack's definition- foraging in such weather rarely paid off- but he would not be defeated by the bleakness of autumn! A rosy image hovered in his mind: a huge bonfire lit in the center of Vistaville, surrounded by music, dancing and feasting- there should be a hero's welcome for a grandson of the town's founder. But the image melted away like the snowflakes on his forehead.

Should be? Used to be, in the old days, not more than a decade ago. No celebration the last time Jack returned from foraging: more like a dirge of grave disappointment, as it had taken a while to sort out the edible from the poisonous mushrooms- one hungry and impatient fellow, clutching his stomach, had died in post-prandial agony that night. What if they gathered now around Jack's sled and threw back the tarp? How would his friends react to the heap of pine cones in there, and to the painstaking task of digging out the tiny edible parts? But wasn't it worth the trouble, having something- anything- to eat besides the endless supply of lyophilized corn (large sacks stamped "Courtesy of the Pan-World Electorate") stashed in the village storehouse? Even if some of the roots he had dug up, boiled and mashed to a bland paste, gave people gas? In winter, edible vegetation was scarce. And of course no weapons, not even hunting knives, were allowed in the Quarantine Zone, so hunting was impossible. His attempts at trapping had failed: a coyote had stolen the one rabbit he had trapped, right before his eyes! It was all up to Jack and his bare hands. How ungrateful his fellow citizens could be- they should all try foraging sometime, or simply shut up and eat their freeze-dried corn mush, reconstituted with high-fructose corn syrup. Jack scowled: feasting was out, and oh yes, he suddenly remembered- so was the bonfire. "Due to a shortage of dry wood," the mayor had announced at the last meeting of the Vistaville Committee, and everyone had given him a long and meaningful look, as though firewood was also his responsibility. Jack felt his face flush. How much longer before they banned music and dancing too?

As he passed the outer streets of the village, Jack sighted a commotion ahead: dozens of his neighbors were hurrying along Folsom Street, toward the park in the center of town. Ah, they had seen him coming- and there would be a big welcome after all. About time, thought Jack, easing the scowl from his face but only managing to pull his chapped lips back in a stiff grimace. He dragged the heavy sled onto Folsom Street with one hand, and with the other, waved- in a grand manner, he hoped- at several passers-by. Oddly, they failed to reciprocate, in their haste to reach the park. Here I am- over here! Trudging in perplexed silence along the main street, Jack felt - yes, a little hurt. But he straightened his back as he reached the park. Maybe it was to be a surprise, and they were busy setting up the....

The nothing. Folsom Park was quite vacant. But the old Methodist church, which faced Folsom Street on the far side of the park, was filled to overflowing. The steps leading up to the front entrance were packed with people straining to see inside, many standing on their tiptoes, pressed forward by the horde on the sidewalk. Staring for a long minute, Jack slowly absorbed the fact that the people had not gathered to welcome him at all, and his scowl returned. He grabbed a passing policeman by the collar of his uniform.

"What's going on, what's this all about?" he demanded.

The young man gawked at the giant and struggled to break free, but Jack had a woodman's grip.

"It's Maggie Sullivan! She's come to see the Martians! They've got 'em in there, now let me go!" Jack released him.

Maggie Sullivan! And Martians? Jack laboriously rolled the weighty thought over in his mind. No little green men. Colonists from Mars. But they're not from the new colonies, right? The ones called Martians, they came from the old colony- what was its name? The PWE must have sent them to the Quarantine Zone. So the PWE was rounding up the old Martians now. Not too surprising, since the old colonists came from original Americans, didn't they?

Reaching the back of the crowd, Jack effortlessly brushed his puny fellow citizens aside and stormed into the church. The pews were completely filled with spectators- council members, reporters, policemen off duty, the idly curious, entire families bearing popcorn, invalids who had been carried in; others, including souvenir hawkers, sat or squatted in the aisles. Undaunted, he slogged forward as though wading through a thigh-deep human river, and soon found himself at the edge of a clearing which surrounded the altar. A mass of enraged and battered citizens lay in his wake, screaming at him in a babble of different languages. They were yelling in Chinese, or Vietnamese, Tagalog, Farsi, Catalan, Czech, Swahili, Yiddish, Greek or whatever: it was all non-white noise to Jack Folsom.

Maggie Sullivan, standing behind the altar with her hands on her hips, groaned as she watched Jack approach; she barely suppressed a roll of the eyes at his usual nonchalant mayhem. Jack the dim-witted giant. Just being a scion of the Folsom family gave him a bloated sense of self-importance. He came from- how did he put it- the "original Americans," and acted as though that were comparable to arriving in America aboard the Mayflower. But unlike the Pilgrims, Jack Folsom had contributed nothing to nation-building; on the contrary, his sense of entitlement and careless behavior had undermined the image of the United States of America. After all, the Quarantine Zone was populated by outcasts from all the former nations of the world, not just the USA. They all hated the PWE with a passion and clung fiercely to the hope of one day reviving their respective nations. But many bristled at Jack's arrogance, which resurrected an even greater hatred, fueled by memories of the United States prior to the War of Unification; Jack Folsom reminded them constantly of why the PWE had been created in the first place. It was fortunate, thought Maggie, that only a few in the Quarantine Zone knew of the clandestine USA Collective, which operated independently of the general nationalism- or "Dis-unification"- movement.

In addition to the damage he had done, Maggie found Jack distasteful on a personal level, and had worked steadily to marginalize him. Everyone knew that he indulged in recreational therapeptides whenever he could get them. She had also whispered certain untruths to the Berkeley Grand Council, regarding Jack's "problem" with fermented products of freeze-dried corn and, under its influence, a tendency toward deviant sexual practices. The Council, composed of self-righteous individuals sworn to political correctness, had immediately fired Jack from his proud position as Vistaville's representative to the Council. But for Maggie, whose penchance for extreme thoroughness was widely known, that would not suffice.

"Hey Maggie! Come all the way from Berkeley," Jack stated the obvious, his large paw raised in a tentative greeting. Even big Jack felt intimidated in Maggie's presence. A short, stocky woman dressed in faded denim overalls and mud-stained boots, Maggie kept a modest appearance which belied the extent of her influence. After the actions of the Berkeley Grand Council two years earlier, she had further diminished Jack (without a whimper of protest by the Vistaville Committee, he noted sourly), moving him by fiat from his inherited seat on the Committee to a position described by a mere footnote in the Vistaville Charter: Sergeant of Provisions. Ha! Caretaker of the corn! Head gatherer of roots and berries! It's a key role, she had reassured him with her best straight face, and for that he despised her to this day. Still, as Chief of the Berkeley Grand Council, she had power; he also knew that the hopes of the secret USA Collective rested on her, and a few others. At least for now he would co-operate, but one day soon, he would show his true colors.

Maggie decided to ignore Jack's hollow greeting, but remained keenly aware of everyone else in the church. This was highly unusual- in fact, it was preposterous- to process new arrivals to the Quarantine Zone in such a public setting, but word of the Martians' arrival had leaked out days ago, and the Vistaville Committee, always pandering to their constituents, had set up this deplorable spectacle before notifying her at Berkeley. What were they running here, a circus? That's exactly what this was. Even though she had been expecting the newcomers for a week, Maggie felt quite unprepared for this encounter. She groaned again inwardly and turned to face the Martians.

* * *

Benn strained to open his eyes, but only managed to raise his eyebrows slightly. He was still sedated from his long journey in the nuclear waste transport. Behind his lids swirled blurry clouds of colors, and his whole body seemed to spin in tandem. Even when the spinning had subsided, he felt like a boat being rocked one way then another by powerful waves. Tossed by high seas with his head pinned underwater, Benn fought motion sickness. He tried to breathe, to focus on the one prominent smear of color he could see- green, straight ahead- but staring at green only made the nausea worse. The green smear was speaking softly, barely audible, but gradually he was able to distinguish words; he also identified the speaker as female. Green was addressing someone else, not Benn.

"Tell us where you're from." Green's steely voice carried authority.

"M-Mars." Another female voice, timid and tremulous. Lora?

"Mars, I see. And do you know where you are now?"

A long silence, then sadly, "No." Lora was crying, he thought.

"You know, don't you, that you have arrived in the Quarantine Zone?"

Silence again, followed by the noise of a restive crowd rustling in the surrounding darkness. Green was starting to pace back and forth.

"Why don't you answer? You must know where you are."

"I... home..." She was still crying.

"Home? No, my dear, you are far from home. Why have you been sent to the Quarantine Zone?"

"Home... fly... out... then..." Suddenly, for some reason, she giggled.

Green's voice sharpened. "What's the matter with you? Do you find this amusing? I want to know, why have you been sent here?"

Another long silence, and Green got louder: "Are you working for the PWE? Was it the PWE that sent you here?" The crowd's rustling grew louder as well.

"Tell... Rion..."

"What did you say? Did you say Rion?"

"Rion. Tell..."

"Rion is an uncommon name. Are you referring to..." Green appeared to be consulting a list. "Rion ...Rion Salkend?"

"Tell...Rion..." She giggled again.

"Rion Salkend is on our list of secondary agents of the PWE!" The crowd noise intensified. "What is your connection to Rion Salkend? The PWE did send you here, didn't they?"

"Fly out...fly out...fly out...they..." she intoned in a dreamy, sing-song way.

Benn pushed hard to clear his sensorium; the sedative was beginning to wear off. What was the matter with Lora? The injection must have caused some sort of dementia- hopefully the damage to her brain would only be temporary. But he himself felt locked in somehow, and powerless to help her. It was the sedative- Neelin's formula, Lou Hunter had said- which prevented him from projecting. Dr. Neelin! He had probably ordered Lora's injection as well, some mind-altering psychopeptide. And Dr. Neelin would not have known about the earlier injection, the one Rion Salkend gave her at Eunigen. Together, the interaction or cumulative effect of two psychopeptides in one day...

"Tell me the truth! You are working with Rion Salkend, aren't you? You are a spy of the PWE! We know all about Rion Salkend- so you might as well tell the truth." Green's voice paused.

Benn's mind had partially cleared, and he could sense that Green was bluffing about Salkend, waiting to see Lora's reaction. Green already knew that he and Lora weren't spies. But then why was she pressing on with this harsh interrogation? Benn kept his eyes shut and read the aura as best he could, but details were obscure. She seemed to enjoy tormenting Lora while at her most vulnerable- but that wasn't the only reason. It was the public exposure: an opportunity to enlarge her image as a champion of the people. Just our luck, thought Benn: sadistic, self-aggrandizing and opportunistic, another dangerous combination- this world seemed to be full of such bad combinations- and for now, she had complete control of both Lora and Benn.

"What has the PWE instructed you to do in the Quarantine Zone?"

He forced one eye open just a crack, and now could make out the indistinct figure of Green; he was surprised to find her dressed like a farmer in a children's picture book. With one hand she gestured vigorously in a direction off to Benn's right; the other hand rested on her hip.

"Your mission has failed! The PWE has no authority here." That wasn't true; all inhabitants of the Quarantine Zone- including this Green person- were essentially prisoners of the PWE. With one eye on the crowd, Green pounded her palm with a fist, like a good politician: *We will search out and eliminate the spies among us. No stone will be left unturned.*" Scattered, anxious applause broke out from Benn's left side, and he could see the shadowy crowd shifting uncomfortably in their wooden pews at the thought, for better or worse, of a witch-hunt in their divided village. He then became aware of his own discomfort, his wrists and ankles bound tightly to a cold metal chair.

"Lies! Lie lie lie lie lie LIES!" This outburst, followed by a sobbing sort of laughter, came from his right, and Benn worked his leaden eyes in that direction.

And there he saw- no more than two meters away- Lora, tied to a chair, just as he was. Her eyes were closed, and her chin rested on her chest, which rose and fell rhythmically. To Benn's surprise, she seemed to be fast asleep. The merciless Green, quieting the crowd with a gracious wave of her hand, resumed her interrogation.

"What was your mission? Tell me!" Lora was still sleeping. So who had Green been questioning, who was she shouting at? Benn stretched his head forward and squinted beyond Lora. By craning his neck, he could now see a third chair, to which a tall, disheveled woman was bound, quite askew. She was still- it was hard to tell- either sobbing or laughing, in either case out of control. Her brilliant red hair had fallen forward and obscured her face, but Benn didn't need to see the green-tinted irises and twin Aresite cheek studs to recognize the woman: it was Nema.

The sudden movement of Benn's head caught Maggie Sullivan's attention, and she turned quickly, like a snake catching sight of a mouse in the corner of its vision.

"Good! You're with us now. Benn Marr: you, I have been expecting. Along with your friend, Lora Wheeler." At the sound of her name, Lora stirred and opened her eyelids slightly.

With both arms raised, Maggie turned to address the crowded church pews, like a prairie preacher bringing good tidings. "People of Vistaville, fellow citizens: as Chief of the Berkeley Grand

Council, I have received intelligence that these two are not spies, but fugitives from the PWE. In fact, they come from Tharsis Colony on Mars; they are Americans, and therefore our friends. A PWE transport left this other woman unannounced at a border checkpoint, which aroused our suspicion. I will pursue her interrogation at a more secure location in Berkeley." Like a growling stomach denied food at the last minute, the crowd rumbled with disappointment.

Jack Folsom suddenly spoke up: "I come from original Americans too!" He stepped forward, his large hand raised hopefully.

"Not now, Jack. I have work to do. As soon as these two are fully awake, they will come with me to Berkeley; these things are not for public consumption- and 'public' includes you." Jack scowled at Maggie, and the crowd, having waited so patiently for a spectacle, a quick trial, a burning at the stake, hissed and booed. Ignoring them (the Circus is over now folks, go home), Maggie Sullivan stooped between Benn and Lora, and said quietly, "My name is Maggie Sullivan. Dr. Neelin sent you to us, along with a warning: he says you have the ability to read minds, Benn. We can't have that sort of thing here- not yet- so we'll be keeping you on a mental suppressant. Anyway, I do hope you understand that we're on the same side." But Benn doubted Maggie's sincerity; for one thing, he and Lora were still tied to their chairs.

Berkeley, the administrative capital of the Quarantine Zone, may actually have been a far less secure place to continue the interview: the PWE had a number of known- and probably many more unknown- listening posts within the city, and certainly had infiltrated the local committees, agencies and bureaus- not to mention the Grand Council itself. In fact, Berkeley had overt ties to the PWE: a century ago, after the Great War of Unification, the majority of Berkeley residents had actually welcomed with open arms the creation of one world government. The PWE had rewarded their support (and also incidentally recognized that the first United Nations had been born right across the bay) by establishing Berkeley as the capital- but had still enclosed it within a prison zone.

Maggie gave this long explanation in a cheerful voice-sounding more like their tour guide than captor- as they rode into town on a questionably reliable farm truck, barely able to cruise at a steady two meters above the road. Benn pressed hard to decipher her true agenda: what was she planning for him and for Lora? The last injection of the sedative, given at the beginning of their journey from the Sierras, now prevented him from reading her thoughts. He made several vain attempts to project himself out of body. Frustrated, he finally had to ask aloud, "Why bring us here, then, to hostile territory? Aren't we surrounded by informants?"

"It's the last place they'll look for us- the PWE figures they know just about everything that happens here, so they look elsewhere for conspiracy. In fact, there's a funny story, Benn. A few years ago, someone- some PWE spy- leaked the name of our American resistance group. Since we'll be working with you soon, you might as well know, it's called the USA Collective. And based on that- just the name, Benn- the PWE swooped down on a small community north of here, a small town formerly called Colusa. Col for Collective, U-S-A, get it? The mighty forces of the PWE against defenseless Colusa. They mounted a full military assault on that simple farming town, met no resistance of course, and wiped most everyone out within seconds. The unlucky survivors, though, the PWE tortured for days, and naturally they had to make up some secrets to spill. Which led to other towns being destroyed. Ha! All of it just because one town was crazy enough to have that name!"

That's a funny story? thought Benn with a shiver. He abruptly switched his attention over to Maggie's driver- mostly because he found Maggie's abrasiveness hard to take, but also because the driver had started to moan softly. He was seated alone in the front compartment- Maggie had planted herself between Lora and Benn in the back seat of the truck- and his unblinking eyes had stared suspiciously at them in the rearview mirror for much of the journey. The driver's jaw muscles twitched under sunken cheeks, and his arthritic fingers gripped the steering wheel harder as the moaning grew steadily louder.

"Just ignore Stefan," said Maggie in a stage whisper. "He often goes on like this. Stefan's family lived in Colusa, and they were all wiped out by the PWE attack- did I tell you that the survivors were all tortured for days?"

206

Yes, with gusto, thought Benn. He glanced at Lora, who was staring out her window as they passed a deserted playground, then an untended park bordered by buildings badly in need of repair. In front of these, a half-dozen men loitered without purpose or interaction. One, missing his right leg, leaned on a crutch; one slept in a doorway; four others sat on the curb with their heads bowed. Out his own window, Benn spied an older woman crouched on the litter-strewn sidewalk, muttering to herself. Her face was badly swollen and blotchy, as were her bare feet, which protruded from a pair of tattered blue overalls.

"Where are the children?" asked Lora suddenly. "I haven't seen a single child since entering the city. Are they kept indoors for some reason?"

"There are no children, Lora- not in Berkeley, nor in the entire Quarantine Zone," Maggie answered casually, as though merely noting the absence of elephants, polar bears or other extinct species. "We haven't had a live birth here in over fifteen years."

Lora listened in stunned silence as Maggie continued, "There's no official explanation for this, but to the Grand Council it's quite obvious that the PWE doesn't want our population, and the political beliefs of the Quarantined Class, to proliferate. We suspect that the PWE is adding some sort of toxin to our environment- water, air, maybe in the corn they send from the Midwestern Quadrant- in order to inhibit fertility."

Lora was aghast. "They're trying to wipe out dissidents by forced sterilization? And to do it secretly! That's inhumane, a crime against humanity! But you must have medical people: can't they identify the toxin and neutralize it, or at least create a therapeptide to correct the defect?"

"A therapeptide? Wouldn't that be simple! My dear, do you think you are back at YaleConn, or in New York Metropol? Believe me, the PWE does not supply the Quarantine Zone with technology to practice twenty-second century medicine. Do you see those people in the park? They're victims of disease- both mental and physical- and we have virtually no means of diagnosing and treating them. Most have been badly scarred by psychopeptides, courtesy of the PWE. We provide food and shelter for them, but little else. For example, your friend Nema, who was dumped by the PWE at the border, will be placed in a housing complex just like that one."

207

Maggie pointed at a faceless gray building in the next block. "She'll be free to wander the city- and wander she will- like these people here. But the damage to her mind can never be repaired."

Stefan, whose moaning had stopped as soon as their conversation shifted from the horrific atrocities at Colusa to the more subtle atrocities taking place in Berkeley, steered the truck along ancient, winding roads upward into a range of coastal hills overlooking a shimmering, wind-ruffled bay. A deep fog bank was blowing in from the west. At this considerable altitude, Benn and Lora spotted the truncated remains of two perpendicular bridges which had once spanned the bay, but now consisted of a pair of long stumps extending from the ruins of the city and disappearing below the choppy waves. So sad, thought Lora: it looks as though the city is reaching out with mangled arms, pleading for help.

"That's San Francisco," said Maggie, without any of Lora's sentimentality. "At least that's what remains of San Francisco- after the Great War, the city was so severely damaged that the few surviving residents had to abandon it. The PWE could have rebuilt, but decided to leave San Francisco in ruins, as an example to others: a grand monument to the futility of resistance. Ha! It's a giant obscene gesture directed at the entire Quarantine Zone, if you ask me!" She suddenly raised her right fist, index and little fingers protruding in the coarse manner of ill-bred teenagers; Lora frowned and glanced at Benn, who had stopped paying attention a while back.

The truck jerked to a halt, and Stefan opened his window, then strained to reach a sensor, which Benn could see was hidden deep in the bushes next to an anonymous-looking, but very heavy wooden gate. At first nothing happened, drawing a string of muttered curses from Stefan, but the gate finally creaked open on his fourth try. He followed a dirt road downhill and parked on the edge of a broad flagstone terrace, facing an ornate two-story mansion. At least two centuries old, thought Benn- large cracks in moss-stained whitewashed walls, intricately carved wooden front door, faded red Spanish tile roof, surrounded on three sides by an old-growth forest. A dilapidated shed was barely visible among the trees behind the mansion. Maggie followed Lora out of the truck and headed toward a low wall at the far end of the terrace. As Benn climbed out the other side, glad to stretch his legs at last, he caught a breeze carrying a scent which suddenly brought to mind...

"Dr. Neelin."

Maggie whirled around. "What did you say, Benn?"

"It's that smell in the air. I just thought of Dr. Neelin. He hosted a wine tasting at Mellon College- it seems so long ago. One of the wines he served that night came from the Australian District, and it had a distinctive smell of..." Benn took a moment to recall, "Eucalyptus?"

"Oh, the eucalyptus. Yes, we have lots of those trees here in the hills." Maggie made a mental note: That showed some insight, connecting the two smells, connecting Dr. Neelin to the safe house: we'd better check the dose of his sedative. She led them to the wall, which stood at the edge of a steep, rocky cliff. Far below, the flat wasteland of Berkeley stretched alongside the bay, and the ghostlike silhouette of San Francisco crouched in the fog just beyond.

Maggie said, "Actually, it's funny, but you know what reminds me of Australia, Benn?" There's something else funny? Wasn't the Colusa story funny enough, wondered Benn.

Maggie went on, "It's not just the eucalyptus trees. It's the whole damn Quarantine Zone! Do you know the history of the Australian District? In its early days, Australia's population was dominated by prison inmates- all the worst, the most incorrigible, criminals from Ireland and England were isolated at a safe distance from the homeland, on a huge island colony in a faraway sea. Australia was one giant prison. And that's exactly what we have here in the Quarantine Zone, Benn: we live in a prison colony of the Pan-World Electorate."

Chapter Twenty

Except for meals, Benn and Lora had been locked together for over a week, inside a wood-paneled bedroom the size of Benn's tiny apartment on Tharsis. Large windows overlooked a lush, shadowy garden which lent a greenish cast to the snug, cozy interior. Under late-November overcast skies, the deep stillness of their room kept both of them in a brooding mood until almost noon. Benn's brooding took the form of frustration in his efforts to project out of body, to assess their situation and to escape. For Lora, the source of frustration was Benn himself: his transformation back to nonchalant, uncaring Benn-of-no-visible-reaction. The change was painful to her, and she blamed Benn for his seeming rejection of the complete intimacy they had shared as auras- even while acknowledging that she wasn't being quite fair. Lora realized that Benn was being restrained by a chemical suppressant, but couldn't help feeling ignored. She longed for the profound sense of mutual vulnerability which had opened up as their two auras had merged, all too briefly, in the Eunigen lab.

On one particularly snug and cozy morning, she took decisive action. Despite the closeness of their quarters, Benn had maintained a decorous level of modesty; on that morning, he was sitting on his bed, dressed in the self-laundering undergarments he had brought from Tharsis. Lora emerged from the adjacent bathroom wrapped in a short towel, hair in wet strings across her face, her eyes glazed with determination. Benn arched an eyebrow as she approached, his attention suddenly drawn to a lavender-colored birthmark on her right thigh. Lora stood facing him, and as he looked up in puzzlement, she let the towel fall to her feet.

Now *there* was a visible reaction.

* * *

Progress. That was one big step- so let's take another, Lora decided. She would clear the air about a worry that had nagged her since their escape from New York:

"Benn, can you read my mind?" she asked suddenly.

"What, right now?" They were lying pressed together in bed, so understandably Benn took Lora's question in the wrong context.

"No, not just now. Can you read my mind anytime."

"Oh. Well, only when I'm connected to the bioweb, and for a short while after disconnecting, I can hear echoes of thoughts. Remember- at Eunigen- I found that if I stood perfectly still, I could impact other auras, but that fades quickly. I'd have to project out of body again in order to..."

"I want you to promise me something, Benn. Promise you won't read my mind without my knowledge."

"But why? I thought we had gotten comfortable..."

"Really, Benn, for someone with such a gift, you're incredibly dense! Don't you care about privacy, or personal space? And that includes my privacy- in case you've stopped thinking of me as a separate individual."

Benn fell silent. Personal space. He thought of the students' auras in the Harkness courtyard steering clear of one another, their aversion to contact. Distance must be maintained. And yet he had learned, just this morning, that closeness was a good thing. He glanced at Lora's lavender birthmark- yes, closeness was incredibly good. There had to be a balance. He began to ponder the optimal ratio between closeness and distance... and Lora, once again mistaking his thoughtful silence for mere indifference, turned away disappointed.

"Forget it, Benn. Just promise me." So he did, with a casual shrug which only reinforced Lora's impression that Benn simply didn't care.

In any case, it was a moot point, since Benn's efforts to project or to read thoughts went nowhere. They had not seen Maggie for almost a week. Promptly at noon every day, Maggie's assistant Evlin administered Benn's injection, then marched them to the dining room for lunch, where she left them under the watch of a security man. They appreciated her departure, not least because the lack of adequate dental care in the Quarantine Zone had left Evlin with faintly sour, bacterial breath. In addition, Evlin provided no

211

explanations and always seemed angry for no apparent reason; everything spoken to Benn and Lora came abruptly in the form of commands, and the other staff members had apparently been forbidden to interact with them. When they entered the dining room with Evlin, several workmen nearby hurriedly gathered their belongings and returned to their duties- whatever those might be.

"Benn, what do you think Maggie's planning? What does she want from us?" Lora asked apprehensively. They were by themselves, finishing their simple lunch in the capacious and ornate dining room, a remnant of a more gracious era. Its entire western side was built of glass, and through the surrounding forest appeared a filtered view of the bay.

"I can't tell," Benn replied. Something to do with Star and Stripe, presumably. He had told Lora about that underground organization, and its goal of restoring the United States to power, but had omitted details of his conversations with Dr. Neelin and Alden Hayes, as well as the overnight stay at Mellon College; Benn felt an unspoken obligation to keep parts of the story confidential, which would have pleased even the suspicious May Acheson. As he pointed out to Lora, Star and Stripe, through Lou Hunter, had kidnapped them and turned them over to Maggie- but what was in store for them next?

"Maggie's left us alone for so long that something big must be happening," Benn continued. "And those workers have been busy all week, going in and out of the storage shed behind the house."

"Storage shed? What could they be doing in a storage shed?"

"Besides storing things? Not much, clearly- it's quite small, on the outside. Must be an entrance to a larger structure, either below the shed or built into the hillside next to it. But what are they working on? It's all so secretive."

Lora exclaimed, "It's obviously part of the resistance against the PWE. Benn! I bet this is a safe house for that secret group Maggie mentioned: the USA Collective!" After a week of confinement, there was no damping Lora's enthusiasm.

Benn simply nodded, as Lora persisted, "Rion did predict that the Centennial of the PWE would bring about acts of rebellion: some of them violent, he told us. And remember? That V.P. of Colonial Affairs- a Russian man, I think- reported violence in

Beijing and Paris. Do you think Maggie has anything to do with those events?"

"I wouldn't be surprised."

"Then maybe the USA Collective wants to use your... you know, special abilities. You could lead an attack on the PWE, knocking out their troops with a single thought!"

Benn laughed at the image of himself, waving an American flag, strapped to the front of a tank and driven into battle against the PWE. They could blow him to bits with a Razer blast: talk about turning E Pluribus Unum on its head! "That's fairly unlikely, Lora. As far as Maggie knows, my abilities are limited to mind-reading. Don't forget, Dr. Neelin's people didn't see what happened inside the Eunigen building, so they have no idea that I can project out of body, or even deliver a punch."

"Oh, that's right." Lora trailed off and set her fork down, as Evlin had returned to the dining room and was now heading purposefully in their direction, with two heavy-set workmen right behind her.

The long ride down reminded Benn of the descent into Hydra Mine Three, but this elevator was much slower, and uncomfortably cramped. Lora, Benn and the inexplicably irate Evlin stood pressed together for over ten minutes, and fortunately Evlin was facing the door, minimizing their exposure to her exhalations. Talk about personal space, thought Benn, trying hard to keep his breathing shallow. The storage shed turned out to be the top of a very long elevator shaft, and now they were all visibly relieved to reach the bottom. The elevator opened onto a narrow platform, next to which sat a compact, box-shaped railcar on a single track. Made of a dark plastic material with transparent doors that hinged upwards, the railcar was no more than five meters long and barely accommodated the three of them.

Evlin had the controls in the front; as soon as Benn and Lora had squeezed into the back and fastened their restraints, she lowered the doors and set the railcar in motion. They entered a dark tube and rode along at a slow crawl for many minutes before emerging into a much larger tunnel. Light panels spaced along its black-stained walls, partially obscured by furry patches of moss and lichen, provided minimal illumination. As the car crossed a connection onto a perpendicular track, now heading westward, there was a loud and jarring clang. Benn, who had estimated that the ride would take, well, forever at that speed, was startled: the railcar didn't float over magnets; it actually touched the track! This was truly primitive technology: the track must have been built by Maggie's people using crude, salvaged materials, and carefully hidden from the watchful eye of the PWE.

The car now mercifully accelerated, and a rhythmic rattling noise filled the passenger cabin. Benn had to shout his question at Evlin: "Did the USA Collective build this tunnel?" Evlin glanced sharply back at him, but said nothing. What did he know about the USA Collective? Maggie had assured her that these two were not spies, but Evlin wasn't sure at all: that was just the sort of question a spy would ask!

As they proceeded to the west, Benn reached his own conclusions before long: he could make out four parallel tracks on the wide tunnel floor. Their tiny carriage clattered along the first rail, so the other three were superfluous: in fact, they were remnants of a pre-existing train system built before the PWE came to power, over a century ago. After a kilometer or so, he saw the wreckage of a much larger train, overturned onto the third and fourth tracks and surrounded by debris blocking most of the tunnel.

Then suddenly came a whisper of voices! Or had he imagined it, against the track noise? Benn closed his eyes and focused: the suppressant they were giving him must have lost some of its effect, because he felt a familiar, haunting sensation, recalling that dank tunnel under the Branford warehouse. He was still unable to project, but could definitely hear a rising murmur, punctuated by shouts and screams; thankfully this time there was no vision of people aflame. The noises he heard now were echoes of past events, their sounds recorded in... a large body of water. The tunnel must be crossing under the bay.

The suppressant was definitely wearing off. He let his thoughts roam in all directions, seeking a vision to add to the voices, which now faded as they passed by the wreckage. Eyes tightly closed, Benn pushed to project out of body. He succeeded only in reaching a boundary, where he could feel the beckoning presence of the Bioweb, but could not fully connect with it. All around him was pitch black, except- Benn focused harder- there! In the tunnel, not far behind them, a faint gray light, barely distinguishable in the darkness. The gray light kept a steady distance and moved purposefully back and forth in a way that reminded Benn of the auras he had seen before.

Someone was following them.

As the track came to an abrupt end, the remnants of a large sign on the wall announced their arrival at a station: EM ARC DERO. The significance of these three words was a mystery to Lora, and she looked inquiringly at Benn, who, for some reason, kept staring back into the tunnel from which they had just emerged. There was no point in asking the hostile and suspicious Evlin what the sign meant. But the condition of the station needed no explanation; it was a shambles, with fallen columns leaning against fractured walls, most of the platform missing, and a huge gaping hole in the roof, exposing the subterranean station to the overcast sky above.

They picked their way carefully up the stairway to the remnants of Market Street. There was no throughway; large sections of collapsed buildings lay on their sides, the spaces in between them clogged with jagged chunks of concrete, twisted metal beams, and shapeless, glassy masses of stone/aluminum/steel/people/plastic/sand fused together for eternity. The adjacent hillsides all looked the same; not a single street had escaped the crush of the giant falling dominoes.

For a long moment, Benn and Lora stood in silent awe at this death-mask of a city. The heat of battle must have been incredibly intense, with temperatures well over a thousand degrees. Benn imagined (or was he really) hearing the roaring collision of skyscrapers toppling against one another, and the crackle of burning wood, paper, skin and fiber. He could almost smell the explosive combustion of oil, bones, flesh, starch, sulfur: any substance whose molecules could combine with oxygen had turned incendiary. Completely callous to the horrific scene and even ignoring Benn and Lora, Evlin muttered angrily to herself as she hurried along a meandering route through the ruins, to a rough path along the waterfront. Because of global warming and subsequent flooding, a seawall had been erected long before the war, to prevent the rising water level from claiming prime bay-front real estate. Sections of this seawall had been severely damaged, forcing them to detour around wide flooded areas. At one point, they had to turn westward to higher ground, where charred stumps of former skyscrapers huddled like an encampment of the homeless. Only one building had not been completely leveled; judging by the sloped angles of its four corners, discernible as they got closer, Benn guessed that the building had originally been shaped like a four-sided pyramid, and still reached about one-third of its original height. Here they traversed a small, serene forest of redwood trees which had miraculously survived the conflagration and spread to cover several blocks.

Forced to climb in and out of deep craters, wade through algae-filled pools, and squeeze through tight gaps in the rubble, they struggled for several hours to cover the circuitous route to the southern face of what was once called Telegraph Hill, a barren, rocky promontory near the old seawall. A barely-legible sign lying on the ground indicated that they had reached the remains of Filbert Street. Benn, who had been listening intently to the surrounding water issue echoes of raging battles, stumbled along in a trance, his face locked in the fierce expression that had always frightened Jace during Waterhunts. Ever since emerging from the oasis of the redwood grove, Lora's attention had repeatedly returned to a tall white monument overlooking the cliff, the only intact structure within sight. Evlin suddenly stopped and pointed her trembling finger at the monument; it was the first time she had acknowledged their presence in over an hour.

"Look! The PWE destroyed the rest of the city, but they couldn't bring down Coit Tower!" Catching her breath, she continued but now spoke flatly, as though reciting something memorized in childhood, "Coit Tower is a good omen for us. It was built to honor the brave firefighters, who saved the city long ago. Six times, like a phoenix, San Francisco has risen from the ashes of great fires. Coit Tower survived the war, and that means, for the seventh time, San Francisco will rise again!" Eyes brimming with tears, she whirled to face Benn and Lora, who quickly glanced at one another, sharing a single thought: even the previous sullen, uncommunicative version of Evlin, to whom they had become accustomed, was preferable to this expressive version.

"Maggie says you can help us in our fight against the PWE: the war criminals who enslaved the whole world. Maggie says you'll help us bring them to justice. She says you'll help to bring back the USA. Our USA." But then her eyes and voice turned hard and sharp. "I think you're agents of the PWE. All those questions you've been asking. You won't help us: you're spying for them! But how can we really know? We need proof! We shouldn't trust you- but Maggie does. Maggie says you'll help. But you're spies! Maggie says… we need… have to trust… Maggie says… no other way." Evlin trailed off, the tears streaming down her cheeks. Then, without any warning, she spun around and ran back along the narrow path, leaving them on their own. What, no farewell or safe travels? No welcome to San Francisco? Benn shook his head and let out a soft whistle: everyone in the Quarantine Zone seemed to be possessed by one demon or another.

Although pulled away by her particular demon, Evlin had not abandoned them, after all. A very narrow door, obscured by the wreckage at the base of the hill, now opened inward, and a short, solidly muscular man with a cat-like grace stepped out into the hazy sunlight. Here was another Abe or Zak- only this version was noticeably older, perhaps by ten or fifteen years.

"I'm George," he said, with a tilt of the head, his keen eyes fixed on Benn. Like Abe and Zak, he spoke bluntly, offering no words of welcome. "Follow me, and be careful: it's dark in here." They squeezed through the door, and George led them some distance into the hill. Against the nearly-black background of the tunnel, Benn was surprised to see a faint greenish glow around George: only a millimeter wide, practically skin-tight, so he might have just been looking at reflected light.

Yet another dank tunnel, thought Benn: unfortunately, I've had too many opportunities to get used to them by now, as the rebels have a true underground movement! Soon they came to a fork in the path and surprisingly, instead of climbing up to Coit Tower as Benn had expected, they turned westward, heading directly away from Telegraph Hill. For several hundred meters, Lora stumbled along the foul-smelling tunnel with her hand cupped over her nose and mouth.

"Be careful," George repeated. "There are some steps ahead."

Steps, indeed. A long stairway led upward in a wide spiral, and they had to clamber up hundreds of uneven steps in near-darkness. This underground shelter was ancient, and had probably been constructed rather hastily. George sprang upward two steps at a time, followed by Benn, then Lora, who fixed her eyes as best she could on Benn's heels. Before long, Lora had fallen far behind, so Benn had to try and slow their ascent. He addressed the back of George's broad shoulders:

"George? I'm curious about your name. We met your... brothers, Abe and Zak."

George paused; he was not even a little winded. His eyes, glowing faintly yellow in the dark, scanned the stairwell until Lora finally caught up. "Abe, Zak and Teddy stayed in the Northeastern Quadrant. The rest of us were sent to the Quarantine Zone."

Teddy. Benn figured that Teddy might have been the unfortunate Lint Man, assigned by Dr. Neelin to protect him on his journey from Mars. An ill-fated mission, carried out to perfection, Benn noted grimly. Teddy, Abe and Zak: three oddly old-fashioned names. Wait- Teddy was another way of saying Theodore, wasn't it? Abe stood for Abraham. And Zachary might be shortened to Zak. Bits of Benn's grade-school education now filtered back to him. In defiance of mandates and warnings issued by the Mars School Board, which was based at Highland City, the Tharsis Academy- and especially Mr. Otis Walker- had continued to teach a condensed version of American history.

"George. Were you and your brothers by any chance named after presidents of the United States of America? Lincoln? Taylor? And Roosevelt?"

George replied softly, "Yes. Presidents. We were named in order of birth. My brothers are named John, Tommy, Jim, Andy, Marty, Bill, Zak, Abe..."

"Aha, I see, in order of birth. And you look a bit older than Abe and Zak, so you can't have been named after the Bushes, who would be much younger."

"No, there is no other George. I was the first-born," he answered with justifiable pride. After all, he was George Washington- the first in a line of multispecies recombinant clones created at YaleConn in the final days of the Great War. George turned back to the stairs and resumed climbing at his merciless pace: pretty impressive, thought Benn, for someone over a century old.

Chapter Twenty-One

Peter V. Annenkov, Commander of Flight Group Four, Quarantine Zone Forces of the Pan-World Electorate, smoothed his mustache needlessly; he bristled whenever Dmitri Lezhev referred to him as Comrade Peter. How was that appropriate in front of his crew- who had come from all corners of the world, from all the former nations- to give them the impression that they were serving on a Russian warship? The PWE had taken pains to give every ship an international character: they provided acupuncture in sick bay and gamelan music in the mess hall, where the crew could munch on fish and chips. Even the exit from his command deck was labeled Sortie. Yet that was how Lezhev had persisted in addressing Annenkov (at least he had given up on using the Russian form of his name, Pyotr), when briefing the officers that morning. He had flown out from New York Metropol, he said, with urgent warnings that the "authorities" had received evidence of some unspecified new weapon in the hands of the quarantined rebels. Although never on friendly terms, Annenkov had known Lezhev for several years, and suspected that these "authorities" were in fact his bosses at that center of capitalist corruption, Eunigen Corporation.

And now they had sent a shuttle to a pickup point in the Central Valley of California, as directed by Lezhev, to bring this, this creature back to his command ship. The Missing Link, Lieutenant Wu had whispered. What this man lacked in intelligence, he made up in sheer volume: he was as massive as the statue on Putin's Tomb! The giant was unshaven, disheveled, unpleasantly aromatic, and now, passively following Wu over to the data screen on the Command Deck, he tracked clumps of drying mud onto the ship's immaculate floor. Annenkov smoothed his mustache again.

"Comrade Peter," began Lezhev, not helping matters a bit, "This is Jack Folsom."

Hearing his name, Jack raised his head and looked dully around the room at a dozen unfamiliar and skeptical faces, a dozen black uniforms. They had stopped their work at various modules, just to gape at him. Jack's contact at the Nevada border had instructed him to wait at a prearranged site for the shuttle, and that was all he knew. The blond fellow sitting in the command chair with his legs primly crossed was obviously not happy to have him on board, and the other officers openly regarded him with disgust- but Jack was used to that. The well-dressed fat man standing next to the commander, on the other hand, stared at Jack the way a coyote might regard a trapped rabbit- yes, he had seen that hungry look only a month before, just before the coyote stole his rabbit.

"Jack Folsom, report!" the fat man barked.

He is like a coyote, thought Jack. "Report?" He watched the blond man uncross his legs impatiently, then focused his attention on the other. "You're the one in charge? All right, but don't forget what I was promised..."

"Yes, yes! We don't have time for that now. You were instructed to follow the two captives when they left the Sierras: what did you learn, Comrade Jack?"

"You mean the Martians? Yeah, well, I followed them in a truck from Vistaville, and they were going slow- taking a tour, I guess. I could stay a few cars back without losing them, so that wasn't too hard. Until I came to the Berkeley limits, where there's no traffic at all. I figured Maggie's driver would spot me soon after that, so when they started up into the hills, I turned off and set up a tent at the bottom of a canyon."

"And who is this Maggie?"

"Maggie Sullivan."

Lezhev consulted his da-disc. "Chief of the Berkeley Grand Council."

"Yup." Jack rolled his eyes. "Maggie the big chief. The Berkeley Grand Council was set up by you folks after the war, you know, to enforce the peace. But that's not all they do! What you don't know..."

Jack played his trump card slowly, the better to savor it: "What you need to know... is that Maggie Sullivan doesn't just work for the Berkeley Grand Council. She is also one of the leaders in that rebel group, the group of original Americans? The USA Collective?"

There- Jack had said it! As long promised, he had now shown his true colors, and Maggie's downfall was all but guaranteed. He watched the two men exchange quick glances. Now

221

he had their rapt attention, maybe they would be more respectful of who he was and what he knew. Pleased with his newfound importance, Jack straightened out of his habitual slouch before continuing: "The USA Collective keeps some sort of a safe house up in the Berkeley hills. That's where they plan their operations, hide agents, transport them underground, all kinds of activities. Since I couldn't follow Maggie in my truck, it took me a while to find it."

"Where is this safe house, and how did you locate it?" At a gesture from his commander, Lieutenant Wu brought up a large map of the Berkeley area on the wall screen.

As if recounting a dream, Jack now spoke more hesitantly. "I used those new shots. The vials you sent me after the Martians arrived. They're amazing, better than anything I've tried before: I could close my eyes and actually move out of my body, seriously! Like my mind was floating. But once floating, it was hard to control my direction, and first I had to teach myself how to steer."

Move out of body? *Mind floating*? What insanity were they listening to? Annenkov, completely baffled, glared at Lezhev, who kept a straight face.

Jack pressed on, "I floated up the hill and searched in all the old houses, one at a time. Most of them were empty, unoccupied for years. It didn't take long to go through a neighborhood, but those shots only last a short time, so every day I had to call off the search after an hour or two. And did you know that going back into my body would be so painful? It was so rough that I couldn't leave again until the next day! That's why it took me a week to find the two Martians. They were kept locked up in this old mansion, a couple of canyons over." He indicated a location on the map.

"Did you say they were locked up?"

"By Maggie and her assistant- don't know the assistant's name, but man, she was even tougher than Maggie. Ran around like a maniac, until she got mad- then watch out! There were also about a dozen workmen or security guys, and they were all scared of her."

"What did you do when you found them?"

"It was lucky I did. They were just getting ready to leave, the two Martians and Maggie's assistant." Lieutenant Wu made some notations in a data-disc as Jack described the hidden elevator in the rear of the house, the train they had taken through the old subway tunnel crossing under the bay. "I followed them into the city, but then moving forward suddenly got a lot harder. Even in the tunnel, it felt like something was pushing me back."

Lezhev stiffened. "Pushing you back? What do you mean?"

"Like walking into a strong wind. You had to push forward. When we came out the other side of the bay, I could only follow them a short while before the shot began to wear off again, and I couldn't keep pushing. So I turned around- but not before I saw them stop at the bottom of a hill. That's where Maggie's assistant left the two Martians." Wu changed the map, and Jack indicated his route along the Embarcadero.

Lezhev stared at the map. There was a familiar name, from the days of the historic siege of San Francisco, in 2096. He suddenly lost all interest in the tedious meanderings of Jack Folsom.

"They have a hidden base on Telegraph Hill! This may be a huge catch! But Comrade Peter, you will approach our target very slowly: it is critical that we take Benn Marr completely by surprise."

"I am Protem Two," the slender, white-haired humanoid introduced itself to Benn and Lora, who were perched precariously on a wobbly wooden plank in a barren, windowless room. Benn estimated that they had climbed almost to the top of a hill he had observed earlier, lying a considerable distance to the west of Coit Tower. Protem Two had been waiting for them in this room. "For the past 85.2 years," Protem continued in its androgynous voice, "I have served as President of the United States of America."

Lora gasped. "Eighty-five years?" Benn stifled the question that immediately popped into his Under Mind, regarding presidential term limits. It was a much better idea to ask, instead, "Protem Two? So what happened to Protem One?" Maggie Sullivan, standing next to the president with one hand behind her back, shifted her weight impatiently. Benn's Under Mind had another amusing idea: as the president spoke, Maggie barely moved her lips, like a ventriloquist working her dummy. Was Maggie running a puppet government? Ba-da-*Bing*.

"My predecessor Protem was destroyed. 8979323. By blanket cyber-attack. 9298752491. Launched by the Pan-World

223

Electorate against the Quarantine Zone. 0112358132134. The remnants of Protem's files were emergently transferred to Protem Two. 594720386."

Maggie cut in. "Over forty percent of its memory was lost, but we saved many important government records, historical and cultural data, state secrets, you name it. Fortunately, our scientists down in San Jose who were responsible for Protem had a back-up system, but even that was corroded by the PWE's powerful pan-virus."

"But why is the data-bank so important, now that you're all prisoners in the Quarantine Zone?" asked Lora.

Maggie reddened. "Because we don't plan to remain prisoners forever! Protem Two carries the framework for the new US government, the blueprints we'll need in the years following Dis-unification!"

"File 84229. File ROSS. File Berlin. 74211786."

"Um, how reliable do you think Protem's records are, Maggie?" asked Benn.

"There are problems with spontaneity, random memory popping up, as you can see. The glitches come up whenever it draws on the memories of the original Protem; all data acquired over the past eighty-two years is intact. But Protem is not just a storehouse of records. Dozens of intelligence reports come in daily from Beijing, from Europe, New York- from our agents embedded in PWE centers all over the world. Protem synthesizes vast amounts of data, detects patterns and connections nobody else would notice- in other words, sees the big picture. In fact, Protem alerted us to the fact that Eunigen was importing you from Mars."

"File M463," said Protem in a confiding way, tilting its head toward Benn.

Maggie groaned. "Yes, File M463. It keeps mentioning that file, but refuses to elaborate, or even give a hint as to the contents. Probably just another confabulation, like some of its other spontaneous statements."

"Protem, what is File M463?" ventured Benn.

"I will open File M463 for you, Benn Marr," replied Protem, and Maggie's jaw dropped.

Protem spoke smoothly now, without any spontaneous interruptions. "Reports from Tharsis One, and later from New

Haven, indicate that your genetic code enables you to decipher, or read, energy signatures in your environment. This is an ability of great potential use. Ever since your arrival on Earth, CIA has followed you closely."

"Wait, Protem. Did you say the CIA?" Maggie interjected. "By CIA, do you mean the old Central Intelligence Agency? That damn-scary company of spies and assassins?" Clandestine operations carried out by the CIA against so many of the dissolved nations- and their aggrieved citizens, now living in the Quarantine Zone- remained a major stumbling block in building group trust. The Berkeley Grand Council had worked especially hard to reassure these suspicious multinationals that the CIA was indeed gone, and would never be resurrected after their respective nations were restored.

"Yes, Maggie. The core of CIA never disbanded, even when the PWE dissolved the US government. Some of the 'agents' to whom you referred- the agents we allowed you knowledge of- are indeed independent contractors working toward Dis-unification. But the majority of our agents operate covertly under the aegis of CIA, and they are unknown to you."

"Why wouldn't you tell me about something as important as the CIA?" Maggie sputtered. "As Chief of the Berkeley Grand Council, I should have been told!"

She added sarcastically, "And by the way, I also run a little organization called the USA Collective. You've heard of it? It's a group of dedicated patriots. People who place themselves in serious danger every day, for a noble cause. As you seem to have forgotten, we both serve the same purpose, which is to return the United States of America to its former glory!"

Benn imagined the Battle Hymn of the Republic playing in the background as Protem listened patiently to Maggie's flag-waving speech. "You have inadequate security clearance, Maggie," was Protem's simple and devastating answer. "But now that Benn Marr is present, I will speak about CIA and File M463." As Maggie looked ready to explode, Protem took a more conciliatory tack. "Maggie, your people have been very helpful to us indeed. The USA Collective, by gathering intelligence at the borders and in the urban areas of the Quarantine Zone, has successfully distracted the PWE from our true efforts."

This explanation failed to assuage her. Maggie could hardly form the words: "Dis... distract the PWE? You mean we're... we're... a *decoy?*"

"Decoy: yes, that is an apt term," replied Protem matter-of-factly. "As I said, your group has been most useful. For example, informing the PWE about the existence of the subversive USA Collective resulted in a diversion of their armed forces away from San Francisco and the peninsula. We planted their first suspicions that the rebellion was based in Colusa."

"*You* leaked the information about us, about the USA Collective? But then the PWE destroyed Colusa and the surrounding towns because of you! The carnage and torture...all of that was because of you."

Watching this exchange, Benn felt increasingly sorry for Maggie. Colusa wasn't quite the "funny story" she had shared with them. And her central role in the campaign to restore the USA turned out to be marginal at best. Under Mind had jokingly suggested a puppet government, but what Maggie ran was much worse, and she was now being stripped of her power piece by piece, diminishing right before their eyes. It also occurred to him that Maggie could not be allowed to return to the USA Collective, now that she knew the truth about the CIA. And indeed, George had gradually positioned himself in front of the only exit. This was all part of Protem's plan, of course, now that Benn had arrived.

"The destruction of Colusa was unfortunate but necessary," Protem explained to Benn and Lora, without any semblance of remorse. He stopped addressing Maggie altogether. "The vital networks and control center for CIA remain hidden along the Peninsula. As far as the PWE is aware, only roving bands of homeless scavengers live between the ruins of San Francisco and San Jose. But in reality there is an extensive community there, many reassigned from other parts of the world: receiving intelligence, conducting research, building equipment for the war ahead." Benn pictured Maggie, "reassigned" to some underground data-processing unit in San Jose.

"File M463 was created years ago, when our source at Eunigen Corporation first alerted us to a covert project on Mars- a project involving the mental ability to read environmental energy signatures. We intercepted company memoranda in which your

226

name and location appeared. CIA has several operatives remaining at Tharsis Colony, and they monitored your activities up to the time of your departure." Operatives? Benn suddenly thought of Bry Yelic, his school principal.

Protem continued, "The agent assigned to accompany you on your journey died by accident on Mars, so we lost contact temporarily, but simply re-attached at YaleConn. Although the details are unclear, the PWE appears to have plans for you as well- so we extracted you emergently to the Quarantine Zone for your own safety. As you know, we have been suppressing your telepathic ability with a psychopeptide up to this point. You may have noticed over the past two days that we are now letting the suppressant wear off, so that we can begin the next phase."

It was true: Benn had begun to sense Maggie's green aura again, and Lora's familiar presence next to him was unmistakable. He looked over at George, who stood in the shadowy doorway, and saw that he had been correct before: a light greenish glow did surround him. The ability to see an aura while still conscious was surprising and new; his abilities must have continued to evolve, even while suppressed by drugs. George's brothers resembled him in almost every way- but unlike Abe and Zak, George possessed an aura. It stood to reason: George was the first soldier created from recombinant DNA, not a clone. Which raised another question: since Benn was a clone, why did he have an aura, the energy he was able to project? It had to be his Martian DNA, which…

Protem, noting Benn's drifting attention, gave its voice a ringing, metallic edge and abruptly interrupted Benn's ruminations. "Benn Marr, CIA has brought you here to undergo complete analysis. The first step in this analysis is to measure your ability to read energy signatures, and to determine its strategic implications for the resistance movement."

Startled, Benn looked up. How would the measurement of his ability be taken, and its strategic implications determined? These sounded like passive procedures, but so was having one's teeth pulled. And what would be the second step in this "complete analysis"? Why had Maggie called the CIA "damn-scary"? Lora squeezed his forearm tightly, while Maggie Sullivan glanced around the sealed room. She made eye contact with George, who turned his head from side to side, crossed his arms and showed no sign of budging from the exit.

Professor Neelin added a generous pinch of salt to the lovely stew of root vegetables simmering on his stove. The dignified sweetness of parsnips, carrots, and onions: three-part harmony, in parallel with the strains of a Bach Cantata drifting in from his living room. Add textural overtones: the pillowy comfort of soft-cooked potatoes contrasting with the mild firmness of beets. Ah, nuances! Earthy, seductive perfumes of cumin, coriander and cardamom. The challenge of cayenne and paprika. A distraction of lemon zest. Magnificent.

You really should watch the salt, he reminded himself- but the cautionary thought passed as quickly as a false alarm ringing in a distant corridor. Hypertension, vascular disregulation, auto-inflammation, endocrine imbalance: what did those matter, in this context? The stew was a masterpiece, destined for an important dinner with the Senior Fellows of Mellon College- blood pressure was several levels of concern beneath that. Now, what about the wine? Neelin glanced at the snow flurries outside his kitchen window, the heavily bundled students hurrying along High Street, a Campus Police car pulling over to the icy sidewalk. A red, certainly: full-bodied, warming, with peppery spice to highlight the stew, low in intellectual gravity, perhaps, but high in immediate gratification. He smiled at the thought. Grenache would be perfect. Yes, a Garnacha from the Spanish District- algo muy especial, verdad? There were only a few old bottles of Garnacha remaining in his cellar three stories down, but why not- they probably should be drunk up, now that their youthful tannins had melted away.

The Senior Fellows of Mellon College- also Directors of Star and Stripe- were gathering that evening to discuss recent developments and next steps. Benn Marr had made it safely to Maggie Sullivan, and she would be delivering him to Protem Two very soon, if not already. He would help the movement immeasurably, what with his stunning powers of perception- could he really read thoughts in detail? And of course Benn would eagerly co-operate: he was a sensible, if reticent, fellow who surely saw that their cause was right. Perhaps he could listen in on high-level PWE meetings. Or help with interrogations. Yes, reading thoughts would be an improvement over the barbaric interrogation process still practiced by the CIA. Doubtless hundreds of PWE captives worldwide had been tortured: justified as a necessity of war, of course, but nevertheless a point of severe contention among the Directors. Neelin shuddered in distaste at the concept of torture, but nowhere in his thoughts was the possibility that Benn himself might soon face the same process.

He gave the stew a final stir, carefully turned off the stove, took a wicker wine basket from his pantry, and donned a comfortable pair of leather slippers kept by the front door. Life as Most Senior Fellow was good, undeniably, and yet he held an image in his mind of a peaceful retirement in the wine country of far Northern California- if only it weren't in the Quarantine Zone. The classic vineyard a hundred and fifty years ago would have been on a mountaintop overlooking the Napa Valley, but over the past century that had become too hot and dry, thanks to global climate change; the southernmost latitude suitable for the cultivation of cabernet sauvignon- or any variety of vitis vinifera- lay on the upper slopes of Mt. Shasta. Still, far-northern California was a beautiful area. Neelin hummed with contentment as he opened his front door.

A campus policeman, obviously in poor condition, was laboring heavily up the last few steps to his landing. Neelin recognized the man as head of security, often seen stalking around the Old Campus- and hadn't his picture been on a poster denouncing drug abuse in the YaleConn community? His name was Haley, or Halsey, something like that. He waited patiently for the cop to pass by, but instead, Halsey stopped at his door.

"Dr. Neelin?" he asked in between gulps of air. "I'm. Torch Halsey. Security. Have to ask you. To come with me, sir. Routine questioning. Recent events on campus."

Ah, thought Neelin, his wicker basket dropping to the floor. Here at last: inevitable, really. He closed his eyes. Perhaps the dream of retiring to Northern California wasn't that farfetched, after all.

Chapter Twenty-Two

Leader Chou Xia-Yu had a lot on his plate. Literally, the stir-fried vegetables and synthetic protein gel (it looks like pink tofu, he sniffed) piled on brown rice was much more than he could eat for lunch. But a dozen issues, inquiries, schemes, plans, tasks, and pending outcomes- each one requiring his undivided attention- currently competed for space on his crowded plate. The China Zone Committee on Global Warming would begin a two-week conference at the Forbidden City today, coinciding with a PWE Council vote on the continuation of global population reduction. The development of nuclear fusion plants a half-century ago had substantially slowed, but not halted, global warming. The polluting activities of over ten billion humans, many felt, were largely to blame, so strict birth limits were enforced; how fortunate that the Great War of Unification, along with its ensuing century-long complications, had already reduced the world population by 13.6 percent.

There was, of course, zero population growth in the Quarantine Zones in North America, Eastern Europe, and Southeast Asia. Elsewhere, the average life expectancy had increased over the past three decades of theragenomic advances to an astonishing 107 years, but that was supposedly a good thing, was it not? Should medical support be withdrawn past the age of 99? Chou made a small amendment to his pre-vote address to the PWE Council.

He turned his attention to bulletins reporting violent protests and acts of sabotage worldwide, on the centennial of the PWE. Over two hundred such events in just the past month! He recalled with rage the bombing last month, killing his loyal chief of staff, along with his good friend General Hugo Respighi and two aides, right outside this very building! Posted anonymous messages had then claimed that Comrade Respighi had been responsible for certain atrocities in the Mideast Zone, and that the bombing was meant to avenge his innocent victims. There had been numerous examples of such outrageous propaganda, seeking to justify acts of pure terrorism. These were tragedies re-written as historical fiction.

Benighted reactionaries, ignoring the great tidal flow of history! Unification of the human race was mankind's destiny, not the mutually destructive agendas of national governments, the exploitation of colonies, or the oppression of entire continents by expanding empires. One group, whether ethnic, political or religious; whether a tribe, a nation, or a civilization; would make advances on various fronts, only to see those advances destroyed by the next group. True, the PWE itself had been compared to an oppressive empire, but that was unavoidable in the first two or three centuries of establishing a truly unified human race: a frictionless and efficient engine which would allow mankind to achieve its full potential.

During this transitional phase, it would be simple enough to arrest the petty saboteurs and protestors, banishing all the opposition immediately to the Quarantine Zones. But the PWE Council had wisely adopted the Thousand Steps policy, based on the enlightened concept that yielding- in a strictly controlled way, of course- to the opposition would actually hasten the transition, whereas an overpowering show of force could prolong the resistance indefinitely. The power of the state was not without limits, and history provided many cautionary tales. Attempts to brutally crush insurgencies in Northern Ireland, Vietnam, the Middle East, South Africa, and China itself, had all led to catastrophic domino effects, throwing fuel onto smoldering fires. Even the most conservative and hawkish members of the Council understood this (so did the rebels, as General Respighi's case showed: if the PWE purposely avoided shows of force, the rebels would resort to fabricating accounts of atrocities). And so the PWE allowed the insurgents to carry on their circumscribed rebellions, and maintained Quarantine Zones rather than standing armies, PsySoc Rehab centers instead of mass-execution grounds.

But on that subject, Chou reminded himself, the warship bearing Comrade Dmitri Lezhev to San Francisco should have arrived by now. He consulted his data-disc. For some reason, they were taking a circuitous route, 50 kilometers to the north, then out over the ocean and back over the mountain range running the length of the San Francisco peninsula. Consistent with Thousand Steps, Commander Annenkov had been instructed by Lezhev not to fly in with guns blazing, but this seemed a needlessly timid approach.

Annenkov was to send men down to capture the mysterious Benn Marr, and Lezhev was to restrain him from killing more rebels than absolutely necessary. Thousand Steps: let the pitiful resistance movement in the San Francisco Peninsula survive, and let that symbol, that fountain of false hope- he paused to recall its name, Coit Tower- stand unharmed.

Not surprisingly, Benn Marr had the ability to read minds and send his consciousness out of body- in the manner of his predecessor Owen Marr- but the exact usefulness of this ability remained unclear. Perhaps Lezhev's prudence was justified. Chou had received sketchy reports on the experiments carried out by Eunigen, but that pharmaceutical company had not been forthcoming. It was typical of the giant international, or interplanetary, corporations to keep industrial secrets and hold themselves above the laws of the PWE. So untrustworthy, these capitalist partners! The beneficence of the Thousand Steps approach should not apply to them: Chou made another mental note, to bring this issue before the Council.

Eunigen's experiments progressed only at the discretion of the PWE, and any notion of corporate autonomy was self-delusion. Unbeknownst to Eunigen and the Mars Wellness Institute, PWE agents at Tharsis and the New Colonies- including the key operative Sool Tamura (a sociopath, nonetheless highly effective)- had monitored and reported on large-scale trials of psychopeptides on Mars for many years. Ranging from mere attitude adjustment to full control of the conscious mind, and even- when absolutely unavoidable- total neutralization of thought, the wide spectrum of such interventions had proven invaluable as an adjunct to Thousand Steps. Chou silently nodded his satisfaction at the inherent justice of it all: descendants of the American colonists had paid a steep price to atone for the imperialist policies of their ancestors. And now, he speculated, this Benn Marr represented another level of reward for years of experimentation. The ability to read and to project thoughts was similar to what Chinese monks (particularly in the Tibetan District) had been practicing for a thousand years. The difference was that Eunigen had given Benn his abilities by modifying his genes, so that they could be passed on to future generations in large numbers: the hypothetical implications for the PWE were staggering! Unfortunately, Benn Marr, although of Chinese descent, had lost touch with his ethnic roots on Mars, and had no understanding of his rich cultural heritage. As with all traditional Chinese, Leader Chou harbored the conviction that the Chinese civilization had greater value- it was simply superior- and should be promoted above all others; Benn was unlikely to feel such loyalty.

In his disciplined manner, Chou curbed his enthusiasm and placed Yin next to Yang. Yes, the implications were staggering, but that was good and bad: danger and opportunity rode together. Benn Marr had already escaped once from Eunigen, and if he could not be reined in, he would be a threat rather than an asset, and would have to be destroyed. For that matter, if all the descendants of Tharsis colonists had evolved similar abilities- as hinted by Eunigen's findings- the PWE may have to neutralize them all. A fourth Quarantine Zone may well be necessary on Mars.

Benn knew that he was dreaming again. What was unclear to him: how much of the dream came from his own mind, and how much was generated by the input leads attached to the back of his head? Some of the images in the dream had a stiff, artificial character and were probably being fed to him by the psychometric computer, which also analyzed his reactions by way of leads placed at his temples and a surrounding scanner highly sensitive to energy emissions. But the fact that he was standing on a baseball diamond, specifically at third base, leaning toward home as the opposing pitcher glowered at him, had to be his own creation.

Admittedly, the fusion of computer-generated graphics and his spontaneous dream was almost seamless: Benn provided the scenario, and his positronic psychoanalyst steered the events within the scene. It was jarring to see the game through the eyes of the baserunner, and at the same time watch it as a spectator: as though he were sitting in the bleachers next to Protem and whole damn-scary CIA (and figuratively, they were indeed in the bleachers, Protem and several CIA department chiefs watching his dream on monitors in remote locations within the Russian Hill complex).

Benn recognized the pitcher, a formidable right-hander from the championship game against the Meteor Dodgers. Just keep leaning that way, the pitcher was thinking: just one more half-step.

At bat was none other than his pal Jace Cohn, who waved the bat in a cheeky way and winked at Benn from the far side of home plate. That distracted Benn a little, but despite that, he found himself suddenly stretched out on the ground with his hand touching the base, just as the pitcher was beginning his pick-off throw to third. The ball arrived with a snap while Benn was getting back up. "Safe!" shouted the umpire. "Negative reaction latency: impressive," said Protem, on a separate line to his department heads. Still one out. A moment later, Jace tapped a soft grounder toward the shortstop, tossed the bat aside and began to sprint toward first base. But before he could even exit the batter's box, Benn had already crossed home plate, sliding quite unnecessarily.

Protem's Vice-President, the titular head of the CIA, said, "So he reacts by premonition, before the situation develops. That would be useful. Let's see what else he can do."

Rising to his feet, Benn felt a strange lightheadedness. There was a flash of blue, and the scene shifted, first breaking up into numerous flickering points of light, as though he had stood upright too quickly. Then it reassembled itself into an enclosed space which he promptly recognized as the cockpit of a Worm, only with a modified configuration. Benn sat in the pilot's seat as usual, but now there was a co-pilot: Lora. She faced a navigator's screen, which normally would have been located in Jace's compartment in the rear. He quickly turned around to check, but no, Jace was not sitting behind him. Bright splashes of red and green moved across the screen, signaling minor obstacles in the area, but none requiring the Worm to change direction. Q! Lora was surrounded by her familiar deep yellow aura, and Benn recognized her unhesitating sense of purpose, the way her strong focus extended so naturally from the rest of her character. He couldn't help gushing: she was just so impressive! His giddy thoughts turned again to melody, tension and interwoven themes, as when he had secretly visited her dorm room: she was a complex and harmonious composition.

Protem commented to the others watching: "Note the closeness of their relationship, the way she captivates him. That might have tactical utility at the proper moment."

In the midst of his admiration for Lora's musical qualities, Benn gradually became aware of a different melody playing. At first it was a distant, vague background noise to Lora's rich emanations, but as the Worm drilled closer to water, the sound grew louder. It sounded like wind blowing over an open bottle: at first a sigh, then a hum, steadily gaining volume and focus. Soon a piercing, flute-like sound was dancing to a rapid beat in his ear. As always, Benn had to lean his head back and close his eyes. His arms flopped to his sides. His jaws clenched. Jace had seen it just this way: a wisp of steam rose from his shiny forehead into the coldness of the chamber (bringing to mind a steaming hardboiled egg that he and Jace had once gawked at, in nutrition class). The leads attached to his temples tingled rhythmically, and Benn realized that the positronic reader was listening to the same tune.

"What's happening to him? Why does he look as though he's in a trance?" the lead psychometrist, who was basically in charge of the CIA's torture program, wondered aloud as he searched his data-disc and found large spikes in the energy readings.

Then came another blue flash, and the Worm's cockpit split apart into thousands of gray dots. This time they reassembled into a completely unfamiliar scene, on board some sort of vessel.

"Where is he now?" demanded the general of the Air Force. "He's off our grid- projected himself out of body. Marr's flying on his own, and I'll be damned if that isn't the command deck of a PWE warship!"

There were a dozen men in plain black uniforms, some standing at attention while others faced control panels. An irate-looking blond man with a sharp face and small mustache, dressed in a gray uniform with red stars on his shoulders sat in a dominant position raised two steps above the surrounding modules. This was certainly a warship, and Benn was looking at it through another person's eyes.

"Carefully, now, Comrade Peter. Use a slow approach," Benn heard himself saying in a tone usually reserved for small children. The ship's commander, the blond man named Peter (last name Annenkov, gleaned from the mind Benn was occupying) glared at Benn- or rather at the speaker- making no effort to disguise his simmering anger. He was master of one of the fastest and deadliest ships serving the PWE, and here was a mere civilian bureaucrat, pulling back on the reins of his charger, urging a slow approach? This corrupt health official, this creature of the pharmaceutical industry! Giving orders in front of Peter's crew.

Intruder! Pirate! With each of these thoughts, Peter's red aura issued a small eruption, like a solar flare.

Without any conscious effort, Benn suddenly discovered yet another new telepathic ability. As though surfing Peter's wave of emotion, Benn jumped his viewpoint over to the angry commander (causing considerable confusion among the CIA chiefs), and now found himself looking back at the original speaker, who turned out to be a doughy-faced, overweight man dressed in fine New York Metropole style. He recognized the man as Dmitri Lezhev from the long-ago opening meeting in New York. Protem had Lezhev's face on file, and clarified his position in the PWE, for the benefit of the CIA chiefs. Less familiar to Benn was the person looming behind him: an unshaven, roughly-dressed giant who looked even taller in comparison to the short-statured Lezhev. Benn vaguely remembered that he was one of the excited crowd Maggie Sullivan had addressed in Vistaville, but that whole episode remained quite fuzzy.

What was the giant doing there? And why was an MWI official giving orders on the control deck of a PWE warship?

Only Benn could see that Lezhev had a dark green aura, which pulsed with excitement as the ship drew ever closer to its destination. To the CIA chiefs, Protem pointed out the image on the main screen at the front of Annenkov's command deck. Coit Tower stood prominently in the center of the view; amidst century-old piles of rubble, collapsed buildings, scarred hillsides, there was defiant Coit Tower, seemingly untouched by war.

"Carefully now, Comrade Peter," Lezhev repeated. "We are not to damage the tower, and must capture the target with a minimum of bloodshed." Leader Chou Xia-Yu, with whom Lezhev maintained steady communication, had been unambiguous on that point, something about a thousand steps. But it was clear that Comrade Peter had different ideas. Benn felt another solar flare erupting from Annenkov's troubled mind, followed by his own sense of alarm: he had a feeling that he was "the target" to be captured, and that Annenkov planned to fully employ the massive battery of Razers mounted at the front of his ship, to level the tower and most of the hill, before sending down his soldiers. Why put troops in harm's way, in a battlefield about which nothing was known? Lezhev had hinted at an unspecified, fearsome new weapon, no less.

Pre-emptive firepower was the way to minimize bloodshed, at least on his side of the battle.

Benn concentrated and tried exerting his thoughts: No bloodshed. Power down. Do not use the Razers.

Unmoved, Annenkov entered a code number at a small display located on his armrest. Red lights came on at several control panels around the chamber, and his officers began to set up the attack sequence. Coit Tower was no more than five kilometers away.

Benn tried again: Delete the attack order. Lift your hand from the panel.

To no effect. At this distance, although he could read their thoughts and even had the newly-discovered ability to see through their eyes, Benn could not control their actions. He decided he'd better return quickly to his corporeal state, which was in real danger of coming under fire.

The rise in activity in the command center, Comrade Peter suddenly getting up to confer with Lieutenant Wu, the blinking red lights- all this did not escape the notice of Dmitri Lezhev. "Comrade Peter! *Kuda idosh, Pyotr!* Did you not hear me? What are you…"

Benn opened his eyes to the dark internal surface of a psychometric scanner. He felt the cool pinch of the leads attached to his temples, the uncomfortably hard surface on which he lay. And then he heard the blare of alarms and the loud clatter of running footsteps.

Chapter Twenty-Three

It took only a few minutes to evacuate the dozen-or-so operatives from Telegraph Hill, but that was just barely enough time. As the supervising engineer ushered his last technician into the tunnel, took a final look around, then shut the heavy steel door behind him, booming vibrations began to rock the tunnel. He held his data-disc over his head and ran the entire dark and winding distance to Russian Hill.

The highest point in the vast underground complex inside Russian Hill was a camouflaged gun-deck built into a collapsed apartment building on Larkin Street. The deck afforded a 360-degree view of the city, but at that moment, all observers clustered at the portals facing east. Although not present on the gun-deck, Benn, Lora and their keeper George Washington shared an identical view, which was projected around a virtual observation room fifty meters below. Protem Two had been waiting for Benn, and started to speak as soon as he walked in.

"In your dream, you were on board the PWE warship. You addressed the commander as Comrade Peter, and you ordered him not to damage Coit Tower- yet he is launching an attack. How were you in a position to issue an order, and why did he disobey? There was another man, Dmitri Lezhev, who is PWE Associate Secretary of Security. What is his role in this?" This last fact caught Benn and Lora by surprise; they knew Lezhev only as V.P. of Colonial Affairs for MWI. However, Benn had gleaned something more important from Protem's questions: the psychometric scanner had recorded all that he saw and heard in his dream, but not what he thought- nor the thoughts he was able to read from others. Only input from the five basic senses generated decipherable patterns in his brain. Therefore they had no explanation for many of the actions taken, and must have been quite confused when he jumped from Lezhev's mind to Annenkov's!

It was clear that Protem had an incomplete picture of Benn's abilities and even less of an idea how to use them. Nor did Benn feel the need to help Protem on either count: being exploited as a major weapon of the CIA was not remotely in his plans. But now the PWE was bearing down on him, firing major weapons of their own, so he had few options. "I can't explain it, Protem. It just happened the way you saw it. But I would consider knocking out that ship, if you have the capability."

Protem's sensors told it that Benn was lying; he was hiding the explanation for what they had witnessed. The psychometric analyzer had failed to provide key data, so CIA would have to resort to a more basic and direct approach to analyzing Benn Marr. But they would deal with that later. "We have not fired on the PWE ship, as it would be ineffective and would reveal our position on Russian Hill. Benn, what is their plan of attack, and how can we best counter it?"

Again, Protem had no idea how to exploit Benn's abilities; the answer was self-evident: "Their plan of attack is to destroy Telegraph Hill, then send troops down to search the entire area. They will eventually discover the Russian Hill complex, Protem. Our best bet is to clear out of here, and to do it as soon as possible."

The PWE ship aimed its fierce Razer fire at the base of tall Coit Tower, sending up an equally tall tower of black smoke as the stone super-heated and quickly began to melt. Within minutes, the tower toppled over and rolled a short distance before crashing ignominiously down the side of the hill. For such a symbolically momentous event, the fall of Coit Tower actually seemed quite trivial. But not trivial to everyone: as Protem ushered Benn and Lora out of the observation room, George and a CIA general bringing up the rear, Benn suddenly thought of Evlin, who at that moment might be watching from the safe house across the bay: if so, her fragile mental state might tip over the edge, just like the tower!

Lora also thought of Evlin, but with greater sympathy than Benn (naturally): poor Evlin had pinned her hopes for the USA Collective, for Maggie's ambitions, on the legend of Coit Tower. To her it was a grand symbol of resistance and survival. Now that Maggie was no longer leading the USA Collective- in fact, would never return to Berkeley- the fall of the tower would send Evlin into a tailspin from which she would never recover.

Coit Tower was just the beginning. The Razers blasted and sliced deep into the hillside, excavating a warren of chambers connected by winding stairways and corridors: Telegraph Hill looked like an ant colony, cut right down the middle. But the exposed network seemed suspiciously modest to Commander Annenkov- much too small to be the rebel headquarters. And where were the occupants? Detecting no human bodies in the wreckage, he ordered his gunners to fan their coverage out over a wider area. The rebels had evacuated the hill but were still somewhere nearby, and their energy emissions -not to mention their machines- would easily trigger his ship's sensors.

By this time, Lezhev was shouting obscenities in Russian and stamping his feet like a child in a tantrum. He looked desperately about the room, then turned as a last resort to Jack Folsom. He could see no other option. Without any confidence that he would actually receive help from that direction, he blindly fired an order, "Jack Folsom! Arrest Commander Annenkov for treason! Jack, I order you to arrest him- now!"

Annenkov calmly countered, "Lieutenant Wu, take Comrade Lezhev to the brig, and remove his com unit." Of course he was gambling with high stakes. But arresting Lezhev was not exactly an act of mutiny, since he, Peter, was the ship's commander. If he could capture Benn Marr unharmed and, at the same time, expose the rebel headquarters and round up its leaders, the PWE and Leader Chou would excuse his disobedience of a civilian's orders, wouldn't they?

Jack, usually slow on the uptake even under normal circumstances, was completely bewildered by this point: Lezhev was the man in charge. Peter looked like he was mad at him the whole time. Lezhev ordered Peter not to attack the tower, but Peter attacked anyway. Then Lezhev was screaming at Peter, and wanted Jack to arrest him. But Jack was not a policeman. And now Peter was arresting Lezhev. But why, what did he do?

Jack Folsom's plodding thoughts came full circle: Lezhev was the man in charge. So he took two long steps toward Peter, reaching out with large, soil-stained hands to arrest the Commander. Before he could take a third step, Lieutenant Wu drew his handheld Razer and blasted a hole in the middle of Jack's chest. As usual with Razer wounds, the intense heat cauterized all affected blood vessels, so there was no visible bleeding. There was, however, an eerie haze and a soft, sizzling sound in the air. Jack, sitting slumped against a module, was able to contemplate the gaping wound in his chest for fully a minute before his vision finally faded.

The commotion gave Dmitri Lezhev a split-second to take out his com unit and send a pre-designed message to the PWE in Beijing. Lieutenant Wu spotted his action and lunged at him, but it was too late: Beijing acknowledged receipt.

Outside the observation room, a large armored car with three additional heavily-armed guards had been waiting since the warship first appeared. With everyone safely aboard, the car whisked silently along a paved tunnel, headed toward a hidden base in South San Francisco. In the front compartment, the CIA general spoke urgently with Protem, while George stared fixedly through the back window. No-one knew that, at that moment, a blip was flashing on a screen near Commander Annenkov: a single vehicle moving quickly in a straight line south, whereas other energy signals were weak and drifted in random directions.

In the car, Benn looked out of the corner of his eye at the deep golden glow surrounding Lora. His telepathic ability had indeed continued to evolve since their escape from Eunigen- despite being suppressed by a psychopeptide for several weeks. No, it occurred to him: it was because of being suppressed for several weeks. Like a loaded spring, his abilities were expanding rapidly now that the resistance to the spring was gone. Although still conscious, he could see all the auras in the car- only Protem had none. He remembered vaguely seeing Maggie's green aura while half-awake in Vistaville, but now his vision was clear. Could he jump to another point of view while maintaining his own? Several efforts failed; he had to be unconscious to inhabit another person's mind, as there was no way to split his own aura into two. Still testing his limits, he reached out and touched Lora's hand with one finger.

"Lora." He had not spoken a word.

"Benn! I can hear you. But we're not out of body. I thought you had to..."

"Yes. I'm changing, Lora. I don't have to be out of body in order to share thoughts or see auras, although I admit it's much easier if we're actually touching. Now that the drugs have worn off, I'm discovering new abilities; still experimenting, but I may even be able to influence others without projecting out of body."

"Can you make them let us go?"

"I think so, except I can't control Protem or other machines. George has an aura, so I might force him to control Protem. But right now, they're helping us get away from the PWE warship, so I won't interfere."

"Then what, Benn? You don't want to stay with these people, do you? You'd be experimented on by the CIA for the rest of your life."

"No, but even if we do escape from Protem and the CIA, we can't go back to Berkeley, where Evlin is now in charge. She is seriously paranoid, and if we come back without Maggie, Evlin will be sure that we're the enemy. Anyway, Lora, the Resistance is a dead end."

After a long pause, Benn withdrew his hand and sat alone with his thoughts, listening to the hum of the car speeding along smoothly. What next? The past few weeks seemed to have flashed by, and his mind was racing ahead, as usual. After they had barely escaped the grasp of Eunigen and Father, Star and Stripe had kidnapped and shipped them in a radioactive waste transport to the USA Collective. Maggie Sullivan, head of a decoy organization, and Evlin, in turn, had delivered them into the hands of the CIA. And the CIA would stop at nothing to exploit Benn's abilities for their own ends. In their global game of chess, the CIA saw him as a pawn with the powers of a knight; in fact, they all did, and if he proved useful to any one group, another would try to destroy him. Much more urgently, a PWE warship was trying to destroy him *right now!* There was no place left to run!

More than anything, he wanted to grow further with Lora, to explore his evolving abilities and to grasp the unsolved mysteries wrapped within himself. He was tired of running: but where could he stop and focus on anything but escape? As with *any* question-even the most complicated and difficult- the answer spontaneously appeared in Benn's mind: Home, of course! But where would that be, home? A cozy room in a Berkeley safe house with Evlin breathing outside his door? A student dormitory at Harkness, Theo Coffin and Nestor Neelin plotting in the room above? A cramped underground apartment at Tharsis Colony, with Wila supervising? All of the above? Why shouldn't he have a multiplicity of homes: many people did, and some even went as far as to dream of their mothers' wombs! His choice immediately became obvious, and he just had to hope that Lora would go along with it. After another moment's thought, Benn began to reach for her hand again, when a sudden jarring stop sent everyone in the car flying forward.

Just ahead of them, sustained Razer fire, blasting through the roof of the tunnel, had sliced a deep trench across their path. Beneath the pavement's concrete shell, a layer of old petroleum-based asphalt burst into flames. The robotic driver immediately reversed direction, then stopped again, with nowhere to turn; George was already watching a unit of PWE troops approach from the rear, no more than a hundred meters away. Without any hesitation, he leapt through the open skylight, rolled smoothly onto the road, and positioned himself between the troops and Protem Two. In the tradition of his long-ago predecessors, the US Secret Service, he would protect the President of the United States- even if POTUS was a machine- at any cost.

The others abandoned the car and fled to the far side of the tunnel, where the flames had begun to subside and the burnt-out trench was shallowest. Protem managed to cross easily on his metallo-polymer legs aided by cybernetic stabilizers, but the general and his guards had to gingerly navigate the steep sides, molten surfaces and extreme heat of the trench. At that rate they would never make it, unless George could delay their pursuers. So Benn and Lora chose not to follow; they waited and watched in suspense as George, standing alone in a peculiar stance with knees flexed and both arms raised, encountered the first wave of PWE troops.

Or rather, the troops encountered George, who proved to be quite a formidable obstacle, for an old man. With astonishing speed, he leapt upwards, arms and legs spinning in a crackling blur, then landed in a deep crouch. All about him lay a dozen groaning soldiers in various degrees of disfigurement. But others continued to arrive, quickly surrounding George on all sides with their Razers drawn. Like a ferocious animal- most dangerous when trapped in a corner- George snarled and began to mount another attack. Again he spun around, but then a heavy steel net launched from the periphery caught him in mid-leap, bringing him to the ground in a loud clatter and rendering him completely immobile. Even so, the soldiers approached him only with great reluctance and extreme caution.

"Now's our chance, Benn, hurry, let's go!" Lora grabbed Benn's arm and tried to pull him toward the smoldering, smoke-filled trench.

Benn yanked his arm free, then stood in silence awhile, regarding her with a complex expression on his face. During the brief overlap of their auras, the touching of hand to arm, Lora sensed many reasons for that expression, joining fear for their safety with a supreme confidence, mixing an open-ended sense of hope with iron-willed determination. They were in great danger, and yet everything was well under control. All possibilities remained wide open, but there was only one path forward. Although Lora read all of this clearly in his expression, she failed to understand.

"Benn, what are you doing? How are we going to get away?"

Ignoring the arrival of PWE soldiers who were bringing up a second steel net behind him, Benn replied in an unnaturally calm voice, "This is how we'll get away, Lora."

With that, he raised both hands into the air and turned slowly around. "We surrender."

Peter Annenkov turned out to be tragically mistaken regarding Leader Chou's capacity for forgiveness. Yes, he had captured Benn Marr unharmed, and yes, he had exposed the rebel headquarters. Annenkov smoothed his mustache. But no, he had not succeeded in rounding up the rebel leaders, who had located another vehicle on the other side of the trench- yes, the same trench his Razers had carved and which had prevented his troops from giving chase. At least that was how he explained the recent events to Chou, whose angry three-dimensional image now dominated the main screen on his command deck.

"Leader Chou, you will be pleased to learn that I've already released Comrade Lezhev, and he is on his way up to this deck. No harm came to him while in custody, and the subject, Marr, as well as his female companion, have replaced Comrade Lezhev in the brig. In addition, we were able to capture alive a unique specimen, a fighter who is now in restraints in our sick bay. He appears to be some sort of genetic recombination, and dissecting him will yield significant information. So overall, I would say we've made a large net gain, despite the fact that the rebel leaders..."

"There is a serious strategic loss of which you are sadly ignorant, Annenkov," interrupted Chou, and Annenkov knew that the omission of "Comrade" in addressing him was a bad sign. "It was not for you to take an independent course of action, and to ignore the orders of the PWE, as transmitted to you by Comrade Lezhev..."

"Lezhev did not make sufficiently clear his..."

"... so I am relieving you of command, effective immediately. Lieutenant Wu, you are now Commander of this vessel."

Having fully anticipated his rise in rank, Commander Wu wasted no time: he snapped his fingers at the two guards holding Annenkov by the arms, and just as Dmitri Lezhev burst through the doorway to the command deck, Peter Annenkov was being roughly escorted, head bowed, in the direction marked Sortie. Lezhev shouted a Russian expletive, lunged and took a swipe at Annenkov's head en passant, but missed. Then he noticed the image of Leader Chou on the big screen, and quickly stretched a surprised smile across his face.

"A thousand thanks, Comrade Chou. That traitor! I heard that he let the rebel leaders..."

"It was never our intention to capture the leaders, Comrade Lezhev. Now that many of their operatives have been killed and Coit tower destroyed, the resistance movement may grow stronger. Commander Wu, leave the area as quickly as possible; make it look as though we are unaware of the one they call Protem. You have Benn Marr, at least: deliver him to Eunigen for the next phase of their project, which is of the utmost importance to the PWE. But," Chou again stacked Yin on Yang, "if Marr tries to fight you, tries to escape, or causes you trouble in any way, Commander Wu, do not hesitate to throw him off your ship."

* * *

Peter Annenkov stopped shouting for a moment and stared down the hallway at the cell diagonally across from his, where Benn and Lora sat placidly on one of the narrow beds- holding hands! *They* were the basis of the capture mission? These two were the reason he had been tempted into attacking Telegraph Hill, the cause of his arrest and probable execution? Two young fools in love? "What makes you so important to the PWE?" he demanded. "*Why* did they go to such trouble, take such incredible risk, to capture the two of you? Why? You are nothing! I could destroy you both with one hand! I could take..."

But suddenly Annenkov could take nothing at all- not even his next breath. At a glance from Benn, he found himself unable to inhale. A minute passed, with Annenkov turning purple, punching himself in the ribs, shaking in rage and panic.

"It works. I was getting tired of hearing him shout," Benn thought to Lora. She agreed, but then gently reminded him to release his control of Annenkov.

"Oh. Right. Sorry." Annenkov gasped loudly once and slumped onto his bed, heaving and clutching his chest.

"Benn, you could make them let us out of this cell right now."

"As that very rude man over there asked, before he mysteriously started choking, why? We're together, we're fed and housed, we're comfortable...." Benn chuckled.

Lora's eyes narrowed. "Benn. We have to leave eventually, you know."

"Sure. I know. So where would you like to go?"

"Back to New York. From there we can find a way up to New Haven. But we would have to avoid Lou Hunter, and even Dr. Neelin. Of all the people we've met so far, the only one I can think of, who has no hidden agenda regarding our freedom or captivity, abilities or usefulness, is Cira Vincent."

"I agree. We'll try to get to Dr. Vincent."

"Can you make these people bring us to New York?"

Benn nodded with a confident smile. "That's where this warship is headed right now, Lora. By surrendering to them, we've hitched a convenient ride with the PWE."

Chapter Twenty-Four

Nestor Neelin was as puzzled as anyone else. May Acheson repeated the question: "Why did Security arrest you, then release you again?" Well, it wasn't quite that simple, thought Neelin. As already described in detail to the Directors of Star and Stripe, that Chief of Security, that Haley fellow, had dragged him to an interrogation room somewhere beneath Phelps Gate, where he spent a cold night without food and water. The next morning Haley came back with a couple of thugs- not employees of YaleConn, judging by the rough manner in which they handled their prisoner. The University would never have permitted security officers to slap and shove one of their professors about like that. Not one with *tenure*, anyway! Then, when physical abuse and threats yielded no results, they resorted to chemical means, injecting a vial of some psychopeptide into his neck. They wanted to know about the resistance movement on campus. Neelin recalled involuntarily answering, but had managed, by means of heroic effort, to keep his statements either fictitious or nonsensical. At many points, his interrogators could see that he was making things up, and would return to physical coercion. He spent a second night alone in that room, groggy, bruised, and once again without sustenance. Not until late the following day did Haley return, this time by himself. In a resentful tone, he informed Neelin that he was free to leave- but clearly it wasn't his idea. Neelin did not see himself as a vengeful man, but he made a mental note to ask Abe and Zak to pay the chief of security a not-so-friendly visit.

"Are you sure you didn't co-operate in some way with them?" asked Alden Hayes. Realizing what he had insinuated, Hayes added quickly, "While under the influence of the psychopeptide, of course."

"Not that I can recall. No, Alden, they did not release me because I made a deal." He should have seen this coming, thought Neelin: even he would have considered such a rapid catch-and-release quite fishy. At the very least his old friends would forever temper their trust in him and keep their distance. Someone would have to replace Neelin as the leader of Star and Stripe.

Lou Hunter, recently promoted to Senior Fellow of Mellon College, sensed the same thing. "No, never mind- nobody's implying that you're lying about making a deal with them, Nes." No-one had brought up lying before Hunter placed it squarely on the table, coloring all further discussion. He continued, "We've known you too long not to believe you, when you say that you put up a valiant fight, despite painful torture. *You wouldn't lie to us*." There it was again- the idea that deception was something the Directors should keep in mind. Fair enough. Neelin nodded at him and began to speak, but Hunter wasn't finished. "However, we also know that a psychopeptide can force you to co-operate, and to forget that you did. One of our members, Theo Coffin, reports that he saw you released from Phelps with courtesy and concern for your comfort; the security officers even waved good-bye, he says. Theo wasn't implying anything, he was just glad that you appeared unharmed, but you can see how it might look suspicious."

Should have seen that coming too. *Damned opportunist*, thought Neelin, turning to face Acheson, Hayes and the other Directors, none of whom would meet his bitter gaze. But they hadn't been the ones to plant the dagger. He looked back at Lou Hunter, his protege since... so many years ago. Neelin had practically changed his diapers, watched him grow up, mentored him. As the son of Nathaniel Hunter, former Dean of Mellon College, young Lou had (narrowly) gained admission to YaleConn. Neelin had advised him on his master's thesis, later invited him to become a fellow of the college, and then had gone as far as naming Lou a Director of Star and Stripe! Neelin had introduced him to Cira Vincent in the hopes that the two would become a couple, but that had turned out disastrously. Having no family ties before the age of forty, following his friend Nathaniel's death, Neelin had raised Lou like an adopted son- or so he imagined- and now his reward was filial disloyalty and betrayal. Enough, he concluded: he was innocent, but how could he ever prove it? Giving up on his defense would be tantamount to an admission of guilt, but he had gone through too much humiliation already. Mustering as much dignity as he could, Dr. Nestor Neelin shook his head, rose slowly from his chair and, with an air of finality, walked out of the Great Hall of Mellon College.

Maggie had not seen Protem Two for over a week, and when it finally paid her a visit at the Event Co-ordination Center in downtown San Jose, it stayed for no more than fifteen minutes. "After all the recent events, I want to be sure you are comfortable in your new setting," said Protem, and Maggie supposed that she was. Unlike San Francisco, almost half of the buildings in San Jose were still standing, and of those, two-thirds had been restored to a functional condition after the Great War. Maggie's office at the corner of the fifth floor had a fine view of an old sports arena, where tattered signs continued to advertise tournaments of a century ago, involving a game called hockey- which suggested the cliff hockey Maggie had played in her school days, but this version had been contested, apparently, on ice.

"Not too bad," Maggie replied coolly, and she meant it. Although she had rebounded from the shock of discovering that the USA Collective was merely a decoy organization, she would never admit that to Protem. Never let 'em see you sweat. There was actually a surprising degree of relief, no longer to be responsible for the anguished hopes of American dis-unificationists in the Quarantine Zone, many of them- such as that foolish oaf, Jack Folsom- so difficult to deal with. The CIA and Protem were more than welcome to handle the challenge; for the moment at least, Maggie felt as though she had retired from a long and taxing career. Let Jack Folsom annoy someone else, for a change!

"Is the work level in the Event Co-ordination Center to your satisfaction?" asked Protem solicitously. In truth, Protem could not have cared less about the level of her work satisfaction, and Maggie knew it full well.

She tried not to sound too sarcastic. "Yes, my part in co-ordinating protests around the world is very important, I feel."

"How would you rate it, compared to your former role with the USA Collective?" Protem's questions sounded to Maggie like a generic workplace survey.

"No, it's not as important as that, of course. But as you've made abundantly clear, even *that* was not as important as that."

Despite its advanced QI circuits, Protem had some difficulty following the logic of Maggie's statement, so it decided to reduce ambiguity by asking her a more direct question. "Maggie, do you intend to communicate with the USA Collective?"

"No," came the reply, slightly too quickly. "What would be the point of linking up again with the USA Collective? Their only purpose was to distract the PWE from the true resistance movement, after all." There was a large pinch of bitterness in her tone. For the first time that afternoon, Protem's sensors indicated that Maggie was lying. She had identified with that organization for years, and it might take an equal number of years for her to surrender her authority. Human thought carried such tedious momentum, Protem had found. It tended to travel at a steady speed and in a straight line indefinitely; inducing any change in direction required a major perpendicular vector. But Maggie's resistance to her changed circumstances was only a state of mind; she would take up her new life, then travel in a straight line from that point on. In any case, there were no direct lines of communication between Berkeley and San Jose. Since Maggie currently posed no definable threat to the security of the resistance movement, Protem was free to move on to more important matters. It would allow her to remain alive, for now.

Maggie stared out the window and said nothing as Protem departed. Poor Evlin, she was thinking. Somehow she would get word to Evlin, about the CIA and its exploitation of the USA Collective. Evlin would avenge their dishonored group. True, she suffered from severe psychological damage, but then who, in the Quarantine Zone, did not? By definition, they had all failed extreme Psychosocial Rehabilitation: that's how people got assigned to the Quarantine Zone in the first place. Evlin was the best hope for moving the USA Collective forward, giving it true purpose, independent of the damn-scary CIA. In their conversation, Protem had not mentioned Benn Marr at all- so maybe he had escaped from the CIA, and hopefully would find his way back to the safe house in Berkeley. Poor Evlin could certainly use the help of someone like that.

* * *

Several small craft rapidly scattered as the PWE warship descended out of a dark, rainy sky and touched down on a landing platform at Queens ElegnaPort. A portal beneath its debarcation chamber slid open, and a sloped walkway reached the ground.

"Finally, the time has come to deliver Benn Marr," said Leader Chou, returning to the Command Deck's center screen. He seems distracted, thought Commander Wu. Despite Chou's most careful plans, human error and the unpredictable actions of others always introduced an element of chaos. Not only had Annenkov's precipitous actions jeopardized a fundamental strategy of the PWE, Chou had just been pulled away by reports of a change in leadership in the USA Collective. In addition, a sensitive situation involving Dr. Nestor Neelin had developed in New Haven. That would probably lead to another change of leadership. Knowing who and where the leaders were, had enabled Chou to apply the Thousand Steps policy to greatest advantage. And now, apparently some fool from Eunigen or YaleConn had placed Dr.Neelin under arrest! Chou's subordinates were dealing with it: the current situation- as with everything else on his agenda- demanded his full attention. "We are fortunate that Benn Marr did not force you to throw him off your ship." Commander Wu, entering copious notes on his datadisc, did not confuse Leader Chou's wry comment with an attempt at humor. He looked up at the screen expectantly.

"Commander Wu, your sole task is to bring Marr to Director Walther Beame at Eunigen, along with his female companion Lora Wheeler- who, obviously, can be used for leverage in case he chooses not to co-operate. Maintain a significant troop presence in the Eunigen building until the next phase of their project has been completed: we cannot blindly trust our capitalist partners to turn over the results of the project to us. And one more thing, Commander Wu: put Annenkov aboard the next ship to Beijing."

The Commander smiled grimly. "I will see to it myself, Leader Chou." When Chou emphasized that delivering Benn Marr was his sole task, it meant that Wu's neck was now on the block. As for Annenkov's neck...

In the brig four floors down, a guard unlocked the cell door and waved Benn and Lora out toward the main corridor, where six more guards joined the parade. As they passed Annenkov, who was lying uneasily on his bed, he quickly turned to face the wall: he had said nothing during the two-hour flight from San Francisco.

"They're taking us off the ship now," Lora whispered to Benn. "I guess you'll wait until we're someplace inside the airport, before, you know, influencing them to let us go? You must figure that the probability of escape would be higher outside this ship with fewer soldiers around, right?"

Benn joked easily, "The probability of escape is somewhere in the area of, let's see, eighty-six-point-three percent, if you want to be exact. Watch this, Lora." He sent a test impulse to the first guard, who watched his right arm rising mysteriously in an old Euro-Fascist salute; as the other guards stared, the arm remained extended for several humiliating seconds, then slapped back to his side. Lora barely suppressed a laugh, and the wide-eyed guard turned to glare, first in anger at her, then in disbelief at his own mutinous right hand.

Lora whispered again, "That was great, Benn! This should be no problem at all." For days on end, she had suffered unabating anxiety, which had peaked to terror during the warship's attack. Even afterwards, the tension had dragged on, stretching her resilience to its breaking point- up until the moment she watched the guard salute involuntarily. There could be no better feeling: suddenly the endless anxiety dissolved into a rush of confidence that everything would end well, after all. They only had to wait for the most opportune moment to escape, but Benn could make their captors do anything he wanted, at any time. At least- as Benn had so considerately pointed out- he could do so about eighty-six-point-three percent of the time! Benn was sensitive to her stress; he had clearly made that joke, and the guard salute, for her sake- and it had worked.

Commander Wu was waiting tensely for them in the debarcation chamber. Charged with such an important job- his sole task- he would take no chances: he held his Razer in one hand, ready to fire at the slightest provocation. "We'll proceed to Six, the military terminal, where a transport is waiting for us. Guards: follow behind the two of them, and if Mr. Marr makes any move to escape," Wu barked out the order, "shoot his friend." That drew a sharp look from Marr, he noted, but otherwise the leverage that Leader Chou had promised worked well: his prisoners were

252

completely acquiescent during the short march into Terminal Six, a large converted hangar where PWE pilots and other military personnel began and ended their missions. Wu pointed at a Glidebus parked on the opposite side, and the guards behind them nudged Benn and Lora across the wide central atrium and onto the vehicle. Wu boarded last, his Razer still drawn. What did he expect, a surprise raid, some sort of rescue party? Benn just hoped he wouldn't pull the trigger accidentally, waving the gun around like that.

He and Lora were pushed to the back of the Glidebus, which departed Terminal Six in the direction of the Long Island Tunnel, with Wu and seven guards positioned between them and the exit. As it passed near Terminals One and Two, where the majority of civilian commercial transport companies operated, the bus slowed to a crawl, for no apparent reason. Observing no other traffic in the area, Commander Wu yelled to the driver, "Why are you slowing down? Keep going!" With a slight jerk, the bus came to a full stop, and the door at the front end slid open; Wu saw that the driver's head was leaning against the side window. He rushed forward to investigate, but was surprised by two guards in front, who leapt up from their seats to grab Wu by the arms and knock the Razer out of his hand. He shouted obscenities in Mandarin, as the guards flipped him hard onto the floor of the bus, where they pinned him down with their knees. Wu watched the other five guards, all beefy specimens of soldier-hood, run up the aisle as if to rescue him, but they heaved themselves onto the pile, like clowns in a circus act.

If only Wu hadn't made that threat to Lora, Benn thought grimly, he might have simply frozen everyone in place. Now crushed under the considerable weight of his own troops, Wu cried out and struggled furiously, in vain, to reach his com unit; in any case, his muffled cries for help would have been incomprehensible.

Lora, clapping her hands with delight, laughingly pointed out to Benn that the probability of escape had just risen to the vicinity of ninety-nine percent.

"Good work, Benn!" Lora jumped up from her aisle seat and paused to admire the stack-up of soldiers ahead of her. "We'll have to climb over them, I'm afraid."

She began to step carefully onto the back of one of the guards, then hesitated and turned to look at Benn, who remained seated by the window. "Benn, we've got to go. What's the matter? Benn, are… are you crying?" Bewildered, she returned to their row and reached out to touch his shoulder. Light reflected off a tear on his cheek, which he quickly wiped away.

"What's the matter?" she repeated. But once her hand touched Benn, she knew what the matter was: "You're not coming? But Benn, you've got to come with me- please. Terminal One's right there! We can easily catch a flight to New Haven. Then we'll be safe with Cira. And one day, somehow, we'll find a way back to Mars. We'll go home: don't you want to go home?" Benn nodded, but made no move. "Please, Benn, please." Tears were streaming down her own cheeks.

Benn was thinking of his recurrent dream: his descent through light and shadow, a storm thundering overhead, his trail fading away in the blizzard. He had left something back on the mountain. "I'm sorry, I can't come with you, Lora. Go on to New Haven, find Cira and stay with her as long as you can. When I'm finished here, I'll join you- I promise."

Lora saw that his face was now dry, his jaw firmly set. Her own mind squirmed and twisted with doubt, but one thing was certain: she would not be able to change Benn's mind. Despite his promise, she knew that the probability of meeting Benn again had suddenly plummeted to the vicinity of zero.

The biometers ticked softly as before. The Dataframe ES and the Hyper-Probot sat in their respective corners. The laboratory was still kept uncomfortably cold. The shiny black cylinder lay on its side, on the control panel. Nothing had changed. The same circle of blue light surrounded by darkness, the same chair in the center of the room. To the sluggish guard back at the elevator, he had sent the impulse, *Get Dr. Beame.* Now he sat under the blue light and waited.

"Hello, son." Owen Marr stood in front of the control panel, a faint trail of blue haze securing him to the black cylinder. "You have decided to return to us. Why?" he asked, his voice skeptical and slightly tremulous. Already he sensed that Benn had grown much stronger in the weeks since his abrupt departure, but was unable to penetrate, and, more urgently, to gauge the nature and extent of his son's abilities. Benn could feel his father's anxious efforts to probe him for more details, and decided to plunge ahead with his newfound ability.

He closed his eyes, took a deep breath, and jumped into Owen's mind, absorbing his entire consciousness. Unlike Lezhev and Annenkov, who had felt no trace of Benn's presence, his father was instantly alarmed, and on the defensive. He bucked against this outrageous intrusion, a violation never before imagined! Within his bio-energy field, he grappled with Benn and tried to expel him, but Benn resisted without much difficulty, at the same time telling Owen to stop struggling. Please, Father! Far from stopping, Owen shoved, kicked and slapped, so Benn darted aside, changed his grip, parried easily before pushing back. The more desperately Owen fought, the more forcefully Benn countered, drawing from what seemed an endless reserve of strength. Finally straining at the limit of his endurance, Owen grunted, "You've gotten so much stronger! So it's true: you have come back to destroy me. I knew it would come to this."

"No, Father, not to destroy, but to read you." Benn suddenly stopped pushing. "You attacked before I could explain. Now that we're joined, I can see it all clearly: you fear that I might surpass you, diminishing your achievements- and that, in the end, people will forget how important you were. You tell me that I've done well, but at the same time, you hate how much progress I've made. It's ironic that you're threatened by me, because I've always felt I could never begin to match your great accomplishments! It amazes me, Father: after a lifetime filled with one success after another, why do you feel so afraid, so insecure?"

Owen screamed in rage and pushed hard again, but he was rapidly losing strength. Somehow Benn's presence drained his strength, and Benn would not budge.

"How dare you talk to your father with such disrespect? As though you can even begin to understand me. Afraid? Insecure, you say? Are you accusing me of weakness?" Owen sputtered. He lunged at Benn, who dodged to one side.

"What I was pointing out is your strength, and again you take it in the worst way. The only thing I accuse you of, Father, is passing your fear on to me, crippling *me* with it! There's no need for that, don't you see? You have your own achievements, your own success."

"But that's nothing compared to your ambition, is it? I'm nothing compared to you, that's what you're telling me?" He made a final, futile shove.

Benn could feel himself wearing thin. "No, Father. I'm trying to say that you don't have to be insecure, or to be afraid of ..."

"TELLING. BEAME. ACCUSE. DES... DESTROY."

Dr. Walther Beame burst into the laboratory and quickly surveyed the scene. It's about time, thought Benn, who had just about run out of ways to placate his father. Had Dr. Beame possessed the ability to see auras, he would have been astonished by the violent storm raging in the middle of the room: the tumultuous blue cloud twisting and turning, pulling in one direction then another, bright flashes erupting like lightning within a towering thunderhead. He only perceived Benn Marr sitting unconscious in the chair, deceptively innocent and vulnerable, like the first time they had met. But he knew better this time: keeping a wary eye on Benn, he removed a Dermamist from its drawer, loaded it with a sedative, and slipped it into a pocket of his lab coat. He did not see that the bright flashes had gradually ceased, and that the giant blue cumulus had unraveled into two separate cirrus clouds, one promptly retreating to the black cylinder. The other dominated the space above Benn and, when no further challenges came from the direction of the cylinder, slowly descended into the inert body. Now watching his prize clone begin to stir in the chair, Beame sprang forward into the circle of light, one hand buried in his pocket. Finally, a chance to get the project back on track! However, after his tiring struggle with Father, Benn needed a few moments- just a few, he insisted patiently, to gather his thoughts- and, although Walther Beame rarely accommodated anyone with such requests, he suddenly found himself frozen, unable to move or speak, grateful simply to be breathing.

Benn opened his eyes and stared at the ceiling, where tiny silvery flashes still darted about. His father was dying. And while wrestling with his aura, Benn had caught a vision of his own death: although decaying much more slowly, he was still doomed to the same fate. He watched the flashes fade away and turned his gaze toward the hollow black cylinder, which throbbed sullenly with fear and hatred. He shut his eyes again and thought of Lora, his desire and need to be with her. Anchoring his thoughts on her, Benn let himself slip into a dream. A benign breeze stirred sparkling snowflakes about aimlessly. He dreamt of swirling auburn hair that smelled sweetly of the sea and melting wax and berries of all colors; gold and green auras flitted down a corridor; tearful children marched two-by-two on an endless red plain. Then he steered at the speed of thought, through a dank tunnel filled with flames and smoke; covered his mouth with hands stained red by Martian soil. He descended to the edge of a black ruffled sea; watched a hapless young man sink beneath the waves, his face stretching painfully into nothingness. In the distance he heard a hum, like the sound of wind blowing over an open bottle, a dancing flute, music bubbling up from deep underground aquifers. A sensation new, yet familiar, wrapped around him like a giant sphere. He could hear and feel his mother's heartbeat. Overhead, a creamy voice said, High Five, Benn. He was standing in a ballpark, leaning at third base... leaning a little more... just half a step further. From here it would be easy, simple, to steal home. He was close now: so very close! Using that practiced turn of his mind, Benn pulled up and away from the dream. Quickly he focused his ranging thoughts again on Lora, and when they had finally settled, he spoke to the surrounding darkness in a clear, steady voice, a compelling voice that sent a chill down Walther Beame's spine.

"The Owen Marr Chimera has been problematic from the start, and now the inevitable failure of the OMC Project is complete. Only a hundred percent fusion can succeed, and that goal is within our reach." With a light wave of his hand, Benn released his paralytic grip on the Project Director, who almost fell to the floor. "Dr. Beame, you may dispose of the OMC, and proceed immediately with the final phase of the BMC Project," the Benn Marr Chimera said evenly. "I am quite ready."

Walther Beame shook his head, overcome by a heady mixture of resentment, relief and triumph. Stepping forward once again with the Dermamist squeezed tightly in his trembling hand, he uttered through gritted teeth, "Welcome home, son. Welcome home."

Made in the USA
San Bernardino, CA
24 June 2020